Morning Light

For
Maria Thaddeus
and
Frances Silverstein

Morning Light

Nancy King

Tasora

Morning Light
© Nancy King 2009
nanking1224@earthlink.net
www.nancykingstories.com

Tasora Books
5120 Cedar Lake Road
Minneapolis, Minnesota 55416

ISBN 978-1-934690-17-8
LCCN 2001012345

Portrait of the author on p. 329 courtesy of Kim Kurian.

Printed and bound in the United States.

CHRONOLOGY

1910   Sadie Dubrowsky Baum is born

1915   Herschold (Heshie) Baumgartner is born (Baumgartner
        is later changed to Baum)

1916   Sadie and her friend Minnie meet in first grade

1948   Sadie and Heshie marry

1950   Anna Baum is born

1967   Anna graduates from high school

1971   Anna graduates from college

1975   Anna receives her master's degree

1980   Sadie moves to Florida

We remember in connected images. The mind has no sense of time as far as the emotional life is concerned. Time is liquid in this book. Like a wave that rolls over itself. I'm bending time.

Timebends by Arthur Miller

1

Sometimes I think I have two minds and the one I like best takes the longest to get strong enough to tell the other to go to hell. I wish I knew what would speed up the process.

As a child, when I was in need of consolation I crawled under my bed or hid behind a large upholstered chair we had in the living room—any place I couldn't be seen. Then, I'd close my eyes, imagine myself in another world, and pretend I was a heroine performing amazing feats in spite of fierce monsters or soldiers in thick armor. In my stories, I was always loved and cherished and honored and wanted. I even had an imaginary companion I created after reading a collection of Aboriginal myths. I don't know where he went or how I lost my stories but they're gone.

After graduation, when most of my classmates marched in twos from the doors of college advancing toward the ark of marriage, lone-liness was the least of it. There was no chance of my getting on board. I was stranded on an island while the ark kept moving farther and faster away. I watched them leave, wondering if my turn would ever come. You need a mate to climb the gangplank, and none of my male encounters stayed the night, much less the course.

From the outside, I didn't look much different from the women in my classes. We all wore short skirts or bell-bottomed hip huggers, Indian prints, and beads. I wore my earrings long, dangling and shimmering, having spent hours meandering in and out of jewelry shops on West 4th Street in Greenwich Village that catered to low budgets and active imaginations. Like many of the girls, my hair was long enough to braid in a single plait that knocked against my butt as I walked. Still, when I looked at my classmates I felt different. As I watched them choose spouses and careers, I felt pushed and pulled by mysterious forces that made me wonder about my inability to make choices. Sartre wrote that choosing not to choose was still a choice. Yet he didn't explain how will becomes so paralyzed you can't remember having a choice to make.

I'm still not sure how I chose to major in education rather than literature but when I met the Dean of Education, a huge man with a body that looked as if he'd been a football player, I had a chance to find out. He got up from behind his imposing desk and came around to shake my hand. "So, Miss Baum, why do you want to be a teacher?"

"I believe kids need to be in a classroom where they feel safe. Where they can make mistakes without anyone laughing at them. Here in New York, many kids come to school, they don't speak English, they can't read, their parents don't know how to help them, and they just keep falling behind until too many of them quit. I'd like to give them a better chance."

"And you think you can do that with thirty children in a class? A small woman like you?"

"Size has nothing to do with competence."

He grinned. "Well done."

For years I believed my degree in education was a second-class degree, but I loved my current job, teaching preschool. I can't imagine how close I came to making a career of teaching literature to restless adolescents with raging hormones and thirty-second attention spans. Still, I hated almost every minute of the four years it took me to graduate. I survived by taking literature courses with any professor who encouraged intelligent adult discussions instead of the inanities we were forced to treat seriously, such as finding the "right" tone of voice to say "Good morning" to first graders. I hated the officially sanctioned phoniness; we were being taught to be untruthful.

At the time, I didn't know why it bothered me so much but now it was pretty clear. My mother, Sadie, could change her expression in an instant. One minute she was hitting me and in the next, she was smiling at a neighbor who came to borrow a cup of sugar. What upset me most was that people fell for it. To me it was as phony as a seven-cent coin, yet it seemed genuine to the public before whom she performed. Somehow, my father, Heshie, managed to keep a smile on his face no matter what number of derogatory expressions my mother hurled at him or who heard. I remember one Thanksgiving when my grandparents and Aunt Lilly and her family came for dinner. My father spilled cranberry sauce on the white tablecloth and my mother started yelling about how clumsy he was and how she'd never get the stain out. "Sadie," he smiled, looking at me, "It's pretty. White is so boring." He winked at me and I wanted to wink back, but I knew if my mother caught me she would make sure I got "what I deserved." I sometimes wondered what would happen if he caught her choking me. Would he wink and smile, pretending it hadn't happened?

Despite my dissatisfaction with the education program, what kept me going were the children. Early on I volunteered to tutor a child. Kaisha, a fourth-grade student, was having trouble reading and, according to her record, refused to speak in class. A tall skinny kid with braids carefully wrapped in pink and red ribbons, she sat on the edge of an orange plastic chair in the principal's office, looking like she was ready to run. When we were introduced her lips tightened, then pursed in disappointment.

The principal spoke sternly. "Kaisha, stand up and say hello to Miss Baum. She's been kind enough to take time from her busy schedule to help you."

"Hello, Miss Baum," said a low voice from a bowed head.

"Kaisha, you and Miss Baum will be working in room 203-A. Miss Baum, when you're finished, please walk Kaisha back to her room. She'll show you where it is, won't you, Kaisha?" Kaisha nodded, staring at the tile floor.

"Kaisha, what do we say?"

"Yes, Mr. Brown." The principal showed us to the door.

We started walking, her head still bowed; a grim expression on her face. *She hates me. How the hell am I going to help her?* I followed as she showed me to our room, little bigger than a janitor's closet. It smelled of disinfectant and lemon wax. Kaisha sat down and stared into space. I moved a chair from behind a desk and put it next to hers. *Now what do I do?* We still had twenty-five minutes.

*****

My mother sees my report card with an "S" for satisfactory behavior instead of an "O" for outstanding and smacks me across the face. "You know better, Anna. When you gonna do better?"

Although I try to hide my feelings I'm not very good at it. The less my mother knows what I'm thinking, the more likely I can avoid being hit. She sees me looking at her and hits me again.

I can feel my mother's eyes boring into me from behind when she shows my father my report card. He shakes his head and says, "This is not acceptable, Anna. Your mother and I expect you to do better."

He touches the bruises, and I wince.

"How did this happen, Anna?" he asks.

"I fell."

"How did you fall?"

"I slipped. Daddy, Mommy made carrot cake for dessert."

"Well, then, let's eat. I'm hungry."

He puts his arm around me and walks me to the table. "What did you get on your arithmetic test?"

"Eat your soup, Heshie, it's getting cold."

*****

Years later, my mother, bemoaning the lack of men men in my life campaigned as if she were a general strategizing to win a strategic battle. I remember one time she called, just as I was leaving for work. "Have I got a man for you! He's a dentist, makes lots of money. You won't have to work. It's all set. Saturday, 6:30, I'm making strudel. His mother told me he loves strudel. He's gonna love you, too."

Right. And then he'll propose so he'll never have to be without strudel again. I take thee strudel to be my ever loving wife till hunger do us part.

I didn't have to pretend when I spoke to Kaisha; it was all too easy to remember how bad I felt about myself growing up. Maybe she was feeling like a failure as well.

"Kaisha, I'm really glad we're going to be working together."

"Why?" she asked, her eyes locked on a brown spider crawling across the floor.

"I'm studying to be a teacher but there's a lot I don't know. Maybe you can help me. You think you could do that?"

"Me?"

At least she looked up.

"I don't know nothin'. Teacher say I'm stupid. That's why I be here. She say she can't do nothin' with me."

I want to be a fairy godmother with a magic wand so I can put a large red pus-oozing pimple on her teacher's nose.

I put my arm around her. When she didn't move away I felt a glimmer of hope. "Well, when I was a kid my mother kept telling me how stupid I was but here I am in college, doing pretty well."

This time she looked straight at me. "Your mother say you stupid?"

I nodded.

"And you in college?"

I nodded again. Out of nowhere came a burst of laughter. Her reaction eased a hurting place inside me. The two of us laughed until tears rolled down our cheeks.

"I guess she wrong," said Kaisha, wiping her face with the crumpled tissue I found in my bag.

"Yup," I said, "she was definitely wrong." *About a lot of things.*

I opened a book of stories. "Is it all right if I read to you, just to get us started?"

She looked anxious.

"Kaisha, you don't have to worry. We're going to have lots of fun."

She didn't react and made no move to stop me when I put my arm around her bony shoulder. I held one side of the book, gave her the other side to hold, and started reading. After awhile, she read, hesitating when she came to a word she didn't know. I waited without comment until she got the word right. Her face lit up in triumph. I gave her a quick hug and began to write.

"Whatcha writing?" she asked.

"I thought of a story."

"What's it about?"

"A girl who thinks she can't read or write but she can, she's just too afraid to try."

"I know a girl like that. She be smart but she don't know it."

"Want to write about her?"

"Me? Write a story?"

"Why not?"

"Hunh," she said, grinning.

Nobody Knows
the Trouble They've Seen

"Kaisha, wasn't the homework assignment to write two paragraphs about George Washington?"

"Yes, Mrs. Jones."

"How many paragraphs did you write?"

She hesitated. Kaisha could hear the girls behind her giggling. "One, Mrs. Jones."

"Where is the missing paragraph?"

Kaisha sighed. She wasn't about to tell her that the baby tore her homework while she was washing the breakfast dishes and she wrote what she could remember. Mrs. Jones would just tell her to be more careful.

"Silence is not an answer, Kaisha. How do you expect to learn if you don't do your homework?"

Kaisha sighed again. She hoped the teacher would ask her to stay after school to do her homework. At least then she could do it without worrying. "I'm sorry, Mrs. Jones. I'll do better next time."

"Next time will be this afternoon. I'd like you to stay after school and do your homework."

"Okay," she said, remembering to add, "Thank you, Mrs. Jones."

Recess was the only time Kaisha felt she could breathe. No matter what anyone said, she wasn't stupid. Sometimes she knew the answer but by the time she found the words, teacher had already called on someone else. Maybe the lady she saw the other day could help. At least she didn't get mad at her when she didn't answer right away. Bouncing the ball helped. "One my name is Addie and my friend's name is—"

Someone fell against her, knocking her down, the ball flying out of her hands. "Hey!" she yelled.

"I'm sorry, Kaisha, I didn't mean it. Jason was chasing me and I was running so fast I didn't see you."

Kaisha looked up and saw Mary, her best friend at school. "Help me find my ball."

Mary nodded, relieved that Kaisha wasn't mad at her. The two girls looked around. A bunch of girls were jumping rope. Hordes of boys were passing basketballs. Two boys were fighting as a crowd gathered, cheering on their favorites. "I think it's over there," yelled Mary above the din. She took off, Kaisha at her heels, oblivious to the screams and shouts of children jumping and pushing and running.

Two boys blocked their path. "Where you goin' in such a hurry?"

"None a your business," screamed Mary.

"Oh yeah?" the taller one jeered. "Who says?"

"I say." Kaisha pushed her way through the two boys, taking them by surprise as she grabbed Mary's hand and charged, running past them as fast as she could. The boys followed only to be interrupted by a flying basketball that hit the smaller boy smack in the face.

Kaisha and Mary skirted the playing field, avoiding much of the action. "Look," shouted Mary, "there it is." She ran over to the curb where the ball lay in a puddle of water. Shaking off the water, she rubbed it against her coat, leaving a muddy stain on the dark green wool. The warning bell rang. Five more minutes. "How come recess goes so fast and everything else goes so slow?" complained Mary. Kaisha shrugged. She felt the same way. "I failed reading again. Teacher say I have to repeat fourth grade if I don' pass," said Mary in a voice so low it was almost a whisper.

"What you gonna do?" asked Kaisha.

"Don' know." Mary stared at the mud on her shoes, spit on her fingers and began wiping it off.

"I got a lady who's helping me. She pretty nice. Maybe you could get one too."

Mary shook her head. "Teacher say there ain't no more. I got to wait till someone volunteers."

"You sure?"

Mary nodded. "I hate school. I wish I was older so I could walk outta here and never worry about having to come back ever again."

"What you gonna do if you don't go to school?"

"Go someplace real far from here. Where it's clean and quiet. No gunshots. No one sleeping on the sidewalk. No one screaming at me—."

They heard the bell. Mary sighed. Kaisha stood up, feeling Mary's misery.

"Come with me. When I go see the lady. Maybe she take us both."

"She won't. Teacher say volunteers can only take one student. It no use."

"Well, just the same, I gonna ask her. She real nice, Miss Baum. I bet she say yes."

"I bet she won't. Everyone be too busy. Don' even bother."

"I gonna bother so quit asking me not to."

2

I was in a bookstore rummaging through the sale section when I saw a novel I'd been dying to read. I wanted the book so badly I shoved everyone out of my way. My fingers were just about to clutch the binding when I felt a strong, masculine hand on mine. "Hey babe, take it easy, it's only a book." *In New York City, you take it easy, you get nothing.* The hand sent me into a state of involuntary meltdown. All of a sudden I felt safe and cared about. *It's only a hand for chrissake.* I looked up at him. He was drop-dead gorgeous—tall, well built, with a smile that warmed my toes. His blonde hair looked real and his eyes were so green I was ready to dive in and swim. His hand on mine kept me from telling him to get the hell out of my way.

He started talking about how great it was to find a woman who liked to read. *It's not so hard, all you have to do is turn off the TV and walk to the nearest library.* The next thing I knew, he was handing my book and his credit card to the cashier. "I'll pay for this," he said smiling seductively at the cashier. She blushed.

I grabbed the novel. "I can pay for my own book, thank you." Waiting for change, I looked at our image in a mirror on the wall above the cashier. There we were, a gorgeous man next to a trim, bright-eyed young woman in a blue Indian print dress and dangling blue-beaded earrings. I expected him to walk away, but instead he grinned. "Okay, you buy your book and I'll buy you a drink or coffee—whatever you fancy."

I fancy you.

Before I could object, he was holding my arm, leading me out of the crowd, walking at a good pace down two streets and into an outdoor café where we sat at a great table with a panoramic view of the botanical gardens.

Max ordered two espressos, two pieces of French pastry, and two glasses of Italian brandy. I thought about protesting, but the pleasure of drinking dark, strong, spectacular coffee and eating delicate pastries, washed down with a brandy so smooth it felt like liquid velvet made me renegotiate my view of the world.

We sat in the tree-dappled sunshine talking until the waiter let us know it was time for him to set the table for dinner. Max did most of the talking, about his latest advertising account, the way he had to fight to become an accounts supervisor, and a whole lot about how in a business like his you have to keep attracting clients or you're out in cold storage. It all sounded much more glamorous than teaching twenty-five first graders to read, write, and figure. The whole afternoon, his eyes never wandered. He asked what I was doing Saturday night.

I couldn't wait to tell my mother that I was oh so sorry but there was no way I would be able to come for dinner on Saturday to meet her Mr. Absolutely Right For Me. I hoped, when I told her my excuse, I could make up a reasonable sounding lie, avoiding any mention of Max, at least for the time being. My mother had a way of ferreting out information that would make the CIA change their interrogation practice if only they knew. On the telephone it was a bit easier; at least she couldn't see my face or read my body language.

When I started looking for a teaching job I was hoping I wouldn't get one. I wanted an acceptable excuse to go to graduate school. Although I filled out application forms, unlike my classmates, I didn't use the professional résumé service offered to graduating seniors.

I was called to account. "Ms. Baum, a professional application is not the place for creative writing. What on earth possessed you to do such a foolish thing?" The university counselor sat in a straight-backed chair at a desk so neat I wondered if she used it. "Although you have an otherwise outstanding record, we pride ourselves on producing graduates who know how to fit into the system."

If that's the case, the system stinks.

"Ms. Baum, I asked you a question." She tapped her pencil on the spotless desk, waiting for me to answer.

"I wrote a story to show what kind of teacher I am."

"You don't know what kind of teacher you are. You have yet to teach. And, given your actions, you may never find out. Next time, omit your story. Good day, Ms. Baum."

Good day, Ms. Tightass. May no children have you as their teacher.

When I got my contract I had half a mind to wave it in the face of the counselor who had done her best to convince me I was "unhireable."

The time came when I followed Max into his apartment, not sure I was ready for whatever was going to happen. After hanging up our coats, he sat down on the lush chocolate brown leather sofa, and motioned for me to join him. I noticed how orderly the room was, everything in its place. *Where was my place?* I asked to use the bathroom. He got up and showed me the way, taking time to brush his fingers across my cheek.

"You're lovely, Anna. Really lovely."

I murmured thanks and hurried to the bathroom where I threw up. Fortunately cleanup was minimal and a bottle of mouthwash was handy. *Why am I so tense? I like him. I've been fantasizing about him. What's the matter?*

I let him lead me into his bedroom, feeling awkward and torn. Most of my previous lovers might generously be categorized as blissful gropers. None of them emanated Max's sexual energy. The quiet tones of the beige sheets, comforter, and curtains were soothing. It was only when I noticed the thick brown rug that I felt an overwhelming urge to run.

Good thing Max was no mind reader. He took my trembling for shivers of pleasure and began to slowly undress me, never taking his eyes off me. Basking in his appreciation, I unbuttoned his shirt and kissed the hair on his chest, delighted by his muscularity. Maybe it was going to be all right after all. He pulled back the sheets and led me to his bed, seemingly in no hurry. I didn't know it was possible to feel terror and pleasure simultaneously. After that night, all he had to do was touch me, anywhere, and I melted into bliss.

My mother met Max and it was love at first flirt. When people look at my mother they see an ordinary middle-aged woman who has been married to the same man for a quarter of a century. Let a good-looking man come into her sight and, **bam**, she turns into a laughing, teasing, simpering coquette. Forget age—taste—sense. Absolutely forget she's the prospective mother-in-law. I shook my head wondering if it was in her genes. Maybe she couldn't help herself. I stood, amazed at the sight of the two of them talking, staring into each other's eyes. There we were, my father on one side of the living room, me on the other, watching what could only be described as a mating dance. At first I felt relieved. If my mother and Max liked each other, I wouldn't have to hear about my bad taste in men or mothers. I thought about asking my father if he wanted to go out for ice cream. I doubted Max or my mother would notice. What I noticed was my trembling.

After a few minutes of seeing my mother act as if Max was the only person in the room, I started to feel weird. Jealous. And it only got worse when she led us to the coffee table, filled with goodies that would have made a pastry chef weep for joy. A mother isn't supposed to seduce her daughter's boyfriend, is she? Especially with a gazillion cakes that she keeps telling him are little nothings she's whipped up in no time at all, just for him. Even if it's true?

Max was the perfect audience. "Yes, Mrs. Baum. No, Mrs. Baum. Certainly, Mrs. Baum. This is the best cake I've ever eaten and I've eaten cakes made by the best, Mrs. Baum."

"What's with the Mrs. Baum? Call me Sadie like all my friends," my mother said .

"Max," my father said, "Did you hear the joke about the grand-mother who's walking on the beach with her grandson?"

Max looked at him as if surprised to hear his voice.

My father continued, ignoring my mother's, "Max darling, have another—" "So, they're walking and out of nowhere, a huge wave crashes up on the beach. Suddenly, the grandson is gone, washed away with the sand. The old woman looks up at the sky and shakes her finger. 'God, he's my only grandson. You made a big mistake. Bring him back.' Suddenly, a gigantic wave washes the grandson up on to the beach. The grandmother hugs him tightly and looks up once again. 'God! He was wearing a red hat.'"

My father and I laughed.

Max kept eating rugelach from my mother's fingers.

"Max, did you go to the beach when you were a kid?" I asked.

"I don't think about my childhood," he said, his mouth full of almond-filled pastry.

I felt invisible. Grabbing my chance during a second of silence while people were chewing, I blurted out, "I'm baking sugar cookies in the shape of the first letter of my children's names. Before they eat one they have to—."

"Max, try this, I made it specially for you," said my mother, bat-ting her eyes.

He savored the strawberry tart, licking his lips. "Sadie, it's scrump-tious. You missed your calling." Max described a restaurant where she was better than the chief pastry chef.

My father winked at me and said, "Anna, just imagine! All this time we could have been rolling in dough." Enjoying his pun, he grinned his famous Heshie grin. I tried to respond but I kept won-dering how he could sit there, calmly eating cake and drinking coffee, unaffected by his wife's loving looks at another man. My man.

The room was closing in on me. I felt dizzy and jumped up to open a window, knocking over a vase of flowers. Water spilled everywhere. I picked up the flowers and went into the kitchen to get a sponge. I could hear my mother cooing sweetly, "Poor Anna, she's such a klutz." I kept my burning face glued to the floor as I wiped up the mess. Silently, I refilled the vase and set it down next to my father. Let him worry about it.

Suddenly, everything that was wondrous about Max and me felt spoiled. I knew his mother died when he was twelve, so I understood how he might want a mother in his life, but my mother was as far from being motherly as I was from being a mother. Besides, who wants to be jealous of her mother?

I was not looking forward to her inevitable phone call. "He's absolutely perfect." *He looks into your eyes and you're finished.* "How did you find such a gem? What a catch. Such a gentleman! Remember, Anna, nothing happens the way you think it will. You got a good man. Grab him while the grabbing's good." *As if he's nothing more than the gold ring at the merry-go-round.*

"What about love?" *What about trust and honesty and respect?*

My mother made a sound I can't reproduce. "Love lasts about as long as a good meal."

"Didn't you and Dad love each other?"

"Bring Max for dinner on Friday. I'm making matzah ball soup and gefilte fish, just the way he likes it."

About a year after I started teaching first grade, I was sitting in the lunchroom with Carmen, a first-grade teacher who ate even faster than I did. She was also the only teacher besides me who needed to stretch her legs and close her eyes before going back to the classroom. We started talking, mostly her telling me about the ups and downs of her relationship with her boyfriend, Angel. I would listen saying, "I know what you mean," and "I understand," in all the right places, but the truth is, her Angel sounded like an angel. When I heard how caring and kind he was, it made me feel too ashamed to talk with her about Max.

Most of the time I was with Max I felt like the luckiest woman in the world; but there were times when he frightened me. His sarcasm was cutting. When he pronounced judgment, I had no recourse. Occasionally he broke dates and then insisted I had mistaken the arrangements. He had what he called "first truth" — his decision about what had been said or done. No facts or logic I offered could change his mind. Although we seldom quarreled, resolving our disagreements by letting them fade left me on the edge of nervous.

One Saturday afternoon he called to say he was coming over for lunch after his workout. The night before, we'd had a pleasant evening and were both feeling mellow. The night air was crisp and clear. We'd taken an invigorating walk in the park before dinner. Now our snuggling in the cab seemed a good time to raise an issue that had been bothering me. "Max, why is it you get so angry at me so quickly? Not only don't I have a chance to explain myself, you don't even give me the benefit of the doubt. It's like you choose the worst imaginable scenario as the only possible explanation." He turned away from me and stared at the passing landscape. When we arrived, the cabbie opened the door. I got out. Max stayed in. The driver drove off.

Now, hearing about Angel, Carmen's life was so different from mine that I had difficulty imagining it. From what she told me, no matter how people in her family fought, nobody stayed so mad they didn't come to family dinners or hug and make up. After accidentally admitting I had a boyfriend, I said just enough to remind her of something she wanted to tell me about Angel or her sisters and brothers. Carmen, who had too many relatives for me to keep track of, often grinned when she spoke about her family. It seemed to me they might live in an apartment with too little space, but they surely had more love than I could imagine.

I was getting ready to throw the remains of my lunch in the trash basket when I heard, "Anna, I got to ask you something." She looked so nervous I thought she was pregnant. Terrified she needed my help to get an abortion, which at that time was illegal, I immediately began worrying about how to find a doctor.

"Anna, Angel and I are getting married. We want you to be our maid of honor."

I was speechless. A thousand no's leapt to my mind, but one look at her eager smile and all I could do was wonder. I had a ton of questions starting with *Why me?* I liked Carmen, but we never saw each other outside of school, which was not her fault. She asked me to go shopping many times and even suggested we double-date. I wouldn't have minded; I liked Angel. When he came to our school to talk about growing up in the Dominican Republic, I enjoyed how he struck a fine balance between politics, geography, and his experiences, especially since he was talking to young children. But a foursome? I could just picture Max in the same room as Carmen in her bright colored blouse tucked into her short tight skirt. We would all be polite but I would feel his derision. So I told her my boyfriend worked nights. "We don't go out much."

"I understand," she said. I believed her. She and Angel worked two, sometimes three, jobs to save up for a formal wedding with bridesmaids and flowers and music. "I've been dreaming about my wedding day since I was a kid," she said. "And it's not gonna be a five-minute rush job in City Hall like most of my friends. We want a day we can remember. Somethin' we can tell our kids and grandkids about. You know, show them pictures in an album—stuff like that."

I desperately wanted to ask her to find someone else. What about a family member? From what she told me, she had enough to fill a whole apartment house. She read my mind. "I got a lot of cousins who've been letting me know they're available but the trouble is, if I say yes to one I'm gonna hurt everyone else's feelings. Who wants to start married life with your whole family mad at you?"

What made me say yes was the look of love in Carmen's eyes when she talked about Angel. She gave me a big hug and for the moment, I felt great. It was only when the wedding announcement came addressed to Ms. Anna Baum and Guest that I began to get cold feet. If I made up a good excuse not to be in the wedding Carmen would say she understood, but I knew she'd be hurt. I was her friend. Friends come to friend's weddings. So I said yes to everything except bringing my boyfriend. "He'll be out of town for a job interview," I said carefully, wishing Max was as easy-going as her Angel.

When I told Max I couldn't go to dinner with him and his out-of-town clients because I had to be in a wedding, his voice was hard. "I've been counting on you to help me entertain my clients. You're my wife. They want to meet you."

"Your what?"

Max looked like he'd swallowed a fish bone. "Wife, girlfriend, what's the big deal?"

Do you want me to be your wife? Do I want to be your wife?

I knew I had a lot to be grateful for. Max introduced me to a life filled with sophisticated people and a way of being beyond my imagination. He introduced me to new museums and galleries, talking about paintings and sculptures with knowledge and appreciation. He cheerfully paid for meals that cost more than my weekly salary. And I liked the adventure of traveling with him. Being with him. I figured if I could just keep things going the way they were, life would definitely be good enough. It certainly was the best it had ever been for me. After too many of his withering looks and snide remarks, I taught myself not to bring up my feelings or his actions because I never knew when something I said or did would trigger his disapproval or anger.

What gave me a little bit of confidence was I knew he liked the way I was in bed, the one place where he sometimes let go of the self he showed to the world. After we made love, when we were lying close together, he was surprisingly tender and responsive, giving and taking like the man of my dreams. I convinced myself that the pleasure of being with Max was worth my worries. For once in my life I felt normal, deserving of this newfound largesse. Yet even my powers of rationalization were strained to the breaking point when we met for lunch after his Saturday workout at the club. He got there first. As usual, he had ordered for me. I received a kiss and a hug just as the meal was brought to the table. I stared at the two fat sausages dribbling juice on either side of a large slice of grilled meat. Although Max was eating like a starved warrior, he noticed I hadn't picked up my fork.'

"What's the matter, Anna? Why aren't you eating? The food's terrific."

"I don't like sausages." My eyes were glued to the bleeding juices.

"Don't be ridiculous. The sausages are superb. Try them." He stabbed one of mine and tried to put it into my mouth. I backed off so he couldn't reach me.

"Do you know how they make sausages? They grind up bits of intestines and organs…."

"You think I'd eat unhealthy sausages? These are made of turkey. And apples."

"Yeah, but even turkeys have intestines. If you don't mind, I'd rather you didn't order them for me." I hesitated. "In fact, I'd rather you didn't order for me period."

"I order for you because I know what's good. And, you have to admit, you've enjoyed my choices." His voice had the edge I'd come to fear, but the oozing juices wouldn't go away.

"That's because I didn't want to start a fight."

"So don't start one now. Eat your food like a good girl."

"I'm not a girl, good or otherwise, and I prefer to order what I want to eat."

His eyes turned almost black. I lost my nerve.

"Max, I appreciate your taste. Can we just agree; no more sausages? Please?"

"Waiter," he called to a blur passing our table. "Our bill, please." He paid, took my arm with his usual gallant manner and guided us out of the restaurant. I relaxed a little when he didn't complain about the taxi driver's choice of music and put his arm around me, telling the cabbie to take us to his apartment without asking if I wanted to come for a cuddle or a drink. I snuggled against his chest, ignoring his clenched hands.

He shut the door and grabbed me, feverishly pulling off my clothes. I tried to take his shirt off but he wouldn't let me. When I was naked, he pushed me to the floor, held my jaw open and forced himself into my mouth. I was choking and fought back, gasping for air. Surprised, he loosened his hold. I wrestled myself out from under him, threw on my clothes, and ran out the door, racing toward the restroom in the lobby.

The doorman saw me. "Something wrong, Ms. Baum?"

"No, Mr. Pritchett, I'm fine." I pushed open the door. In the mirror was a terrified, disheveled woman who looked anything but fine. Still trembling, I straightened my clothes, combed my hair, and left quickly. In the subway, waiting, I wished I'd thought to hail a cab.

I didn't see or hear from Max for a week, a very long week. When I came home from school Friday night, there he was, wearing my favorite blue-green jacket, the one that matched his eyes. He grinned seductively, cradling a huge bouquet in his left arm. Bestowing the flowers into my arms, ever so gently he held each side of my face with his strong, powerful hands. "I missed you, Babe. I missed you a lot." I felt him down the length of my spine.

"How about dinner at Le Blanc's? Perry and Jill asked if we could join them."

I took a deep breath. "Come upstairs. I'll change my clothes."

In the taxi, holding me close, Max asked, "What's been happening?"

My answer was to snuggle closer, enjoying the spicy smell of his after-shave lotion. I had nothing to say. My two minds were at war. One piece felt lucky to be wanted, the other yearned for Boonah. Where had he gone? Why had he disappeared? And if he were here, what stories would I tell him. I wasn't so sure I liked what came to mind.

Birth Days

Normally, walking up Fifth Avenue, peering into store windows, was one of Minnie's secret pleasures. She liked to imagine herself in the couture clothes worn by exquisite manikins, setting her kitchen table with the handcrafted porcelains and tableware from around the world. Today, nothing tempted her. All she could think about was the birthday party in a few hours. It wasn't that she'd left buying a present for the last minute. She just couldn't think of something special enough to buy. As always, on Anna's birthday, she remembered how Sadie had called. "Minnie, could you come over? I talked to the doctor and he says I'm only in the first stage and I got lots of time but the pains are really bad. What happens if he's wrong? Heshie's working until six. He says he'll be home in time to take me to the hospital but I'm afraid to be alone."

She had turned off the stove and rushed over to find Sadie writhing in agony. Although Minnie was no expert it seemed there wasn't much time between contractions. She was afraid to say anything that might worry Sadie and scared to call a cab. What if Sadie had the baby on the way? Minnie remembered in the movies—they boiled water, though she wasn't sure why. Still, it was something to do. And then Sadie screamed so loud that Minnie froze. Sadie, who prided herself on never asking for help or letting anyone know how she felt about anything, was pleading and begging. Crying, sobbing, and yelling, "Help me, Minnie, the baby's coming!"

Minnie was terrified. Her Sarah was born in the hospital and she had been so groggy from the anesthesia she didn't remember anything except the pain when she tried to sit up. She pulled the covers off of Sadie and even as she thought to get the receiving blanket, out popped the baby's head. Minnie grabbed the towel she'd used to wipe Sadie's face and caught the baby. "What is it?" asked Sadie.

"A girl," said Minnie, knowing enough to cut the cord and wipe the mucus from the baby's eyes. The blood and smell was too much. Minnie barely held on to the baby as she collapsed in a chair, grateful the child was a healthy pink color and breathing normally. Minnie noticed the baby didn't cry and hoped everything was all right.

"Heshie wanted a boy."

Caught between anger and awe, Minnie stroked the newborn child's forehead, kissing her smooth tiny face, murmuring, "You are beautiful, little one. I love you. May you live a long and happy life."

Now it was Anna's sixth birthday. As usual, Sadie had been no help when she asked her what Anna might like. No six-year-old wanted practical gifts like pajamas, at least no six-year-old Minnie ever met. She went into FAO Schwartz and looked around, horrified at the prices, delighted at the ingenuity and beauty of the toys. Nothing she could afford struck her fancy. Not that Anna had a lot of toys, but somehow Minnie didn't think a toy was what Anna wanted. She walked out of Schwartz's, toward the large bookstore four blocks south.

"May I help you?" asked a woman in her early forties, dressed in an impeccably tailored dark blue suit.

"I'm looking for a present for my friend's daughter. Her birthday's today. She's six."

"The children's section is to your right." Minnie sighed. She had the feeling Anna wouldn't want a children's book. She was such a good reader, much better than her Sarah. But so serious—. Minnie could not remember a time when Anna giggled. She worried about Anna but Sadie always said everything was fine. Minnie scanned the children's books. Nothing caught her attention. Well, if all else failed, she could always buy pajamas. At least Sadie would be happy.

She left the children's section, wandering around the aisles, looking at books, paying no attention to where she was going. Then, she stopped. Her eyes fixed on a large book with a brilliantly colored cover. The title, *Myths of Aboriginal Australia,* was exotically lettered. Curious, she opened the book, gazing at the photographs, scanning the stories. Her imagination, caught by the strange images and oddly named creatures, kept her turning the pages. She couldn't put the book down. Sadie would kill her. "It's too much money," she would say. "Whoever heard of giving a six-year-old a book of aboriginal myths?" Minnie bought the book anyway, hoping Anna would love it and that Sadie would let her keep it.

Slightly apprehensive, she watched Anna open the package. Anna's face lit up.

"Oh Aunt Minnie, this is the best present I ever got in my whole life." She couldn't stop hugging her mother's friend. Minnie held Anna on her lap, smelling the child's clean sweet scent. "I'm so happy you like it. Somehow I just knew it was something for you." Minnie refused to meet Sadie's accusing eyes.

Engrossed in reading the stories, Anna had to be called to the table three times. And even as she blew out the candles on her birthday cake, images of a strange little brown-skinned man filled her head. She forgot his name but she remembered his kind eyes and wonderful stories.

3

I'm in fifth grade. I have a homework assignment to write a biography of a family member for school. My mother is out visiting so I ask my father to tell me what his life was like when he was my age. He shrugs and mumbles, "Nothing special," then goes into the kitchen.

"But Daddy, I need to write at least five pages. You have to tell me something. There's no one else to ask."

After shrugs, two cups of coffee, and too many sighs, he finally tells me a little about growing up poor, the youngest boy in a family of four children. "In Russia, my father was a *yeshiva bocher*."

"What's that?"

"A person who studies Talmud all day."

"So who makes the money to buy the food and pay the rent?"

"Am I telling the story or you?" He stands up and starts walking out.

"Wait, keep going. I won't ask any more questions. Please!"

"All day, he studied at the *yeshiva*; it was his life's work. He was engaged to a woman who worked in a grocery store. She would support him while he spent his days studying. But after being drafted into the Tsar's army—for Jews that meant twenty-five years—he escaped, came here, found another woman, got married, and had four children. What did he know? Nothing. All he ever did was study. When he was little he had helped his mother sew clothes for the villagers, and from what he remembered, he taught himself to sew."

My father pays no attention to my look of surprise.

"Fourteen hours a day he worked in the shop and then he took piecework home to do at night. After supper, my parents would sit in the kitchen, sipping tea in a glass through a piece of sugar in their mouths, sewing while they listened to the radio. Sometimes my older sister helped out, but my brothers refused even though it would have meant more money for the family. 'Women's work,' they'd sneer in disgust. My father just nodded and sewed. I used to get so mad at him; it wasn't right they didn't help. I wanted him to yell or argue but he would tell me, '*Sha Heshele*—by me it's no problem.'"

"How did you meet Mom?"

"I knew her friend Minnie through my cousin Asher."

"Was it love at first sight, Dad?"

"You read too many books, Anna. Now what else do you have to know?" He answers the rest of the questions on my list but I feel unsettled. When we finish, he smiles the same smile he always smiles when he doesn't want to answer any more questions. "Now you know everything, I'm going for a walk."

I'm writing up his answers to my questions when my mother comes in. She asks, "So what's the assignment tonight?"

"Oh, just an essay, nothing special."

After our talk I feel a kind of softness for my father, like he deserves something special from me that he isn't getting from Momma. When he comes home at night I make a point of asking how his day was and if he wants a glass of tea. If Momma notices, she doesn't say anything.

*****

When did I stop? Why?

At work, I ate lunch with Carmen. When I agreed to be her maid of honor I had no idea what it meant to plan a wedding. Carmen excitedly told me about menus and flower arrangements and reception plans and guest lists—details I wouldn't have thought of if I had ten million years to prepare. Our talk made me wonder, if I ever got married, what kind of wedding I would have. I couldn't imagine wearing a billowing white wedding gown surrounded by attendants. For starters, who would I invite? On a good day I could possibly fill two seats. And then there was the not-so-small matter of the groom.

My mother was more than ready to welcome Max as her son-in-law. Her hints grew into a full-scale campaign calculated to make him propose. After listening to yet another monologue about how to get Max to propose, it hit me like a ton of bricks—with all her strategies and lines of attack, she never once suggested I ask him to marry me. *No matter what you want, you can't ask for it.*

As Carmen's wedding day approached, my tension increased exponentially. When I told Max I had to be at Carmen's apartment by three in the afternoon, he was livid. "I've already made reservations for a one o'clock lunch at the Golden Sun, and you know how difficult it is to get a table there."

"Why did you choose a restaurant so far downtown? You know I have to pick up my dress. Can't you make the reservation for noon?"

"My clients do not eat at your convenience."

I winced.

His tone of voice changed. Caressing me he said, "Besides, she isn't your kind."

"My kind?"

"Honey, don't you know it's more than business? My clients like you. They see you as what's great about New York." *He isn't the top salesman in his company for no reason.*

"Okay, Max. I'll figure it out."

"That's my girl," he said, massaging a shoulder I didn't know was tight. I let him take me into his bedroom. I allowed him to undress me. I gave him what he wanted, but it wasn't making love. Still, Max was more observant than I realized. When I tried to get up he held me, nuzzling my neck, waiting until he felt me relax. I heard him say, "Oh, my sweet Anna." I wanted to get up immediately. I stayed.

Sometimes feeling wanted didn't feel so good.

I walked into the church hall, nervous and tense. Carmen and Angel's families immediately surrounded me with open arms and more hugs than I've had in a lifetime. *Why can't my life be like this?* The wedding went just as Carmen hoped and dreamed. The dozens of nieces and nephews, sisters and brothers, all dressed in shades of blue, made an adoring backdrop to the radiant couple. Carmen and Angel's parents were everywhere, touching, talking, tasting, arranging, making sure everything went as planned. I held Carmen's bouquet as she exchanged rings with Angel, tears trickling down my face. When he lifted her veil and kissed her, I thought of Max. My relationship with him felt like trying to sip a thick malted through a thin straw.

Despite my initial qualms about majoring in education, I grew to love my first-graders as I focused on their struggles and triumphs. When Antonio, who gave up speaking when he discovered Spanish was not the language of the classroom, spoke his first sentence in English, I cheered along with his friends. Dow Young cried the first six months and was almost demoted to kindergarten but I used my powers of persuasion to convince the administration to give me more time. The day Dow joined the children in their circle games I was so happy I promised everyone cupcakes. Yet despite my involvement, my brain yearned for intellectual involvement and I was weary from fighting the administration's determined reliance on standardized testing to assess student progress.

Toward the end of my second year of teaching, Max moved from subtle hints to an out-front high-pressure full-scale campaign. "You're too smart to spend the rest of your life teaching six-year-olds. You can find a better job."

"What's wrong with teaching first grade?"

"I say use your brains or make money. Why waste time on kids who won't remember your name the minute they leave your classroom?"

Who says? I remember my first grade teacher, Miss Mathews. She made me a milk monitor. She told me I was intelligent.

"I'm flattered you think I'm smart but I'm not wasting my time. I make a difference in their lives." There was no point telling him about Latisha, who had refused to talk in any language. Yet just yesterday, in the middle of storytelling, she put up her hand. When I stopped talking, without missing a beat, she told the rest of the story. And then there was Marco who started first grade with his fists. Now he's too busy building marvelous structures out of boxes I collect from stores and stuff thrown out on the streets to start fights. I never tell Max about the frustrating parts of teaching—too many kids with too many problems I can't fix. It's discouraging to realize that if I want to permanently improve their lives, I'd have to be as strong as Hercules, rich as Croesus, wise as Solomon on his most inspired day, and lucky.

"Hey," he said, holding up his hands in surrender, "I'm only making a suggestion."

"You sound like a snob." I walked out of the room. *Fuck this.* I walked back into the living room and said, "I'm going for a walk."

"Good idea, I'll get my jacket."

The cool air felt bracing. He took my hand in his and put our hands in his pocket. *How is it possible for the warmth of his hands to make my body tingle?*

A few nights later, we went to a Thai restaurant on the Upper West Side that had recently opened, so popular you had to know the owner just to get a decent table. The place was filled with sleek young people in designer clothes. Before meeting Max I would have felt out of place, wishing I could leave before I stepped inside the doorway. Now I felt comfortable, my clothes were right, I looked good and we made an attractive pair.

I was sipping Chardonnay, when a tall willowy blonde named Veronica, the cosmetics editor at a sleek fashion magazine, asked, "What do you do, Anna?"

Max beat me to it. "She's starting graduate school in the fall. Congratulate her; she just got a prestigious fellowship."

I stared at him. He continued without hesitation.

"She's going to major in English, which is pretty silly I think, given the job market, but one thing about Anna, she's determined to do what she wants to do. Who knows? When she's finished, there might be an opening writing copy at Bender and Shanks. Besides, I make enough to support both of us. Nice thing about marriage is you don't have to pay rent on two places."

I sat, too stunned to move while Max's friends wished me well and smiled slyly at Max. The willowy blonde came over, pecked my cheek and cooed, "I'm so happy for you."

When a couple stood up to leave, I announced, "We have to go, too. Thanks for a wonderful evening." I kept my mouth shut until we were in the car, even counted to ten.

"Why did you lie? How could you tell them such a load of crap?"

Max put his hand on my thigh and purred. "I asked you to marry me."

"What was all that stuff about graduate school? And the fellowship? Prestigious no less!"

"Anna, forget that shit, I asked you to marry me."

I never thought I'd hear those words yet here they were and I wanted more. "Who would know? What about something a wee bit romantic, like a candlelight dinner for two, soft music, beautiful flowers—?"

He spoke seductively. "Anna darling, would you be so kind as to consider marrying me. Anna darling, would you do me the great honor of agreeing to be my dearly beloved wife? Anna darling—" His laughter stopped the words but his hands kept seducing my inner thigh.

"Okay Max, stop laughing. I'll marry you."

I remember wondering how I could be dancing on air because a man asked me to marry him and, at the same time, be falling down a black hole. Now, when I think back to that time, I lived life as a divided self, one part saying yes, the other, no. I was so busy trying to please the world, especially Max, that I gave no thought to what mattered to me. Didn't even realize it was an issue. I thought being taken to expensive restaurants and fancy hotels was the same thing as a satisfying relationship.

I didn't have to worry about wedding plans. As soon as I said yes, Max designed invitations, made a guest list, and, most important, decided where the ceremony and celebration would take place. I might have been upset by his control but I liked his choices. For the service and reception, he picked a restaurant run by one of his friends that had just been awarded an unprecedented third star by Gourmet Associates. When we told my parents, my mother immediately called five people. Even my father hugged Max, opening a bottle of expensive champagne to welcome him into our family. "*A shtik naches*," he said as we toasted. (*A great joy.*)

"Oh, and by the way," said Max, as we were sitting around my parents' dining room table, "I talked to an old college friend yesterday. He's a minister and he said he'll marry us so that's one big worry off the list." He popped a piece of my mother's cheesecake into his mouth.

I surprised everyone, even myself. "No. I want to be married by a rabbi."

My mother recovered first. "Since when, all of a sudden, you're so Jewish?"

Max sneered. "I didn't know you were religious."

My father looked as astonished as I felt.

There's a lot about me you don't know. "It's not negotiable. You chose the invitations and the place. I'll decide who marries us."

"Do you even know a rabbi?" asked Max, with a controlled edginess in his voice.

"Yes," I lied. "I was waiting to make the arrangements until we chose the date and place." I left no room for objections. "I'll let you know who's going to do it as soon as I get a confirmation." I cut my cheesecake into pieces too tiny to eat.

Strangely enough, it was my father who broke the tension. He had a look on his face that I read as yearning. *For what?* "Mazel Tov, Anna." I took that for acceptance, grateful to have an ally. In a city of so many Jews surely I could find a rabbi to perform the ceremony.

There was no real waiting room, just a nook in the secretary's office, but there were lots of books and she said to help myself. I picked out a book of Jewish stories and only looked up when I heard a warm voice say, "Ms. Baum?"

She's a rabbi? So young? What can she possibly know? I had no idea how to begin.

"You wanted to see me?"

I nodded and followed her into her office. It was small but cozy. Bookshelves filled with books on top of books covered most of the walls, but in one corner there were two small chairs covered in a pale blue pattern, separated by an oval table. She gestured for me to sit in one of them. The Oriental rug was a deep blue and the walls, what I could see of them, were painted a lighter shade. On her desk was a photo of the rabbi with her arms around a grinning man and a young girl.

"So, Ms. Baum, tell me, why do you want to be married by a rabbi?"

I wish I knew. It's all happening so fast. "I don't really know."

"There must be some reason."

I avoided her penetrating stare.

"When Max told me he was going to ask a minister friend of his to marry us, I started to think about the stories my grandmother used to tell me and I got really upset. I told him I wanted to be married by a rabbi, not a minister or a judge or—a ship captain for that matter." *As if I knew one.*

"And what did your fiance say?"

"Nothing. I guess he was shocked. He's never shown much interest in spiritual stuff."

"What does it mean for you to be married by a rabbi?"

"I need a friend when I get married." *Where did that come from?*

She gave me a searching look. "I was thinking more about what it means to you to be a Jew, and why, from what you tell me, it's suddenly so important for you to be married in a Jewish ceremony. Do your parents go to synagogue?"

"No. At least not very often, but we always lit Chanukah candles and fasted on Yom Kippur. When I was a kid, I went to synagogue with my grandmother."

"What do you think about when you think about being Jewish?"

I paused. "Telling stories."

*****

For two days Momma hasn't gotten out of bed. I bring her food on a tray but she doesn't eat. I must be a bad cook. Daddy says she has to go to the hospital and I have to stay with Grandma but he isn't sure how to get me there. I tell him, "I'm nine years old. I can take the bus. I know how to go." He looks doubtful, but after I repeat three times what bus I'll take and how I'll walk once I get to her stop, he gives me twenty-five cents and makes me promise to go straight there, not to talk to strangers, and if I get lost I should go into a store and ask for help from someone with a kind smile. He says he will call from the hospital when he can. I feel very grown up.

The first thing Grandma does is give me such an enormous hug I have to take huge gulps of air. I hug her back as hard as I can. Then she makes me a cup of hot chocolate with lots of tiny marshmallows in it. I stir the marshmallows until they melt, sipping the gooey sweetness slowly, not wanting to burn my tongue or rush the deliciousness of the moment. When she brings a plate of freshly baked sugar cookies I dip them into the chocolate and slurp. She smiles. Knowing Momma would not approve of making so much noise, I slurp even louder, ignoring the ringing of the phone. I think I'll stay here forever.

"So, how about I tell you a story? You're not too big for my lap?" I gulp the last of my chocolate and snuggle against her, inhaling her lavender smell. "It's almost Purim. You want I should tell you about Esther and how she saved the Jews?" I have heard the story so many times I know it by heart, but I love it, especially when Grandma makes all the noises of celebration. Later, when she tells me I have to stay for two nights, I hug her and she kisses me and calls me her *shaineh maidele*, her pretty little girl. I use her toothbrush and sleep in a pajama top that Grandpa used to wear. Grandma found it in her rag pile.

*****

I was still wondering how to approach Max as we walked in Central Park along a route we often took to work off Sunday brunch, when he turned to me. "So when do I get to meet our rabbi?"

Our rabbi? I didn't like his tone of voice. "As soon as you like."

He rubbed my neck. "Forget this Jewish thing. Ralph is happy to marry us. He's a nice guy. You'll like him."

"It is not a Jewish thing. I am a Jew. You are a Jew. I want us to be married in a Jewish ceremony. When can you meet with the rabbi?"

"How much time do we need? And what's he going to do? Check me out and decide whether he thinks we should get married? Some clown who doesn't even know me?"

"First of all, he is a she."

"No shit, a female rabbi? Where'd you find her? You're amazing, Anna."

"Thank you. Second of all, the meeting is standard procedure, not an inquisition. A chance for us to talk about our feelings, to discuss what we want from our marriage and what we want her to say during the ceremony. Some couples write their own vows. Any ideas?"

"No." He started walking fast. I kept up with him. He walked faster. I walked even faster. "Anna, can't we forget the Jewish stuff? It's too complicated. With Ralph, he reads a few lines, we say 'I do,' and it's over, in five minutes. What's the point of a rabbi?"

I walked to a large moss-covered rock and dug my shoes into the earth. "If we don't get married in a Jewish ceremony, I'm not getting married." *I don't believe I said it.*

"You're not serious? You'd wreck your whole life just for a few stupid words?"

It got easier. "The words are not stupid. They have meaning." I looked up at him, meeting his accusing eyes. "I want to marry you in a way that feels right to me. That means us being married by a rabbi, especially a woman rabbi." I pulled a Max. I put my hands inside his jacket and massaged his back, feeling the warmth of his body touching mine. He moved closer to me and nuzzled his face in my neck. I could feel his body respond and for a moment I felt a sense of triumph that had nothing to do with sex.

"Okay, if it means so much to you, I'll do it. But I sure don't understand."

I did it! I really did it. Rabbi Berman, here we come. I set a record for speed walking.

Deciding who would hold up my two poles of the chuppeh put my life in disturbing perspective. There were only two people I knew to ask, Carmen and Angel, both Catholics. Max offered to invite two people for me. "I'll do my own asking, thank you very much," I told him.

At staff meeting on Monday, I made sure to sit next to Carmen, who seemed to be blossoming as a married woman. She radiated happiness and her skin, at one time covered with acne, was clear. When the meeting was over I asked, "Could we talk for a few minutes?"

"Sure," she said. "What's up?"

I flushed. "Tell you over coffee. Let's get out of here."

I staved off the question on her face by ordering. "You're looking terrific, Carmen. Married life definitely agrees with you."

She blushed. "My Angel, he truly is an angel. I'm the luckiest woman in the world. What did you want to talk about?"

"I'm getting married."

"Oh, Anna, that's great. Who's the lucky guy?"

"Max." I showed her my ring.

"It's lovely," she said without emotion. I guess she was remembering the one and only time I invited them for dinner. Max could hardly contain his sarcasm. Although Angel and Carmen acted as if Max was joking, the evening gave me a stomach ache. Afterward, while we were cleaning up, Max told me that if I ever invited them again, he would make sure he had another engagement.

"Anna, are you pregnant? Are you marrying Max because you have to? There're other alternatives; I'll help you. Me and Angel, I promise."

"I want to marry him." I ignored her look of incredulity. "I know when we had dinner the three of you didn't get on so well but he's not always like that, really he isn't."

"Does he treat you good, Anna? Does he make you feel loved and special?"

We met in the secretary's office in the synagogue, too small for Max to pace. He paid no attention to the secretary's suggestions of books we might find interesting and stared at the closed door. When Rabbi Berman came out of her office she had her arm around a young boy, his face wet with tears. "It's going to be all right, Stephen, but it takes time." He nodded, not comforted. "I'm here. Whenever you want to talk, just come. Promise?" He leaned against her as they left. I felt Max staring at me as I pretended to read about art in ancient Egypt.

She greeted us warmly. "You must be Max. I'm Rabbi Berman. It's a pleasure to meet you. Good to see you again, Anna. Why don't you go into my office? I'll be right there."

I peeked at Max's face and stifled my laughter.

"Anna, are you sure she's old enough to be a rabbi? She looks like a kid."

Rabbi Berman entered, shook Max's hand and then mine. The three of us sat around the oval table. "Max, I told Anna it's my practice to talk with couples before I marry them. I want to know what the two of you think about marriage, what you want from each other, what you're prepared to give up, what's important to you—I'm happy to have this opportunity to get to know you a little. Who wants to start?"

Max flashed his megawatt smile, taking my hand in his. "Rabbi Berman, I want you to know I consider myself a lucky man. Anna is smart, beautiful, energetic, and a good cook. What more could a man want?"

"I don't know, suppose you tell me." Her manner was kind, not at all confrontational, but I sensed an edge in her voice. "What makes you want to marry Anna?"

"Since we've been seeing each other, I've never been so happy. All my clients think she's the greatest. And, to tell the truth, it makes me feel good to know I'm helping her do what she wants to do, get her master's degree. And when she wants to go for her Ph.D., I'll be there for her too. I like the idea of being married to a smart woman." He laughed. "But it doesn't hurt that she's got a wonderful sense of humor and loves Thai food."

Rabbi Berman didn't respond to his smile. "What about you, Anna? Why do you want to marry Max?"

Because I love how he touches me. The way his fingers play with my hair. "Well, of course Max is handsome and talented and hard-working and very successful, for starters." *I left out smart.* "And I appreciate that he supports my going to graduate school. We have a lot of fun together. My parents adore him." *Something's missing—what?*

"What about your parents, Max? Do they like Anna?"

"My parents are dead. They were only children, so I don't have any close family. I appreciate Anna's parents. They've been so welcoming."

"What kind of marriage do you want, Max?" He let go of my hand. Rabbi Berman's gaze seemed to have less warmth than before. She might be young but she wasn't easily thrown or seduced by him.

"That's a good question, Rabbi. Maybe some men don't think about things like this, but I do. My parents fought a lot. As a kid I heard more screaming than talking. I never saw my parents touch each another. Forget hugging or kissing. I used to wonder if they even liked each other." *How come you never told me this?* He hesitated for a moment and then continued. "I'm marrying Anna because we have a good time. We like the same things. We don't fight. We see the world in the same way."

"And what way is that, Max?" The more directly she looked at him, the less able he was to return her gaze. I could feel the tension rising in his body. *Maybe this wasn't such a good idea.*

"Well, it's hard to put it into words, but I guess you can tell by the way we solve problems. Like finding an apartment to live in. We just picked the one we thought was best for us. That's what I mean." I noticed she didn't ask me.

"Tell me about a time when you disagreed."

Max paused, an innocent expression on his face, as if he were searching his memory. "I can't think of a situation, can you, Anna?"

Carmen's face loomed large. "Well, maybe. Is asking Carmen and Angel to hold up the chuppeh poles a disagreement? I know you didn't care for them when they came to dinner."

"Carmen? Angel?" Max sneered, quickly catching himself. "It's not that I don't like them. I just met them once. Aren't they Catholic? Still, you were Carmen's maid of honor; they're your friends, asking them makes perfect sense." He smiled, leaning back in the chair. "See Rabbi? Even Anna can't come up with a disagreement."

I didn't know I was holding my breath until I let out such a big sigh I had to cover it with a cough, then two more.

"Is something wrong, Anna?" asked Rabbi Berman. I couldn't look at her.

"What could be wrong? I'm marrying Max," I said, taking his hand in mine.

She kept searching Max's face, as if looking for something she couldn't find. I wondered what she was thinking, but then she shifted gears and told us how she conducted weddings, the prayers she liked to read, and the way she structured the ceremony. "Do you want to write your own vows?"

"No," said Max.

"Yes," I said at the same time.

We laughed nervously. She looked at me. "You don't have to decide now. We have time to settle the details."

We began having dinner with my parents regularly, sometimes once a week. After hearing too many "Sadie's" from Max, I called my mother Sadie. "What's with the Sadie business," she shot back, "I gave birth to you, remember?" Each time she heard Max call her Sadie, she beamed. I suppose it's difficult to flirt with a man who calls you "Mom."

Once I signed the lease for the apartment, waiting made no sense. We set a date and sent out invitations. The thought of cordially inviting people I didn't know to witness me becoming Mrs. Max Leitner made me wonder why I was doing this. What purpose was served by Max and me having to stand up in front of people I didn't know to say "I do?"

A week before the wedding, I was home grading papers when I heard a knock on the door. *Max has a key. Who could it be? It's late.* I peeked through the eyehole. "Angel?" He was unshaven and wild-eyed. "What's wrong? Come in. Can I get you something?" He wobbled into the room. "Angel, what's the matter? "

"It's Carmen." I stopped breathing. "Carmen—is—dead."

"NO! We had lunch this afternoon. We're shopping for shoes to-morrow—."

"Carmen wouldn't have wanted me to tell you over the phone."

"How?"

"We finished dinner. I heard her say, 'Angel.' I caught her as she fell. No time for 911."

"But Carmen looked so healthy. She was so happy about the baby—."

He wiped his eyes and blew his nose. "I cannot be in your wedding, Anna."

At school the next morning, children cried when they heard the news. The principal ran from one room to the next trying to reassure and comfort, but Carmen was a popular teacher and one of the youngest. How do you make sense of a person who looks the picture of health dying at twenty-four? At lunch everyone bombarded me with questions I couldn't answer. All of us kept repeating the same words over and over, "She looked so healthy. She was so young. How could she die of a stroke?"

When I asked Max to go to the funeral with me he said, "Anna, you know I have a meeting with the people from Aztec. I'll send a spray of flowers." I didn't press the issue.

The funeral was held in the same church where the same priest who now conducted her funeral service had baptized Carmen and married Carmen and Angel. Father Joseph didn't try to hide his tears. I have no idea how he managed to say the prayers and lead the singing of Carmen's favorite hymns. There were so many flower arrangements ushers had to put them in the aisle, on both sides, and at the back of the church, even in the entryway and on the steps outside. There was hardly room to walk. Afterward, we gathered in her parents' apartment, hugging and crying and telling stories. Carmen was right. There might be too little space, but there was so much love.

Three days later, Max and I were married on a balmy Saturday evening in July 1973. It was a quiet wedding, pleasurable despite my mourning the loss of Carmen. Rabbi Berman's presence helped the most. Her husband's and daughter's willingness to hold the chuppeh poles made me feel connected to a family, even if it wasn't mine. Her nine-year-old daughter asked if she could be my maid of honor since she was taking Carmen's place. I said yes, appreciating the dignity with which she held the pole and handed me the ring. I was grateful I had held out for a sit-down dinner with no dancing. No band. No DJ. No shtick. I was in no mood to be embarrassed by some clown who didn't know good taste from none.

While we were waiting for the cake to be served, Minnie made a beeline for us. "Darling, you are absolutely beautiful," she said, enveloping me in her hug. She took Max's hands in hers since she couldn't reach his shoulders easily. "One gorgeous bride, you hear me?" I blushed. "You are a lucky man, Max. Take good care of our Annale, she is one in a million." I blushed even more.

He smiled at her, "Ma'am, I intend to do just that."

Minnie snorted. "Ma'am, I'll ma'am you. Call me Minnie. I knew Anna when she was just a tickle between Sadie and Heshie. A good girl she is, you hear me. But serious! Even when she was a toddler she looked like she carried the world on her shoulders. I tell you, the day I made that child laugh I knew I'd done a mitzvah." She hugged me again, whispering, "I hope he's as good as he is handsome."

I hailed a waiter. "It's time to serve the cake."

My father stood up and spoke in a strong, take-charge voice, holding his glass of champagne. "Friends, as the father of the bride, I'd like to make a toast." I was sitting to his right, with Max on my other side, my mother next to Max. Although she made the seating arrangements, my mother didn't sit herself next to my father. I thought this rather curious. Didn't wives usually sit next to their husbands?

"We are gathered here tonight to celebrate the marriage of Anna and Max. My Anna, she has always been a very special daughter, always trying to please, always wanting to make people happy. So tonight, let us drink to Anna's happiness. Let us drink to Anna and to Max. If I have to lose the love of my life, after Sadie of course, at least it's to Max, a man who knows a good woman when he sees her. May their marriage be a source of joy for them. May they be loving life-long partners. And, may Sadie and I have healthy grandchildren." He tilted his glass to us and everyone joined in, echoing his toast. "L'chayim!"

I looked at my mother who was staring at Max. Almost in a daze, she stood up. "Since Max's parents didn't live long enough to see him married, I'll make the toast they might have made. "Here's to our beloved son, Max. May Anna appreciate the happiness Max will bring to her life. May she be a loving wife to him." *What about him being a loving husband to me?*

Minnie stood up and winked at me. "I been knowing Anna all her life. They don't come any better. So, here's to Anna, the woman who makes Max's dreams come true. And here's to dreams, theirs and ours, may they all come true."

Job Action

He needed a job. Waiting in line was not his forte. Max looked to see how many people were in front of him. Too many to count. He wondered how to convince the landscape architect that he was the best and only person for the position. Looking at his wristwatch, he sighed. An hour since he first got in line. At the rate the line was moving he'd be here all day, if he was lucky and they didn't hire someone before interviewing him. He looked at the man just coming out, smiling, cocky. Max hated him immediately and couldn't help himself. "How did it go?"

"Great. The guy asked me to draw a plan. I guess he wants to hire me."

Max forced himself to ask, "What kind of plan?"

"For taking care of a garden in a drought. To show him I know my stuff, I guess."

Thank you, thank you, thank you, Max thought to himself. "Good luck."

Afraid to just leave the line, he waited a few minutes and then smiled at the woman standing behind him.

"I need to go to the men's room. Would you be willing to hold my place?"

"Sure," she said, "if you'll do the same for me?"

Nodding, Max left. Walking slowly, he looked for a clean piece of paper, cursing himself for not having thought to bring any. Just before the men's room was a small office with a glass window. A gray-haired woman was typing intently. He took a deep breath, put on a wistful smile, and knocked.

Annoyed, she said, "Yes?" not looking up.

"Excuse me," he said, catching himself before he called her ma'am, thinking this would not endear him to her. He hoped he looked appreciative. "I was in such a rush this morning I left my brief-case home. I'm supposed to make a presentation and the drawings are in my briefcase. Could you by any chance save me from myself and give me three sheets of paper?" She looked less annoyed. "I can't tell you how much I would appreciate your help." He grinned seductively; looking at her with what he felt was convincing admiration and approval. She returned his gaze and smiled wryly.

Shit, he thought, she sees right through me.

"What's it worth to you?" she asked.

"My life. A job. A way out of living with a slob who thinks picking up his dirty clothes is women's work." He hoped his lies would hit their target.

"Sounds like my husband."

Max held his breath, wondering how long the woman behind him would hold his place.

"Please," he pleaded. "I really need your help." He avoided looking at the stack of paper on a shelf behind her desk.

When she put an inch-thick stack of clean white paper into his hands he almost cried. This time his thank you was genuine, his relief, palpable. "If I get the job, the drink's on me."

"Make that dinner and I'll say yes."

"It's a deal." Just to show he meant it, he said, "My name is Max. I'll phone you either way."

Back in line, he wasted no time. Ideas flowed. He ran out of ink and had to borrow a pen. Now he was grateful for the long line of people still ahead of him. He could use all the time he had.

It was almost five when he walked inside and shook the hand of the man standing behind the desk. Max knew how to wait patiently for the right moment, which came sooner than he expected. "It's late. I know you've been standing in line for a few hours. What can you tell me about your qualifications that would make me interested in you?"

"Well, sir, I've been thinking. I read in the paper that the reservoirs around New York are at less than half capacity. As a gardener, it would be my job to irrigate the plants, using as little water as possible. I drew a plan of how I could reduce water usage and protect the plants at the same time. Would you like to see it? It's rough; I had to do it standing up, while I was waiting. I could—."

"Never mind. Let me see what you have."

Max appreciated the thoroughness with which the man looked

at his plans. He sent a silent prayer of appreciation to his drawing professor who'd insisted on his learning drafting. He knew his lines were clean and elegant even if he had had to work freehand and without his drafting table. Max watched the man's every move, trying to read his thoughts without looking as if he were staring, which he was.

"You're the only applicant who thought to bring me a practical solution to a real problem. When can you start?"

Max already knew the restaurant he would take her to. On his way out he stopped by her desk. He was a man who paid his debts promptly.

4

I finished graduate school with high honors, funded by enough fellowships to leave me free of debt after graduation. A friend of Max's helped me find a job teaching high school English at a prestigious private school for girls. Shifting from teaching first-graders struggling to learn English to figuring out ways to reach bored, privileged adolescents was more difficult and less satisfying than I could have imagined. I lost my sense of purpose, of being a teacher where it mattered what I did.

Despite my feelings of dissatisfaction at work, life at home and our marriage, was wonderful. Max was an attentive husband and I enjoyed the role of loving wife. Aside from being nervous that I'd say or do something to set off Max's temper, we had fun eating out, going to the theatre, and visiting galleries and museums. He graciously listened to my tales of trying to interest students in the books we read and almost always attended school functions with me. I especially enjoyed the way we planned vacations that appealed to both of us. His income made it possible for us to travel in a style I thought belonged in books about the rich and famous. Even after trips to Thailand, Peru, and Switzerland, I still pinched myself. Like the time in Paris when the concierge saw me looking tired after a day of sightseeing and had a glass of wine and *petite* sandwiches sent up to help me regain my strength. I felt a little guilty about staying in luxurious hotels, but not so much that I didn't savor every minute of the staff's pampering. I even began to enjoy meeting my husband's clients from Europe and Asia.

One lunch period, the high school teachers' room was full of talk about the school hiring Dr. Rosalia Chavez to head the counseling program. I thought she must be pretty damn good to impress a Board of WASPs enough to hire a Latina. I was looking for the right moment to introduce myself when one of the girls in my class fainted smack in the middle of Chaucer. For quite some time I had been wondering if she was suffering from an eating disorder, but since we were not allowed to "meddle" in the personal lives of our students, I kept my thoughts to myself. Dr. Chavez stopped me in the hall.

"Are you Anna Baum, Brittany Field's teacher?"

I nodded. "Tell me about her."

"Brittany is dangerously thin. I think she needs to be in treatment for anorexia."

"How about a cup of coffee after work? Sal's Place?"

Dr. Chavez was a short round woman in her late forties, with cropped jet-black hair that fit her head like a velvet cap. Her dark eyes looked directly through me with no stopping to be polite. Sometimes, in faculty meetings, just the sound of her voice made me feel safe, a curious sensation for which I had no explanation. She wore ethnic dresses rather than business suits and long dangling earrings with stones that matched her dresses, like me. The ring she wore on her left middle finger looked like a wedding band. I particularly admired her confidence and ability to address controversial matters. She was the only person in faculty meetings who pressed the issue of what we teachers should do when one of us found a forbidden pot pipe on a student. We were supposed to believe that the student's parents' large and unexpected contribution to the school played no part in the headmaster's decision to go against the rules and keep the student in school

I found a table in a corner and waited, wondering why Dr. Chavez wanted to talk with me. Had I done something wrong at school? Upset a student without knowing it? In a school like ours, before you could blink, a parent would be in the headmaster's office complaining about how their poor little darling was being mistreated.

"How do you like teaching at the school?" she asked.

Something gave me the courage to want to speak honestly. "Can we keep this between ourselves?"

She nodded, her earrings tinkling as she leaned toward me. Her gaze felt comforting.

I put down my coffee. "I feel empty. Like what difference does my teaching at this school make? I know it sounds silly but—"

"Doesn't sound silly to me." She ordered another coffee.

"All I've ever done is teach, and I like teaching. That's what I don't understand." I was surprised by the intensity of my feeling.

She put down her cup. "I turned down Yale to study at a state university. At the time, everyone told me I was crazy, but I got a good education and, afterwards, I didn't lack for interesting job offers that gave me the opportunity to make a difference in my clients' lives."

"Forgive me if I'm being rude, but if that's the case, why are you working at an exclusive private school for girls?"

"Good question. Stay tuned."

She grinned.

I grinned.

"My treat," I said. "Let's do this again. Soon."

On my way home I discovered I could whistle.

About a week later, I literally bumped into Dr. Chavez. "Anna, just the person I was looking for. I'm raising money for a new Head Start program for troubled kids. Interested?"

Something inside me perked up. "What degrees do the teachers have to have?"

"We're still working out certification requirements. Well?"

"Me?"

She nodded.

"I've never worked with such young kids."

"We'll give you preliminary training and I'll supervise." She looked confident.

I stared at her. A previously unseen door was opening. "Well, if you think I can do it, I'm willing to try. The best day for me is Wednesdays. Max plays racquetball with friends and he's never home for dinner." Her smile felt like a gift.

On the first Wednesday I was to volunteer, Dr. Chavez offered me a ride.

"Dr. Chavez—."

"Please, call me Rosa."

I felt uncomfortable using her first name. "I'm about to dive head first into mile-deep water and I don't know how to swim."

"The kids will love you."

We pulled into the school's parking lot and six kids from the playground cheered when they saw her car. The next thing I knew I was being introduced to Jameeka and Jose and Roberto and Lupita and— Jameeka immediately asked me to push her on the swing. Lupita was quick to protest. "You awready been pushed. It's my turn, ain't it, Miss?" She hurled herself at Jameeka, fists outstretched. I caught her just in time.

"No problem," I said, "the swings are close enough for me to push you both." Their squeals filled the air and me with pleasure. The kids might be emotionally fragile but they hadn't forgotten how to giggle. Three hours passed so quickly I thought Dr. Chavez was teasing when she said it was time to get them ready to leave. I couldn't remember when I'd been so involved.

Wednesday afternoons became my treat for the week. Not that everything was wonderful. After the first day it didn't take a genius to realize how much I had to learn. What surprised me was my interest. Not only did I ask Dr. Chavez for stuff to read, I read it. And thought about it. And asked questions. Sometimes, I spent more time thinking about what I'd do with the Head Start kids than I did planning my literature classes. The hole inside me grew smaller but now I couldn't ignore knowing how much I hated teaching in the private school.

One Tuesday night, I was preparing for work when Max said, "I'm not going to the club tomorrow night. I'm bringing Bill Jackson from the Greene account home for dinner." I nodded and continued looking for a story to read to the children the next day. "Didn't you hear me? I invited Jackson for dinner."

"I heard you. I'm busy."

"You're always busy. What's going on? You were so late tonight I wondered if you forgot where you live."

"Dr. Chavez was shorthanded and asked if I could help out." I found a story, put it in my book bag and went into the kitchen to make a salad. I was cutting up tomatoes when Max came into the kitchen, took the knife out of my hand, and pushed me against the wall.

"You're a volunteer for chrissake. No one's paying you. Right?" His face, inches from mine, was contorted with anger.

I tried to get away. "Let me go. I have to finish making the salad."

He glared at me. Hard eyes. Tight mouth. "You're fucking another man."

"No! If you don't believe me call Dr. Chavez and ask her. Let go, you're hurting me."

"This is just in case you're only thinking about it." He whacked my head against the wall. My vision blurred. Blinding pain filled my head. Blood poured from my nose.

*****

I'm drinking a glass of milk in the kitchen. My mother comes into the room and I look up at her. The slap hits me full on the right side of my face. I freeze. The milk dribbles down my chin and wets my skirt. She knocks me against the refrigerator door. The telephone rings and she storms out to answer it. I hide behind the couch, curling into a little ball. I hear her call me but I stay there until my father is home from work. When he's sitting at the table and my mother isn't looking I come out from behind the sofa and sit in my chair. My mother serves dinner. We eat. I do my homework. I go to bed. I lie awake all night, wondering what I did wrong.

*****

"Let me go or—"
    "Or what?" sneered Max.
    "I'll kick you in the balls."
    "Just try." He twisted my arm. I stopped struggling. "Remember what I said. Don't fuck with me." Angry red welts outlined his fingers on my arm. He stormed out of the room.
    I threw dinner away and cleaned up the kitchen. Wrapping myself up in a quilt as tightly as possible, I put my head under the covers and tried to find my stories. I begged Boonah to come back, to tell me stories again. "I need you, Boonah, please!" Maybe he left because I lost myself and he couldn't find me. Maybe what I really needed to do was find myself.
    We didn't talk about the incident.

*****

I spent hours reading material I had previously ignored just to plan classes, staying long hours at the high school where I tutored after school, increasing my afternoons at Head Start from one to three. I was a horse with blinders, looking only at what was directly in front of me. Before leaving to teach, I played with my face in front of a mirror until my smile looked reasonably genuine but four-year-old Rico was not fooled. His mother was in rehab for the third time, his father was in jail. He spoke to no one and responded to nothing. I wanted to help, but no matter how gentle I was, I scared him. I kept trying. Part of me hoped that if I helped him I could fix what was wrong in me. When I saw him scrunched up in a corner, face to the wall, I quietly put my hand on his back. Then, so softly I wasn't sure he could hear me, I said, "I love you, Rico." He didn't move away. I cradled him with my body. We stayed in this position long enough for all my muscles to ache. After a while he got up and went to the swing, me following behind. He stood watching until a child got off. He got on. I carefully pushed him. "More!" he giggled, the first word we heard him speak.

Each time Max hit me I grew smaller and more helpless. When I left the apartment I became Anna the teacher. When I returned, I was Max's wife. I took my cue from him and gave no sign that anything was amiss. We cooked. We cleaned. We discussed his work. We had sex. We continued to go out with his friends. When women called and hung up after hearing my voice, I pretended it was a wrong number.

Why didn't I call the police or get a divorce? How was it that Max's hitting me made me feel like a child who had done something wrong—who deserved to be punished. I remember how confused I felt about his behavior. One minute Max would be hurting me, the next minute, kind and caring. I kept thinking the change in him was my fault. If only I was smart enough to figure out what I had done wrong, I could fix it and everything would be all right.

My master's degree graduation was different from college and high school. I didn't ask anyone to come see me receive my diploma and awards. No one sent cards of congratulations. When the ceremony ended I struggled to disengage from tangles of hugging people. Diploma in hand, I went directly to the headmaster's office. "Mr. Brevoort, I'm here to tender my resignation."

His shocked expression pleased me. "Mrs. Leitner, I thought you were happy here. May I ask why? Your students give you high marks and your Chair has nothing but praise for your work and participation in faculty governance."

"I've taken a position with a Head Start program for at-risk children effective July 1."

He looked even more stunned. "Will that be enough of an intellectual challenge for you? I expected you to leave us for a Ph.D. program."

I smiled. "Who knows? In a few years, I just might do that." Leaving his office I made another decision. From now on I would be Anna Baum. Mentally, I kicked Mrs. Max Leitner out of my way. The legal change took longer but was no more satisfying.

My hunger to know about the children with whom I was working knew no bounds. I poured over studies that Rosa and others were conducting, researching ways to reach damaged children. After reading one more study that had been received with great acclaim but left me dissatisfied, I told Rosa we needed to talk. Two days later we met for coffee.

The waiter came by to take our order. I thought about the studies I'd read and compared them to my teaching experience. "There's something missing from the research studies you lent me," I told her. She looked more than a little surprised.

"Those are refereed studies. What could possibly be missing?" she asked.

"Stories."

"What do you mean?" she asked.

"When I tell my children a story, they tell me one back. Even if the story they tell me is not about their lives, it tells me something about how they're feeling."

She frowned. "For example?"

The waiter brought our coffee giving me time to think of a good one. "I told them a Korean story about a boy who always asks for stories but will never tell one. When he's about to be married, an old servant notices a wriggling bag high in the young man's room. He hears the spirits of the stories the boy wouldn't tell plan to hurt him. So the servant finds a way to outwit the spirits. When the young man finds out what the servant did, he promises to tell stories to anyone who asks.

"What stories did they tell you?"

"Lupita told me about a time her uncle kissed her and said if she didn't tell anyone he would buy her a big candy bar. Raul told about a big bird that was stealing food from the little birds. Big Bird said if they told, he would smack them. When a bear came, the big bird gave him the little birds' food and the bear and the big bird laughed. 'The little birds got dead,' he said." *I wish I could tell you my story.*

"You might have something here. Have you kept records of the stories you told and the responses you got from the children?"

"Some. I can't always do it right away and sometimes I forget, but I'm absolutely sure the stories are an important part of their language acquisition."

"Interesting. There's a conference coming up that's focusing on children's language development. Want to submit a paper about your findings?"

"Me? All by myself?"

"Why not?"

"Couldn't we collaborate?"

Rosa thought for two seconds. "Why not?" We laughed as we made a big deal of shaking each other's hand.

I got used to a new routine, going to work two hours before school started and coming home so late I skipped dinner most nights. Max made no comment about my changed schedule. I made no comment about how frequently he didn't come home to sleep. Writing the paper with Rosa gave me a desperately needed new purpose. As part of my research, I visited the homes of some of my children so I could talk with whatever adult might be around. The hole inside me grew smaller. I paid no attention to my clothes becoming too loose.

All marriages have their ups and downs. This is just one very long, very bad down. The misery felt familiar, like it was my natural state of being. I wished I had the courage to call Rabbi Berman, but I was too ashamed to tell her I was living with a man who kept hurting me. *Yes, it's wrong for Max to hit me. Yes, I'm afraid of him. But, I must be doing something wrong to make him so angry.* I decided if I changed, so would he. I made an extra effort to dress well, make nice meals, and be especially attentive to his clients. I learned to conceal the worst of the bruises with makeup. I chose clothes that covered my body. I swallowed bottles of aspirin. I had nightmares.

One Wednesday Max was drinking whiskey when I came home after teaching the preschool kids. I was still thinking about the change in Jacinta, a child who usually had to be prevented from hitting or kicking anyone who got too close. Today, she actually sat in my lap while I told a story. Max hadn't started supper so I went into the kitchen and took out steaks, humming, feeling happy and grateful I'd been able to help her. He followed behind me. "Forget the steaks, babe, I've got a present for you."

Pulling me into the living room, he held me close, slowly unzipping my skirt, like the overture to a first act. I could feel my body melt as his hands danced on my body. When I tried to unbutton his shirt he moved my hands behind my back, a little too firmly.

I stopped humming." "Ouch, what are you doing?"

He laughed salaciously, unbuttoning my blouse, tossing it to the floor. He took off my bra and pants, pinching my breasts together before he kissed them. "Having a good time? I want you to have a really good time, Anna."

I tried to unbutton his shirt but he pushed my hands away. "Max, stop."

He ignored me. I tried to pull away. "You're hurting me."

"Come on, baby, don't spoil the fun." He crushed me to him, my back to his body. I could feel the hardness of his erection as he snapped a black satin strapless pushup bra around my breasts. Then, still crushing me against him, he lifted each of my feet to pull up a string bikini with satin garters dangling, cold against my skin. Caressing my crotch, he stuck the thong between my buttocks. I could feel the heat emanating from his body as he took out sheer black stockings from his pocket and slowly unrolled them, licking me as he pulled them up my legs. His hands held me firmly as he caressed my body while attaching the stockings to the garters, putting black high-heeled shoes on my feet. As I struggled to pull away he abruptly turned me around, his face contorted with lust. He forced my mouth open, kissing me, his tongue so deep in my mouth I gagged.

"Max!"

He gripped my shoulders, looking at me with glazed eyes. I was too frightened to move.

"Dance for me, baby." He sang a slow blues ballad, his deep seductive voice enveloping me. I stood stone still. He stopped singing. "I asked you to dance."

"Let me take off your clothes. Let's dance together."

"What's the matter, sweetheart? You only dance for your boyfriend? You think I believe that volunteer shit? You're fucking another man."

I started to run but he caught my leg and yanked it so hard I crashed to the floor. Before I could roll into a ball and protect myself he kicked me. "Whore! I'll fix your ass." The first kick knocked the breath out of me. The next blow was so hard I was flung halfway across the living room. He pulled me up with one hand and punched me with the other, screaming obscenities and hurling accusations. I passed out.

Coming to, I heard the silence. I felt blood trickling from my nose and mouth. I crawled to the toilet bowl and managed to wash my face before everything went black.

When my eyes opened all I could see was blood. I coughed, and there was more blood. Dragging myself to a standing position I looked at the bloody, swollen face, the black and blue eyes. My stomach ached. My bones hurt. Every breath was painful. My left arm stuck out at a peculiar angle. I called the school to say I was sick and then passed out. This time when I came to, I called Rabbi Berman. "I need a lawyer."

Before I could make an appointment to see one, Max offhandedly handed me divorce papers. Despite his objections, I knew I needed to find my own attorney.

I put off saying anything to my parents, yet I wanted to tell them before Max did. We were just finishing dinner one Sunday afternoon when my mother asked, "So how come Max is suddenly too busy to come to dinner? He doesn't like my cooking anymore?"

"We're getting divorced."

My mother's coffee cup crashed to the floor, spilling brown liquid over the starched white tablecloth. *Almost like my blood on the sheets.* Her mouth contorted. She pounded the table with clenched fists, spitting out curse words I didn't know she knew.

I looked at my father, needing him to come to my aid and offer consolation. Instead, he picked up the cup pieces and said, "I'll get a sponge."

My mother grabbed the tablecloth and yanked it off the table. Dishes crashed to the floor. Water, coffee, wine, mixed and spilled. I picked up shards of broken glass and china, watching rivulets of blood flow from my hands. My mother ran out of the room.

My father returned with paper towels, a sponge, and a plastic bag. We cleaned up the mess without looking at each other.

"Dad..."

"*Shah*, Anna, it's best not to say anything."

A few weeks later my father talked about how tired he was. Three weeks after that, I was getting dressed to go back to the hospital to visit him when the phone rang. I barely recognized my mother's voice.

"Your father's dead," Her tone was devoid of emotion.

"I saw him two hours ago."

"I saw him fifteen minutes ago. He's dead."

I was speechless. I hadn't counted on my father "disappearing" with no warning. "I'll call Minnie." I crumpled onto the chair.

"She's on her way."

"I'll take a taxi. Wait for me."

"Where am I going? Thirty-two years we been married. In a month he was gonna be sixty-five. Didn't even have time to retire."

"I'm leaving now."

"They were making a party for him at work. Well, that's life. Can't count on anything to work out the way you want it to." She hung up.

There were over two hundred people at the funeral service. As soon as I entered the room my mother made a beeline for me and snarled, "Where's my Max?"

"Your Max?"

"I bet he wanted to come and you told him no."

I stared at her, unable to speak.

"You should have tried harder. He's one in a million."

"Mother, it's enough already."

"I'm so embarrassed. People ask why. I should tell them you just let him go?"

Like he's a charm on a bracelet? Lose one, get another? "If I told you the truth, you wouldn't believe me, so why bother?"

"I know the truth. You didn't give him enough and he found it somewhere else."

The truth, huh? You wouldn't believe the truth. You'd say it was my fault.

"Have you signed the divorce papers?"

I shook my head,

"Then there's still hope."

Hope? Hope for what? That he'll stop hitting me? That he'll stop seeing other women? That he'll love me as much as he loves himself? It felt as if she cared more about losing Max than she did about the death of her husband. I felt as if I had lost the only man who ever loved me.

Rabbi Goldman spoke about my father as a man of intellect, a person who questioned authority. He said that although my father seldom attended formal services, they met regularly to talk about issues of Jewish identity and the consequences of personal action and repentance. *Is he talking about my father?*

After the rabbi spoke, Minnie got up. "I knew Heshie from when he was five. Sixty years is a long time to know someone. He was a good friend, a decent human being. And when he had troubles he never complained. Just did what he could. When he made mistakes, and he made plenty, he felt bad. *What kind of mistakes?* I want to tell just one story about him, to show the kind of man he was. When I was fifteen, I was walking home from work one night and a bunch of hoodlums attacked me. They stole my money and left me crumpled on the ground. After they ran off, I didn't know what to do. My best dress was in shreds, my nose was bleeding, and my legs forgot how to walk. I was terrified but I managed to limp over to where Heshie lived. He was just walking up the steps when he saw me. One word I didn't have to say. He helped me inside, gave me a cup of tea, and found clothes I could wear home. To make a long story short, he got my clothes cleaned and repaired so they were almost as good as before. He wouldn't take any money, and I'm sure it cost him plenty. When you were in trouble, Heshie always did the right thing."

Suddenly the world started spinning. I put my head between my knees and felt a hand patting my back. "Take a deep breath, *neshomeleh*, it will soon be over."

After the funeral service people came back to our apartment for cake and coffee. My parent's neighbors and friends brought platters of food, telling stories about my father as they sipped and ate. I listened, trying to comprehend that the man they were talking about was my father, a man who, in our house, seldom ventured an opinion about anything. Now I was learning he had a whole life outside the family. Did my mother know? I eavesdropped shamelessly. What struck me was how many people he had helped. *Why hadn't he helped me? Why hadn't he stopped my mother from hurting me? Didn't he know how much I needed him?*

A pot-bellied gray-haired man with sad eyes told a woman who cried softly, "Heshie lent me money when I couldn't borrow from a bank. Never once asked for his money back. He knew I'd give it to him when I could. How many people you know would do that?"

A dark-haired woman with large glasses overheard him and said, "I know what you mean. One time he went to the drug store for me to get medicine for my daughter because she was too sick for me to leave her." *How did he know you were all alone?*

I walked away from their stories only to bump into a man who grabbed me. He didn't even try to hold back his tears. "Annale, darling, your father took a whole week off from work to sit shiva with me after my wife, blessed be her name, died. If it hadn't been for your father, like a brother he was, I don't know what I would have done. No one should sit shiva alone. But that's what would have happened. Me sitting shiva, with strangers." He hugged me as he cried, his hot tears soaking my dress.

I looked to see how my mother was faring. Her face remained impassive as people came up to her, telling stories about their Heshie. Always, Minnie was close at hand, acknowledging people's condolences and moving them on. I felt like an outsider observing a strange ritual for an unfamiliar person I was told I should know.

My nonreligious mother decided we would sit shiva for the full seven days. Minnie stayed the whole time, never letting my mother out of her sight. Long after I had gone to bed I could hear them talking and crying and laughing. Before she left, Minnie hugged me. "Take good care of your mother, Annale. She needs you." In the living room, my mother was crying. *And when he was alive? Did you care?*

About three months after my father's death, my mother called. "I'm moving to Florida next week. Do you want anything? Otherwise I call Jewish Federation."

I was too stunned to speak.

"So Miss Snooty Pants, I got nothing you want?"

"I never thought you'd leave New York. Why go to Florida? You don't know anyone there, do you?"

"I want to stick my toes in warm sand."

"What about Minnie?"

"Maybe she'll come down, too. She hates the cold even worse than I do."

"Won't you be lonely?"

"So what's new? If I need company I'll go to the JCC."

"But you hate those places."

"So I'll unhate. I need a change. I've been here all my life. It's time for something new. Are you gonna look or what?"

"I'll come tomorrow after work."

"Why not tonight?"

"I have a late meeting."

"With a man?"

"With Child Protective Services—about one of my children."

"One of your students, you mean. I shoulda known."

"I'll see you tomorrow. And for once, can I please take you out to dinner?"

"I suddenly forgot how to cook? We'll eat here. I'll make pot roast."

"Let me bring something."

"I got everything I need."

When I moved out of my parents' house, all I could think of was getting away from her harshness, his quiet, and a kind of disappointment I couldn't define, as if each blamed the other, but I didn't know for what. When I started teaching, I hoped my life would be better than theirs—lighter, happier, but I seemed to have inherited their heaviness. Even now, after remembering so much, I still couldn't figure out what went wrong.

The coughing bouts were getting harder to deal with, lasting longer and coming more often. I knew that something was wrong with me, but I wasn't willing to find out what it might be. Rosa kept telling me I needed to see a doctor, but not going meant not knowing. I was too tired to deal with any more bad news. Sometimes it felt as if my whole life was about avoiding something I didn't want to know. Maybe if I could have talked to Boonah, and we told each other stories, I would know what went wrong. Maybe then I wouldn't have been so afraid to see a doctor.

Moving

Sadie hunched her shoulders and turned her back to Minnie, a gesture each of them knew meant the discussion was over but Minnie refused to stop. "Look, Sadie, you lived here all your life. You know your way around, where the stores are. Why do you have to have to move a thousand miles away? Just like that. Poof, you're gone. You have no people in Florida. No friends. Here you got me, you got Anna . . ."

"Hah! Anna! I might as well be dead as far as she's concerned."

"Oh yeah, who took you out to the ballet two nights ago? In spite of your kvetching about the cost of tickets. Who sends you Mother's Day cards?" Minnie put her arm around Sadie. "We've been friends since grade school. Almost sixty years. Who's gonna make you laugh down there? Who else knows you like I do? Who knows me like you do? Sadie, don't just throw it all away. I know you're lonely. But it'll get better, believe me."

"So move to Florida with me. Herb don't care where he lives long as he gets good hot dogs. They sell Nathan's in Florida. The sun will do him good. Make him feel like his old self again."

"What about Sarah and the grandkids? I'm their only grandma."

"When you want to see them you get on a plane. A few hours later, you're there. No big deal."

"Why Florida? You and Heshie used to make fun of people who moved down there. What was it you said? Blue Hairsville? People too old to see they're old?"

"Yeah, well, Heshie's dead. I got no one to look after. I can go where I like."

"Why do you have to go anywhere? Almost seventy years you live in New York and suddenly it's not good enough for you any more? Makes no sense. Give yourself time to get over the shock. Heshie died so suddenly."

"I'll make tea." Sadie walked into the kitchen. Minnie followed. Sadie took two mugs out of a cabinet. Staring at them, she put them back. Tight-mouthed, she pulled out a small ladder and slowly climbed up to reach a cabinet over the refrigerator. Minnie watched silently as Sadie took down two delicate cups and saucers, one at a time, put the ladder away, and carefully washed and dried the cups and saucers, a faraway look in her eyes. Sighing, Sadie took out the ladder again, climbed up, opened the same cabinet and peered in. Rearranging dishes, she took out an oval tray wrapped in tissue paper. Cautiously climbing down, she placed the tray gently on the counter before putting the ladder away. Sadie unwrapped the tray and deliberately folded the tissue paper. "This was my grandmother's. She gave it to Momma when Momma was leaving Russia. With the cups. There were six but only two survived the trip."

She took out a flowered teapot, filling it with hot water. When the teakettle sang, Sadie poured out the water and filled the teapot with two teaspoons of loose tea. She poured boiling water into the teapot, covering it with a tea cozy she had made when Anna was a baby. Blue and purple flowers against a yellow and white background, the same blue as the flowers on the cups. The color of the violets Avi gave her the day he first kissed her. She put the cups and saucers on the tray, with a plate of apricot bars freshly baked that morning. She tried to keep from showing her feelings. "Here Minnie, you take the tray and the cups, I'll bring the teapot."

They sat at the small round table in a corner of the living room, covered with a starched white tablecloth Sadie had embroidered when she was pregnant with Anna.

"Sixty-one years I know you and I never saw these cups. What else don't I know? I can't imagine life without you," said Minnie tearfully.

"I been saving them for a special occasion," Sadie said, blowing her nose, handing Minnie a tissue, avoiding her friend's incredulous expression.

"You and Heshie were married thirty-two years. It takes a while to get used to living alone. Maybe you'll meet someone— at least give yourself time to recover, to get over him going so suddenly."

"You think I want to spend the rest of my life washing a man's socks? I'm finished with all that business."

"That's what you think of marriage? Washing socks? Anyway, what's the rush? Wait a year. See how you feel. Maybe you'll change your mind. You got the rest of your life to be lonely down there."

"Minnie, I been taking care of people all my life. I gotta do something for me even if it's only moving to Florida. I'm not gonna die in the same city were I was born, where I lived all my life. Florida's nice. I'll find a place near the water; I always wanted to walk on the beach. Feel warm sand between my toes. Watch seagulls fly. Smell clean air. Something besides noise and dirt and sirens and a telephone that never rings."

"I call you," protested Minnie.

"I'm telling you, you should come with me Minnie. Herb will do anything to please you."

"Please, Sadie, don't go."

"There's an empty apartment two doors down from me."

"Sadie—" Minnie couldn't stop crying.

5

Rosa and I spent hours each week discussing material for our upcoming presentation. Although the collaboration began because of my experience with stories, it quickly became an issue between us. I was at my desk, writing, when she opened the door, holding the first draft of my part of the paper.

"Anna, all your evidence is anecdotal. It won't hold up under professional scrutiny."

"Screw professional scrutiny. We know telling stories makes a difference."

"Our experience is irrelevant. What we need is scientific data. Numbers. Before and after. Certifiable results."

I glared at her. "You've seen and commented on my children's language development compared to children in other people's classes. The kids are randomly chosen and they all come from the same projects."

"Maybe you're a better teacher."

I threw down my pen and stood up. "What makes me better, if in fact I am, is that I'm the only teacher in this program who uses stories to teach language. My kids are no different from the other kids who start school in September refusing to speak, yet in a few months my children know enough English to tell stories. The others don't. That's what our research is about!"

Rosa sat down. "So how are we going to document this? Anecdotal evidence has no scientific basis. It doesn't prove anything and it won't hold up. I know our audience."

Barely able to control my anger, I spit out my words. "And I know what I'm talking about. Maybe it's time for that to mean something. I'm not saying our research is conclusive, and I'm not saying telling stories is the only way to reach these kids. What I am saying is we definitely have enough information for a phenomenological comparison study."

"Yes, but how do you prove it's the stories?" she challenged.

"And how do you prove it's not? Those so-called professionals, who probably haven't been in a classroom in forty years, and maybe never in a classroom with kids like ours, should, just for once in their lives, shut up and pay attention to people who are helping kids heal. That's what I'm saying." I took a deep breath.

"But how can you be so sure? You're not being reasonable."

"And you're the one to decide, I suppose." I slammed the draft down on my desk. "You come into a classroom, test the kids, and leave. And that makes you an expert in what changes screaming, hitting kids into children who can listen and share and work together? Please!"

She recoiled, holding her hands in front of her face, as if to ward off my verbal blows. "Look, it's not that I think you're wrong. I know my colleagues. I don't want us to be laughed off the podium because we can't cite scientific evidence for the changes in the kids."

I started to pace, then stopped and looked her in the eye. "You may be worried about being laughed at but I don't give two shits. Someone, somewhere, has to be the first one to do something." I stopped and took a deep breath. "Who did Newton cite, for God's sake? Or Galileo? But if you're so worried about what they'll say, I'll write the damn paper myself. I'll use my 'anecdotal' evidence and if they want to laugh, fine. In the end, I'll have the last laugh and I'll keep laughing for as long as children leave my class able to tell their stories in any language they choose."

Rosa put her hands up in surrender. "Whoa. I give up. I've never seen you like this. Mama tiger protecting her cubs."

"If not me, who? Someone has to help kids talk about their lives." *I need someone to help me. But with what? My mother?* I tried to calm down. "Have you finished collecting your data on the children in our control group?"

"Just about. Why?"

"What would happen if I taught the other teachers how to use stories with their children? If you document the changes, that should give the audience something to munch on. If there's not enough time to do it in all the classes, we could at least do it with one."

"What happens if there's no change?"

I shook my head. "Oh, ye of little faith —. There will be a change. Big enough and clear enough for you to document it to the satisfaction of Scrooge."

I was trying to stop coughing while transcribing one of Eric's stories when Rosa came in waving a piece of paper. She looked disapprovingly at the pile of cough drops on my desk and then said, mimicking the children, "Ms. Baum. Ms. Baum, I got something for you."

"What?" I asked, grateful when the coughing stopped.

"Come and get it," she teased.

My office isn't exactly huge but she managed to fend me off until I lunged, grabbing the letter out of her hand. Not only was our paper accepted, we had been given prime time. My jubilation knew no bounds. I hugged Rosa. I would have hugged the janitor had he not escaped, laughing. "We have forty minutes before the children come. I say we celebrate."

"You're on," I said. I threw my sweater over my shoulder, remembering that Max had given it to me after I'd won a teaching award. I wish I'd known then how much I would enjoy teaching preschool and working with Rosa.

I began our presentation. Although I'd never told a story to a large, crowded room filled with adults, once I started, it was like I was in my own world, telling it as much to me as to them.

"This is a Native American story," I paused.

"The People were bumping around in the dark and the cold, huddling together for warmth. Although it was the only life they had ever known, one day someone asked, 'Is this all there is? Is this the whole world? Will we never have a better life?' No one could answer the question."

Just like my children, the adults grew quiet. I could feel them listening. They had stepped into the world my words created.

"One day, a strange creature appeared, burrowing its way into their dark, cold world. Someone had the courage to ask, 'Is this all the world there is?'

"Mole, for that was the creature's name, answered, 'Well, sometimes I go to a place that *feels* different.'

"Mole prepared to leave. The People were anxious and uncertain. 'How is it different?'

"The People edged a bit closer to Mole. 'I don't know,' he said. 'I can't see it because I'm blind. All I know is that it *feels* different.'

"Can you take us to the place that feels different?' asked someone else.

"Yes, but when I travel, I dig the earth from in front of me and put it behind me. If you choose to come with me you must do the same. You will never be able to return to this place.'

"'Ooh,' moaned a lot of the People, terrified at the idea.

"But some thought differently. 'Please, Mole, take us to the place that feels different.'

"Eventually, despite their worries, all the People followed Mole, passing the earth he dug in front of him to the People behind. It was a long, hard journey.

"Suddenly, Mole said, 'This is the place that feels different. It is time for me to leave you.' The People were shocked. It didn't look different. It was still dark. But soon, some of the braver People walked toward something that felt different and stepped outside into the bright light, where they screamed in pain.

"'If only we could go back to where we lived. At least we were used to the dark and the cold.' But they knew there was no way to return to the place and the life they had known.

"A voice spoke to them.

"'Courage, my children. Listen to me and all shall be well. Your eyes hurt because you looked directly at the sun. Do not do this. When you go outside, keep your fingers in front of your face and your eyes closed. Slowly open your fingers and even more slowly, open your eyes.'

"When they were able to see they asked her, 'Who are you?'

"'I am your Grandmother Spider. Follow my advice and you will find a home. Do not go east to the red mountain for you will bleed to death from the wounds of wild creatures. Do not go west to the black mountain for you will starve to death in the dark where nothing grows. Do not go north to the white mountain for you will freeze to death. Go south, to the green mountain. It is far away but if you journey there you will live and prosper. Your children will thrive.'

"'But if it is so far away, how will we know when we arrive?'

"'You will see a creature that reminds you of Mole but is not Mole. It will remind you of your Grandmother Spider but it will not be me. When you see this creature you will know you have arrived at the place that is home.'

"The People huddled together during the longest night they had ever known, waiting for their first dawn.

"With the coming of the light, a few of the People grew restless and looked around.

"'Green mountain is too far away. Let us go to the red mountain.

We are brave enough to kill any creature that attacks us. When we return we will tell you what we found.' But they never returned.

"Some of the People decided not to wait any longer. 'We are going to the black mountain. We know how to survive in the dark. When we return we will tell you what we found.' But they never returned.

"A few, not trusting the advice of Grandmother Spider said, 'Let us go to the white mountain. We know how to live with the cold. When we return we will tell you what we found.' But they never returned.

"Now, only two people remained; a man and a woman. They decided to follow Grandmother Spider's advice and began their long journey to the green mountain, a place they could barely see. They walked and they walked and they walked. They grew tired and discouraged and thought about stopping but where would they go? So, they did the only thing they knew to do; they kept on walking.

"While they were resting, the woman saw a creature she had never seen. The man urged her to keep away, that it could be dangerous, but the woman edged closer to it. 'Look,' she said, 'the creature has pulled in its head. It reminds me of Mole.'

"The man joined the woman and noticed the patterns on its shell. 'Those markings remind me of Grandmother Spider's web.' The man and the woman looked at each other and smiled, grateful. They had come to the place that was home."

There was a suspense-filled moment of silence before applause filled the room. *I am a storyteller.*

The rest of the presentation was like a dream. Rosa followed up on my observations, people asked questions, and not even the most skeptical could burst my bubble. Afterward, about fifteen audience members followed us down the hall to an empty room where we continued discussing the issues raised by our presentation. My passion for stories and their effects on children created a space where anything was possible. The story I told and the question it posed, 'Is this all there is?' kept me focused and inspired. It was the best day of my life.

The next morning I was still high from our presentation. Normally, I arrived at school about an hour before the children to have a cup of coffee and think through my plans for the day. Often Rosa joined me and we talked about the kids or our research. Since she became Chief of Psychological Services for Head Start, we saw each other quite a bit. She had an easy way about her that I admired. Everything seemed more possible when she was around.

This morning, our talk began with a progress report on Abdul, a painfully shy four-year-old whose mother died in a house fire when he was a baby. His father's whereabouts were unknown. Until three months ago, Abdul lived with both grandparents, but when Mrs. Kareem died of pneumonia, Abdul stopped speaking. Mr. Kareem asked me to talk with Abdul, who refused to leave his grandfather to come to school. If I thought Mr. Kareem was skinny before his wife died, he was positively wraith-like afterward. I usually brought homemade cookies or cake that he received with unabashed delight. In return, he made me a cup of tea and gave me the magazines he'd collected for the children who liked to cut out pictures.

I began to notice that my coughing was becoming uncontrollable. Even more puzzling was how unusually tired I felt. Still, I enjoyed my time with Mr. Kareem, drinking his special blend of tea, eating my carrot cake and his sugar cookies. I laughed every time I thought about his foray into cookie making that started after Abdul asked, "Are the sugar cookies living with Gramma in heaven?" The first few batches were inedible but Mr. Kareem persevered. One day, he baked some that were shaped funny and burned, yet Abdul was so pleased he ate them all in one sitting.

When I was ready to leave, Mr. Kareem handed me a bundle of magazines. Although it was no bigger than the usual stack, it felt much heavier than the one two weeks ago. I hoped I had the strength to carry them to school.

As I staggered into my office, I was so focused on not dropping anything I bumped into Rosa. The string burst open and magazines flew everywhere. "You better slow down," she said. "If I were a cop I'd give you a speeding ticket." I could feel her staring at me as we picked them up. "Anna, your color's really bad. When's your annual physical?"

"I just need more sleep. I'll catch up this weekend. Boy, the kids go through magazines like wind through an empty street. I can't keep up with their scissors." Rosa kept looking at me. I shrugged and told her my observations of Abdul.

"Sounds like he's making good progress. When did you say you were seeing your doctor?" Her tone of voice was not pleasant.

"We also need to talk about Julio. His father was arrested for smashing his mother's face into a wall while he was watching. Yesterday, he asked to live with me but I told him his grandmother would be lonely if he left. He asked if she could come too." I opened a file drawer. "Here, I made these notes about his behavior this past week."

Rosa put on her glasses and read while I left the room until I could stop coughing. Suddenly my nose started to bleed and I wondered if one of Max's punches had ruptured something inside me. I didn't like the look on Rosa's face when I returned. "He definitely needs help," I said, showing her some of his drawings and stories.

"So do you."

"We're talking about Julio."

When my assistant, Pilar, entered, much to my relief, Rosa stopped staring at me and started organizing her notes. I pulled out two folding chairs, managing to make room for the three of us. Cozy is good sometimes.

Rosa began, as usual, laying out the facts without making the situation seem hopeless, never losing sight of reality. Pilar wasted no time in pleasantries. "So, what's the plan? Julio needs a lot of help. The sooner the better."

"Keep telling stories and encourage him to make up his own from the stories you tell him just as you've been doing," said Rosa.

"And what about Eric?" asked Pilar. "He's so tense it's a wonder he can breathe. It's like any moment he expects to be hit."

"Yeah, and Shalana who cries if you look at her without smiling," I added. "Well, we'll write down as many of their stories as possible." I grinned at Pilar, "What about you and me submitting a paper next year? 'Anecdotes from the Field.'" I sent a sly look to Rosa. "Lord knows we have enough material for a book. I can see it now—the book-publishing phenomenon of the year—'Stories By and For Young Children.'" *Written by two people who know!*

Pilar looked thoughtful. "Why not? Some stories our kids tell would fry the hair off a lot of people's heads." *Might be just the thing to take the wind out of those windbags.*

That afternoon, we were huddled on the storytelling rug listening to Rajana tell how she came to this country when Rosa walked into the room holding a little girl's hand. My first reaction was anger. Why didn't she tell us we were getting a new child? Why hadn't Pilar and I been given her records so we could create a plan to help her feel comfortable? First impressions are crucial. Rosa avoided my eyes.

She spoke to the children. "I'd like to introduce you to Marina. I hope you will make her feel welcome." Marina hid behind Rosa, clutching her leg. The children stopped giggling and squirming. All eyes focused on Rosa and the little girl. She was tiny, either very young or small for her age. "Marina, I'd like to you to meet Ms. Baum and Mrs. E. They're going to be your teachers. Ms. Baum, could you say hello to Marina?" Walking over to them, I could feel the children's stares.

Marina was holding on to Rosa's leg so hard her knuckles were white. "Dr. Chavez, perhaps the three of us should go for a little walk?" I suggested. Rosa nodded.

Opening the door, I smiled at Marina, who buried her face in Rosa's thigh as Rosa practically carried her into the hallway. Rosa shook her head to the questions my eyes asked. Maybe Marina had been foisted on her and she was as clueless as I was. "Ms. Baum, I really have to go to my office, a child is waiting for me. Could you tell Marina a story?" Her voice was unusually desperate. Marina continued to cling to Rosa.

I knelt down until I was eye to eye with Marina. Speaking softly, I said, "Marina, when I was a little girl I told myself stories about a friend I named Boonah. Whenever I was afraid, he would find me and tell me a story. Do you like stories?" She hid behind Rosa. I held out my arms and gradually moved toward her. "Marina is a pretty name. I'm happy you're going to be in my class. We have lots of fun." Although she refused to look at me I sensed she was listening. "Dr. Chavez has to talk to another child but she'll come back to see you. While she's gone, you and I can be special friends. Okay?" Slowly she released her hold on Rosa's leg. "Is it all right if Dr. Chavez goes now, just for a little while?" She nodded and squeezed my hand so tightly it was all I could do to keep from wincing.

Rosa brushed away the tears on the little girl's face. "I'll come back, Marina. I promise." She left quickly. I held the frightened child until my leg muscles demanded that I move.

"Marina, will you come with me so I can tell you a story?" She nodded, but remained frozen. Holding her frail body against my chest, I carried her to my office. When I closed the door she whimpered so pitifully I quickly opened it. Sitting her on my lap, she curled against me, silent, taking up as little space as was humanly possible, her eyes wide open. "Once upon a time, there was a little girl who was very lonely," I began. "She didn't have any brothers or sisters."

In the classroom, Marina looked at what everyone else did before making a move. Some kids talked to her, not bothered by her silence or the way she watched them. Mostly, she huddled in a corner. While I was helping the children make a circle, we heard a loud noise like a truck backfiring. Marina let out a strangulated sound, put her hand over her mouth and ran into the closet. I had to use all the sweet-talking I knew to coax her out. She burrowed into my shoulder, her fingers digging into my body. I held her, crooning words I always use when kids need to hear safe sounds. "Hey, hey, it's okay. Hey, hey, it's okay." Her taut body cuddling against mine made me feel strong. As she calmed down and her grasp loosened, with me by her side, she joined the others in a circle game. I felt a surge of energy when she looked up at me or put her hand in mine. For the rest of the day, she followed my every step; but when it was time for us to get the children ready to go home, Marina hung back. Pilar tried to put on her jacket, but Marina again hid in the closet. I opened the door and she fell into my arms, sobbing. Remembering times I spent in the closet my knees buckled, all I could do was croon, "Marina. Marina. Sweet Marina." When she stopped crying, I said, "You have to go home now, but tomorrow you'll come back and we'll tell more stories." She refused to look at me. I wanted to take her home, to erase the fear in her eyes, to help her laugh and play. I tried to move her out of the closet, but she wouldn't budge.

Pilar came over. "Marina, there's a lady here to pick you up. She says you like her." *Who is she?* I saw the fear in Marina's eyes and tried to hide my own. "Let's go see the lady, Marina, you and me." A caterpillar on a hot day would have moved faster.

The social worker rushed toward us. Marina hid behind me. The woman slowed down, putting a smile on her face. Marina's nails dug into my leg. I introduced myself and said, "My aide and I need to talk with you."

"Maybe tomorrow. Marina, we have to go." Marina was squeezing my leg. "Say good-bye to your teachers." Marina burrowed into my back. "Come now, the others are waiting for us." Grasping Marina firmly by the shoulder, she led her to a waiting van where children peered out of the windows. Marina tried to break away but the social worker tightened her grip and whispered something to her. Marina stopped struggling and mechanically waved to us. Soon the van was just another vehicle in rush-hour traffic.

Back in the office I tried contacting Rosa but she'd left for a family emergency. I could only hope she'd be back in time for us to talk before morning. "Pilar, what do you think?" I asked, looking through my files, wondering if I'd missed Marina's.

She let out a deep sigh. "I wish we knew more about her."

"You have a good feeling about that social worker?"

She shook her head. "Something is definitely wrong."

I dialed Rosa's number again. No answer. "Well, you have to pick up your kids. I'll close up shop and call when I get home. I'll let you know if I learn anything."

It was after ten when Rosa called me back, sounding as stressed as I felt.

"Why didn't you tell us about Marina when we were discussing Julio?"

"Would you believe I didn't know she was coming? Let's talk tomorrow. My mother-in-law's surgery took much longer than we expected. I'm exhausted."

I couldn't sleep. Wherever Marina was, I knew it wasn't a place she wanted to be.

*****

Momma is home from the hospital but she doesn't have the baby. She won't talk to me. She says she is tired. I want to ask why she left it there but she is crying and crying and crying. Maybe somebody took it. When she stops being so tired she tells me we have to go see a lady. Momma dresses me in my new dress and braids my hair. She even puts blue bows that match my dress on the ends of each braid. "Why do we have to see the lady?" I ask.

"Stop with the questions. Wash your face and brush your teeth."

It's a long way to the lady's house. We take a bus and a subway and another bus and by the time we get there my dress is rumpled. I'm thirsty. I hope the lady will give me a drink. She lives on the second floor of a one-family house and there are a lot of steps. The lady says she is oh so sorry and Momma says something about he was perfect but I don't understand what they are talking about. "Momma, what does perfect mean?"

"Go play with the blocks."

"Momma, I'm thirsty." The look on her face makes me sorry I spoke. When the lady goes to answer the phone she smacks me across my face.

"We're guests. Where are your manners?" She keeps hitting and pushing until I'm falling down the stairs, tumbling backwards.

I hear the lady say, "Sadie, I think she's going to be all right. It doesn't look like she's broken any bones." Momma is glaring at me. The lady has tears in her eyes.

*****

I arrived at school much too early but Rosa came in just after I made coffee. She took one sip after another, all the time staring out the window. "The stepfather used her as his personal ashtray." She sat down, stood up, stared out the window, and sat down again, trying not to look at the file in front of her. "It seems Marina's older brother decided to take out his misery on her after his girlfriend left him. The mother's been arrested for selling crack. A neighbor called child protective services and a social worker finally got an order to take her out of the home, but not before she'd been beaten and who knows what else."

I gasped. "Is that the same social worker who took Marina home yesterday?"

"Don't know. What I do know is she's in temporary placement."

"Does that mean someone like me could take her in? Be a foster mother?"

"Yes, but you have to be approved—."

"How do you do that?"

"You apply. And wait. And wait some more."

"There's no time to wait."

"If you're interested, I'll tell you where to get the forms."

I started coughing and couldn't stop. Rosa got me a glass of water.

"When are you going for your physical?" Her tone of voice was harsh. Her look was worse.

The gulf between my success at school and failure at home widened each day. Max's relentless determination that I use his lawyer unnerved me. Although I hadn't formally consented to the divorce, I agreed to meet with Max at his lawyer's office, hoping this would ease his anger. Before I could answer the question his attorney asked, I began coughing uncontrollably. Max looked at me with disdain, as if unable to imagine that this pale, sickly looking woman was actually the woman he had married. His wife.

"Is something wrong, Anna?" he asked, backing away from me.

I wanted to say no but I couldn't stop coughing.

His lawyer brought me a glass of water. I looked at Max, stupidly hoping that he might, even now, care about me.

"Is it contagious?"

I shrugged, unable to speak. I didn't know what was wrong. I didn't know why I agreed to meet him in his lawyer's office. I didn't know why I couldn't stand up for myself. Not with Max. Not with my mother. Not with anyone who seemed to have power over me. Not even when my life might be at stake. It was Max, standing near the door, handkerchief over his nose and mouth who said, "Maybe we should postpone this meeting."

Marina charged into the room after recess, elbows out, shoving everyone out of her way. She ran into my arms like a sprinter, holding on to me until Emily, Abdul, and Shakira knocked her aside. Marina fought back, clutching tightly to my left side. Pilar called out, "Who wants to pour the juice?" The children headed for the juice pitchers; Marina held on. Although she never spoke and insisted on staying as close to me as skin permitted, I paid enough attention to the other kids so they didn't complain. All too quickly it was time to get them ready to leave.

When the good-looking, well-dressed man appeared at the door and said he was there to take Marina home, something inside me clenched and I panicked. Using my most professional voice, I asked, "Who are you?"

His smile reminded me of my father and a voice inside me said I was being foolish, that there was nothing to fear. I told myself to relax, that my imagination was working overtime.

"None of your business, lady. Get out of my way."

Definitely not prepared to hear him say this, I was figuring out a response when Marina saw him. She let out a strangulated scream.

I turned to see her running toward the front door. I yelled, "Marina, stop!"

Pilar and I raced back into school. The man disappeared.

Later, when the police asked for his description, neither Pilar nor I could say anything definitive; we described him as tall, stocky, and middle-aged, with dark hair.

We looked for Marina all afternoon and evening, combing the school, nearby neighborhoods, and a park. We even went door-to-door and house-to-house in the area surrounding the school. I kept telling myself somebody must have seen her. Surely someone would find her. We called her name and gave her description to everyone we met. Pilar and I were prepared to look all night but the police told us to go home. They promised to call if they had news. I heard the "if" and silently screamed.

I cursed myself for not keeping Marina safe inside until the social worker came. Later, it occurred to me that no one else had come to pick up Marina. Who was the man? How did he know who she was? Why was he there to get her? Where was the social worker? When Marina saw him, why did she run away from Pilar and me rather than trust us to keep her safe? The last bit was the worst. I hadn't protected her though I told her I would.

Sergeant Weissman, the policeman in charge, talked to the kids quietly and carefully. "Boys and girls, I'm sure you know that one of your classmates is not in class today. We're here to help find her. Have any of you seen Marina?" The children shook their heads. "Do any of you play with her after school?" Again they shook their heads. "Well, if any of you do see her, or if you hear any news about her, would you tell Ms. Baum?" Heads bobbed up and down. "Thank you very much. I want you to know we're doing everything we can to find her."

I had to admire his skills. He went out of his way to reassure me too.

"Ms. Baum, there was absolutely no way you could know Marina would run away when she saw the man."

"I promised I'd keep her safe."

Each day that passed with no news confirmed my worst fears. The police were pretty sure the man who came to pick up Marina was her stepfather, but when they went to find him, no one knew where he was or where Marina might have gone. It got to the point where I began to wish her body would be found. At least then I would know something.

The next day Eric came to school ignoring the blood dripping from cuts on his face, arms and legs. Even his swelling face didn't stop him from pummeling anyone who blocked his way. Paying no attention to classmates' threats, he shrieked, "Ms. Baum. Ms. Baum. Ms. Baum," and with a final burst of energy, hurled himself at me. I caught his quivering body, masking the horror I felt, ignoring the blood staining my clothes.

With practiced composure I spoke to the children. "Eric needs my help. Please sit on our storytelling rug. Mrs. E. will tell you a story." The children, experts on trouble, reacted as if a windstorm had suddenly entered the room. Previously cooperative children fought over toys, knocking down blocks. A few of the youngest cried.

It took hours before the children were comforted, Eric quieted, I had reported the incident, filled out the paperwork, and we had returned to some semblance of normalcy. Later, as we were putting away toys and wiping up traces of blood, I kept shivering though afternoon sun still warmed the room. A fit of coughing seized me, draining my last bit of energy. On my way to boil water for tea I took two steps and crumpled to the ground. Getting up, I slipped again. Although we thought we'd cleaned up all the blood, there they were, four puddles of dark red on the green linoleum tiles. Pilar brought wet paper towels to clean it up. "Are you all right?" she asked. I nodded, hoping the swirling in my head stopped before I enlarged the puddle with undigested lunch. Then, despite my embarrassment, I began to cry. Pilar brought tissues. "Blow!" she said as if I were a child. I blew. We both laughed nervously

After she left I sat at my desk. How foolish I was to hope we could keep misery and pain out of the lives of our children. They lived in places neither Pilar nor I could go. I yanked upward on my bloodstained denim skirt. Wrestling to get it off, something pressed into my left eye. I dragged the skirt back down and felt for the hard thing. It was the key to the basement door. I stared at it, put the key in my desk, changed clothes and left the school, my eyes searching for a five-year-old girl with big dark eyes.

The next morning Eric did not come to school. Rajana, in braids tied with red ribbons, asked, "Where Eric?" Without waiting for an answer she socked Emily who punched Abdul who whacked Maya—a chain of misery that reflected their anxieties.

David, who peered at the world through thick glasses too large for his face, cried as he ran to the closet. "Eric dead!"

As I went to calm the chaos, tiny Filomena started to sob. "Eric dead. I wanna go home. I don' like this place." Soon half the children were in tears, the others ready to join them.

I kept seeing the police report in my mind's eye, reading like a bad play.

"Can you tell me what happened, Eric?" asks Detective Hawkins, a specialist in cases of child abuse.

"Man hit me."

"Tell me about the man."

"Don' know."

"How big is he?"

"Big."

"As big as Mr. Demetrius over there?" Hawkins points to a six-foot-two police sergeant.

"More big!"

"What's the man's name?"

"Don' know."

"Why did he hit you?"

"Don' know."

"Did you do something?"

"No."

"Where was the man when he hit you?"

"In the bed."

"Who else was there?"

"Momma."

"Were you talking to your momma?"

"Yes."

"What did you tell your momma?"

"I wan' a cookie."

"Were you hungry?"

"Yes."

"Then what happened?"

"Man hit me."

"What did you do?"

"I falled down."

"Did he hurt you?"

"Yes."

"Where did he hurt you?"

"He hurted me all over. He hurted my legs and my arms and my face and my tummy. I was bleeded."

"What did your momma do?"

"She yell."

"Then what happened?"

"Don' know."

The children kept asking where he was and what was wrong. "Eric didn't feel very good this morning so he stayed home but he'll be back soon, maybe tomorrow," I said. The children stared, waiting. "He just needs to rest for a day or two." Pilar handed out musical instruments and eventually succeeded in getting the children to dance with her. I couldn't tell them that a man hit Eric in his mother's house because Eric was hungry and asked for something to eat. The worst part was when I spoke to his mother—all she could do was complain. "It's Eric's fault. I tell him all the time, 'Don' come in the bedroom.' He's a troublemaker, that kid. No matter how much I beat him he still trouble." *Do you hug him? Is a man in your crotch worth more than your son?*

*****

An image and a memory. Momma and Daddy are yelling at each other. Daddy is holding me, pressing me against him. Momma yanks me away. Daddy grabs me. I cover my ears to keep out the screaming. Why is Daddy holding me so tightly? Why is Momma pulling me away?

*****

After what felt like years, it was time to get the children ready to go home. Aljulio, a mischievous newcomer from Texas, bronzed from the sun and his heritage, put his five-year-old arms around me and asked, "Why you sad?"

"I'm not sad," I lied.

"If no, why you look sad?"

"I don't know."

"Then you sad!"

"Go away," I said, trying to keep my voice light. "You ask too many questions." His dark eyes glared at me before he stiffly turned away, refusing to say goodbye. I felt bad. I knew I'd hurt his feelings so I hurried after him. Stooping down until we were eye to eye, I said, "I was wrong. You don't ask too many questions. It's good you care how people feel."

"Why you sad?" he asked once more, solemnly buttoning his third button in the fourth buttonhole, still not looking at me.

I rebuttoned his coat and carefully chose my words. "Sometimes we don't always know why we feel sad. I didn't even know I looked sad until you told me. But I'll think about it and I'll tell you if I figure it out, okay?"

"Is it promise?"

Lord, why don't I work in a tollbooth? "Yes, it's a promise." Giving me a dazzling smile and a quick hug, he wiggled his way outside.

Still thinking about my so-called promise, I walked to the closet to get a large piece of paper but the shelf was bare and all our supplies were kept in the basement. Cursing myself for not remembering our need for it sooner, I tried to think of ways to avoid going down there but I was the one who had promised the children the large painting project. I was tired. It had been a hard day and the coughing spells that were lasting longer and coming more often left me depleted. I opened the top drawer to put in my lesson plans, saw the key and closed the drawer.

After changing into my "real life" clothes, I walked outside and stood on the stoop. "Go home," I told my feet. They refused to move.

Joe Weissman, the policeman who'd been so kind when Marina disappeared, walked by. "Any problems?" he asked.

"I just realized I forgot something and I'm wondering if I should go back for it."

"If you're like me and you don't go back, you'll be thinking about it all night." He waved, whistling as he turned the corner. I stifled the impulse to ask him to come with me.

I went back inside and searched in my bag for matches, knowing we had emergency candles in case the switch didn't work. The connection was loose and we'd called maintenance several times but the repair which was supposed to be fixed this week had once again been rescheduled. I reminded myself there was no reason to worry. I knew how to use the crowbar lying near the steps if I had to, though I knew I wouldn't need it.

I wasn't pleased to discover the switch didn't work, but after lighting the candle I felt better. I walked down the stairs, one step at a time, allowing my eyes to get used to the dim light. There were nine steps. At the bottom of the seventh step my feet gave way. The candle went out and the ground reached up to meet me as I tumbled into black.

I lay in the darkness. Hearing footsteps. Seeing a light. "Hello? Anybody down here?"

I felt a hand gently touch my head and began struggling to get away. The deep voice was gentle. "It's me, Joe. We said hello to each other a little while ago."

"How did you find me?"

"I was walking toward the patrol box and saw your front door was open. I didn't see no lights so I thought I better take a look. What happened?"

"I fell."

"Looks like you're bleeding pretty bad. I better call an ambulance."

"I'm all right."

Paying no attention to what I said, he put his arm around my waist and helped me up the stairs. At the top he turned on the light switch. The sudden illumination hurt my eyes. Turning off his flashlight he asked, "Why didn't you turn on the light?"

"I did. The switch didn't work. We've been having trouble with it."

"Get it fixed. Broken switches are a code violation." He helped me sit. "Wait here, I'll get you a glass of water." I slumped against the back of the chair. Blood dribbled down my face, flowing onto my blouse and skirt, making dark red puddles on the floor. *Just like Eric's.*

Joe came back with a glass of water and a bag of ice cubes. "Drink this while I hold the ice against your cuts. If the bleeding doesn't stop I'll have to call for help."

The next thing I knew, he was washing my face with a wet towel. I heard him say, "Welcome back to the land of the living." I managed to mutter a few words of thanks before I started coughing. "You need a doctor."

"No." *Something happened. What was it?* I tried to stand up but my legs buckled. I tried again. And again. He put his arms out as I slumped. "I'm calling an ambulance. Don't move." We both laughed at the absurdity of his words.

Ambulance lights flashed. *This isn't necessary. I just need to rest. I need to remember what happened.* When they put me on the stretcher and began to strap me down, I fought with a burst of animal fear, screaming and coughing as if my life were at stake.

"Stop!" Joe yelled at the paramedics. "She's had a bad shock. Tell her what you're doing, for godssake." He bent close to my face. "They don't want you to fall off the stretcher, that's why they have to use straps."

I drifted into a void.

Wafting in space.

Peacefully floating.

I will fly like this forever.

No!

Emma sat on the bench, trying to keep her nervousness from showing. They had said the meeting would be over by three, at the latest. It was now half past three. What could be taking so long? She didn't notice Jacob's arrival until he sat down next to her. "What are you doing here? It's your day off."

"You sat with me when I was waiting to learn if the Board would use facts instead of Seward's accusations, when he tried to say it was my fault that Mr. Hancock was given the wrong medication."

"Thanks, you're a good soul." They sat in silence, listening to the sounds of the second hand making its way to the next minute. When the door opened, Emma went in, her face impassive. She left the room the same way.

Despite being exonerated, nothing the doctors said made her feel better. Her patient, a thirty-four year old woman with no history of lung disease or smoking had come into the hospital with an apparently straight-forward case of pneumonia, yet one hour after Emma checked her vital signs and found them to be perfectly normal, she returned to inspect her IV and found the woman dead. Why? The IV was working properly. Oxygen was flowing smoothly. Although the hearing was standard procedure, no one's words eased her feelings of guilt or her sense of responsibility.

"Mrs. Wahieloa, wait up." Emma kept moving, ignoring the nurse who followed behind.

Jacob walked quickly to catch up with his supervisor, finally moving in front of her. "Emma, have coffee with me, please? Don't keep beating up on yourself."

"I'm doing nothing to myself. It's already done."

"When I was upset you kept telling me, 'You need to talk. Don't keep your feelings bottled up.'"

"You live alone. I talk to my husband."

"He doesn't face life and death every day the way we do."

"She's dead, Jacob. There's nothing to talk about."

Jacob led her into the staff cafeteria to a secluded place behind a potted ficus tree. "I'll be right back. Don't go away, please." A nice boy, she thought, young enough to be her son. She'd done a good job of training him. Even the grumpiest and sickest patients had trouble resisting his smile. The very same smile he was using on her now, she noticed wryly as he returned with coffee.

On the floor, when others were around, it was Nurse Wahieloa and Nurse Holder, but when the two of them were alone, it was always Emma and Jacob. Had been from the very beginning, when his was the only brown face on the ward beside hers. He took the cup off the tray and put in one and a half teaspoons of sugar.

"Don't fuss, I'm all right. I just don't understand what happened. If I knew, I —"

"But you don't. No one does. The autopsy showed she died of pneumonia, nothing unusual, nor was there any sign you did anything wrong."

"Jacob, you're a good person, I appreciate your concern, but even you can't change facts. I'll tell you one thing, this will not happen again. Not on my watch!"

"Emma, even you can't control death."

"As if I didn't know. Maybe I'll take Sam and we'll go back to Hawaii. Raise pigs."

"Pigs don't die?"

"You raise them to die."

"When I was in trouble you kept telling me, you do what you can and when it's over, it's over and you have to move on and let it go."

"You were accused of doing something you didn't do. Jacob, stop worrying, I'm fine. I just need a good night's sleep. I think I'll go and sniff the roses."

She walked to a small garden area just off the employees' restaurant that was usually empty. A woman was sitting on the bench, crying. Emma felt a surge of frustration and anger. The garden was clearly reserved for medical personnel. What was she doing here? The woman looked up. Emma pretended she didn't see her, turned, and walked toward the parking lot, then turned again when she saw two nurses from her ward. She sighed. There was only one place she could be by herself.

She hurried off to the employees' lounge, avoiding eye contact. Locking the door of the toilet stall, she took off her shoes, and squatted on the toilet seat, closing her eyes, imagining herself on her favorite beach. Black sand sparkled. The deep blue sky was cloudless. Huge waves crashed against ancient bits of lava. The brilliance of the sun warmed her soul. She saw herself running along the hot sand, dipping into the violent surf, but only at the edge, hot and cold. Free.

6

I was floating amidst a clamor of voices. One demanded attention. Drifting back into nothingness, pushed and pulled into hearing and feeling.

I tried to shield my face but the covers wouldn't move. I opened my eyes and was immediately sorry. The comforting darkness had disappeared, giving way to a cold hurtful light. A round woman the color of cafe au lait looked at me with concern. Although she had a kind face, which fit the lilting voice I'd been ignoring, I turned my back. Wanting to float peacefully. I couldn't find the darkness.

He was perched on top of the blanket, halfway between my head and feet, a tiny man, his small brown face haloed by white bushy hair. Wearing a flowing garment made of shades and patterns of brown, he looked older. Still, he was here, his grin just as I remembered it.

"Boonah!" I whispered. Stunned.

He sat peacefully, legs crossed, arms resting lightly on his lap. "Hello, Luv." He acted as if it hadn't been years since I last saw him.

"Where have you been?" I asked.

"At your service."

"Why did you leave me?"

"I believe it was you who left me. Close your eyes and open your heart. I will tell you a story."

I listened, just as I did when I was a child.

"Once upon a time the world was not yet as we know it. Earth was covered with flowers and trees and grasses. When the People arrived and saw this abundance they sang songs of joy and gratitude, planting and harvesting many crops. Life was good and food was plentiful.

"But there came a time when no rain fell. Children asked questions no one could answer. The time of dying was near. One woman struggled to fight the lassitude of death. Each dawn, she called to the spirits. 'Where are the rains?' Seven dry days and seven dry nights passed.

"Flowers from her garden, led by a graceful blossom, spoke to her in a

vision. 'We will share our knowledge if you choose to find the rains. But be warned, the journey is long and arduous.'

"'I must go. Death's song is everywhere.' The flowers transformed into a map, dancing their way into a path, disappearing when the woman asked questions.

"'Who will come with me?' People turned from the woman, too weak to care. Too tired to offer blessings for her safe passage.

"Tucking the map in her belt, she climbed rocky mountains that lay to the east, crossing huge expanses of withered grass. At dawn, she woke to find herself lying on hot desert sands. Despair, like a giant vulture, hovered.

"She did not die. A wind funneling sands into a spiral sucked her up, carrying her over the desert to a place of boulders where she moved toward a fragrant scent of moisture. Giving thanks to the spirits, she followed the faint sound of dripping water, clambering up and down huge rocks with no end in sight. 'Spirits, do not abandon me,' she begged. 'Show me my path.'

"She drifted in a dream state until a breeze pushed her through a small opening between two giant stones. Jagged shards slashed her clothes and pierced her skin. Her blood painted the earth, staining her ragged garments.

Too proud to admit defeat, she cursed herself for undertaking an impossible journey, yet images of cool water beckoned. The woman let the warm breeze take her where it wished. Sharp edges rounded. Boulders of black gave way to blue, merging and melding until they glowed brilliant green. Puzzled, she moved toward a patch of sun.

"Walking toward the bright light, her eyes aching from radiating spears of gold, the woman stumbled and fell on the root of a tree. As she lay on the earth, she heard water splashing. With renewed energy, she ran toward the sound, yet at day's end she found no water.

"Desperation and fury propelled her into the waterfall she did not see. Gratefully, she honored the spirits for helping her reach the birthplace of water where she drank and bathed and swam in the delicious wet coolness.

"Images of lush greenery collided with faces of dying children. She found shells and filled them with water, dreading the loss of a drop.

"The woman's loneliness was greater than her anger and despair. She let her feet guide her through hot sands, dry plains, and steep mountains until she reached the gnarled old tree standing at the outskirts of her village. Thankful for her safe return, she poured water on the dry earth and blessed the flowers of her vision. She woke to the fragile promise of returning life.

"The woman dribbled water on parched earth all around the village, creating designs of life on depleted ground. Without hope, she retraced her steps, amazed to see tiny blades of grass growing from each drop of water she had poured on the dry roots.

"Following the path of tiny green shoots back to the gnarled tree, she saw a small bubbling spring. Delighting in the water, she splashed her face, enjoying the rivulets that filled each crevice of her body.

"She heard crying and looked to see a gaunt old man covered by dried leaves, cradling an emaciated child. She watched him use his tongue to catch tiny drops of moisture as they rolled down his face, putting them into the mouth of the dying child. Repelled, the woman turned away, yet in her mind's eye she felt their silent misery and found herself walking to where they lay.

"Cautiously, she took the child from the old man and brought the girl to the spring where she moistened every inch of her body. Carrying the old man to the water, she dripped tiny droplets into his mouth.

"The old man and the young girl survived, nurtured by earth's bounty which flowered as the rains returned.

"With winds to the east and west and north and south, this story ends."

"Thank you, Boonah." I give him a hug.

"You are welcome," he says, his eyes crinkling just like they used to.

"I am so happy to see you."

"Now it is your turn. Tell me what you see."

"No. I'm afraid."

"Look. I will keep you safe."

"A man plays with a baby. He rubs himself against her. A woman sees him. She screams and grabs the baby. The man and woman wrestle. The man pulls the woman to him. He kisses and hugs her. The baby dangles from his arm."

"There is more," says Boonah. "Tell me what you see."

"The dangling baby is changing into a little girl, cowering. Her arms are covering her face. She is backing into a corner."

I stop, too upset too look anymore.

"What are you seeing?" asks Boonah as he caresses my forehead.

"I see my mother beating me."

A more horrible picture forms. I scream.

"No! No! No!"

Two nurses responded to my yells. "What's the matter?" asked a stout woman with bleached-blond hair and a voice like fingernails scratching a blackboard. "What happened to your oxygen mask? And your IV is disconnected. Are you trying to kill yourself?" The tall skinny woman's voice was terrifying.

The fingers grabbing my wrist hurt. My right hand and arm were cold and swollen.

I struggled to keep the blonde from putting the mask back on my face. "Don't hurt me," I begged her. Cold metal chilled my skin. I gagged as a thermometer was thrust into my mouth.

The second woman, her dark hair pulled into a tight bun, said sharply, "You've come loose. I have to reconnect you." Something was holding me down. I couldn't move.

"Please don't hurt me," I screamed.

"Should we request a transfer?" the skinny nurse whispered.

"Give her a shot."

I felt the cool swab of the alcohol pad and then screamed again when I felt the piercing pain of the needle.

My thoughts thickened. I began to drift. This was not the peacefulness I yearned for.

A greenish-blue warm light surrounds me, carrying me away from the blackness, from the pain. "Boonah, I'm in trouble."

"Let us begin. Tell me who you are."

I speak from a panic that lies outside my self, in a dumping place I refuse to acknowledge or enter. Forming words is difficult. "You know I am Anna, mother of no one."

"And? The daughter of?"

I am sweating profusely.

"I am the daughter of Sadie and Herschold Baum."

"Dive into the blackness," he says. "Jump before it is too late."

I jump.

The baby lies on her mother's body sucking at her mother's breast. The baby falls asleep. The mother tries to wake her. Frustrated, the mother pinches the baby, who cries but does not suck. The mother puts the screaming baby in the crib. Later, the baby wakes and cries. The mother refuses to feed her.

The baby transforms into Marina. The woman puts her in the crib though Marina's feet stick out. The woman bumps into the feet and curses. She returns with an axe. I scream, "Run!" Marina runs out of the house. I run after her. The woman reaches out and grabs the back of my neck. The cold axe slices my cheek.

An undertow pulled me down every time I surfaced but I heard a deep voice. Something wiped strands of hair from my face. I tried to open my eyes but my lids were too heavy. My face was being washed. I kept trying to float to the top of whatever was keeping me down.

The smell of coffee. The sound of words.

"Coffee—momma's—you." My eyes didn't know how to open. My face felt warmth.

A male nurse was holding a cup of steaming liquid close enough for me to feel the heat. Smiling. The aroma was heavenly. Even better, I understood, "Have a sip, it's made from Jamaican beans—the best in the whole world." My spirit was ready. My body wasn't. He leaned forward and put his arms under my back. "Let me help you sit up." Changing positions made me dizzy. He brought the cup to my face. "It's hot. Be careful." I drank a tiny bit, exulting in the rich taste. "What do you think?"

My words were garbled.

When I was able to hold the cup we drank in companionable silence. "My name is Jacob. I'm the duty nurse."

I tried to speak. If my kids could learn to tie shoelaces, I could figure out how to tell him my name. It was more difficult than lifting a thousand pounds.

"I'm Jacob Holder." Nodding, I swallowed the steaming liquid, fully absorbed, able to do only one thing at a time. There was a knock and then the door opened.

"Well, well, do I smell Jacob's brew? Where's my cup?" It was the lilting voice.

Jacob grinned. "You keep watch, I'll get you one." He left the room.

The woman spoke hesitantly. "Ms. Baum, I'm the floor supervisor. I'm real glad to see you're awake. I believe we need to talk."

Fear flickered through me. "Toilet—."

"Let me help you." Vertigo overwhelmed me but with her help I kept moving forward as she pushed the IV pole, me leaning on her.

"Good girl," she murmured, "you're doing fine. Just put one foot in front of the other and you'll make it." Going to the bathroom was harder than opening a bushel of oysters. Studiously avoiding the mirror, I splashed water on my face and hands. The nurse practically carried me back to bed. "Don't be discouraged. We'll have you racing around the corridor before you have a chance to develop bed sores." *I guess that's a joke.*

Once she settled me in my bed, I held out an unsteady hand. "Thank you—."

"Call me Emma." After checking my IV she started to neaten my tray. "The night staff recommended you be committed to the locked ward."

"What? Why?"

"They think you're a danger to yourself."

"Huh?"

"You haven't spoken to anyone. You've had bouts of violent yelling and crying—. It's all in your record."

"Who says it's true?"

She shrugged. Jacob came in with Emma's coffee. They exchanged worried looks.

"The doctors are beginning rounds," said Jacob.

"What do they want from me?" I asked.

"To be healthy, of course," she said quickly. "And, they want to help you recover. That's why they work in a hospital."

"Why should I talk to them if I don't want to?"

"If the staff believes you're acting against your own best interest then it becomes a medical problem," explained Jacob.

Emma's voice took on an urgent tone. "Ms. Baum, please be careful how you talk to Doctor Adams. If you need more time, ask to use the toilet—get some water—whatever you think of. Just present yourself as a sensible and cooperative person." *I thought that's who I was.*

The door opened. A tall man entered, followed by a group of men and women in white coats with stethoscopes around their necks. All deferred to the tall man.

Emma and Jacob spoke almost simultaneously. "Good morning, Dr. Adams." The tall man nodded then studied papers in my folder. "Ms. Baum does not appear to be the unruly person described in the chart. Nor does she look uncommunicative. Nor is her face turned to the wall." He looked up at Emma. "What accounts for the discrepancy?"

She spoke carefully. "My report will state that I found Ms. Baum awake and alert. I believe she is making significant progress towards a full recovery."

"Very well, Ms. Wahieloa, you may go." He turned to

Jacob." "What condition was Ms. Baum in when you came on duty this morning?"

"She was sleeping, sir."

I had to defend myself. "Dr. Adams, please, let me explain. I had a nightmare last night and yelled in my sleep. The nurses wouldn't listen to me when I tried to explain what was going on. I have nightmares all the time and I know what do to when they happen, but they didn't give me a chance. Just gave me a shot that knocked me out."

Dr. Adams thrust a stack of records into the hands of a young man who scrambled to keep his balance. His voice was a controlled bark. "Ms. Baum, we have been trying to save your life for more than a week with no help from you. I hardly think you're in any position to criticize the actions of staff who've been acting on your behalf for your own good."

"Dr. Adams, I didn't need an injection to calm me down. All they had to do was turn on the light and ask if I wanted a drink of water." He made me shiver. *Why am I so afraid of him?*

"You were unconscious when you were brought in. When you might have spoken, you chose to turn your face to the wall. You cannot blame the nurses for not knowing what you need. *I just wanted to float.* "Now, if you will excuse me, I will proceed with my examination." *Is he going to open my gown and use his stethoscope with me naked? With everyone watching?* He loosened the ties and slipped the stethoscope down under the gown, apologizing that it might be a bit cold. He listened to my chest and back. "Sounds much clearer," he said. I had trouble connecting the softness of his touch with the harsh tone of his words. *Something feels familiar. What is it?* I kept shivering the whole time he touched me. Inside my head was a kaleidoscope of frightening images, whirring too fast for me to see any of them clearly.

He read my chart and then spoke in tones befitting a judge. "Ms. Baum, you are under my care. I will do what I deem necessary for your recovery." The white coats looked like they were trying to make themselves invisible. Jacob appeared to be holding his breath. I got the message.

"Dr. Adams, I'm really sorry, but I need to use the toilet. Please excuse me for a moment." With Jacob's help I made my way to the bathroom and gratefully noticed that he looked away. I could hear a lot of talking but not the words. Counting to twenty-five, I flushed the toilet and walked back to bed with as much dignity as I could muster, given that Jacob was following behind me, keeping all the tubes in order.

With icy calm the doctor said, "I've finished my examination." He turned to a woman whose soft green dress contrasted sharply with her starched white coat, mumbled something, and walked out with everyone else in tow, leaving behind a dense silence. The woman checked my ability to breathe into a tube, took my blood pressure, and made me cough a few times.

Before she could scurry away, I asked, "Do I have the right to change doctors? Preferably one with at least a passing connection to the human race?" No response. She left.

Noticing a clean hospital gown and towel I said to my IV pole, "I need a shower."

Easier said than done.

Boonah is sitting on the arm of my chair, legs crossed, hands clapping. "What a performance! Four stars." Shamelessly, I wait for him to say more. "Well done, Luv. Well done. Now we must prepare."

"For what?"

"You are fighting for your life. We have much to do."

He sits down, cradles his head in his hands and chants. When he looks up, his dear face is filled with concern. "The pictures you see—"

I flinch. "Where do they come from?"

"From you. Trust them."

"How can I trust what I don't remember?"

"In time you will. Right now, you need strategies and allies. Even with the help of Great Spirit, we face much danger."

"Who is Great Spirit?"

"Long before Earth formed there was Great Spirit, carried by Wind, not yet Wind. Great Spirit touched everything everywhere, leaving SeedSpirit in its wake, an imprint for the future.

"And in all of life SeedSpirit nestles. Waiting. Your SeedSpirit called to Great Spirit for help. I am one of Great Spirit's messengers with knowing beyond why or how. Listen to your inner voice. You will hear the voice of Great Spirit."

"Tell me a story about SeedSpirit"

"It is your turn."

"I lost my stories."

"Stories never leave us. Remember the story you liked to read, about the

beginning of the world? It was your favorite. You often told it to me. Let it lead you to a new story."

I took a deep breath. Words tumbled out of my mouth.

"Before the beginning of World as we know it, there was SeedSpirit. It lived on the crest of a soft warmth that cradled and nourished its vitality. When World began to form, SeedSpirit flew unseen, touching, tapping, blowing, prodding, pushing, poking, giving something of itself to all Earth's beings. The more SeedSpirit gave of itself, the stronger it grew, filling emptiness with the richness of potential.

"In the beginning, SeedSpirit found only welcome. Yet just as light must have dark to be known, SeedSpirit encountered DeathSpirit. They fought for the right to enter the heart of Beings. While they struggled, the world continued to be shaped by forces of earth and air and water and fire.

"From the depths of the turmoil came a powerful yearning for an end to confusion, for pattern and habit and peace, yet chaos and cacophony prevailed.

"Suddenly, all was still. Beings took a collective breath. The silence was bewildering. The fighting Spirits were swept into the vacuum until there was no beginning and no end. Each was irrevocably part of the other.

"As the two-now-one Spirit flew into the hearts of Beings, it brought pain, suffering, joy, and hope in equal measure. But in some, Spirit disappeared and could only be recovered through yearning and searching.

"Even now, those who seek are often lonely and afraid, yet they continue, probing for the deepest truths about life and death. Once in a great while, two seekers meet and create love—a miracle for all times and ages."

Oh, Boonah. Thank you.

Off the Beat

"Josie, I'm home," Joe yelled, waiting for her customary, "I'm in the kitchen," or "I'm in the bedroom." This time there was no answer. He yelled again, "Honey, I'm home." Silence. Suddenly drenched in cold sweat, he roared, "Josie, where are you?" and quickly ran into the bedroom, afraid of what he might find.

Josie walked out of the bathroom wearing a yellow maternity dress, her hands cupped around her swelling abdomen. "I've gained two pounds and the doctor showed me how to listen to the baby's heartbeat."

Joe's relief was palpable. "Oh, honey, that's terrific." He steadied his voice. "When you didn't answer me —." He avoided looking at her and cursed himself for showing his anxiety.

"I'm not made of glass," snapped Josie.

"I know." He changed the subject. "Did you get responses to your newspaper ad?"

"Three. Quit worrying about me! You act like we'll never have this child. We will!"

"I don't know how to stop worrying."

"Figure it out. Fast." She poured herself a cup of milk, sipping slowly to calm herself.

"Who answered your ad?" asked Joe.

Josie snorted. "You can't imagine the weirdness of some of them. God knows why they apply to work in a florist shop. One applicant actually admitted she was allergic to roses! Can you believe? Two others seemed less interested in flowers than I am in washing windows. Why would they even bother to apply?"

"What are you going to do?"

"Run another ad. Require a minimum of five years experience. Who would think people would answer an ad for a job as a florist with no experience or even an interest in working with flowers?"

"Reminds me of some of the applicants to be cops. I wonder if they toss a coin: 'I like guns. Should I be a criminal or a cop?' This is a big city. Someone's got to know something about arranging and selling flowers."

"I certainly hope so. I'd like to have a few months to train them before the baby's due. Oh, well, how about dinner? I'm starved." She put her arms around him. "Mmm. Your body feels good."

He returned the hug, relieved to feel her welcoming warmth. "So do the two of yours."

She rubbed the back of his neck. "How was your day?"

"I saw Ms. Baum on my lunch hour. Turns out the fall was the least of her troubles. She's got a bad case of double pneumonia and is all hooked up to oxygen and a bunch of tubes. Gives me the creeps just to look at her."

"Oh, no!" Joe loved the way Josie cared about people, even strangers.

"Seems her blood counts are too low. When I went in she was sleeping. The charge nurse said I was her first visitor."

"Really? Well, tomorrow, on your way to visit O'Neill in the hospital, stop by the shop and I'll give you flowers for both of them. Maybe they'll make her feel better."

Joe grinned. He admired Josie's common-sense approach to what for him would be a problem. "You sure you don't mind me giving flowers to a strange woman?"

"Not as long as I'm the one who chooses the flowers for her." She turned serious. "Stop worrying. It makes me feel bad. It's not good for the baby, or my state of mind, or your blood pressure—."

Trying to keep the anguish out of his voice, he said, "Give it a rest. We have other things to talk about." Josie waited. "I told you about that kid who disappeared—well, we have new clues to go on; some guys have been arrested on suspicion. The Chief wants me there when they're questioned. I don't know how long it will take or when I'll be home. Maybe Shelly can come stay with you." He didn't say what he was thinking. *What do we do if you have another miscarriage while I'm away? One more botched-up mess?* He tried to push the fears out of his head.

She pulled back. "I'm not a child. Don't give me a hug and think that takes care of everything. You were on extra duty last week. Why can't someone else do it? You're not the only one who investigated the case." She looked at his face. "Forget it, I'm in no mood for a lecture on how you're a cop and I knew it when we married." She turned away, not wanting him to see the unwelcome tears in her eyes.

"Look, you worry about getting a new employee and I'll worry about what happened to the kid." He rubbed her neck.

She poured another cup of milk and drank slowly.

"Josie, look at me, please—." She turned around. Kissing away the smudge of milk clinging to her upper lip, he tried not to think about what his life would be like if she were not his wife.

7

Voices in the outer world have no regard for inner travel.

"Ms. Baum. Ms. Baum." Emma of the lilting voice was shaking me, breathing a sigh of relief when I opened my eyes. "Ms. Baum, Dr. Adams will be here any moment. I just learned he's committed you to a psychiatric ward. In his judgment, you're a danger to yourself. Is there a family member we can call?"

"My mother lives in Florida."

"What about friends?" I shook my head. "What about the man who called the ambulance? He came once while you were asleep. And there are messages from a Mrs. Escondido and a Dr. Rosa Chavez. That would be good, another doctor. No, she said she'd be out of town for a few weeks, but Mrs. Escondido said to call her if she could help."

"She's got too many troubles as it is. I don't want to add to them."

"How about Mr. Weissman? His being a cop might make a difference—."

A loud insistent knocking disrupted the conversation. Dr. Adams entered with a sheaf of papers in his hand, followed by two orderlies. Trying to control my panic, I smiled. "Good morning, Dr. Adams. I'm sure you're pleased to know I don't need the oxygen mask anymore and all of my vital signs are normal."

Dr. Adams looked irritated. He cleared his throat. "Ms. Wahieloa, don't you have a staff meeting this morning?"

"Yes, but I asked Nurse Holder to take charge because I thought you might require my assistance. I've put Ms. Baum's charts in order."

I couldn't help blurting out, "Dr. Adams, I'm feeling much better."

Dr. Adams chewed on his cheeks. "Well, Ms. Baum—naturally we are pleased. All we want is for you to make a complete recovery."

"Dr. Adams," asked Emma, "do you wish to review your orders

for Ms. Baum with me? I mean in view of her improving condition?"

Dr. Adams turned to the two orderlies. "You may leave, gentlemen, I don't believe we need your services at the moment." When Emma left she gave me the thumbs-up sign. After the door closed and all the footsteps dimmed, I hugged myself.

"Boonah, you're my best friend."

He pats my shoulder. "We are not separate."

"Ms. Baum?" Joe Weissman was standing just inside the door. "Josie sent you these daffodils. She thought you might like them."

"Who's Josie?"

"My wife."

"They're beautiful. Any news of Marina?"

"No. We combed the neighborhood. Interviewed her family. Talked to people who knew her. Nothing! I don't understand how a five-year-old kid could disappear without a trace in broad daylight. I keep hoping someone's rescued her, waiting for things to blow over before they notify the authorities. I've heard of cases like that." He put more water in the vase.

"What about the man?"

"He's definitely been identified as her stepfather. No one's seen him since he came to your school." I gestured for him to sit down but he kept standing.

"Is anyone still looking?"

"Not officially, but a couple of us cops keep an eye on the family just in case he decides to come back home. We've got a few guys being held for questioning but it's mostly circumstantial evidence. I'll let you know if there's any news." Finally, he sat down on the edge of the seat.

"I think about her all the time. I just wish I'd kept her inside."

"Give yourself a break. You got enough to think about, like getting well enough to get out of this place." He stood up again. "Man, hospitals give me the creeps. Bad news city!"

"I don't think I'm ready."

"Who is? Yesterday, I'm walking on my beat. The sun is shining. The air smells real sweet. It's just about time for me to meet Josie for a quick bite at the diner when I hear three bangs. A guy's blood splashes all over the sidewalk. I'm thinking lunch and instead I have to deal with murder and telling the guy's family —."

"That's awful."

"It's my job. And your job is helping kids, not lying here in some smelly hospital."

He looked at his watch. "Yikes, I'm supposed to relieve Gonzales in ten minutes. Sorry to run out on you like this."

"Thank you for coming."

The room seemed smaller and colder.

I drifted into what Max used to call my "state," where I'm not awake or asleep. I'm walking in a strange place that I'm supposed to know but don't. Nothing looks familiar. I hear a voice calling, "What are you going to do? Anna, Anna!"

I curled into a ball under the covers and was just about to have a severe bout of *pity party* when Emma's voice pulled me back into the waking world. "Anna? What's going on? Where's my ferocious, feisty freedom fighter?" She uncovered my face. "Last time I saw you, you were feeling real spunky. What happened?"

"I don't know."

She stroked my cheek.

"Emma, do you ever feel like giving up?"

"Sure, but where I come from, any time I was ready to throw in the towel there was always someone around with a thousand platitudes to lecture me as to why I needed to keep going. Give me your mouth, sweet pea. Time to check your lungs."

"What was it like, where you came from?"

She had me blow into a tube and wrote down numbers. "On an island, you grow up with sisters and brothers and aunts and uncles and cousins and people who have nowhere else to go. I still remember my shock when I came up north and saw how many lonely people there were. I mean we certainly have plenty of troubles where I come from, but there's usually someone who's willing to love you. Especially on an island." Her face darkened. Emma stared at the water as she filled a glass.

"You look like you're a zillion miles away."

"Sorry, it's a bad habit."

"Do I have the right to refuse a doctor's treatment?"

"There's a patients' rights pamphlet in the drawer of your table."

What else have I missed?

After she left I read the pamphlet. There was nothing in it about how to change doctors.

I'm sliding into an all-too-familiar swamp of depression. I think about Boonah. Instantly he's walking on my outstretched palm. His footsteps tickle. "Anna, what keeps you from asking for help?"

"I don't know."

"Where are you?"

"In a closet."

"Time for your blood test," the technician called out as he pushed the squeaky cart.

Gallows humor time. "How am I supposed to get well if you take all my blood? My veins are exhausted. They need a rest."

"Which arm do you prefer?"

"Neither." I dreaded feeling the needle. "For all I know it's a secret plan to use my blood without paying for it." The technician was in a bad mood. He tied the rubber tubing around my arm, tighter than he needed to, and scrubbed me roughly with an alcohol wipe. I flinched as he tried to stick in the needle.

"Hold still. Your veins are slippery."

I looked away. "When can I find out the results?"

"Ask your doctor when he comes to see you."

"How does a person know they're well enough to go home?"

"The doctor says you're ready." He untied the elastic cuff and took the needle out. It was time to see how many times I could walk up and down the hall before I had to stop. I forgot how much energy it took to organize the tubes on my IV pole.

"Anna?" Pilar was standing at the door holding two envelopes. "Am I interrupting?"

"Never. Come in, Have a seat. Water is all there is but the ice is fresh. The maid just brought a new container." She laughed. Already I felt better. I opened one of the envelopes she handed me, filled with drawings and paintings from the children. Someone should invent windshield wipers for the eyes. A few of the pictures had messages printed in a neat hand that could only be Pilar's.

"Feel better."

"I love you."

"What's happening?"

I saw a funny look on her face as I read the children's messages. "What?" I asked.

She shook her head. "It's nothing."

"Already I know it's something. Tell me."

"Well," she said reluctantly, "you know our kids. No matter why, we don't show up, they think we're gone forever. As they say in the psychological jargon—abandonment issues."

I sighed, knowing exactly what she was talking about. "So who's doing what to whom?"

"You mean, who's hitting the most, crying the loudest or knocking down whatever's in sight?" She looked at my face and said quickly, "It's normal. Better they should act out than keep it inside. Besides, having them make drawings for you was a big help. It gave me a chance to remind them you were sick and when you were well, you would come back."

Yeah, if they don't hire a permanent replacement. My heart lurched when I looked at Julio's painting of splattered red hearts with the words, "Come back!"

"Pilar, let's put them up on the walls. It will give me something else to think about beside my blood counts."

Nodding, she searched the huge bag she always carried and after messing about, emerged triumphant, a roll of tape in hand.

"What's in the second one?"

"I was told to put this picture in a special envelope. Not only did he watch me put it in, he taped over the top so I couldn't put any other picture inside."

I opened it up, no easy matter; you could have mailed seven packages with less tape. Inside was a huge red heart with two stick figures in the middle, one much smaller than the other. On it was written, "You are in my heart." It was signed with Eric's shaky but readable signature. "Oh, Pilar," was all I could manage. She brought the chair closer to my bed and sat down. We both needed a tissue.

We studied Eric's heart. "It deserves a special place," She said.

"Put it over my head so it's the first thing Dr. Adams sees. Maybe it will remind him that I'm a human being, not an illness. When is Rosa getting back?"

"I'm not sure. Her mother-in-law had a relapse."

I kept thinking about the children feeling I'd abandoned them. "I need to do something more than just have you thank the children."

Pilar rummaged in her bag, pulling out a pad and five magic markers. "If you're not too tired, you could write a little note to them." With the yellow, blue and green markers I printed a great big thank you and surrounded it with red hearts of various sizes.

"The kids will be thrilled. Next time I'll bring you paints," she teased. "Who knows? You could have hidden artistic talents hitherto undiscovered." I threw one of my pillows at her. She grabbed it. Arching her body as if going up for a lay-up shot, she threw it back at me, hitting the top of my head. "Slam dunk." It felt good to laugh.

"I'd better go. I'll tell the children you hung their pictures up in your room and when I get Eric alone, I'll tell him where you hung his."

The lump in my throat was so big I had trouble thanking her for coming.

Just as she left, a nurse came in with fresh ice water. I made an extra effort to be nice.

"Where did you get all these pictures?" she asked.

"The children I teach."

"Seems like they miss you, huh?"

"Probably not as much as I miss them."

"Is there anything you'd like before I leave?"

"Yup. I want to go home."

"Anything else?" she asked, friendly as could be. I kept smiling until she left, leaving me with an aching jaw and the realization of just how boring it was to lie in bed so much of the time. I got up to walk. My back ached and my legs were cramping from inactivity, yet I knew if I didn't get up I'd lose too much muscle tone to teach all day. What a motivator fear can be.

"Boonah, what does fear taste like?"
"Some say like dry rust."
"Where does fear come from?"
"Memory."

I smelled food and it wasn't enticing. When the attendant brought the tray, whatever appetite I might have had disappeared. Plopped on the white plate was a slab of white turkey perched on a mound of white speckled dressing, white potatoes, whitish-gray gravy, and cauliflower. A dab of cranberry sauce, like an uninvited guest, sat on the edge of the dish. I could hear my mother. "Don't those dieticians know anything about color and texture? Why not yams and broccoli or string beans?"

Daddy is away on business. Momma dresses me in the pink dress that used to be Sarah's. I hate wearing Sarah's dresses and when Sarah opens the door and says, "How do you like my dress?" I want to punch her.

"She likes it fine," says Momma, grabbing my fists, pushing me inside. The apartment smells terrible. Something is burning. For once, Momma and I look at each other and giggle under our breaths. Momma says Minnie is a wonderful person but she can't boil water.

Minnie wipes her hands on her apron and leaves big brown stains on the white cloth. I look at Momma but she doesn't say anything. I love the way Minnie hugs me, smuggling hard candy into the pockets of my dress. She smells like lemon drops.

When we sit down to dinner, Minnie passes Sarah's daddy the food. He says, "Oy vey," and makes a horrible face before laughing. I eat all the burned potatoes and onions on my plate. The chicken is so dry I have to chew it with water before I can swallow it. The mushy string beans are hard to get on my fork and I spill some on the tablecloth.

Momma notices and quietly hands me bread to use as a pusher. For dessert we have store bought cookies. I eat everything. Even Minnie's bad food tastes good to me.'

*****

Tossing restlessly, I inadvertently pushed the call button. Embarrassed by her quick response I murmured an apology. "Could I ask you a question?" The nurse nodded, adjusting my IV. "I'd like to go home. What's the procedure?"

"I'll make a note on your record. Patient requests release."

"What if my doctor decides not to?"

"Doctors have to have a reason to keep you here. You got someone to help you when you go home? You know, shop, cook, clean, pick up meds, take you to the doctor, stuff like that? Be a good thing to have."

I don't even know the names of my neighbors. "Do you know anyone who does this kind of work?"

"No."

"Do you have any idea what it might cost?

"No."

I watched the door close. The room always seemed smaller when I was alone. It occurred to me that some people fill a space with hope while others make the world feel wrinkled and old. If I was going to have to live by myself for the rest of my life I would have to learn to make the room as spacious as I needed. I got up and walked unsteadily to the closet, surprised to see that the clothes I'd worn to the hospital were now clean and neatly pressed. I tried to remember how this happened but I drew a blank. *Make a plan.*

I had just taken a hot shower, put on a clean hospital gown, and was sitting down when Dr. Adams strode in, followed by three white coats. He quickly masked his look of surprise when he saw me sitting in the chair, alert and clear-eyed. "Good evening, Ms. Baum."

"Good evening, Dr. Adams."

"How are we today?"

"I'm doing well. I want to go home."

"That may be a bit premature. I've ordered additional blood tests to give us necessary information about your condition. There are problems with your clotting time and we still don't know why your white counts are so low."

"Can't the tests be done as an outpatient? I'm arranging to have help when I go home."

Dr. Adams gave instructions to the white coats in a terse voice, using terms I didn't understand. I had to bite my tongue to keep from asking him to speak English. Given the way they jumped when he spoke, I was surprised that any of them had the courage to speak in his presence.

A woman, wearing a necklace made of rows of intricately beaded jewelry, asked, "Do you have a ton of children or what?"

"I teach."

"Seems they really like you."

Dr. Adams paused briefly to look at the pictures. "I'm sorry to interrupt, but I need you to get in bed so I can examine you."

When he finished, I asked, "Is there a special reason for this evening examination?" He gave me an unreadable look. "You usually come in the morning."

The white coats shifted uneasily. With a "Humph," he read my chart, left instructions and walked out. A prematurely gray-haired young man listened to my heart and lungs. The others watched, taking notes as he called out his findings.

"What do you think?" I asked.

He spoke reluctantly. "Your vital signs are good, your lungs sound clearer, and you are making good progress."

"So? Am I ready to leave the hospital?"

"That's up to Dr. Adams."

"Can't you make a recommendation?"

"Please, Ms. Baum, I'm just doing my job."

I was thinking about my options when the duty nurse came back in. "I thought about your wanting to go home. Here's a paper if you want to look at the Help Wanted section."

"Thanks. You ever hire someone from Help Wanted?"

"No, but somebody must. Good luck!"

Retired nurse looking for long-term position caring for invalid.

Older woman available for light housekeeping and cooking. No driving.

Unemployed professional looking for job with room and board. Willing to do light housekeeping, odd jobs, and act as companion while searching for permanent position.

I stopped reading, wishing the right person would appear by magic. Closing my eyes, I drifted into a gloomy world where nothing was clear and no one made sense.

"Boonah, I'm sinking."
"Reach up and take my hand."
"Why did you leave me for so long?"
"You left me."
"Why would I do that? You were my only friend."
"Because you were so afraid."
"I'm still afraid."
"No, you only think you are. If you were, you wouldn't have challenged Dr. Adams as you did. And, you have allies now."

Walking in a Minefield

The memory still burned. The teacher asked in English, "What is your address?"

Pilar didn't understand. "No sé," she said apologetically.

"No say? What kind of a response is that? If you want to be an American you better learn how to say where you live. Right, class?" People uh-huh-ed. "Now who can tell me their address, using proper English?"

Pilar left the class feeling as big as a pea and as mad as a tornado. She didn't feel better when Miguel met her at the door with a big grin on his face, his arms ready for a hug—and more.

"Tomorrow's your birthday, the big twenty-one. How do we celebrate? I hired a sitter."

"No more kids. You or me, one of us got to get fixed."

"I can't do that. Besides, the Pope says—"

"Screw the Pope. Might do him some good. I'm not having fourteen kids like your mother. Who knows how many my mother would have had if she hadn't died so young. There's more to life than cleaning up messes."

"But Chica, I thought you liked being my wife. And you were the one who talked about having a daughter." His face darkened. "What's wrong? You got another man?"

"Twenty-five." She moved away from him. "One night a week I go out to learn English. You got a problem with that?"

"So what do you want?"

"I want to be a teacher."

"How you gonna be a teacher?"

"I will find a way, Miguel. This is a vow I make on this night, to myself and to you. This is my present. This is the celebration I want." She avoided looking at the hurt in his eyes.

Here she was facing her thirtieth birthday. She'd made some progress. Her English was pretty good, and she no longer cleaned houses. But, being a teacher's assistant was not the same as being a teacher. She didn't realize just how big the difference was until Anna got sick. She'd been in charge until they found a licensed substitute. Just out of college, no experience, and the bitch thinks she can tell me what to do, when to do it, how to do it. Anna never made her feel inferior or less capable, but this woman—she acts like she has a stick up her butt. Well, she's not walking over me. Not for any reason. Not if I can help it.

Pilar unlocked the door, noting with satisfaction that the teacher was late. Humming, she arranged the clay on two tables, making the first initial of each child's name. She heard the door open and looked up. "Mrs. Escondido, why are you playing with the clay? I did not tell you we would use clay today."

Pilar stared at the woman in front of her. Tight-lipped and tight-assed. She forced herself to use a pleasant tone. "Ms. Jones, we usually put out clay. The children love to find their initials. We make it seem like a game but they're really learning their letters."

"We? Ms. Baum trained you to do what she thinks best, but I'm the teacher now, and you will do as I tell you. I have carefully prepared lesson plans and I expect you to follow them exactly as they are written."

Pilar took enough breaths to find her voice. "Ms. Jones, how many years have you been teaching?"

"This is my first full-time position, but I have experience. You do a lot of teaching when you study to be a teacher. And, I graduated third in my class."

Pilar resisted the impulse to say, how many in your class, three? She unclenched her fists. "Do you know how many years I've been teaching in this program?"

"You don't teach. You're an assistant. You do what the teacher tells you to do. Now, put the clay away and get out the crayons. Today the children will learn how to color inside the lines." Pilar fought the impulse to shake her. She'd been teaching the class for almost two weeks by herself and she knew she'd done well.

"Excuse me, Ms. Jones. I'm supposed to meet with the school psychologist before the children come. I'll do the crayons when I get back." Pilar stormed out of the room before she exploded. Went to the bathroom. Splashed cold water on her face. Formed a plan. She knocked on the door of Dr. Chavez's substitute.

"Dr. Feldstein, you got any brochures on how to be a teacher?"

"Here's a phone book. Try the public library. They might know." Pilar wrote down two telephone numbers she found in the directory. Returning, to the classroom, she took a deep breath and did what she was told. But in her dreams, she was in her own classroom, one filled with books and toys she had chosen, a vase of lilacs on her desk. On the door was her name and her title: Mrs. Pilar Escondido, Master Teacher.

8

The night nurses' voices sounded like the ones who'd given me the injection and requested my transfer to a locked ward.

"Look at the colors on that one."

"Reminds me of jello gone wild."

"You got no taste."

"How would you know?"

Their laughter felt friendly enough for me to pretend I just woke up. "Good evening. How do you like my art gallery?"

"It's great," said the nurse with ample hips and bleached hair. "I should bring my four-year-old to see them. Her teacher says she won't make pictures. How do you get kids to draw?"

"You don't. But if you leave stuff out, the two of you could do it together, just for fun."

"I never was good at drawing, maybe Maggie feels the same way."

The other nurse, the skinny tall one, grinned wickedly. "If you make one for me I promise to hang it on my refrigerator." Big hips swatted her. Tall skinny shook her finger in mock protest. I laughed with them.

I couldn't help noticing the difference in their attitude toward me, even warming up the stethoscope disc before putting it against my chest. Or was it my attitude toward them? Big hips asked, "Would you like something? Juice? Hot milk? A sleeping pill?" They even straightened my bedding and put ice in my water pitcher. The more I thought about how chance actions can change life, the worse I felt. My dream didn't help.

I'm sitting in a courtroom. A judge, sitting behind the bench, is dressed in bright red so shiny it hurts my eyes. I turn to the couple sitting next to me and ask, "What's going on?"

They reply in chorus, "You know." When I protest that I don't, they repeat, "You know." No matter what question I ask, they answer, "You know." When I move to leave, they force me to sit down. I struggle to get away, but guards push me back into the chair.

A man dressed in brilliant purple comes toward me. He's the prosecuting attorney. His tone of voice sounds like he's accusing me of something awful, but I don't understand a word he says.

I ask the judge, "What am I being charged with?" He remains impassive. "May I address the bench?" The judge laughs so hard his eyes tear and he has to wipe his glasses. The courtroom is guffawing. Their clothing changes to brilliant red satin, bleeding crimson onto the floor.

I woke myself up, gasping for breath, terrified, struggling to get away. In the process I pulled out the IV needle attached to my wrist. The pain was so awful I pressed the call button, trying to breathe into the pain instead of fighting it. I couldn't avoid looking at my red, swollen hand. A young male nurse I'd never seen came in. When I showed him my wrist, he clucked comfortingly. Within seconds he'd reattached the IV and the pain subsided. "We better put ice on this. Good thing you called for help." *See, Mother, asking for help is not necessarily a crime.*

The first thing I saw when I woke up was the Help Wanted section. I read a column and pushed the paper aside. The scattered pages made such a mess I felt obliged to pick them up but as I bent over, a bout of coughing left me gasping for air, clutching the rumpled newspapers.

"What's this?" asked Emma.

"I've been looking at want ads. To see if there's someone I can hire to take care of me."

"What are you waiting for?"

With no excuse for not dialing, I decided to phone the number in the third one. The recorded voice was pleasant. "If you're calling about the advertisement regarding household help, please leave a detailed message and I'll call you back as soon as possible. Thank you very much."

While Emma took my vital signs I left a message stating my job requirements and how I could be reached. "What you *doin'*, gal?" she teased. "Your blood pressure thinks it's supposed to hit the ceiling?"

"I would have thought it had gone through the roof."

A few minutes later, the phone rang. I practically levitated, and when I heard the deep male voice I almost hung up. "My name is Paulus Barszinsky and I'm responding to the voice mail of Anna Baum."

"That's me," I croaked.

"I'm looking for temporary work as a live-in companion. I'll do some housekeeping, shopping—whatever needs doing, but I have to have two or three hours a day for job interviews. What do you need the person to do? I'm not qualified to deal with a very old or very ill person but I can give shots and take blood pressure."

In all my thinking about who might have placed the ad it never occurred to me the person seeking employment might be a man.

Emma asked, "What's wrong?"

Putting my hands over the receiver I said, "She's a he. What am I going to do?"

I could hear the male voice asking, "What kind of person are you looking for?" I couldn't think of anything to say. The voice kept on asking, "Hello? Hello?"

Emma's laughter didn't help. I blurted out, "I'm, uh, looking for a person to help me when I leave the hospital. I thought you'd be a woman."

"Are you going to turn me down just because I'm not?"

"Well—it's a little weird to think about sharing my apartment with a strange man."

"I believe you skipped a few steps. I'd be coming to work for you, not share your life. What kind of help do you need?"

I remembered Emma's advice about what to do if I got stuck. "Look, the nurse just came in and I have to get off the phone. Can I call you back?"

"Sure. What time span we talking about? Five minutes? Two hours?"

"How about within the hour?" I hung up realizing I hadn't asked what he'd been doing, or what kind of job he was looking for, or references.

"Emma, what am I going to do?"

She couldn't stop laughing. At first I felt hurt, but then I saw the comic side, especially when she began to act like a coach at a basket-ball game. "Here's what you do. If you decide to hire him, you set the rules. Closed bathroom door means no entry. Telephone calls limited to five minutes. No strange women in the house."

"Huh? Christ, I hadn't thought about what happens if he's dating—."

"Make a list of the questions you want to ask and check off each time he answers, plus if it's positive, minus if you don't like the answer. Get him to ask you questions about what he needs." *What do you mean, he needs? I'm the one with the needs.*

No sense postponing the inevitable. Maybe he turned into a she in the meantime—.

"Ah, Ms. Baum, thank you for calling back so promptly."

I took an exceedingly deep breath. "This is my situation. I'm recovering from a serious case of pneumonia and my blood levels are low, so it's possible something else is wrong. In order to leave the hospital I have to have help; someone to shop, take out the garbage, and drive me to the doctor until I'm strong enough to go to work. Right now, no one knows when that will be or how long it will take for me to get my strength back."

"I used to write for a paper in California but decided to move east. I need a place to stay until I find work. Sounds like we should meet and talk. I've discovered that when I make decisions based on a person's voice I find I got it all wrong."

"Just a moment," I said, putting my hand over the phone. I whispered to Emma, "He wants to meet me. What should I do? He really is a man!"

"It's a job interview, remember, not a date? If it will make you feel better, call Joe and ask him to check if the guy has a criminal record."

When I heard the knock on the door, I could barely spit out, "Come in." The man who entered was short, heavy set, and balding, wearing unrelated rumpled pants and jacket. Yet he walked into the room with dignity and confidence. "Are you Ms. Baum?"

I nodded as I thought a potential employer would. "Please, have a seat. Would you care for a drink of water?"

"No, thank you." His voice was deep and calm. "I appreciate your willingness to talk with me since I'm not the woman you hoped I'd be." *He has a nice grin; that helps.*

"I'm not quite certain what to ask, I've never hired anyone before."

"Well I'm sure you want references. Unfortunately, the only people who know about my ability to cook and clean are my family. Not an unbiased source."

"Oh, I don't know. I wouldn't give my mother as a reference for any reason." *Maybe if I say his name this will seem more real.* "Mr. Barszinsky, how long will you be available to help?"

"Please, call me Paulus. I hope I'll be lucky and find a position on a paper quickly but, when I get a job, if you still need help, I'm sure we can work something out."

"Are you married?"

A shadow momentarily flicked across his face. "No, I'm single. No children. Only a mother who tries her best to introduce me to 'the nicest woman.' I brought my resume so you can see where I've worked for the past few years, but it won't be much help for this job."

"Do you mind shopping, cooking, doing laundry, maybe even a little cleaning? I mean does it feel like a comedown from what you're used to?"

"I shop and cook and clean for me, what's one more to do for?"

"Do you mind driving me to the doctor?"

"Not if I can use your car. I sold mine when I left California."

"What else will you need? To do the job, I mean."

"Hard to say right now." There was an awkward silence

All his answers seemed to point to his being a reasonable human being. I couldn't think of anything more to ask so I brought the interview to a close by saying, "My doctor won't be in until tomorrow afternoon. I'll decide once I've seen him."

He looked disappointed. "Do you need more information?"

"I don't think so. The problem is you're a man. If I hire you you'll be living in my apartment. You'd use my car, talk to people who call me—I don't even know how old you are."

He laughed. "Thirty-seven." *The same as me? He looks ten years older. Wonder what his life's been like.* "And, though you haven't asked, I enjoy a glass of wine with a good meal. What else? I like opera. I have a passion for the Beatles. I'm an incorrigible reader, and not very nice before breakfast. I admit, I have a thing about good coffee and come equipped with a coffee grinder, which I'm willing to share if you like fresh ground beans."

"What roast?"

"Is this a test? I'd hate to lose the job because you preferred light and I was partial to dark. But, since you asked, I like my coffee rich, dark, and hot."

"You're in good company. Although I've been known to drink instant in the past, I've come to see the error of my ways."

"Well then, it's agreed, if I'm hired, I'll provide freshly brewed coffee each morning. Any other requests?" asked Paulus, grinning. *Is he flirting with me?*

"Excuse my saying so, but you seem pretty calm for a man without a job. If I were in your situation—no work and no place to live—I'd be terrified."

He shrugged. "Any other questions?"

Shaking my head I said, "I have your telephone number. If I think of something, I'll give you a call." He held out his hand, which I shook, expecting it to be flabby and soft. Instead, it was pleasingly firm. As he opened the door I remembered a question I'd forgotten to ask. "Wait! We haven't talked about salary."

"What are you offering?"

"What are you expecting?"

"I think it's your call to state a figure and my call to agree or not." *At least he looks as uncomfortable as I feel.*

"Well, I'll provide room and board, that is, breakfast and dinner. You buy your own booze. As for salary, what about three hundred dollars a week and phone calls, but you pay for long distance. That is if I hire you." I said the first figure that popped into my mind.

He hesitated before speaking. "That seems reasonable for now. If either one of us is unhappy with the arrangement we can renegotiate after the first week if that's okay with you." I nodded. He walked out with the same impressive dignity he came in with. He seemed like a man who was his own person, but not aggressive, like Max. Then again, he was applying for a job not a romance. *What am I afraid of?*

Emma came in at the end of her shift. "How did it go?"

"Fine."

"And?"

"He needs a place to live while he looks for work. He's willing to do everything I need done. His only housekeeping references are his family. He was pleasant, reasonable, and straightforward. I realize I can't hold gender or his sense of fashion against him but—." She smiled. "I can tell, you're thinking he's exactly what I need. For all I know he is. I just don't know if I can handle a strange man living in my apartment."

An aide came in to remove my food tray and bumped against the table, spilling grape juice, making a large red stain on the white bedding.

"You're supposed to put the juice on your tray," she snapped. I cringed. Stupid tears filled my eyes.

"I'm sorry," I murmured, wiping my eyes.

"Now I got to come back and change your bed," complained the aide.

"Never mind," countered Emma. "I'll do it. Take the tray and leave."

"You seem upset about something," I said, rolling back the stained sheets that looked too much like blood. "Tell me I'm not imagining it."

She motioned for me to sit in the chair and took off the discolored bedding, sighing. "You remind me of someone I used to know." She remade my bed carefully. Too carefully. *Who?* When I got back into bed she kept fussing with the covers and pillows. *Who?*

She talked so softly it was almost a whisper. "I can still hear her shouting, 'Go away. Stop ruining my life.' I told her, 'Please baby, don't shut me out. I'm a nurse, I can help.' She wouldn't listen. 'I don't need help! Go away!'

"According to the autopsy report she was five months pregnant. Her boyfriend denied knowing anything. Besides, what did it matter? She was dead. No second chances."

Emma stood up, her back turned to me. "I was six when she was born, but right after that Ma took sick. I practically raised her, even though I was still a child myself. Fixed her cuts. Wiped her tears. Made her lunch. When she was old enough to go to school, I walked her there so she wouldn't get lost. In some ways you remind me of her. Not that you look like her, not one bit, but she had a quirky sense of humor, like you, and a grin as wide as the world. A born mischief, always teasing and playing games. No matter how tired I was when I came home from school or work, just looking at her was enough to lift my spirits." Emma smiled.

"After I went off to study nursing, she quit school. Said something about an argument with her art teacher. By the time I heard about it, she was up to her eyeballs in trouble. I came home for Papa's funeral, but Lalani wasn't there. I asked everyone where she was. I knew something was wrong. I kept yelling, 'Where's Lalani? Where's Lalani?' Finally, someone took me aside. 'Look here, girl, don't mess with what ain't yours.' I growled, 'Ain't mine? She's my baby. Where is she?' I think he told me just to keep me quiet." Emma blew her nose. "I ran to the place where he thought she might be, an old wooden shack, right on the beach, with a dune in front so you couldn't see it from the road. I didn't even know the shack was there though I'd been swimming near it for years.

"I pounded on the door but there was no answer so I kicked and banged and hit it with my fists, yelling for her at the top of my lungs.

When the door gave way, the stench almost knocked me out. In the corner, lying on a pile of dirty straw was my baby sister, unconscious. I rushed around like a crazy woman, found a banged-up pot and filled it with ocean water. Only water there was. Cleaned her and cuddled her. Sang the songs I used to sing to her when she was a baby. When Lalani opened her eyes and saw me, she could barely whisper, 'Hey,'Mommasister.' She was too weak to say anymore. I picked her up and carried her home. It was like holding heavy air.

"For days I did nothing but spoon feed her, stroke her hair, bathe her, tell her old stories, anything I could think of to bring her back to life. When she was better, I asked what had happened, but she laughed away my questions. 'You one silly Mommasister.' I couldn't get her to tell me anything. Everyone else said they didn't know. A whole family of people and no one knows anything? Makes as much sense as a leaky basket. When my leave was over, I told her I wasn't going back to school. She wouldn't hear of it. Said I had to stay in school, to make something of myself. Even managed to drive me to the airport, all the time laughing and telling things she remembered about the two of us when we were little. When I got out of the car we hugged. She was nothing but skin and bones. I could feel her tears wetting my shirt, but she was quick and put her fingers on my lips, 'Hey, ole Mommasister, you go. You be the best nurse there is, you hear me? Don't let nuthin' stop you. Nuthin'! You hear me now.' She gave me a hug and took off, her long black hair shining, flying in the breeze. I can still see her."

Emma wiped the tears that flowed down her face. "Two days later they found my sister's body on the rocks at the bottom of the cliff."

"Oh, Emma."

"There was a note for me. Said, 'Hey, 'Mommasister, stay in school and be a nurse, like you always wanted. Do it for your babylove.'" Emma folded the stained sheets into a neat pile. "Today is the anniversary of her death. I left her alone, knowing I should stay. She had her whole life in front of her. I could have made it better for her, but she wouldn't give me a chance. It's hard to accept that one person's love is never enough. It always takes two."

Emma glared at me. "You know what was really happening? She was living with a dumb shit who kept telling her she was useless. Said she was lucky to find someone as good as him. Made her thank him for the beatings and the abuse. Kept her worse than you'd keep a dog. And everyone closed their eyes and pretended it wasn't happening. That's the worst part. All those people—friends, relatives—they saw everything and did nothing but cry useless tears around her closed coffin. What good is family if they don't help when they know there's trouble?" She sighed deeply, shaking her head.

"Later, one of my uncles told me, in secret, like he didn't want anyone to know he was telling me, that everyone was afraid of her man. He had a gun. Well isn't that just too bad, like there's no such thing as cops and courts—. It was all I could do to keep from strangling him so he'd never use such a pitiful excuse again."

Emma paced back and forth, trying to contain her rage. *I wish you would make me feel better, like you tried with your sister.*

"I lost a child in my class because I didn't think fast enough. I didn't protect her when I promised I would. It's the worst feeling in the world. It never goes away."

"What happened to her?" asked Emma.

"I don't know. No one's seen her since she ran away from the man we think abused her."

Emma shook her head. "I shouldn't have told you all this. Forget what I said. You have your own troubles."

"What makes you see your sister when you look at me?"

"Are they still looking for the child?"

"Not really. No clues to go on. How come I remind you of your sister?"

She turned away. "Something in your eyes—maybe the bleeding and bruises when they first brought you in—the words you were mumbling."

"Huh? What did I say?"

"Most of it was hard to understand, especially once you started coughing."

"So what did I say?"

"Something like, 'Don't hurt me.' Mostly it was garbled. Every now and then you'd say, 'I'll be a good girl,' over and over, in a child's voice. Then, when the doctor stuck the needle into your vein to hook up the IV, the ones we could make out were, 'Don't hurt me. I'll be good.'"

I noticed my fists were clenched.

"What was going on?" she asked.

"I don't know." *I wish I had the courage to tell you.*

"No ideas?" she asked, straightening out my covers before she left. "It's okay; we all have stuff we don't want to talk about. Some of us manage to keep our mouths shut." She looked hurt.

"Emma, could I tell you something, in private?"

She nodded and sat down on the edge of my bed.

"Sometimes I have weird images in my head but when I try to make sense of them, they disappear. Then I feel crazy. You ever have anything like that happen to you?"

She shook her head. "What do you suppose it means?"

"I don't know."

"How long has this been going on?"

"Forever."

"Do you remember how it started?"

"No." *How could I tell her my mother used to hit me and throw me into her closet and lock the door until just before my father came home from work. That when the key turned in the lock and I heard her footsteps getting softer I would know the beating was over and it was safe to hold myself and let the pictures in my head begin. Like watching a movie, with stories as real as the closet. That's when Boonah came. That's when I felt better.*

"How old were you?"

"I'm not sure. Pretty young, I think. After a while, the images in my head began to come all by themselves. Sometimes I don't know what's real and what's my imagination."

"Did you ever tell anyone about it?" she asked.

"No. I was afraid they would say I was crazy."

"How come you're so worried about people thinking you're crazy?"

My mother said I was crazy.

"I never met anyone else who has images in their heads."

Emma teased. "How many people you asked?"

"One. You." I snuggled the covers around me.

"Ever thought about seeing a therapist?"

"Why did your sister stay with a man who treated her so badly?"

"I keep asking myself the same question. Lalani was beautiful and smart and talented. If she'd had a family who'd been mean to her or treated her badly, maybe—but everyone loved her. She was the baby. There wasn't anywhere she couldn't go without someone giving her a hug. None of it makes sense. None!"

I lived with a man who beat me. Who raped me. Why did I stay? Why didn't I file for divorce the first time he hurt me? Why did I lie to my parents and his friends about the bruises I covered up with makeup?

I was spinning into a black hole. "Your sister's story doesn't make sense. Unless—"

"Unless what?"

"Well, it's possible, I mean, I'm not saying it happened, but you weren't around all the time. Your mother got sick when you were young. Maybe someone, you know, took advantage of your sister, when she was a kid, and no one knew. I mean bad things happen to kids all the time without families knowing." I started to shake. Emma's expression scared me.

"That child I mentioned? Her stepfather and brother treated her like shit, and the whole family knew about it but didn't do one damn thing to keep her safe." I pulled the blankets closer around me but the shivering wouldn't stop. "I guess you'll never know what made your sister do what she did." She sighed. I wanted to give her a hug and tell her she had done her best.

I surprised myself. "Emma, could we stay in touch? I mean when I get out of the hospital? I really like talking with you." *It feels so safe.*

"Sounds good to me." She poured ice water into my glass and when I had another fit of coughing, stayed with me until it stopped. She massaged my back until the shivering eased up.

This time when I dialed his number my hand didn't shake although his deep male voice was still unsettling. "Mr. Barszinsky, I've made up my mind. If you'd like the job, it's yours."

"Great! When do we start?"

"Could you be here around eleven tomorrow morning to help me check out? My car's parked at Ben's garage on 85th near Warner. Ask the man named Josh for the keys. When he wants to know how you knew to ask, give him my phone number, tell him I'm in the hospital, and you're picking me up. I'll be ready and waiting." I was pleased with his response. And yet—

Boonah lands gracefully in the palm of my outstretched hands.

"I did it! I am out of here tomorrow, caretaker and all. Boonah, I'm scared shitless. I keep thinking about what happened with Max."

"Think about me."

I dreamed men in white coats were chasing me. A man was twisting my arm and wouldn't let me out of an elevator unless I promised to be good. A man and a woman were pushing me into a river of blood. A woman was squeezing my neck as she forced me into an earthen grave. I woke myself up coughing so hard I thought I would choke to death. In my thrashing I must have hit the call button because Jacob rushed in. I couldn't stop coughing. He patted my back and gave me water to drink while he checked my vital signs.

"Your pressure's way up. What's going on?"

"Nightmares. What time is it?"

"About six thirty. Want a cup of coffee?"

I nodded. "Jacob, you got a minute?"

"Maybe two. Why?"

"Did you ever have a dream that was so real you believed it was real, even when you woke up and saw that it wasn't real?" He nodded. "What did you do? When you woke up I mean. How did you make it go away?"

"Mama used to tell me that there's more than one reality. She said there's a world inside us and a world outside us. Sometimes, just between sleeping and waking, she says the two worlds can touch. Then you got to take a deep breath and open your eyes real slow. Pretty soon the inside world goes back inside so you can live in the outside world. All it takes is faith."

He laughed at my expression of disbelief. "Yeah, faith that a couple of deep breaths and a cup of coffee can keep the world in its proper place. Sometimes it takes me two cups."

"You're too much, Jacob." Unwanted tears filled my eyes. "I'll miss you and Emma."

"No reason why people can't join you for coffee wherever you are."

I couldn't imagine Emma or Jacob sitting in my small kitchen.

Usually Dr. Adams made his rounds at ten. I was still recovering from the latest blood tests when he walked in at eight-thirty. I felt a powerful stab of fear.

"Good morning, Ms. Baum," he said, his voice flat.

I nodded. He talked to the white coats in his usual undecipherable technical language before turning to me. *Why can't he use words I understand?*

"I'd like to listen to your lungs."

He put his stethoscope on my chest. "Take deep breaths through your mouth." His examination was thorough, causing my anxiety to rise. After dictating notes, he walked to the door and then turned and said, "I'll leave your prescriptions with the nurse at the front desk. She'll give you instructions about outpatient lab tests and an appointment for your next visit. Take good care of yourself." The white coats followed him out.

I watched them leave, wishing I didn't feel so depressed, so worried about how much energy it took just to get dressed. I tried to make myself believe that if Emma said she'd call me at home, she would.

While I was waiting for Paulus Barszinsky, I wondered what his life was like. Why had he come all the way across the country without a job waiting for him or a place to stay? Didn't he know anyone in the city? What could have been so terrible that he left without a place to go? Maybe I should have had a background check done on him. The more I thought about living in the same apartment with a strange man, the worse I felt.

An End and a Beginning

He saw it as soon as he walked into his office. Someone had cleared the papers from the center of his desk, propping it up against his coffee mug.

As soon as he opened it and read the words, "Dear Mr. Barszinsky," he knew it was bad. Good news always started with "Dear Paulus." He sat down, closed his eyes, and took a deep breath. After reading it, he stood up, as if changing his position would change the message. Slowly, he opened each drawer, took out files of information on upcoming stories, ripped them up, and threw the scraps into large plastic bags that he dragged down to the recycling center. When he came back, his eyes fixed on the photograph, a smiling group of five people—his mother, father, sister, and grandmother—only two still alive. Paulus and his mother. He looked for something to wrap the photograph in but when he couldn't find anything, he took off his shirt and undershirt, wrapped the photograph in his undershirt, put on his shirt, and walked out without looking back. His coffee mug stayed on his desk. It was too full of memories.

Habitually, on Friday evenings, he stopped at Lomax Liquors to see if Charlie had any new wines or special cheeses. Charlie was a wine connoisseur who spent so much time looking for good cheese and crackers to eat with his wine, he decided to sell them himself. Paulus liked the way the store smelled of moldy cheeses and the bouquets of flowers that Charlie sold only on Fridays. Paulus had parked before he realized this wasn't just any Friday. "Hey, Paulus, just in time, I'm about to open a new one, from Chile. Up for a glass? You look like you could use it. And what about a chunk of aged Stilton with cumin crackers from Finland?"

He pulled up the bar stool, happy to watch Charlie go through the ritual of opening the bottle, smelling the bouquet, tasting a sip, and giving his expert opinion. "Good. Not great, but definitely worth drinking with the Stilton." Charlie brought out a large wedge of cheese, a box of brown crispy crackers, two glasses, and set them down on the counter. "Help yourself. Let me know what you think."

The letter in his jacket pocket pressed against his chest. Paulus pushed it away, took a sip of wine, and a bite of the cheese and cracker. "Charlie, you got the best job in the whole damn world."

"I told you, I need a partner, only cost you fifty grand. How bout it?"

"I'd probably drink up all the profits, but thanks for asking. Wrap me up a bottle with a half-pound of cheese, and a box of the crackers. They're really good. Oh, and stick in a bouquet while you're at it."

Paulus was pouring the wine when he felt Mollie's eyes boring into him. "It's written all over your face. You got fired, again, didn't you? I told you if you didn't quit messing with issues that aren't your business—."

"It's not the end of the world, I'll get another job. I always have."

"Sure, and in the meantime, the rent's due on Monday and you have a car payment on Thursday."

"I pay my bills. Besides I have lots of possibilities."

"Bullshit! Nobody wants a bleeding heart on the payroll. They pay you to write, not to cause trouble. You're so busy worrying about other people's lives you never think about your own. I'm tired of picking up the pieces. The last time this happened, you promised you'd keep your mouth shut and your eyes on the deadlines, but you just can't keep your nose out of other peoples' business. What's it been? Four months?"

"Taste the Stilton. It's the kind you like. Remember, we couldn't find it last time—." The No she spat out reverberated. "Please," he pleaded to her stony face, "it's been a hard day. We can talk just as well after a glass of wine and a piece of Stilton. You told me how much you liked it."

"Stop with the wine and cheese crap, for godssake! There's nothing to discuss. It's perfectly obvious that helping day-care ladies or trash collectors or God knows who is more important to you than I am."

"That's not true." His hope flickered when she smelled the freesias.

"Paulus, you have great taste in wine and cheese and flowers, and coffee and food and restaurants, but that doesn't make a relationship."

"Can't we talk about this like two reasonable people who love each other?"

"We could if there were two reasonable people. I 'm sorry but I just can't take any more false promises."

"We've been together three years. Think about all the good times we've had." He looked at her. "I love you."

"I need more security, Paulus. If it's all the same to you, I'd prefer you move out." She left the room.

He took the letter out of his pocket, put it into a metal pan, and burned it, watching flames eat the bad news until there was nothing left but ashes. He poured himself another glass of wine and munched on Stilton and crackers, appreciating the combination of flavors. Maybe it was time to leave California. Put the West behind him. Maybe he'd have better luck somewhere else. Go East, young man, he thought wryly.

9

Moving as slowly as possible still took up too little time. I wanted to say goodbye to Jacob but couldn't force myself to walk to the nurses' station. Any moment I expected to be told that the permission to leave was a mistake.

To distract myself I thought about my new employee. What if he's watching basketball and I want to look at ballet? Even worse, what if he brings a date back to my apartment? And how should I address him? He said to call him Paulus but that felt too casual. Mr. Barszinsky? Too formal. And what should he call me? Probably Ms. Baum. That would give us emotional distance. *I wish there were a book with rules and regulations about hiring and addressing* —

My mother never hired anyone to help her clean. Max and I had a cleaning service, but they came while we were at work. I only saw them once, and that was by accident. They were supposed to be cleaning out the refrigerator, and I suppose, to give them their due, they were, only not as I would have expected. One was eating a leg of chicken and the other was munching on a piece of quiche. I saw them before they saw me. "Lunch break," the skinny one said. The other one threw the bone in the garbage, washed his fingers, and began to wipe the refrigerator door. I left.

What do I say if Paulus eats all my food? In the middle of imagining an argument about him talking on my telephone too long, he walked in pushing a wheelchair with the same quiet dignity that so impressed me the first time. I was grateful he was on time. Cheerful. Ready to go. I was not ready for the wheelchair.

"We didn't discuss what to call each other," he said matter of factly, "but I prefer Paulus to Mr. Barszinsky. Is it all right if I call you Anna?"

No. "I guess so."

He wrapped my flowers in his newspaper which he thoughtfully wet, stowed my suitcase in the space under my seat, and locked the chair. I sat, holding the children's pictures on my lap. Numbly allowing him to wheel me to the elevator, I suddenly remembered I needed to pick up prescriptions and appointments.

While we waited for my take-home bag, I caught him watching me, which made me even more nervous, something I didn't think was possible. "I don't know about you but I feel weird. I'm not sure this is going to work."

"Does that mean you've changed your mind?"

I shook my head.

"Well, then just think of it this way: you're housing the homeless. A mitzvah." *He's Jewish. At least we have something in common.*

Sitting in the passenger seat of my own car felt awkward. The closer we got to my street, the more apprehensive I became. He parked the car in the handicapped parking spot and helped me out. I moved slowly. What a pair, him holding his suitcase and my overnight bag, and me trying to hide my anxiety, hoping I'd make it to the elevator without collapsing. My thoughts were jumbled, too many colliding in too small a space. As I opened the door to my apartment, panic took up residence in my head like it had no intention of moving out.

"Where do you want me to put my things?" He seemed pleased with the room. "Before I settle in, is there anything you need right now? I can pick it up before I park the car." *I need a reliable body. I need a woman to take care of me.*

All too soon, he was knocking on my bedroom door. "How about giving me directions to the nearest supermarket and a few suggestions about what you like to eat. Also, I'll need a key to the front door."

Although I managed to find the extra key I'd hidden in the bathroom, I was a whisker away from hysteria when I gave it to him. No matter that it was a reasonable, necessary request. I lay back down, waiting for him to leave. It seemed like years since I'd last slept in my own bed. *What do I wear to the bathroom when he's around?*

Hearing the key turn in the lock reminded me of listening to Max open the door, worrying about his mood. I watched my housekeeper put two bags stuffed to the top with groceries on the kitchen table. *He is not Max. I am paying him to work for me. When I no longer want his services, he will leave. Why am I so jittery around him?* "I've got two more bags in the car. Be right back." I put the groceries away, relieved to be doing something mundane.

I didn't know whether to watch, help, or direct as he made lunch, deftly slicing toasted bagels, slathering them with cream cheese. I set the table and poured water as he washed tomatoes and cut up red onions. Although he'd bought what I'd asked him to buy, suddenly I wasn't hungry. A feeling of nausea swept over me.

*****

I'm being honored, like everyone in junior high who's been on the honor roll each year. For the celebration, my mother comes home with the required white dress and it is absolutely exquisite. Only one problem, it is too small. "Mom, it's a size three. I wear a five, even a seven some times. Why did you buy it?" I can't help admiring the off-white confection of organdy that has a full skirt and a darker white sash.

"This is the only size they had. It's a real steal. I saw it in Saks for five times what I paid for it. So you'll go on a diet. Wouldn't hurt you to lose a few pounds." She takes the bagel and cream cheese I'm eating and throws it in the garbage. "You got a few weeks; you can do it. You'll look gorgeous up there. So you don't eat for a while. It'll be worth it—believe me."

*****

I watched him wolf down three bagels piled high with cream cheese, tomatoes, and onions. How he managed to get it all in his mouth was a mystery. I moved food around on my plate so it looked like I was making something to eat.

He noticed. "What's wrong? Would you rather have something else?"

I shook my head, put a dab of cream cheese on a sliver of bagel and artfully arranged a bit of tomato but couldn't make myself eat. Instead, I poured a small glass of orange juice and swallowed five of my afternoon pills.

When he ground beans for coffee I felt my stomach muscles begin to relax.

"Want some?" he asked.

"Sure. Smells great."

"I notice you have a large jar of instant coffee."

"Toss it. I've reformed."

After I'd taken a sip he asked, "Did I describe my coffee making abilities accurately?"

I appreciated the effort he was making and forced myself to smile and use his name. "Paulus, I do believe you are a truthful man."

When he left to buy newspapers, I sat in my favorite chair, admiring for the umpteenth time the needlepoint seat cushion my grandmother made before I was born. Kneeling down, I ran my fingers over the even stitches just as I'd done the first time I saw it, stuffed under old shirts in the bottom drawer of a chest in my parents' bedroom.

*****

At seven, I can barely recognize fine craftsmanship, but something about the design and jewel-like colors of deep blues and greens and reds and purples stirs my imagination. I can look at it forever. Even though I know I shouldn't be in my parents' room, much less look in their chest of drawers, I covet the needlepoint with a desire so fierce it becomes uncontrollable. One day, after sneaking in to see it, without thinking, I rush into the kitchen where Momma is making a casserole. "Can I have this, Momma? Can I put it on my dresser? Can I? It's so beautiful."

She looks stunned at the sight of the needlepoint. Right away I know I'm in trouble. How can I explain finding it without admitting I've been looking through her things? She grabs it from me and slaps my face. "How many times I got to tell you, stay out of my room. What's there is none of your business."

I want the needlepoint so badly I ignore the slap. "But Momma, it's in a drawer in your chest. You're not looking at it. Can't I have it? Please?" The second slap stings my face and knocks me into the refrigerator. Pretending she hasn't hurt me, I pick myself up and walk out of the room. Why is she keeping something so beautiful, so wonderful to look at, in a place where no one can see it?

*****

Afterward, no matter where I looked, I couldn't find the needlepoint. I never mentioned it again, fearing she might destroy it, if she hadn't done so already. Only after I graduated from college, teaching certificate in hand, did I dare broach the subject. My mother had invited me to lunch to celebrate my graduation. After buttering a roll, she cut off a piece and stopped. "Your father always talked about wanting to be a professor and teach at a university."

"I didn't know that. What stopped him?"

"Responsibilities, that's what. He had a wife and child and two old parents. He did what he had to do, just like I did."

"But if he really wanted to be a teacher, couldn't you have helped him?"

"What? I washed. Cooked. Cleaned. Took care of you. Lost two babies. What more did you want me to do?"

I tried to hide my shock. "What two babies?"

"You don't remember? After the second I had no more tears."

"That must have been awful." *Two babies?*

"Well, it wasn't easy. The first one I lost when you were about two and a half. I wanted to die but there you were, screaming to be fed, wanting attention, crawling into my lap. But if I thought I felt bad when I lost the first one, it was even worse when I lost the second. He actually lived four days. My last chance to have the son your father always wanted. In those days they didn't have the fancy treatments they have now. The doctors told me to forget about having any more children. I was too old." She looked grim, her mouth tight, jaw muscles clenched. Shaking her head she said, "Well, that's in the past. Nothing to be done about it."

I didn't want to spoil our moment of intimacy by asking why she didn't get a paying job when I was in elementary school or why my father didn't use the G.I. Bill to help with his expenses. Did losing the two babies make her so angry she couldn't care about anything else? "I'm sure you did the best you could." *Why did you hurt me?*

"I did what had to be done. That's what it means to be a grown up. You give up your dreams and deal with reality. Meet your responsibilities. Take care of people who depend on you. You forget about yourself." *What dreams did you give up?*

"What did you dream about?"

"Waiter, we need the bill." My mother poured coffee into a cup that was full.

*****

Daddy comes into the living room wearing socks. I've never seen him without shoes before. His face looks funny and he walks like he doesn't know where he is. "Daddy? Where are your shoes? Should I get your slippers?" It takes a while for him to answer.

He looks at me with an expression I can't figure out. "No thank you, darling. It's kind of you to offer but I need more than slippers."

Ever since he started kissing me with wet sloppy kisses I've been keeping my distance but now he looks so weird, I say, "Tell me what you need. I'll get it for you." I'm eight. I can make him a cup of tea and toast some bread. Maybe he will feel better if I scramble eggs.

"You're my sweetie, my darling girl." I wait for him to tell me what he wants but he doesn't say. Instead, before I can move away he gives me a too tight hug and plants his lips on my mouth. His hands stroke my body. I wriggle out from under him and run into the bathroom, locking the door. "Anna, come back here," he calls. I wash out my mouth but the bad taste stays for a long time.

*****

My mother's loud voice startled me. "Anna, did you hear what I said?"

"Uh, no, I'm sorry."

"What were you thinking about?"

"Uh, my new apartment. I wonder what it'll be like, living all by myself." *No mother poking around. Reading my diary. Listening to my phone calls. Telling me how to live. Complaining about my single state. No worries about locking the bathroom door. Free at last, Lord. Free at last.*

"I still don't understand why you're in such a hurry to move out. Our apartment is plenty big for three people. Keep your money for when you get married. Don't think I'll pay for a fancy wedding. You got to save, same as your father and me. We started from nothing. Now, we aren't rich, but we're not poor either."

"Mother, we've been over this a hundred times. My place is five minutes from my job. If I live with you and Dad I'll spend half my life on the subway."

"Don't come running to me the first time you got no money to pay your rent."

What would happen if I stuffed your mouth with my napkin? "I really appreciate your help. I'll manage. I'll figure it out, just like you did." *Why can't anything I do be okay with her?*

"You'll have to buy furniture and dishes and curtains and a toaster. How you gonna manage on a teacher's salary? You won't earn enough to put money in a savings account, which you should do right away. You never know when you'll need it."

Tired of defending myself, I tried a new tactic. "You look nice,

Mother. That dress is really pretty on you. Amber brings out the color of your eyes." She looked bewildered. I kept going. "It's nice, us having lunch. I felt like celebrating. Too bad Dad couldn't join us."

"His boss wouldn't give him the time off. I got to give him his due; he works hard, always has. We're proud of you Anna. You're the first one in our family to graduate from college. Your father and I want to give you a present. Something we can afford, that is." She looked thoughtful, a bitter expression on her face. "No one gave me nothing."

Her tone of voice shocked me. "If you could have had a present when you were my age, what would you have wanted?"

The hard lines of her face softened. "Anything?"

I nodded, eager to hear her answer.

"World War II would never have happened."

I gasped. "That's not exactly a present anyone could have given you."

"Well, that's what I would have wanted. For starters."

"Then what? What if there had been no war?"

"Nothing mattered after the war. But never mind me. It's your graduation. You're the one who's getting the present."

I knew what I wanted. "I'd like to have the needlepoint that Grandma made."

"What? That old *shmatta*?"

"It's beautiful."

"That's what you want for graduation? I thought you'd ask for something good, what you could use every day, or even for special."

"I'm sure. I want the needlepoint." I hoped she still had it, given her propensity to throw stuff away in a fit of pique and then moan about it later.

"Here I offer you a real present and what do you ask for? Old cloth with stitches. But, that's what you want—okay, it's yours. Just don't come running to tell me you came to your senses and prefer a coffee table or a toaster. Anna, think again. Be sensible for once. I know what I'm talking about, believe me."

"What are you talking about?"

She looked disconcerted. "Well." She ordered more coffee for both of us. "Let's just say there was a time when I wanted something and didn't say I wanted it and when I was ready to say it, it was gone forever. Better not to want, that's what I learned."

"What did you want?"

"That's not the point. The point is about changing your mind."

I sighed. "I'm not going to change my mind."

"How am I going to explain to your father that his dearly beloved daughter turned down the chance to get a real present?"

"Mother, stop! Just for once can we have a peaceful meal, like two normal people?"

"I'm not the one who started. The problem is, you have no sense. You think you know everything." She paused. "But you're right; we're celebrating. I offered; you took."

I was so pleased she agreed to give me the needlepoint I wanted to hug her, not that she'd let me. Still, I couldn't help myself. I stood up and gave her a squeeze before she could object. "I'm so happy. Grandma's needlepoint will look really pretty on the blue chair I just bought."

She scowled, and muttered, "Grandma's needlepoint...*oy vay iz mir*." She shook her head. "Well, let's hope I can find it. Think of something else in case I don't have it anymore."

"Did you love your mother?"

"What kind of question is that?"

"You never talk about her or your family. What was it like when you were growing up?"

"Nothing special. What my father said, that was it, even when he was wrong. Oh, I suppose Momma tried to stick up for us but I think she was afraid of him, just like Lilly and me. He had a terrible temper that he could lose faster than a heartbeat." She sighed, "Well, he didn't have it so easy. His family—most of the village—was murdered in a pogrom in Poland. He survived by hiding in the outhouse with two other Jewish kids. When we complained something smelled bad he would say, 'The smell of shit is the smell of life.' Who could argue?"

"So how did he get to this country?"

"His mother had a cousin who lived in another village. She found him a couple of days afterward. Said he didn't speak for months. She was so determined someone from the family should survive she paid a man to forge papers saying he was her son. He got to America but he never got to school. Told us he paid a neighbor to teach him to read and write." She grew thoughtful. "Some things you never get over, maybe, no matter how good your life gets."

"Was there stuff you never got over?"

"What's with all this stuff about me? We were talking about my family. About Papa."

"What happened to him wasn't your fault. You were his daughter. Didn't he love you?"

"Love, shmuv. We didn't think about those things. Are you sure you don't want a toaster? I saw a nice one on sale the other day. Half price 'cause the label was crooked. A real bargain. Cheap enough for two presents."

I shook my head. "Want dessert, Mother?"

"Anna, for once in your life use your brains. Stay by us and save your money so you can get a nice apartment, more than two rooms. What's so bad about living in a place where your meals are cooked? I'll do your washing, same as before. Are you listening to me? Anna Baum, I'm talking to you! Anna? Anna!"

How do I make her stop? "I'm fine, Mom, just thinking about the needlepoint."

Paulus turned on the radio so loud I yelled, "For godssake, Paulus, turn it down. *This is not your place. You should ask if it's all right to blast me out of the room.* Staring at him, I remembered Emma's advice and mumbled, "Excuse me." I practically ran to the bathroom and stuck my head under the faucet, waiting for my anger to subside. *Paulus is not Max.*

I went into my bedroom and lay down on the bed, falling into a sleep so deep I was dead to the world until the smell of sautéing garlic woke me up. Looking at the clock, I was shocked to realize I'd been sleeping four hours. I crept toward the bathroom, hoping Paulus wouldn't hear me. My desire to be alone, to feel less anxious, was so unbearable I went back to bed and curled up in a ball under the covers.

*****

He caresses me. It feels nice until he holds me so tight it's hard to breathe.
"Oh, my sweet little pussy. My own little puss."
"She's mad at me."
"She loves you."
"She hurts me when you leave."
"She's playing. She loves you."
"She hits me. She says I'm bad."

I shook myself awake but the images continued. What were these voices? Like a stuck note on a damaged record, they kept playing, demanding my attention, but they made no sense? *Do I want to know?*

I walked into the kitchen where Paulus was slicing onions with precision. Around him were dishes filled with uniformly cut, diced, and chopped vegetables. "I hope your tears are from the onions and not my bad manners." I flinched, waiting for his reaction.

Paulus took a huge handkerchief from his pocket to wipe his eyes. "So far so good. My fingers are intact."

"How about your spirits?" I quipped.

"Anna, there's something you don't know about me."

"That's an understatement if ever I heard one."

He laughed.

The next night while he was cooking a delicious-smelling curry, I dropped the glass I was washing. "Damn, I'm sorry. Don't move until I clean it up."

"Let me do it. You might cut yourself. You need all the blood you have."

One silly remark and my appetite disappeared. "Paulus, would you mind terribly if I skipped dinner?"

"It's your house. Do what you want."

Max walks into the apartment though the door is locked and he has no key.

"Leave, Anna. It's my turn to live in this apartment."

"No. I found it. It's mine." I run into the bedroom and lock the door but he walks through it and stands next to my bed.

"Leave or else—!"

"Anna, what's wrong?" Paulus was standing in the doorway. Shaking, I clutched the covers to my body and sat up—disoriented and frightened.

"I'm all right. Don't worry."

"You were screaming and now, look at you, you're shaking. Take pity on a poor man who's scared to death his employer will starve to death before morning. For my sake, have a cup of soup while I regain my composure." He returned with a bowl of soup and put it on my desk.

"Paulus, that bowl's for salad, not soup. There's enough here for six people."

"Eat. What will I tell the cops if they find you dead from hunger?"

"I can't."

"Yes, you can. Try!"

Another nightmare triggers a painful reminder of life with Max, when after a particularly awful nightmare, where I was being raped by a faceless man with a seductively smooth voice, Max shook me so violently I woke up. "I'm fucking tired of being woken up by your yelling. You sound like some kind of monster."

"I can't help what I do when I'm sleeping."

"I can't take anymore. I'm leaving."

"What?"

"You heard me," he said throwing off the covers.

His tone of voice spiraled my fury. "Then leave for chrissake. But I'm no monster and you're no prize." I shouted to his back, "And since you're going, get your crap out of the study."

While Max got out a large suitcase I began throwing his books and papers into a large carton. I pushed his stationary bicycle into the living room and then did the same with his barbells, and golf clubs, and rowing machine. He had so much stuff. Where were my things? Where was my space?

Dragging his suitcase into the living room, he tripped over the golf clubs. "You bitch!" he screamed, rubbing his shin, then moving toward me, fists curled.

I picked up a weight. "Don't touch me."

"What happened to my sweet, darling wife?" His low, sexy voice took me aback.

I ran into the bedroom. Max followed me.

I heard his breathing. I felt his rage.

"Slide the keys under the door when you leave," I said, hoping my voice did not betray my terror.

Knocking the weight out of my hands, he threw me face down on the bed, tearing off my clothes. Screaming. Cursing. Moving down on top of me with all his weight and anger. Smashing into my clenched body. Tearing open the tightness. Crushing. Ripping. Slashing. I crashed into shards of bloody pain.

"It doesn't taste good. I don't want it."

"Swallow." A hand covers my mouth.

I retch. The hand holds my mouth closed. A hand squeezes my nose. I have to swallow. I throw up.

*****

I ran into the living room, expecting to see my tall, trim, curly-headed, handsome, furious, husband. Instead, there was short, paunchy, balding, frightened Paulus. I stopped in my tracks, draping the afghan over my nightgown. "I'm sorry I woke you up. I had a nightmare but I'm okay now. Go back to bed; it's late."

"Sit down and rest," he said kindly, as I had imagined my husband would act. I wanted to bury my head against his chest and hold on for dear life, at least until the shaking stopped, but when he started to put his arm around me I moved away.

Backing off, he said, "I'll make you a cup of tea."

I huddled inside the afghan. My hand trembled uncontrollably; the teacup clattered against the saucer.

"I'll turn up the heat," said Paulus.

"It's not the temperature. It's my memories."

"Feel like talking?"

"It seemed so real, like it was happening now."

"Anything I can do?"

"No."

"I'm doing my best, Mollie. Give me a break."

"Mollie?"

He turned away. "Slip of the tongue."

Images were working their way into my memory like thieves burgling a house. I had the feeling something awful had happened. All I could remember at first was a rainy Saturday. A new girl, six, like me, had just moved next door and I went over to play with her. On my way home I slipped and fell. More of it was coming back. I remembered being afraid to go into the apartment covered with mud so I rang the bell, trying to scrape the mess off my shoes and raincoat.

My father opens the door, something he rarely does. "Look at you. You need a bath."

"No, I don't." I tell him, shivering.

"Mommy wouldn't want to see you all dirty."

He pulls off my shoes and raincoat and yanks off my sweater.

"Daddy, let me go." He holds my arm, pushing me toward the bathroom. "Ouch. Let go."

"Stop pulling away. Daddy just wants to help."

"I don't need help." He turns on the tub faucet.

"Let go, Daddy, I'm not a baby."

"I know you're not. You're Daddy's big girl. You're Daddy's good girl." He's hugging me and holding me. Something hard is pushing against me.

*****

Then what happened? Why can't I remember? Did I tell my mother? What would I have said? Would she have listened? Would she have told me what she told Aunt Lilly?

*****

I haven't started school yet, but I know how to read. The doorbell rings. I hear the surprise in Momma's voice as she opens the door. "Lilly? It's the middle of the afternoon." Momma's older sister comes in alone, without my uncle or cousins. Aunt Lilly is taller than Momma, with shiny blonde hair. Momma hardly ever talks about her except to say, "She was the pretty one" in an angry voice. My aunt walks into the kitchen like she's holding herself together, all stiff and tight. She sits down at the table and begins to cry. Momma puts a hand on her shoulder. "Lilly?" My aunt cries and cries and cries. Momma moves away. "I'll make us tea." Aunt Lilly keeps crying. Momma's voice isn't friendly. "So tell me, what's wrong this time?" I've never seen a grown-up cry before. I move closer.

Momma sees me. "Anna, go read. This is between me and your aunt." I get a book and sit on the sofa, pretending, just in case Momma checks on me. Aunt Lilly's words are all mushed up with crying but

I have no trouble hearing my mother. "Look, Lilly, either take it and keep quiet or make a plan. What's the point of coming to me and crying? What can I do? I can't make him stop. At least he pays the bills. You live in a nice house, in a good neighborhood. The children got new clothes for school. Who's gonna pay for all that if you leave? Where you gonna find a place you can afford? And when you look for a job? Who's gonna hire you? You haven't worked since before you got married. Anyway, what makes you think he'll let you take the children? He's got too much pride."

I tiptoe to the doorway. Momma puts a glass of steaming tea with cubes of sugar in front of my aunt who is slumped over. Her head is lying on her arms. "Drink the tea. It will make you feel better." She brings a plate of cookies and puts them in front of Aunt Lilly. "I just made them. Eat." Momma raises my aunt's head and tries to put a sugar cube in her mouth.

Aunt Lilly pushes Momma and the glass away.

Momma glares at her. "If you're so unhappy, do something. Stand up for yourself. This isn't the old country. You're not living in Papa's house."

In The Rose Garden

Heshie looked at himself in the mirror and sighed. His curly brown hair refused to stay down, but he didn't want to put more pomade on it. He already smelled like a barbershop. He looked at his three ties. Sadie liked bright colors, so he put on the blue and yellow but immediately took it off. Too bright. He settled for the red and blue stripe. Maybe she would think it was too traditional, but that's the kind of guy he was. He put on his polished black shoes and took another look in the mirror. What he saw made him feel a little better. He was tall enough, trim, and had a good job. He smiled. He had good teeth, thank goodness.

He walked to Minnie's house, needing to talk to her before he asked Sadie to go with him to the park. The last time he'd invited Sadie out she didn't sound happy to hear from him. Well, Minnie would know.

"Heshie? I thought you were seeing Sadie today."

"I am. I just need to ask you something. Minnie. You positive Sadie likes me?"

"What kind of question is that? Course she does. You got second thoughts?"

"No, nothing like that. It's just sometimes she gets a funny look on her face, like maybe she's thinking about some other guy. Did she have another boyfriend? Someone she wanted to marry?"

"Before the war there was a man she liked, sort of, but he disappeared and she never talked about him again. If Sadie was in love with him, you can bet I would have known. Besides, that was a long time ago. Nothing for you to worry about, believe me. Your problem is you think too much. Stop thinking and start asking." Minnie smiled. "So go already. Next time we talk I want to say, 'Congratulations.'"

"Okay, I'm leaving. You won't tell Sadie we talked, will you?" She shook her head with mock exasperation, blew him a kiss, and went inside.

He could feel his heart racing as he banged the knocker on the door. Sadie opened it slowly, a suspicious look on her face. When she saw him she said, "Oh, Heshie, it's you."

"So who'd you expect? Uncle Sam? It's such a nice day I thought we'd take a walk."

"I got to clean the house while Momma's visiting Lilly's new baby."

"So clean later, I got something to ask you."

"So ask!" She didn't smile. She didn't look very happy. Could Minnie be wrong?

"No, not here. In the park." He watched her. She had that strange expression on her face, the one that made him nervous. "Is something wrong? Don't you want to go? We could do it another day."

"No. Give me a minute. I'll get my sweater. Only I can't stay too long. I really got to clean. Papa says he'll make me quit my job if I don't help Momma more."

They walked in silence to the park a few blocks away. Heshie envied the children running and shouting, with no thoughts about tomorrow. He took Sadie's cold hand and gently rubbed it. Once inside the park he said, "Let's go to the rose garden. The roses are in full bloom. Besides, we can have a little privacy."

"Heshie, you been knowing me for years. All of a sudden you need a special place to talk to me?" He tried to laugh but was too nervous. He walked her to a bench in front of bushes filled with fragrant blossoms. She took her hand from his and sat down, her face impassive, waiting.

"Don't the roses smell good?" She nodded. "Which color do you like Sadie?"

She stared at the reds and yellows and pinks and whites and shook her head. "You know I like yellow." She stood up and walked to a bush. He followed her. "You look like you got something to say," she said.

"Sadie—Sadie—"

He began again. "Sadie—Sadie—"

She fidgeted.

"That's me. You definitely got the right person. What are you trying to say?"

"Let's go sit over there."

She walked to the bench, not looking at him. "Okay, I'm sitting."

"Sadie—" Why was this so hard? Minnie was her best friend. She said Sadie loved him. Minnie would know. She wouldn't just make it up; she wasn't that kind of person. He straightened his tie, took a deep breath and spoke quickly. "Sadie will you marry me? Will you be my wife?" He saw her stiffen slightly, but maybe it was his imagination. "I love you, Sadie. I want you to be my wife. Will you marry me?" An unreadable look flickered across her face. He took her hands in his. They were ice cold though it was warm in the sun.

Staring at the roses, she said, "Sure, Heshie. I'll marry you." She tilted her face toward his. She allowed him to kiss her.

"I love you, Sadie." She nodded.

10

A huge black cloud moves between Marina and me. I can't see where she's going. I call out to her but she doesn't answer. I keep running. I'm running in blood. I'm drowning in blood.

Another nightmare. More blood. I dragged myself into the kitchen; hoping coffee would make me feel life was worth living. On the table was a note from Paulus.

> Anna,
> I have two interviews this morning and one in the afternoon.
> I'll be back at 2:30 to take you to your 3:30 appointment with
> Dr. Heisenfelzer. I bought the bagels fresh this morning. I
> hope you like onions. They're my favorite.

I forgot to tell Paulus I can't stand onion bagels. The smell is enough to make me vomit.

"Boonah, I'm scared of what the doctor will say."
"Worrying is not useful."
"How do I stop?"
"Use your imagination."
"Everything inside me is dead."
"Illness is like a forest fire burning everything in sight. Underneath, new life is growing. Dig, Anna, you will find it."
"Where? Where do I start?"

"Are you talking to me?" asked Paulus.

Disconcerted, I shook my head. Looking at the clock, I realized I had to rush if I wanted to make my appointment. "Be ready in a second." I sloshed water over my face and accidentally looked into the mirror. A haggard woman with dripping hair, frightened eyes, and a clenched jaw looked at me. Her ugliness surprised me. I used to think she was reasonably attractive.

The waiting room was hot and crowded. Paulus took off and I slumped in a chair, staring at a photograph of an African mother with her child on her back carrying a water jar on her head.

*****

"Momma, teacher says Columbus discovered America but in my book of world myths it says there were lots of people living here and they all had their own stories. How could he discover America if people were already living here?"

"Ask your teacher."

"But Momma, it doesn't make any sense. Who says Columbus discovered America?"

"I'm busy. Go away!"

"How can you say you discovered something if it's already known?"

"Do I look like an encyclopedia? Stop with the questions already. I got potatoes to mash and gravy to make."

"But I need to know." The slap was my answer.

"Are you satisfied now, Miss Anna Baum?"

*****

"Ms. Anna Baum?" Cringing, I looked up to see a gray-haired woman with kind eyes. *Where's Momma?* Around her neck, peeking out from under her white coat, was a multicolored silk scarf—purple and blue and pink and lavender—my favorite colors. She said, "I'm Dr. Heisenfelzer." I took two steps toward her and fainted.

I came to in an elegant office on a purplish tweed sofa. My head was resting on a blue velvet pillow. Sitting up carefully, I wondered how to let someone know I was conscious. Time passed slowly. A nurse came in, relieved to see I was awake. She handed me a pleasantly cool wet cloth. "Wipe your face. It will make you feel better. When you're up to it, drink some water. I'll get Dr. H."

When the doctor appeared it was clear that standing up was a terrible idea. She apparently came to the same conclusion, gesturing for me to stay seated as she took my blood pressure. "Don't get up yet. You need time to recover."

"Why did I faint?"

"I'm not sure, but your blood pressure is very low so you need to move slowly when you sit or stand. It's probably part of being run down. I don't think you should drive until you've gone two weeks without feeling dizzy. We don't want you to have any accidents."

"Is there anything I can do to prevent them, the dizzy spells I mean?"

She shook her head. "Just get up slowly." She looked through a folder on her desk, piled high with books and papers. "I've read your hospital records and I'd like for us to talk before I examine you."

My eyes were caught by three exquisite ceramic bowls, each a different shade of purple, carefully placed on a shelf with jade plants on either end. *Well, we have one thing in common, we both love purple.* I kept staring at the bowls. The doctor looked at them, pleased.

"Do you like them?"

I nodded. "Where did you buy them?"

"I didn't. I bartered them in exchange for medical help."

"You did what?"

Dr. H. laughed. I liked her laugh, which was full and resonant. It made me glad I'd acted on Emma's recommendation, at least so far.

"I have a friend who's a marvelous potter. When I had no money and Miriam was too poor to buy medical insurance, we came to an agreement—her bowls for my medical know-how. Turned out to be such a great bargain we decided to continue it in perpetuity."

"They're exquisite."

"So tell me, what's going on? Are you still dizzy?"

"Not right now."

"I'm puzzled why you turned your face to the wall in the hospital?"

"How do you know about that? Don't tell me Emma said something."

"It's in your records. Besides, she's too professional to talk about a patient. Why did you refuse to talk to anyone, Ms. Baum?"

"I wanted to float."

"What does that mean?"

"It's a peaceful feeling. No worries. No pressure. No anxiety—."

"What stopped the floating?"

"Forced feeding, bad nurses, good nurses, bad luck—who knows?"

"And now?"

"I'm stuck. Can't float. Can't work. I've turned into an illness. Hard to imagine just a few weeks ago I was giving a paper with a colleague in front of hundreds of professionals at a major conference. Now I can hardly stand up without feeling like I'll fall down any second."

"You've been very ill."

I shrugged.

"Although I don't underestimate the severity of your illness, I have the feeling something else is going on."

"I don't understand. Aren't you an internist?"

"Yes, I am, but bodies and minds talk to each other. What they say affects healing."

I was not interested in hearing any conversation my mind might have with my body.

Dr. H. persisted. "What's so great about floating?"

"It's like I'm suspended above the world. Nothing bothers me."

I kept looking at the bowls.

She followed my eyes. "You ever thought about making a bowl like those?"

"Me? Are you kidding?"

"Why not? Did you ever try?"

"No," I snorted. "If I could, I'd consider myself an extremely fortunate woman."

Dr. H. smiled. "I know what you mean."

"How come? Did you ever pot?"

"Yes, but after much effort and considerable soul searching on both our parts, Miriam and I came to the conclusion she should make the pots and I should do the doctoring."

"Does she give lessons?"

"Yes, but I warn you, when you ask what she charges for lessons, she'll ask what you have to offer. She loves to barter as much as she likes to pot."

"What have I got to offer? Shit!"

"What's the matter?"

"I sound like my mother."

"Is that a problem?"

"To hear myself talking like her is not wonderful."

"Tell me about your mother, Ms. Baum."

"What's my mother got to do with me being sick?"

"I don't know. You brought her up."

"Yeah, well—Tell me about Miriam."

"She's very down to earth." We both laughed at the inadvertent pun. What potter doesn't touch the earth?

"You think I can manage lessons? Potting takes a lot of energy."

"Only one way to know. Give it a try and see what happens." She looked at my chart. "Ms. Baum, you get taken to the hospital where they discover you have double pneumonia, a serious condition, but not necessarily a death warrant. You remain uncommunicative until, I believe, it was Emma who finally found a way to reach you."

"She's irresistible."

"Is it possible the trauma of the fall reminded you of something?"

I stared at the carpet.

"Might this have to do with turning your face to the wall and refusing to speak?" I sighed audibly. "Ms. Baum, if I could help in any way, what would it be?"

"Since I got sick, I've been having even more nightmares than I used to have."

"Would you like something to help you sleep?"

"Sleeping pills don't agree with me. When will I be well enough to go back to work?"

"I can't say." She followed my eyes to the bowls. "Would you like to have a bowl?"

"Huh?" *Is this a test where I say yes and she laughs at my stupidity?* I watched stupefied as she reached for the smallest and, to my mind, the most beautiful bowl and put it into my hands. I held it, feeling the smoothness, unable to take it in that she had given it to me.

While we walked to the examining room, Dr. H.'s arm around my waist, I held on to the bowl as tightly as if my life depended on it. I was surprised to notice how grateful I felt that my doctor was a woman.

*****

"Momma, I don't want to go to the doctor. He hurts me."

"He's a doctor."

"Momma, please don't make me go."

"Stop sniveling. He doesn't hurt you. It's all in your head."

*****

"Ms. Baum," said Dr. H. with a twinkle in her eye, "One of the prerequisites of your being my patient is that you have to breathe. It's an absolutely nonnegotiable requirement."

I took a huge gulp of air and started to cough. She patted my back. "Take it easy, there's plenty more where that came from." After listening to my chest and feeling for swollen lymph glands, she said, "Put your clothes on and come to my office so we can talk."

I stroked the bowl; unable to believe she just took it off the shelf and gave it to me. If I had something so beautiful it would be a cold day in hell before I'd let someone have it.

When I entered her office, Dr. H. was standing near her bookcase, poring over a huge book that rested on a stand. My anxiety level zoomed off the charts. Caressing the bowl, I forced my vocal cords to work. "So, what do you think?"

She hesitated. "We haven't identified the underlying cause of your condition. I'd like to give you time to recuperate while we track your blood counts and do more tests. That should help us with our diagnosis. Do you have any questions?"

"Do you have any idea when I'll be able to go back to work?"

"No, I don't."

"How long will it take before you know what's wrong with me?"

"Your fatigue is caused by low red counts. You need to stay away from crowds and sick people. And, Ms. Baum, be kind to yourself."

Am I dying? "How sick am I?"

"You've been very ill and you're not out of the woods yet. We'll know more as we track your blood levels."

In shock, I walked to the waiting room and headed for an empty seat off to the side, near the coat rack. I took a magazine and looked at photos of a volcanic crater before and after eruption. I allowed myself to drift off.

"I've been expecting you," says Boonah, as he helps me off the crater's edge.

"How do you know I'm looking for you?"

"Sit here and listen." I sit.

"Once upon a time, there lived a tiny girl in a family of giants. Her parents hoped she would grow to be big like them, but this did not happen. They had to build a special highchair for her to eat at the table, and steps so she could reach her bed. They even had to make tiny plates and cups and utensils.

"The little girl struggled to live in a house that was many sizes too big for her. One day, when she saw her family preparing to visit her grandmother, she dressed in her best clothes and ran to join them. 'I'm coming,'

she shouted as they walked away. 'Wait for me, please.' She raced to catch up to them, but they quickly disappeared from her sight.

"The little girl cried as she walked back into the house and looked at the too-tall chairs, the too-heavy plates, the too-high table. She would never be big enough for her family. They would never like her. Never.

"She was hungry but the cheese was on a shelf she could not reach. The little girl was afraid she would starve to death before her family came home, so she packed a few belongings, pushed open the heavy door and—"

"Anna? It's Paulus. Wake up, we have to go home."

Suspended between two worlds, I flew around in space, trying to make a safe landing. I saw Paulus take a bagel out of a bag. I grabbed it.

Gobbling the bagel, I avoided his eyes. "Why are you staring at me?"

"You look kind of funny," he said. "What's going on?"

Reluctantly, I told him about the little girl and her family but didn't dare mention Boonah.

"Wow, no wonder you don't watch television. You've got it all in your head."

The nurse handed me three slips of paper with writing, but my eyes refused to focus. "You left them in Dr. H.'s office. You also forgot the orders for future tests." They felt like dead weights. Only Miriam's telephone number gave me hope.

We were close to home and had passed all the potential traffic trouble spots when I took a deep breath and closed my eyes. The cars in front of us immediately slowed to a crawl and then stopped. Soon no cars came toward us. I cursed, feeling closed in. Paulus turned off the engine and got out to see if he could figure out what was happening. A lot of drivers had the same idea. We watched a young black man take off in the direction of a busy intersection just down the road. The silence was eerie after the horns stopped honking. More people gathered together on the street, all of us wondering why the traffic had stopped yet no one else went to look.

In about ten minutes the man returned, his eyes wide with shock. "Some guy lost control of his car and ran into a group of school kids. There's blood and bodies all over the place. My guess is we're going to be here for quite a while." We looked in the direction of the accident. No one moved.

"Paulus, I'm too tired to keep standing here, I'm going back to the car." I wished I could think of something else beside children's bloodied bodies.

"I'll go with you. We can turn on the radio. Maybe there will be some news."

"Think of the phone calls those parents are going to get," I said, shivering. "Today starts out an ordinary day and with no warning, it's marked forever, an irreversible before and after. What if they didn't kiss their kids good-bye? Or there was an argument before the kids left?" My mind raced through possibilities, each more horrific than the one before. I thought about Marina. When traffic finally started to move, I promised myself I would keep my eyes straight ahead, focusing firmly on the car in front of us. But when we got to the scene, I couldn't help looking at the carnage, the bloody sidewalk.

Between the third and fourth floors of my apartment house, the elevator stopped. I sputtered in frustration. "Oh for God's sake, now what?"

Paulus' voice was tight. "Did I tell you I'm claustrophobic?" He kept banging the red emergency button.

Looking around for instructions, I muttered, "Where the hell is the card that that tells you what to do if the thing stalls?"

He could barely whisper. "It's supposed to be right by the buttons." Pacing back and forth like a caged animal, he retreated to the back corner where he hunkered down, mumbling to himself while he chomped on a poppy seed bagel, as if he couldn't eat fast enough. His whole body curved in toward the bagel. I looked at him, slumped against the wall, sitting with his knees as close to his chest as he could manage, his mouth full. I felt like joining him, just for comfort, but my mind was bursting with images of blood-spattered bodies, of dead children.

Unable to sit, I strode back and forth, each time punching the red button. I banged on the door. I yelled. When my throat eased, I yelled again, "Help! We're stuck. Help!"

"Who's going to hear you?" muttered Paulus. "Sit down. Have a bagel. They're still warm, just out of the oven."

The way he was eating reminded me of my mother. A dozen doughnuts could disappear down her throat in seconds when she was upset. "Can't you do anything but eat?"

"I'm sorry to tell you, but I'm no hero. Smashing steel doors isn't my style."

I banged the doors again until my fists hurt.

"Hey, why not finish that story? Give us something else to think about."

Desperate to be distracted, I said, "Okay, where was I?"

"The girl opened the door and left, I think."

"Right." I took a breath, closing my eyes to let the images form. "Well, she pushes open the heavy huge door and walks outside. It's a hot day and she's thirsty. In the distance she sees a pond and runs to it. Cupping her hands, she slurps the cool water. The sun shining down on her makes her sleepy. Soon she's fast asleep. She only wakes because she hears someone calling her name. 'How does anyone know my name?' she asks herself. A fawn, smaller than she is, is standing in front of her, looking right at her. The fawn says, 'I've come to take you home.'

"The little girl says, 'No, thank you. I'd rather go anywhere than home."

Just then the elevator groaned and moved. "Thank you, good spirits. Maybe there is something to you."

After dinner, I watched Paulus pore over a newspaper, studying it so intently my curiosity got the better of me. "Is there something special about that paper?"

"It's put out by my prospective employer. I was offered a job this afternoon."

For a moment the world went black. "What will you be doing?"

"I'm not sure, but if they give me a choice I'll tell them restaurant critic. Imagine being paid to do what I like best. Think how nice it would be, a different restaurant every night. No shopping, cooking, cleaning. All I'd have to do is write about it. All you'd have to do is keep me company."

"Maybe I could help. I used to eat in great restaurants with my husband—former husband, that is."

"Sounds good. I think I'll make a phone call if you don't need to use the phone." I nodded and he went into his room. *Who is he calling?*

The living room suddenly felt empty. I thought about the children in the accident and went to my desk. Writing a story for children was something I could do.

> There was once a small village nestled near the curve of a
> lake that flowed into a large river on its way to the ocean. The
> water was crystal clear. People living in the village fished in

its waters, bathed in the depths, and washed their clothes in shallow pools. Animals came to the shores at dawn and dusk.

One night there was a terrible storm. The wind howled and rain pelted the roofs of the huts. Huge hailstones tore up blossoming flowers and tiny vegetables just peeping up through the earth. People huddled close together, afraid, in awe of the storm's power. They heard screams but no one dared go outside. It was the longest, darkest night anyone could remember.

In the morning, when the worst of the storm had passed, villagers gingerly opened their doors and stared at the devastation. Houses smashed. Trees fallen. Crops, plants, seedlings—all drowned by rampaging waters.

And then, someone looked up.

Soon everyone was looking up.

There in the sky was a double rainbow.

A mother held her child close and said, "We will plant again."

I took out my paints and painted a double rainbow arching over the end of the story. When the paint was dry I put the story and a note into an envelope, addressing it to the hospital where most of the injured children had been taken. I felt peaceful, almost as good as when I was floating. Standing up, I crashed to the floor with a graceless thud.

Easy Come, Easy Go

Max sighed with satisfaction and relief as he sat in his favorite chair and looked around the living room of his apartment. He particularly liked how the new television was carefully hidden behind a Japanese screen. If there was one thing he hated it was moving. No matter how careful he was, something always got lost or damaged in the move. He still mourned the loss of his favorite fountain pen, nowhere to be found since he and Anna split. She must have thrown it out. Sometimes he missed her directness and her sense of humor. And the way she touched him. He'd never met a woman who was so responsive, for good and for bad. He shook his head, still wishing he'd managed to get the apartment as part of the divorce settlement.

"Max? Are you home?" He leaned back, waiting for Sheila to find him. Max smiled, running his fingers through her hair as he hugged his newest love. "The place looks great. I can't believe it's only been a few days since you moved." He basked in her compliment, allowing her to rub his back, enjoying the feeling of her long fingers easing away the tension in his neck. Max liked the way Sheila smelled. It reminded him of when he worked in the college greenhouse, watering, spraying, cutting dead blossoms, and picking up spent blooms. He liked how he had made order out of chaos. Well, chaos might be too strong a word, but he always felt satisfied when he left at the end of his shift, knowing all the branches were carefully pruned, and the dead and fallen flowers had been stashed in the compost bin for use later when he grafted shoots to make new plants from old ones. He sometimes missed the feeling of a job well done, of protecting fragile plants.

Maybe that was why he was so good at his job at the ad agency. Always knew how to prune a jingle so that its essence resonated. Never used two words when one would do. People teased him. Here he was Creative Director and his desk was always neat, in and out baskets usually empty. "I take care of business" was his motto. Don't ask too many questions and do what you have to do. Main thing is to get ahead. He kissed Sheila passionately until the phone rang. "Max, let it ring," she murmured. "The machine will pick it up." But he had already disengaged. He never could hear a phone ring without answering it.

"Hello?" Instantly, he was all business.

"We've got a problem with the Carter account. Smith is furious with the new rep. Said she's too damn aggressive. He's called a meeting. Wants you there and her to be history by morning."

"But I thought Sheila—" He was annoyed. Why couldn't she have done what he told her to do?

"Look, it's your decision, buddy. I'm just telling you what he said. The meeting is at three."

"Shit, I was planning to take the afternoon off. Okay, I'll be there. He likes French Roast decaf and Danish pastry from Marguerite's. Oh, and make sure there's a white linen tablecloth on the round table in A4 with three white roses in the small glass vase." Max hung up, more than a little irritated. He'd warned Sheila to keep her good ideas to herself when she was around the old man. Now he'd have to do a lot of damage control that could easily have been avoided if she'd just followed his orders. "But Max," she'd smiled, "I can handle men like Smith. Give me a chance." Max had let her convince him. Well, so much for that.

Sheila stared at Max as he hung up the phone. "Did I hear my name?"

"Smith says you've overstepped your bounds." He cut off her protests. "Doesn't matter. He wants you out. You're out. I'll write you a good recommendation. Davis and Jones might have an opening." He admired her for not crying or begging for another chance or asking what would happen to all the plans they'd made. A vacation in two weeks—. "You know the way the game is played."

When she touched his thigh, asking, "Doesn't love matter?" he pushed her away.

He hated scenes. "Yeah, it matters. It's just that I have to go. Mizrachi's been waiting for a chance to get to Smith and I don't want this to be his opportunity." He avoided her eyes. "Look, you know as well as I do if we aren't a team we can't be a couple. It's just too complicated and I hate complications. Be a good girl and don't make a scene. I got fancy repair work to do in the next two hours."

There was no point in reminding her she'd done exactly what he'd repeatedly cautioned her not to do. And he didn't want to think about having to find a new woman. Not that it was so difficult; it just took time and energy he could put to better use. He wished she would leave. He certainly didn't want to throw her out. One thing about Anna, she always assumed everything was her fault. Made life easier in a lot of ways. He walked Sheila to the front door, opened it, and gave her a quick goodbye hug, steeling himself not to feel her warmth and softness as he kissed her cheek.

As he walked to the bedroom to changes his clothes, he wondered if Cynthia was free tomorrow night. Only one way to find out. He dialed her number and smiled as he heard the warmth in her voice.

11

The early morning sounds of horns blaring and people yelling woke me up. I walked toward the window and crashed to the floor just as the phone rang. Pushing my body with my feet, I finally reached it as the last ring vibrated into silence. Lying in a pool of frustration, my eyes fixed on a glimmer of sunlight touching the rim of the bowl Dr H. had given me. The purplish-blue glaze sparkled and beckoned. I tottered to the chest of drawers, relieved to be upright. Rubbing my finger around the smooth surface of the bowl made me feel better. Cradling it in my hand filled me with a sense of contentment that gave me enough energy to make a decent breakfast for myself, which I ate until I saw the newspaper headlines, reporting more about the accident. The driver had apparently suffered a heart attack. He was in his early forties, not much older than me.

Staring at the bowl, I had an urge to make an offering to it, to give thanks for its unexpected presence in my life. Feeling slightly foolish, I toasted my favorite bread and took a deep breath as I put toast crumbs in the bowl, swirled them around, and ate them. I did this three times—for the past, the present, and the future. The bowl gave me the courage to call but as soon as the phone rang, I hung up. Two hours later I felt confident enough to try again.

"My name is Anna Baum, I'm a patient of Dr. Heisenfelzer's. I saw your bowls in her office. They're beautiful—." *Babble on, dear girl; she'll really be impressed.* "I was wondering, if it wouldn't be too much trouble that is, if I might see more of your work, I mean if it wouldn't be an intrusion—."

"My studio is open on Thursday afternoons between two and four or by special appointment."

"If tomorrow's good for you, could I come at two?" My stomach felt queasy and when I hung up, I saw Paulus standing in the doorway, his face tight and drawn.

"I thought you were working all day. Is something wrong?"

"Not really. As Mollie would say, 'Time to stop the pity party.'"

"Who's Mollie?"

He sighed. "Mollie, whose name was Martha Miller, and who now calls herself Mollie Mills, is the woman with whom I used to live."

"Mollie Mills? Sounds like a cereal."

"Yeah. But no nutrition."

"What happened?"

"You could say her version of what makes life worthwhile collided with mine. I lost."

"For godsakes, why?" Already I didn't like her.

"Let's just say she preferred her brand-new Mercedes to my old Ford. Stupidly, I thought she'd change." Paulus looked rumpled and tired. I felt a surge of anger. He'd been so kind to me I tried to think of a way to make him feel better.

"You're a writer. Why not send her a letter? Lay it on thick. Tell her how wonderful your life is now. How grateful you are that she provided the, shall we say, impetus for change."

Paulus smiled wanly. "What good would it do? Besides, what would I say? I don't know if the job will work out, I don't have my own place—." He looked small and old.

"Who said anything about truth? Use your imagination. Make her feel she made a huge mistake."

Paulus rolled his eyes.

"Talk about Armani suits, a fancy apartment overlooking the river, season tickets to the New York Philharmonic."

"She'll know it's bullshit. That's what she would want, not me."

"So write about what how happy you are that fate intervened and you left California."

He looked even more upset.

"What if I write the letter for you? You can change what I get wrong."

"She would know it wasn't my handwriting."

"Paulus! I'll type it." I was getting juiced.

"This is a totally crazy idea."

"Why? Make us coffee. I'll meet you back here in half an hour." I was not about to take no for an answer. I needed to write this letter for my own reasons.

"You got yourself a deal."

I started to run to my bedroom and felt the world spin again. This time I grabbed hold of the wall in time, grateful when the world resumed its proper shape. Just in case, I walked the rest of the way like an old woman, each step unto itself. When I sat down at my desk, full of ideas, I felt some of my old spirit return. Positively gleeful, I typed, fueled by all the words I wished I'd said to Max. The words flowed, and when I read it out loud to myself, I thought, *good job, Anna.*

> My Dear Mollie,
>   I'm sure you'll be pleased to know what an amazing favor you did when you asked me to leave so precipitously. I am now Food Editor of an excellent daily paper and have been given free rein, not only to visit restaurants of my choice, but also to develop recipes, and interview famous, and not so famous, promising chefs. Part of my job description includes giving readers information about where they can buy unusual foods, condiments, and cooking equipment, which I will have the pleasure of finding, trying, and tasting. In my wildest dreams I never imagined having such a terrific job or earning so much money.
>   And, if the above weren't wonderful enough, I am fortunate enough to be living with a marvelous woman who appreciates my warmth and caring. It's as if I had been wandering in the desert for a very long time but have now found an oasis in which I can live with my love for the rest of my life.
>   Thank you. Thank you. Thank you. Leaving California turned out to be the most extraordinary gift you could possibly have given me.
>   Warm regards,"

Not wanting to fall down, despite my enthusiasm, I walked slowly to where Paulus sat, grim-faced. "Here you are, my friend." I watched Paulus read, pleased to see the grin slowly taking over his face.

"This is too much. I only wish I were Food Editor."

"Who knows? It might turn out to be true. Besides, what's a little hyperbole between friends? Eat your heart out, Martha Miller Mollie Mills."

"What about the second paragraph?" he asked.

"So it's a bit of embellishment? So what? Why give her the opportunity to say 'I told you so.' She sounds like the type who'd kick you when you're down without a second thought. But, it's a draft. Make whatever changes you want."

"She's not that bad," protested Paulus. "We had a lot of good times together."

I rolled my eyes.

"Well, come to think of it, maybe she is," he said, color coming back into his face.

I cleared the table, happily putting cups and saucers into the sink, feeling like I could burst into song.

I was on my way out of the kitchen when Paulus said, "Oh, by the way, I forgot to tell you, Dr. H. called while you were sleeping. She wants to see you Friday morning. I told her you'd be there, since I figured you had room on your social calendar."

What does she want? I tried to keep the panic out of my voice. "Why didn't you wake me up so I could talk to her? Did she say why so soon? How did she sound?"

"Concerned but not upset."

I was about to dial her office when the phone rang. It was Pilar, telling me she had more pictures from the children and that Abdul and Mr. Kareem had sent me a letter. *I miss our morning tea and his flowers.* I could see Abdul's dark eyes shining in anticipation, ready for a story as he and the other children snuggled against me. Their tiny bodies never completely still, huddling together like puppies for warmth and comfort. I could hear them now. "One more story, please, Ms. Baum." A dizzy spell hit as I hung up the phone.

Determined to keep going, I went to get the mail. There was the letter from Mr. Kareem and Abdul and a big envelope from the Department of Social Services—too late. I opened the letter from the Kareems.

Dear Ms. Baum,

We say prayers for you in your time of illness. Abdul thinks you will not return from the hospital but I believe you will. I have been thinking about what would make you and Abdul feel better. Not far from where we live is an empty lot. It is covered with garbage. I think it would be good to clean it up and make a garden. When I asked Abdul about this he said we could do this for you. I know you are upset about the child who disappeared. I asked him if we could name the garden after her. He said only if Ms. Baum comes home from the hospital.

When you are well enough to write, would it be possible for you to write to Abdul and tell him if you like the idea. I think this would make him feel better. You are in our prayers.

Abdul and Ammar Kareem

Abdul had made me a picture on which Mr. Kareem had written, "Marina's Garden."

Pilar stopped by later that evening to show me what the children had made. "They're mostly pictures, but some of them wanted to write to you so I printed what they told me. I hope you can read my writing." She had a strange expression on her face.

"What's going on? You look like you were about to say something and decided not to."

She shook her head. "It wouldn't hurt you to be less perceptive."

"Speak, woman, your silence is making me nervous."

"It's nothing, just a little acting out."

"Doesn't sound like nothing to me."

She sighed. "You know our kids. They thrive on routine. They don't like change."

"So they're taking out my absence on you. Let me guess, more hitting and crying and everything else that expresses anger."

"And fear, Anna. They're afraid you're not coming back. Actually, a few of them believe you're dead and I'm not telling them the truth." She sighed again.

"Would it help that I'm writing them a story? It's not finished so I can't give it to you."

"The children miss you, Anna. Anything would help. What have you got so far?"

"It's not much but I'll read it to you.

"Once upon a time, in a place far away, there lived a group of children who kept hearing stories about a magical place where birds and animals talked to children but none of the storytellers knew where it was.

"'It doesn't exist,' said one storyteller.

"'It's just a story,' insisted another.

"But the children believed if there were stories about a place where birds and animals talked to children, it must be a real place. They kept asking, 'Where is the land where birds and animals talk to children?'

"'Who knows how to go there?'

"'Who can take us to hear the birds and animals talk?'

"They asked everyone they knew but no one knew of such a place. Yet the children were determined to find it. They were sure such a place existed. One morning, before the sun was fully in the sky, the children met at the edge of the meadow just outside the village, ready to begin the journey that would take them to the place where birds and animals talked to children."

I paused. "That's all there is so far."

"I'll read it to them first thing tomorrow morning. Eric will feel better."

"What's wrong with Eric? It's more than just hitting isn't it?"

Pilar hesitated, choosing her words carefully. "We have a new teacher."

Someone punched me in the stomach. "Of course, how stupid of me. What's her name? Does she have a lot of experience with our kind of kids? How's she doing?"

"Ms. Butcher. She's just out of school. Doing okay, I guess."

My heart sank. "And—do the children like her?"

"We miss you, Anna. We all hope you'll be coming back very soon."

I was sure I had the wrong address. But, the middle-aged woman wearing jeans who met me at the door let me know I'd come to the right place. There was no way I could hide my surprise—a studio in a synagogue? Miriam explained. "My father was the rabbi of this *shul* for more than thirty years. At that time it was Orthodox so men sat downstairs and women upstairs. Only men were allowed to read from the Torah. Now the rabbi is a woman. Isn't it great how times change?"

"Good for her. How did you come to set up shop here?"

"When I started potting seriously, my father persuaded the congregation to let me turn an empty room into my studio. We trade—their space for my Seder plates, menorahs, kiddish cups—whatever they need. It's a perfect arrangement for everyone. Come, I'll show you."

Considering how seldom I went to synagogue, I felt strangely at home. Being there made me think about Rabbi Berman and how helpful she'd been. *Maybe I should give her a call.* Following Miriam through a dark hallway, we walked long enough for my eyes to adjust to the dark. When she opened the door to her studio I gasped. The burst of color struck my senses as if I had walked into the heart of a multicolored, multifaceted jewel. Lemon-yellow madras valences and curtains covered the bottom part of two large windows, allowing filtered light to pour through the gauze-curtained top of each window, caressing vases and bowls and plates and sculptural pieces. I stared at a pot, a huge piece, a cross between a sculpture and a vase, imagining it in a well-appointed lobby, filling the space with its presence. I maneuvered around several half-wrapped pieces to take a closer look.

Miriam noticed my awkwardness. "Don't worry, even at the best of times it's always chaotic. Suits my nature. What do you think?"

"Your work is amazing." Unable to resist, I stepped over a pile of boxes to take a closer look at a group of pots that reminded me of mine. I yearned to touch one.

"Pick them up. They're not that fragile," she said. "Take your time looking. I'll start packing. It's going to be a very long night."

"Can I help?" I asked, pleased to be of use to someone.

"Sure, if you don't mind." *If I can make pots my life will change.* Even as I thought it, a voice inside me cackled and I felt myself slipping backward in time.

*****

"Boys and girls, as part of our unit on dialogue, you will write a piece with at least two characters in any form you choose—a short story, radio play, or one-act play." A loud, collective groan from my seventh grade class follows her announcement but I can barely contain my excitement. My hand, usually close by my side, shoots up enthusiastically.

"Miss Marshall, can I write a puppet play?" Her nod makes my excitement grow exponentially. After school I sit at the kitchen table, writing down ideas faster than my hand can follow, so absorbed I don't hear Momma come in.

"What's all this mess?" she asks, carrying two bags of groceries.

I quickly gather up the papers. "It's homework. I'm writing a puppet show." Her questioning look unsettles me. "The teacher says I can."

"So who's going to tell you how to make puppets? Better you should stick to what you know. What's wrong with writing a story? You're always making up stories. Write one down. You'll be finished. You won't have to worry about making mistakes."

"But I want to write a puppet play."

"Then don't come crying to me when the show doesn't work. Believe me, nothing turns out the way you want it to. Set the table.

Your father will be home soon."

My excitement grows to the point where I can hardly sit still. After school I go to a toy store and look at all the puppets. The wooden ones are too complicated. The cloth puppets have heads made of china. Then I see two puppets that are made from something but I don't know what it is. The clerk says it's called papier maché. I look it up in the encyclopedia and figure out how to make it.

The next day, I take a light bulb from my lamp and grease it before covering the surface with cut up pieces of newspaper that I soaked in a paste made of water and flour before pressing the pieces around the bulb. It takes a while because I have to wait until one layer is dry before I can put on the next. Although I try to be careful, the puppet heads turn out lumpy and I'm tempted to start all over again but then I remember hearing an actor talk on the radio about being a character actor because he isn't handsome enough to be a leading man. My puppets will have character, I decide; they don't need to be pretty as long as they have heads, with eyes and noses and mouths.

When I tell the vegetable man in the grocery store I need a big carton to make my puppet stage, he unpacks a box of canned tomatoes so I can have the carton. I paint it purple with bits of green and brown near the bottom to give the impression of bushes. I can't remember being so happy. When I bring the puppet theatre to class, Miss Marshall offers to bring purple material from home for curtains. I even figure out how to make them so they can be drawn back and tied with purple ribbon once the play begins.

I am in seventh heaven when two of my classmates ask if they can be in the puppet play. It's the first time anyone wants to do something with me. Miss Marshall also brings in scraps of fabric for the bodies and clothes. We have a great time making characters. My classmates even agree to rehearse after school to keep our play a surprise from the rest of the class.

"There's too many words. I can't speak so much if I have to move the puppet at the same time," says Jackie who is playing the part of the baby sitter.

"Okay, tell me what you want to say and I'll cut the rest."

"When the kid knocks over the vase he can hide behind the sofa so when the baby sitter comes in he can say, 'I didn't do it.'" It's the first nice thing Jackie has ever said to me.

"Good idea," I say, happily crossing out words that took me hours to think up. The rehearsal is so much fun I keep thinking of comments just to make it last a little longer.

I go home after school feeling so excited about our performance the next day I leave the puppets on the kitchen table and go to change my clothes. When my parents see them, they laugh uproariously, making jokes about "my daughter the artist."

"You actually get credit for this *meshugener* stuff?" asks Daddy.

"Are you sure you did what you were supposed to do, Anna?" asks Momma.

I feel like smashing my puppets. The only thing that stops me is the zero I know I'll get. Besides, the other kids might be so angry who knows what they'd do to me.

*****

"Anna, could you open the door?" Startled, I knocked over a pot, catching it just before it hit the floor. Miriam was carrying a wooden tray made of odd bits and pieces of wood, with two ceramic glasses of iced tea and a bowl of cookies. I sat on a packing crate while Miriam perched on a small stool, a cardboard box serving as our table. I liked the coziness of sipping tea amidst the mess of half-packed pots. "I hope I'm not taking too much of your time."

"Nope. I need a break from packing."

"That's an interesting tray, where did it come from?"

"When the Russian authorities told the Jews in my grandfather's village to leave, people had only a few days to get ready. Even so, my grandfather made time to cut a tiny bit of wood from as many trees as he could and stuffed the pieces into the lining of his coat, sewing them in so they didn't move. He didn't know why, he said, he just wanted to have something to remind him of the place he loved. I think he knew he could never return. My grandfather was a large man—he carried a lot of pieces—so when he got to Ellis Island he was afraid the officials would ask him about the lumps in his coat but somehow he got through."

"When did he make the tray?" I asked.

"After they had been married about five years, my grandparents, who had been living with my grandfather's sisters, finally had enough money to move into a little apartment of their own. He made the tray to celebrate the beginning of what he called their "real marriage." It was my grandmother's most treasured possession. When she knew she was dying, all she could think about was what would happen to the tray after my grandfather died. He promised her it would go to their oldest child, who in turn would give it to his oldest child. And that was me!" Miriam gently rubbed her fingers over the tray.

I was envious. Although I had my grandmother's embroidery, I wanted stories of my grandparents' lives. My mother always brushed aside questions about her family. Even when my grandmother came to live with us, she didn't want to talk about her life.

When Miriam began to pack, I followed her instructions. Each plate was wrapped in three sheets of newspaper; bowls and vases were filled with plastic peanuts and encased in bubble paper. I was enjoying the quiet camaraderie of wrapping pots and snuggling them inside cartons filled with shredded newspaper when suddenly perspiration drenched my clothes and face. I felt so dizzy it took all my will power to keep from dropping the pot I was wrapping. I sat down carefully, trying not to panic.

I heard her say, "Anna?" but couldn't make the words come out. "I'm calling Dr. H.," Miriam said tersely.

When my tongue was once more willing to work, I tried to joke. "If I were a lamp I'd say someone pulled the plug, but now it's back and I'm okay." I packed a few more boxes, reassuring myself that this was true, but riding home I passed out in the cab, barely coming to as we neared my street.

"Tell me what happened yesterday," asked Dr. H. as we sat in her office.

I made light of my terror. "One moment I was fine and the next moment I felt a little faint, but nothing really happened." I was not ready to face blacking out. "You were right; Miriam's work is stupendous. I'm sorry I didn't ask about lessons."

"Miriam said you couldn't speak."

"I was having a great time. The light in her studio—it's almost like a painting. I've never seen pots like hers."

"How are you feeling now?"

"All right." *I am not feeling all right, not by a long shot, but I can hear my mother sneering, "By you, every time you get a sniffle you think you're dying."*

"I just feel a bit washed out after yesterday. What couldn't wait until next week?"

"I received the results of two tests Dr. Adams ordered just before you left the hospital. He's concerned about your dropping blood counts and the fact that your platelets are so low."

"What does that mean?" I noticed the hole created by the missing piece of pottery and wondered if Dr. H. regretted giving me the little bowl, not that I was about to ask.

I barely heard her say, "It could be a temporary blip. Or you might be anemic, which would account for your low red counts. Low white counts are caused by any number of conditions. At this point we don't know why yours are falling."

I forced myself to ask casually, "What made me feel so peculiar in Miriam's studio?" I couldn't tell her it wasn't the first time I'd blacked out. Or how often I felt dizzy.

"I'm not sure. Maybe you just need time to recover your strength. But before we do more complicated tests, I have to take a blood sample to see where your counts are now."

"What if they're even lower?" *Stop asking what if.*

"With severe infections, such as the one you've had, we expect white counts to skyrocket, not fall, but let's see what effect rest and recuperation has. In the meantime, stay away from crowds and children. Since we don't know what's causing your blood counts to drop and your immune system is definitely compromised, we better not risk another illness. You certainly can't return to teaching until your blood counts are normal."

"You make it sound like I have leukemia or something," I blurted out. Her startled look quickly gave way to a neutral expression. I froze.

"Well, it is possible you have some form of leukemia," she said.

I was only fooling. I didn't mean it. I take it back.

Her quiet voice pushed through the frenzy of my thoughts. "But as I said, at this point, our information is not conclusive. Try what I've suggested and if your counts continue to drop we'll order more invasive tests."

I imagined huge mechanical creatures, with arms poking into every crevice of my body, their heads shaking in disgust.

"If I have cancer, why wait?"

"Whatever you have, neither Dr. Adams nor I believe you're in immediate danger. That gives us a little time to see how recuperation affects your condition."

My mind raced in a thousand directions, all bad.

I stood up, more than ready to leave. "We're not finished," she said.

"I feel quite finished," I said wryly, sitting down.

"After the blood test today, we'll schedule them on a regular basis."

"You might know, given my 'great love' for needles, I'd get a disease where doctors are either sticking needles in to give me blood or sticking needles in to take my blood. What are my options? What are you going to do?"

"First we have to know what's causing your blood counts to keep dropping."

How much time do I have? How will I support myself if I can't teach? If I live?

"Boonah, what am I going to do?"

"You live inside yourself, in a dark place. But even deeper than this darkness is a place of light. You once lived there. Part of you remembers."

"How do you know?"

"I am you. We played in the light."

"If you're here, with me, how come you know the way out?"

"Because your mind flies free. Ride the nightmare out of your prison, into the light. Call to Chaos, leader of primal forces. She rides a wind so powerful you will feel yourself blown in all directions simultaneously."

"This will help me?"

"And when you sense her presence, take the deepest breath you have ever taken and then breathe deeper still. Let your breath become voice. Yell to the life force to guide you. Yell as if your life depends upon it—It does."

"What do I yell? Where will you be?"

"I am you. Do it now, Anna. Call to Chaos."

I took a deep breath that began in a place I couldn't name. As it gathered force I pushed a word forward, pushed until it had a voice. "Yes," I shouted. "Yes. Yes. Yes."

A huge wind, writhing and twisting, swirled in front of me, thrusting me upward. Suddenly, as I was falling, a giant hand placed itself under my back, laying me on the body of a woman with huge breasts and a comfortable stomach. Without warning, I was thrown up once again into the blackness as my breath screamed.

"Yes!"

"Ms. Baum, wake up. You're having a nightmare." I barely saw the blurred shape holding me. "Just relax; you're going to be fine."

"Where's Chaos?"

"Ms. Baum, you're in the waiting room." The blurring faded. I let myself feel a rare sense of comfort as I slumped against the softness of the nurse's body.

"Could I have a drink of water?"

"Sure, just don't get up." When the nurse left, I tried to stand but immediately fell back onto the chair. I was sipping water when Paulus rushed in, apologizing for being late.

"That's okay. I was just talking to Chaos." He gave me a puzzled look. "More weirdness. Let's get out of here."

Normally, torture couldn't make me talk about this waking dream business or whatever the hell it was, but I was scared. I wanted a friend I could talk to. Why didn't I have any friends? Why had I lived so much of my life feeling like an orphan with my face pressed against a window, watching people live their lives? Wanting to talk to someone was a new experience for me. Wondering who it could be intensified my sense of aloneness.

*****

"Momma, the dress is too dark. All the girls are wearing light-colored dresses."

"The material is good. It will last a long time. Besides, it's half price."

"But Momma, the kids will make fun of me."

"There are worse things in life."

*****

Listening and Hearing

"Did I ever tell you that you are insufferable and arrogant? Just because it's Dr. Adams this and Dr. Adams that in the hospital doesn't mean I have to treat you like you're some kind of God, especially when you don't have the wit, wisdom, or sense to apologize when you're wrong."

Archie watched Jane leave the living room. It wasn't the first time they'd had a bad fight, and he knew it wouldn't be the last, unless she gave him back the ring, which now seemed like a distinct possibility.

He sat down on the sofa. He was only trying to do what was best for her. In fact, for anyone he dealt with. Why would he want to cause pain to the woman he loved? Or to patients he was trying to cure? What sense did that make? Why did she keep saying "Don't tell me what to think. Don't tell me how I feel. Don't tell me what to do unless I ask for your opinion, and even then, the decision is mine." Well, if she wanted to leave, she'd have to go through the living room. Thank goodness they were in his apartment where there was only one door out. Then what? Could he physically keep her from leaving? What could he say or do that might make a difference?

When she appeared, dressed to leave, she spoke softly. "Archie, here's your ring. I think it's best to give it back to you. If you really want us to be married, you're going to have to stop thinking you're the only one who knows. You're going to have to stop telling and start listening, because otherwise we're through. And this is the last time I am going to say it." She held out the ring, waiting for him to take it.

He made no move toward the ring. "I do listen. How else would I know what to say?"

"You may listen, but you don't hear what I'm saying."

"Listening is listening."

When he refused to take the ring she put it on the end table and walked to the door. He sensed that if he didn't say the right something she would leave for good, yet he was too angry to be diplomatic.

"Who are you? Ms. Perfection? You say I tell you what to do? What about you? Who died and left you judge? Who put you in charge of our communication? What are you, the word police?"

"I feel sorry for you," she retorted. "It must be difficult to be the great and renowned Dr. Adams in the hospital and Archie Adams at home. It's no accident that you're forty-three and unmarried."

He gasped. "That's a crappy thing to say. You're not exactly a sweet young thing yourself. Just yesterday you were telling me you're the last of your friends to be married."

"And you call yourself a caring person?" She glared at him.

"I love you, Jane. I want us to be married. I want it more than anything I've ever wanted in my whole life."

"You have a peculiar way of showing it."

"What do you want?" he challenged her.

When she didn't answer, he picked up the ring and walked to where she stood, ramrod straight. His eyes misted. "Do you remember when we bought this? How happy we were?"

"Yes, I do."

"I want us to be that happy again, Jane. I want us to be that happy together."

She sighed. "Archie, if and when you discover you've made the wrong decision about a patient's medicine or treatment, what do you do?"

"I correct it. As quickly as possible."

"Do you ever tell the patient you made a mistake?"

"Certainly not. That would undermine her confidence in me."

"Her?" She repeated archly.

"That was just a figure of speech," he responded quickly, adding, "her or his."

"Did you ever think that admitting you didn't know something or that what you tried wasn't helping might help in the healing process?"

"No. I'm the expert. I'm supposed to know what's best. If I don't know, who does?"

"So, it's never occurred to you that there could be a time when you don't know what's best and you have to ask for help? Or let the patient know you're stumped, at least for the moment?"

"I'm a doctor. That's what work experience as an intern and resident is for. I'm trained to save lives and cure illnesses. I'm paid to know the best treatment. That's my job. Just as your job is to design jewelry."

"My mistakes aren't a matter of life or death," she snapped back at him.

"I'm tired of tiptoeing around your feelings," he retorted.

"And I'm tired of you thinking you have all the answers." She walked out.

12

The nightmare struck again. This time while I'm holding Marina she hemorrhages. The blood is seeping into my lap and pouring onto the floor. I throw my arms around her, trying to hold in her blood as I tell the frightened children to call for help. When the tall man comes toward us, I scream, "Go away! Leave Marina alone!" He has a horrible smile on his face as he strides closer, arms outstretched, fingers reaching. When he's within touching distance I wake myself up.

Before the nightmare, while I was still awake, I kept seeing cells multiplying, growing out of control. I whacked them but each blow multiplied the cells. You'd think after a while I'd give it up as a bad job, but no, I just kept whacking away, hoping visualization would encourage my healthy blood cells to be fruitful and multiply.

The nightmare rescued me from my labors. Some rescue! I did not look forward to more nights like this. My days weren't much better. I was going to have to find something to do while I was in medical limbo. All my life I had always kept myself busy. Act or react as quickly as possible had been my modus operandi. Now I had too much time to think about malignant cells attacking my body and the disappearance of Marina.

Miriam's bowl sitting by itself on the top of my dresser looked as lonesome as I felt. Despite a bout of dizziness I managed to pick up the phone and dial Miriam's number. "I was wondering if you have a small piece you might be willing to sell."

"Not right now. Just about everything's been sent to the show."

"Oh." I couldn't believe how disappointed I was. *Time for a new plan.* "Uh, Miriam, I—Do you—Are you giving lessons?" I remembered how many times I'd gone to craft shows and fallen in love with ceramic sculptures I couldn't afford. I even had fantasies about making my own dishes, soft earth colors with a brownish purple glaze.

"Sure, group and private. If you aren't bothered working in a studio so clean it's hard to imagine it ever saw a speck of clay, you're welcome to come by and play with the clay to get a feel for it before deciding if you want to continue."

"What's it like having a clean, empty space?"

"Weird. Doesn't happen often, thank goodness, but when the janitor sees her opportunity, she goes at it as if her life depends on getting up every last bit of dried clay and dirt. Still, as the Zen master says, 'Empty and be full.' When do you want to come?"

"The sooner the better."

"I'll be here most of the afternoon."

"Great! I'll come as soon as I call for the results of my blood tests." I hung up the phone and shouted, "Yes!" at the top of my lungs. I phoned Shirley; positive my test results would be good. Wasn't happiness part of becoming healthy?

Her tone of voice made me shiver. "I'm sorry, Ms. Baum, but your white counts have dropped again. The red counts and platelets are also a bit lower." I tried to convince myself that living life on an emotional roller coaster was better than living in an emotional desert, but I kept hearing my mother's words, "Nothing ever happens like you hope it will." They played inside me like a broken record.

Entering Miriam's studio was shocking. "You weren't kidding when you said clean. I could eat off the floor. Unreal!"

"Horrible!" She shook her head. "I'm babysitting and it's time to put my granddaughter down for her nap. Feel free to look around."

My eyes were drawn to a shelf with three different-sized vases that looked like a group of elders having a conversation. I took a closer look, baffled as to how Miriam could make anything so stunning. The tallest vase was the same purple color as my little bowl, but the glaze was crackled, with shades of blue running up and down it, like streaks of lightning, pouring out energy. One side was taller than the other and leaned over toward a slightly smaller vase which was also purple but mottled, as if Miriam put a purple glaze on the pot and then brushed blue glaze on top. Between the two was a third vase, not as broad or high as the other two, but pushed out at the top, as if it were the connection between the two though none touched. The smallest vase was mostly blue, but it had purple glaze whooshing up and down, the source of energy for all three. I was still staring at them when she came back in. She stood by my side, quiet for a moment, looking at the pieces.

"I see you found my elders."

"I'd like to buy them."

"They're not for sale. They won me my first big prize."

My disappointment was so palpable I was relieved when she left to make phone calls.

Without Miriam, the studio was sterile. A large pile of clay in front of me made me yearn to touch it but I felt inhibited by the cleanliness of the studio. I could just see the janitor storming in, yelling at me for being so messy. Yet my fingers yearned to touch the cool clay. For all my desire to make a pot I had no idea how to begin. I stared at the lump until I remembered seeing a film about an Indian woman who made bowls by coiling circles of clay that she piled one on top of the other and then shaped. I pinched off a bit of clay and started rolling it into a long log, which was much easier than trying to soften the big piece. My fingers quickly tired but I kept going, refusing to be defeated. When the log was as even as I could make it I shaped it into a circle. I kept doing this, piling logs on top of each other until I had sort of a bowl shape but didn't like the straightness of it so I took off the coils and decided to make each one a bit shorter than the one before it. This time, the bowl had a rounded shape. I didn't even try to pretend I wasn't pleased with myself. While I knew it wouldn't win a prize, it was mine. Something I had made out of imagination and memory.

"Well done," said Miriam, who had returned and been watching me.

"Yeah, sure," I said, fiddling with the clay because I didn't know what else to do.

"Let's have a look at your bowl." She took a wire and cut the bowl free so she could hold it. "You did a neat job with those coils. Ready to try something else?"

"I hate to admit it, but I need a nap."

"If you like, lie down on the couch in the room where the baby is. If not, call a taxi."

"The couch sounds irresistible. Also, I'd like to pay you for today. What do I owe you?"

"The first lesson is always a trial for me and the student. Let's leave it for now. I love to barter. Maybe we can make a deal."

I will not ask what I have to offer.

I stood, not knowing what to say. I couldn't imagine what I had that Miriam would want.

She covered up the awkward moment. "See how you're feeling and then give me a call. We'll decide then what we want to do. How's that?"

"Okay." I crumpled up my little bowl.

"Hey! Why'd you do that?"

"No sense pretending it was special. Besides, I read somewhere you have to throw a hundred pots before you make one worth saving."

"That's a bunch of crap. If you don't value your work, what's the point of making anything?" I stared at the crushed mound of clay lying limp in my hands.

"If you want to be my student you have to respect every step of the process."

"Okay, I get the message," I said, wishing I were anywhere else.

Miriam angrily slapped the clay into a plastic sack with a moist rag on top. "I need to get milk. It would help if you could watch the baby while I run to the store."

Too tense to sleep, I wheeled the carriage over to the couch, rocking the baby as she woke and slept. When her eyes opened, I crooned, "Hello, sweet thing." My reward was a big smile. She let me pick her up, even snuggled against my shoulder. *She likes me.*

"Nothing like it, eh, Anna?" said Miriam, holding a gallon of milk. While she changed the baby's diaper and gave her a bottle, I looked around. There were floor to ceiling bookshelves on two walls, overflowing with books. A desk filled most of the third wall, above which was a small window covered with dark red curtains. The fourth wall had a doorway and an artful arrangement of charcoal sketches, some of children playing, others of what looked like religious life in the *shtetl*. Miriam noticed me looking. "My grandmother did those."

"Are they pictures of her village in Russia?"

"Yes. They're part of a series she drew after she arrived. She said if she couldn't be where she wanted, she could at least look at what she wanted."

"You certainly come from a talented family." I watched her hug and kiss her grandchild, aware of an envy I didn't like.

When she put the baby down I asked, "Can I hold the baby?" surprising myself and just as quickly wishing I hadn't asked when the baby began to wail.

"Sure." I was inordinately pleased that the baby's sobs stopped when I picked her up. Holding her against my shoulder, she touched my cheek with her fingers.

*****

We're standing at the bus stop on a cool evening in late spring, some time after midnight. "Josh, the test came back positive."

"Fuck! You said you used a diaphragm."

"I did. I told you I thought you pushed it out of place."

"You trying to tell me it's my fault?"

"Why does everything have to be about fault? We're talking about a life."

His face becomes a mask. "Anna, you have such pretty hair," he says in a detached voice, running his fingers through the length of it, playing with the strands.

"You said if anything happened we'd get married."

"Yeah. Well, it's late, I have to go." He leaves the bus stop and walks to his apartment building without looking back. Cold as death, I watch him disappear. The bus driver yells, "You getting on or what?"

Abortions are illegal. I have no money and no idea how to find a doctor willing to do one. Time is not on my side. After throwing up three days in a row I know I have to do something. Desperation makes me talk with my father as we drive to buy bagels. "Dad, if I tell you something, will you promise not to tell Mother?"

"Depends what it is."

"I'm pregnant."

He stares at me. The look on his face is a mixture of disgust and contempt. I wait for the car to stop at a red light so I can get out. Anywhere is better than where I am. I curse myself for being such a coward, for being unable to open the door and jump out. Maybe kill the baby.

"What makes you think I know a doctor?"

"Forget I said anything. I'll figure it out."

"You got any money?" I shake my head. "What about Josh? He's working."

"Josh left me."

"Just like that? He makes a baby and leaves? Disappears? What's wrong with you, Anna? Why didn't you use contraceptives if you couldn't wait until you were married?"

"I did. Something must have happened." I keep waiting for him to stop for a light.

"Something sure as hell happened. That is absolutely certain." All the city traffic and the one time I need one, we never hit a red light.

When we arrive at the bagel store, he says, "I'll make a phone call." He comes back with a bag of bagels, munching one that reeks of onions. "Here. They're still warm." I shake my head, trying not to throw up, but the stench of onion is overpowering. I use my purse and close it quickly. The smell is foul. My father gags as he opens the windows. He says nothing about the phone call until we are almost home. "The guy I called—he's got connections. He'll call me back tonight." It's an excruciatingly long six days.

The first man I go to looks like a doctor. In the presence of a nurse, he stuffs cotton gauze drenched with horrible-smelling glop up into my vagina and tells me not to take a bath. When I return a few days later, while I'm waiting, I ask the nurse if I can use her phone to call my father. She sneers, "I know your game. Get out of here and don't come back."

The second man meets me at the door and tells me to scram, that the cops are coming. Even as I hurry down the steps and cross the street, three police cars, lights flashing, sirens blaring, turn the corner.

The third man greets me with an open fly. I run down eight flights of stairs.

The fourth man works out of a hotel. He tells me his usual fee is three thousand dollars but since my father has done him some favors, he's willing to take only two thousand. He holds out his hand for the money even before asking how pregnant I am. A second man comes into the room, and while counting the money, tells me to take everything off from my waist down, to lie on the table and put my feet into the stirrups. There is no anesthesia.

The first time I let out a moan one of the men barks, "Keep quiet or we stop. You shoulda thought about babies before you had your fun." When it's over, he hands me two sanitary napkins to put inside my panties, tells me to get up, dress, and leave. There is blood all over my legs and the white paper on the table. I can't make my feet support me. "Get moving. You ain't our only customer and this ain't Rockefeller Pavilion."

I don't know how I manage to put on my clothes and negotiate the hallway and the elevator and the foyer, much less walk to the hotel across the street where I sink into a couch in the lobby. Soon I'm bombarded by gruff voices. "Hey, lady, sleep your drunk off someplace else." Strong arms lift me off the couch and push me out the door but they aren't fast enough to keep me from seeing the red stains where I've been sitting. Outside, I lean against the granite wall, waiting for my father to pick me up. As I stand, slumped over in pain, two guys come by and tell me they can help me, for a price. By the time my father's car draws up to the curb I'm standing in a pool of blood.

In spite of his promise, he has told my mother. He had gone back to comfort her.

She won't look at me and refuses to talk unless I ask her a direct question that she can't avoid answering. I stay in my room except when I have to wash bloodstains out of the sheets and make myself tea. The cramps are arrows of pain, splitting me in two. After five days, I stop expelling fetal tissue and the bleeding slows down enough for me to go back to school.

I take on extra hours at the bookstore in order to pay the money back as soon as possible, working three other jobs, before, during, and after classes, all day Saturday and a half day Sunday. Whatever time is left, I study. My parents and I never speak about what happened. Like a prisoner marking off time in jail, I count the days until all the money has been repaid.

One Sunday, about two months after the abortion, my mother, still unwilling to look at me, says in a flat tone of voice, "Josh called. Here's his number. He wants you to call him back."

"I have nothing to say to him."

"Call. Maybe he'll marry you. Who's gonna want damaged goods?"

*****

I came home from Miriam's thinking about the bowl I had crumpled, feeling as if I had crushed my self. I could hear my mother's voice, screeching inside my head. 'No wonder you have no friends. You spoil everything you touch.' Well, dear mother, that is about to change. Right now! I dialed Josie's number. No reason why we can't be friends.

"What's happening at the shop? How's the new woman working out?"

"So far, so good." *At least she sounds pleased to hear from me.*

"Josie, could you send flowers to Jacob and Emma at the hospital? I want to thank them for all they did for me."

"Sure, what do you want to send? A bouquet? Plants? Cards? One? Two?"

"How about a coffee cup full of flowers for each of them? And a note that says, 'With many thanks from your favorite wallflower.'"

"Sounds fine. What kind do you want to send?"

"Pick something that looks pretty and smells good."

"I'll send them out first thing tomorrow morning. I'm glad you called. I've been wondering how you are, but I didn't want to bother you. I know what it's like to come home from the hospital and be inundated with calls and letters and visits."

I wish I knew.

"Please, call any time. I like talking to you. When's the big day?" *Another baby —*

"One month, three days, and four hours, but I'm as big as a house so it could come today as far as I'm concerned. Oh — oh, I have a customer. Let's talk soon."

Paulus wasn't due home for a few hours, plenty of time to talk to Chaos. I wished I knew how to begin.

"Begin at the beginning," says Boonah.
"Where is the beginning?"
"Wherever you start."
Asking Boonah for answers is like asking the sun where rain comes from. "Okay Chaos, here I come."

I was sitting in my chair, holding my little bowl, breathing deeply, when I heard, "What are you doing?" I jumped up and the bowl fell. My stomach crunched.

"Paulus! You're not supposed to be here for hours." I picked up the bowl, examining it for cracks. "You almost broke my bowl."

"Correction: you dropped it. What's the problem, you expecting company I shouldn't know about?" His tone of voice was unpleasant.

"What?" We glared at each other.

"I didn't know I was supposed to inform you of schedule changes before entering your apartment." Paulus walked toward his room.

"I don't appreciate your deciding that I'm expecting company."

"I didn't decide, I asked."

"It's none of your business."

"I came back for a copy of my résumé." He modulated his voice to sound like an obsequious employee. "As long as I'm here, do you need anything?" I shook my head. He went into his room, came back with an envelope and headed for the door. "Should I call next time?"

Yes. "No."

I spread the children's letters in a circle around my chair in the living room and set the alarm clock to ring in an hour. Surely Paulus wouldn't be back any sooner. I wanted to be awake when he returned, not lost in limbo. Still ill at ease, I took a shower and put on my purple faux silk caftan, daubing perfume on my wrists and behind my ears. It didn't help. I made up my eyes, put on a ring and bracelet I'd bought at a flea market and never worn, went back into the living room, and sat down. *I have to be squeaky clean and dressed up to be acceptable?*

Closing my eyes, I intoned. "Chaos, I would like to talk with you." Suddenly I was shivering with fear and cold. I grabbed the afghan from the back of the chair and wrapped it around me before dropping off into blackness.

"So, Anna Baum, you wish to talk with me?"

I hear a throaty, powerful voice.

"Are you Chaos?" I whisper.

"I am." The voice rises and falls from a vast nothingness.

"I am caught between two worlds. I want to live in one."

"Choose."

"I choose to die."

"Your choice is not life or death. It is between past and future."

"I don't want the past. Do I have a future?"

"Tear down the barricades you built against knowing."

"What knowing?"

"Cry for the child you were. Moisten your parched landscape."

"I don't know how to cry."

"That's what you think."

We're sitting in a hot, crowded train, going to the beach. Next to us, an old woman sways while holding on to a strap she can barely reach. Momma pinches me. "Get up and give the lady your seat." I stand up just as the train lurches, knocking me to the floor. A man steps on my hand as he tries to regain his balance. I yelp with pain. Momma grabs my arm and yanks me

195

up. "Stop crying. It was an accident. You'll make him feel bad."

Running into the kitchen, I slip on newly waxed linoleum and fall against Momma who is pouring Daddy a cup of coffee. The hot liquid burns my arm. I start to cry. Momma yells, "I'm the one who should be crying. I told you not to run in the house."

Some girls on the block invite me to play with them. I'm excited — this is the first time they've asked me. I go down to Mary Catherine's basement, where there are six girls from my first grade class. Mary Catherine tells me to go into the middle of the circle and close my eyes. We're going to play a game and I'm "It." I hear the girls chant, first softly then louder, until they are screaming. "Dirty Jew Christ-killer! You killed Christ. We'll kill you. You killed Christ. We'll kill you."

I push my way through the shrieking girls who are closing in on me. I run up the stairs, out of the house, across the street, into our apartment, and hide under my bed. Momma finds me. "I didn't kill him. I didn't kill him, Momma. I don't even know who he is." She yanks me out from my hiding place. "Stop crying. No wonder they don't want to play with you; you're such a crybaby."

"Cry," commands Chaos.
"I'm trying. Nothing's happening."
"What stops you?"
"Shame on me. Shame on Anna Baum."
Chaos disappears into a black cloud. I run after her. "Don't go! Tell me how to stop the shame." I am suffocating in endless black clouds. Bells are clanging. The sound is deafening.

I fought my way out of the blackness, coughing and gasping for breath. The ringing was too loud to ignore. As I stood up, I knocked over the telephone.

"Anna? Anna, it's Pilar. Are you all right? Your voice sounds funny."

"I'm fine, just a bit of a coughing spell." I coughed.

"I read your story to the children. They want the rest of it. They want answers to their letters and a picture of you. Mr. Kareem convinced Abdul to come to school, but he says he'll only stay if you come back."

"They don't want much, do they?" I hesitated. "What about their new teacher?"

"She's doing her job," Pilar said in a voice that brooked no questions. *At least she's not enthusiastic.*

"Give the children my love and tell them to keep up the letters; they mean the world to me. If I can't finish the story at least I'll send you a little more."

"Do you know when you'll be back?"

"Dr. H. says I have to get through a day without a two-hour nap. Quite unreasonable, don't you think? And can you believe she thinks kids are always coming down with something. Did you ever hear such nonsense?" We both laughed.

"We'll get you a cot. You can sleep when the children rest. I'll wipe their noses. Whatever it takes. We miss you, Anna." My heart lurched as we hung up. *I wish I could talk with you about shame. Why label someone who's hurting a crybaby?*

*****

Momma says tomorrow I'll be four years old. She's baking a cake for my birthday. I ask if I can lick the bowl. As she gives me the bowl it slips out of her hand. It falls and smashes. She starts yelling so loud I run into the closet, hiding behind an old coat. I hold my breath when she opens the closet. "Anna, I know you're in here. You can't hide from me." She grabs my arm and yanks me out of the closet. She's hitting and yelling. I'm crying. "Now I have to buy a new bowl for the mixer. Stop being such a crybaby. Shame on you."

*****

My mother dropped the bowl yet I believed her when she said it was my fault. I didn't know there were mothers who would say, "Look at the mess I made. Well, it doesn't matter; it's just a bowl. I'll buy another one. No one got hurt; that's what's important."

I wonder—maybe there's a difference between knowing a fact and ascribing meaning to it. Maybe we accept the interpretation our parents give us without question. What happens when we question what we're told? Where does meaning come from?

Sometimes, even though she locked me in the closet as punishment, it felt like a safe place, except when I had to pee and couldn't keep it in. I didn't want to think about how I took off my socks to mop it up, knowing there was nothing I could do about the smell.

Then the closet air was hard to breathe and I felt as if the walls were closing in on me.

More memories than I wanted to remember.

I paced around my apartment, trying to stop the movie inside me, but it wouldn't quit no matter how hard I pushed the stop button. Grabbing my coat and keys, I ran out of the apartment, into Paulus as he left the elevator.

"How nice," he said. "A welcoming committee."

Although I laughed, I felt a cold fury that came from nowhere, ready to spew against this man whose only crime was being pleasant. I had no idea where the rage came from, which upset me even more.

Back in the apartment Paulus stopped and stared. "What's all this?" I cursed myself for not picking up. "Looks like letters from your kids."

"That's what they are."

Without warning, my brain turned into a theatre marquee with huge letters in lights that flashed on and off. *ANNA BAUM IS A BAD GIRL. ANNA BAUM IS BEING PUNISHED. ANNA BAUM HAS LEU-KEMIA.* I paced, trying to erase the images.

"What if I never have enough energy to take care of myself? What if I lose my job? What if I need help forever?" The words slipped out. I couldn't take them back.

Surprised, Paulus said, "I've never been much good with forevers, but I think you're going to be fine. You've got guts. You don't take things lying down. You'll get your energy back."

"What good is all that if I have leukemia?"

I could see he was taken aback. "Maybe you've been in basic training for this fight for your life without even knowing what the battle was about."

*****

I'm wearing a navy blue dress, a hand-me-down from my taller and heavier cousin. It hangs loose around my waist and drifts toward my ankles. Daddy yells at Momma. "Why is Anna wearing such a *schmatta*? Why can't she wear something pretty? I make enough money. We can afford to buy her a new dress."

"You never notice what I'm wearing," my mother snaps.

"So when did you notice what I wear?" he hurls back.

*****

Chaos is waiting for me. "Let the image form," she commands.

I run into Momma's closet to get away from the shouting. She's yelling at someone who shouts back in an angry male voice. I can't understand the words, but I hear my name. They're arguing about me. I put my hands over my ears, but the sounds grow louder. The voices are coming closer. Desperate to keep them from overwhelming me, I pull down Momma's fur coat and wrap myself in the softness. Suddenly, there is silence. I am about to leave the darkness of the closet when I hear new sounds. Laughter. Groans. Moans. I burrow deeper into the fur and imagine myself in a place far away. I talk to the lion in "The Wizard of Oz."

I opened my eyes, feeling wetness on my face. I tasted tears. Maybe Boonah was right, that I shouldn't fight the images. Why had my mother been so upset? Who was the man she was yelling at?

"Anna?" called Paulus. "How about some dinner?" Suddenly, I was very hungry.

"Be there in a minute." I kept thinking about the memory, wishing I could remember the missing piece. There was a missing piece, more than one. The images and memories that kept pushing at me had to come from something, for some reason.

"This is great lasagna, Paulus. How did you get to be such a good cook?"

"Practice."

"Hah! Tell me how you learned."

He looked upset.

"Is it a big secret?" I teased.

"No, just something I don't feel like talking about."

"How come? It's only cooking."

"Not when you do it to keep someone from leaving you." There was an awkward silence. "My boss asked if I'd read the journal his father kept during World War Two. I think he wants to know if it's worth publishing."

"What do you think?"

"Good story, bad writing."

"My mother's friend Minnie said my mother kept a diary."

"Have you read it?"

"No, Minnie still has it. She tried to tell me how she got it but was too upset to talk about it. She still felt bad that my mother kept so much to herself. I guess there was a point where my mother didn't trust anyone, not even her best friend. What a way to live." *Do I trust anyone? At least she had a best friend.*

"Do you want to read it?" he asked.

"My mother refuses to talk about her life. Maybe she wrote down what she couldn't say. Minnie's old. Who knows how much longer she'll live. I wonder what would happen if I ask her to let me read it, if she still has it, that is."

Call her. God knows we share a history.

Long Distance

She rested on the twin bed, stroking the quilt that covered it. Her fingers knew every inch of each square; she'd made it when she was pregnant with Sarah, while Herb was in the army and she thought she'd die of loneliness. Now she was living with Sarah. Had been since Herb died. It was the loneliness that made her decide to give up her apartment. How did Sadie manage all these years without Heshie? On an impulse, she reached over and dialed the only telephone number she knew by heart.

"Minnie! What's wrong?" Sadie was brusque. That meant she was worried.

"Nothing! I should call only when I got bad news?"

"It costs a lot of money. Why didn't you wait until the weekend?"

That was her Sadie all right, always telling you what you should do. "I didn't wait because I didn't want to wait. I could be dead in three days." Minnie smiled as she imagined the expression on Sadie's face.

"Are you sick?"

"No."

"Then what's all the fuss about dying?"

"Stop jumping to conclusions. I didn't say I'm dying. I called because I was lonely. I was missing you."

"I told you to move down here with me when Herb died. Right now, there's a place three doors down. Just came empty—two bedrooms, two bathrooms, and a balcony big enough for a table and chair so you can sit outside and drink your coffee and not worry about freezing to death.

Minnie couldn't resist. "Yeah, I'd just swelter to death from the heat. Anyway, it's good living with Sarah. I see my grandchildren and help out a bit. Makes me feel useful."

"Why you got to keep feeling useful? You raised a family, took good care of your husband, it's your turn to rest. I'm telling you,

Minnele, you should come down here by me. The family can visit you. I'll find out how much they want for the apartment. We'll have fun, like we used to. Remember how we laughed?"

"Remember the time we wanted ice cream and we didn't have any money so I pretended I'd lost my nickel and began to cry and the old man took out his handkerchief and wiped my eyes and gave me a quarter. You almost died trying not to laugh. Some pal you were, almost giving away the goods."

"You got to admit, I managed to look almost as upset as you were," protested Sadie.

"Yeah, you did. That was the best ice cream—vanilla fudge with chopped nuts."

"We could eat ice cream every day if you come down by me. We'll talk and laugh just like old times."

Minnie thought about the box she'd found in the garbage. "Sadie, I've been wondering," she said carefully, "what about that man, you know, the one you liked before the war, the one who disappeared? I seem to remember you used to talk to him a lot. Whatever happened to him? Suddenly, you didn't talk about him no more."

"That was a long time ago. Who remembers?"

Minnie felt a pang of sadness. Even after all these years— She wanted to say, "You remember, I remember," but she didn't know how to confront Sadie. Never had, especially when Sadie had her back up. She felt lonelier now than before she called. "Sadie, why don't you come visit? See me and Anna."

"I told you when I left, I'm not coming back. You come down here. The warm weather will do you good. Get Sarah to put you on a plane. We'll have fun, like the old days. Remember those vanilla sodas?

"Yeah and what about the time my mother was looking for me and you hid me behind your skirt and lied right to her face, 'No, I haven't seen Minnie.' To this day, I don't know how you made it sound like the truth."

"It was easy. You were in trouble."

"We had such good times—and now look at us. Whoever thought we'd end up thousands of miles apart. I miss you so much. Life's not so good without you."

"That's the way it is. Nothing happens like you hope it will. No sense trying to pretend otherwise."

"Have you spoken to Anna lately?"

"She's working. Let her pick up the phone. She can afford it."

Minnie sighed. "Sometimes it's nice to be called, don't you think?"

"She calls when she wants to. I can wait."

Minnie wished Sadie would call more often. They didn't have to talk long. Just to hear her voice would be good enough. No one knew her like Sadie did.

13

"We're sorry, the number you dialed is no longer in service." How long had it been since I last talked with Minnie? Too long. Well, one thing I had plenty of was time. After three days and umpteen phone calls to friends of my parents, I got her daughter Sarah's number. Two more days before she answered the phone. Our first conversation left a lot to be desired. "Hello, Sarah, this is Anna calling, Anna Baum."

"Hello, Anna," she said curtly.

"It's been a long time since we've seen each other."

"Yes?"

Why are you so angry? What did I ever do to you? "How's your mother?"

"Not good. It's time for her medicine. I can't talk."

"Please send your mother my love. I'd like to come see her." Silence. "I hope she feels better soon."

"Thank you." End of conversation.

The more I thought about the diary, the more I wanted to read it, but talking with Minnie was even more essential. I kept trying. The next few conversations with Sarah reinforced her hostility. Although she refused to let me talk to her mother, I kept at it. After losing count of the number of times I tried, one afternoon Minnie picked up the phone and we talked. She was as friendly as Sarah was cold. Minnie might be ill, but her sense of humor was exquisitely intact.

"Annale, it's been centuries since I've heard your voice. Why the long wait?"

"I don't know. But, that's in the past. I've changed. From now on, we talk whenever you like. How are you?"

"What's the old joke? Except for my body I'm perfect. I live by Sarah now. She's a good daughter. Always was." *I wish I could hear my mother say this about me.* "So, Annale, when are you coming to see me?"

"Today, if it's okay with Sarah."

Ice would melt ten times faster than Sarah's tone of voice. "I don't know what you and Mama talked about, but she's too excited. That's not good for her. Can't you think of anyone but yourself for godssake?"

"Sarah, please—give me a chance. I know when we were kids you didn't like me, but we're adults. All I want is to see your mother. I would never do anything to hurt her. Ever. She wants to see me and I want to see her. What's wrong with that?"

"I don't remember you asking to see her when she was well. I don't want Mama upset."

"How do you know I'll upset her?"

"Because after talking with you she got really stressed. That's not what she needs."

"And you're the only one who knows what she needs, I suppose."

"You sound just like your mother."

"And you sound like a fucking iceberg."

When I calmed down I tried to think how to get past Sarah. At some point she would have to leave the house. Maybe she had help taking care of her mother. Maybe that person would let me in. There had to be a way to see Minnie.

A few hours later I called again. Sarah answered and I spoke quickly, before she could hang up. "I'm sorry I got so mad, but I need to see your mother. I also think she needs to see me."

"Oh, and you would know, I suppose."

I knew losing my temper was a bad idea. "Did your mother ever talk about a diary she found around the time my mother went to Florida?"

She paused. "No." *Why the hesitation? I think she's lying.*

"Well, just before my mother left, they had a visit."

"They had lots of visits. So what?"

I took a very deep breath. "I know. But on this particular visit my mother threw her diary in the garbage can and your mother took it out and left with it."

"How dare you call Mama a thief!"

"I didn't say she stole it. I said she took it."

"What's your point? I haven't got all day."

"Sarah, you are not the only one who doesn't like Sadie."

"You can say that again."

"Please. I won't upset Minnie. I just need to read the diary."

"So that's it. You don't want to see my mother. You want the diary." She slammed down the phone.

Two days later, I stood in front of Sarah's apartment door, ringing the bell. The woman who opened the door was shorter than I remembered, with a long brown braid that reached the length of her back. She was wearing jeans and a handmade blue sweater that matched her eyes, almost the color of Max's eyes. "Yes, what do you want?"

"It's me, Anna Baum. I've come to see your mother. And you. I'm sorry to come without calling and I'm sorry I upset you. Please let me see her for a few minutes. I promise I won't mention the diary."

"Sarahle, do I hear Anna?" called a weak voice. "Annale?"

She sighed. "Okay, I'll let you in." Whispering, she said, "If you upset her I'll—"

"I love Minnie too, you know," I reminded her, tears in my eyes.

"No, I don't. How would I know? She could have died for all you cared."

"Annale?" Minnie called again.

Sarah glared at me. "I'm warning you—"

I nodded, walking into the living room where Minnie was bundled in a wheelchair. What struck me was her frailty. Gone was the vitality and roundness I remembered, yet I was so happy to see her I ran to give her a hug, trying not to show how shocked I was at the change in her appearance. It was hard to believe she had enough of anything to keep breathing. Only her eyes sparkled. And her grin. Her grin was as mischievous and warm as ever.

Sarah pushed me away. "Mama, you look tired, let me help you into bed. Anna can visit with you there for a few minutes. But you mustn't overdo. She can always come back."

"Sarah, don't fuss. Annale, I'm so happy to see you *neshomeleh*." I gave her as tender a hug as I could, afraid the slightest pressure would break a bone. We were both crying.

As I followed Sarah into the bedroom I thought about how good Minnie had always been to me. As a child I used to wish she'd take me home with her. I liked her softness and the way she smelled of lavender. Her voice was kind and she laughed a lot. There was nothing about her that was hard or sharp-edged like my mother. Best of all, Minnie almost always wore an apron with two big pockets and an inexhaustible supply of hard candy, which she slipped me when my mother wasn't looking. And hugs. *So why did I wait so long to see her? Was it the guilt I felt because I loved her and didn't love my mother?*

"Come here, darling, sit by me. Tell me how you are. You look a little pale? Are you working too hard? You always did have your nose in a book." She patted a space on the bed for me to sit down. When Sarah drew the curtains to give us more light, Minnie winced.

"Sarahle, bring us something to drink, please?" I let my breath out though I didn't know I was holding it.

"Tea all right, Anna?"

I nodded. Minnie took my hand in hers; they were ice cold. She kept looking at me, eyes brimming with tears. Sarah left the room with a warning look to me.

"I don't know why I waited so long to come see you. I'm sorry. I love you, Minnie. You were always good to me. Always."

"You're here now. That's what matters. I am so happy to see you." She kept caressing my hand, kissing it. Then her eyes closed. Her breathing grew shallow.

I kept my voice soft. "Minnie, do you remember the time we talked, just after my mother left for Florida?" *I wish I hadn't waited so long. Why didn't I do this years ago?*

She took a few breaths and opened her eyes. "Help me sit up. Fix the pillows." She was so light I could have carried her in my arms. "It's been on my mind, what happened that night. Ever since, I been wondering what to do. But, when I thought about mailing them back, I got a bad feeling. Maybe if Sadie was here, and we could talk." She sighed, "I don't know." She coughed and I helped her drink some water.

She looked at me. Really looked at me. "You didn't have it so easy with Sadie, I know. Neither did Heshie. But you were a child; it was worse for you." She took a sharp breath and held her stomach. The pain showed on her face, yet she whispered, "Look under the night table. There's a box." *Sarah, it wasn't me that brought it up.*

I bent down, my heart beating wildly as I saw an old cigar box, pushed against the wall. I kept staring at it. *Minnie, please don't let this kill you.*

"Did you find it, Anna? Is it still there?"

"Yes, it's here."

"Give it to me."

I put it on her lap. She looked at it, running her fingers over the dusty top. "All these years I been wanting to give it back to Sadie. All these years it's been between us."

"How do you know? She threw it out, didn't she?"

"Sadie was always doing stuff she was sorry for afterward. Knowing her, she probably went to get it out of the trash as soon as I left.

When she couldn't find it she knew I took it. All these years she's been waiting for me to say I have it."

"Why did you take it?"

"I don't know. I did it without thinking. Everything happened so fast."

"Did you read what was inside?"

"No. Not the letters or the diary."

"How could you keep from reading them?"

"I don't know. All these years—I just couldn't bring myself to do it. I kept thinking if she wanted me to know she woulda told me but I was afraid to send it back. I didn't want to start a fight we couldn't stop. Maybe she wouldn't believe I didn't read any of it." She sighed again. "I even asked Sarah what I should do, but she said it was my decision. Maybe I didn't read them because if I let something slip— Sadie can get so mad so fast. When she doesn't want to hear something, it doesn't get heard. Ever."

"I understand." There was more silence. She closed her eyes. I could see the pain was worse than before. Her breathing grew shallow and her face lost color. I held her hand lightly, waiting. Being with her filled me with a happiness that made me want to weep. Why had I waited so long? I would have given whatever it took for her to be healthy.

She opened her eyes, holding the box to her chest. "You take this, Anna. You read what's inside. I hope it helps you." She handed it to me. Shivers ran up and down my spine.

Minnie sighed. "I thought of sending it to you but I kept worrying, what if you said something, even by accident? Then what? Sadie would never forgive me. Once she gets mad—. You'll be careful won't you, Annale? You won't say anything to your mother? Promise?"

"I promise. And please, don't worry. It's not like my mother and I talk every day. And when we do, it's always about the weather or how the cost of living is going up so fast. She's not easy for me to talk to, even now."

"Yah, I know. Sadie can be difficult, but deep down she's a good person. I wish you could know her like I do. Such a good friend, steady as a rock all these years. Like the time she caught the guy who stole my pocketbook by tripping him and then sitting on top of him until the police came. Amazing, huh? And another thing, there's no one who can laugh like she does. I remember when she went to open a bottle of seltzer and it whooshed all over her clothes and face. You should have heard Sadie laugh. All day, whenever she thought about it, she laughed. Annale, darling, promise me you'll never tell her I gave you the box."

"I promise—"

She shut her eyes again. I could see she was exhausted, but I couldn't stop. "You say my mother was a good person, but she wasn't good to me. It's like we're talking about two people. I never remember hearing her laugh like that. What happened, Minnie?" *Tell me it wasn't my fault.*

"Darling, never mind the past. I just want you should be happy."

"Why didn't my mother like me?"

"You were such a quiet child. Always worrying. I want you should be happy. Be happy, Annale." Her head fell back on to the pillow. *Please don't die.* I put my head against her chest and heard her heart beating.

I knew I shouldn't but the words poured out. "Tell me about my father."

"Heshie was first-class, steady, a good friend all my life."

"Minnie, you know my mother better than anyone else. Could I ask you a few questions?"

"Not now, Annale, I'm too tired. Come back in a few days, I'll feel better. It's so good to see you. You're a sight for sore eyes. Promise me you'll come more often."

I kissed her cheek and neatened up her covers. "I promise I'll come whenever you want. Sarah can tell me when you feel up to another visit. Be well. Please. I love you, Minnie. " She patted my hand. I watched her chest rise and fall, unwilling to leave.

Sarah was putting the tea on a tray when I came into the kitchen. "She's sleeping."

"She's hardly ever awake any more. The doctor says it's a matter of days, maybe a few weeks." She wiped her eyes and blew her nose. When she saw the cigar box in my hand she glared. "I warned—"

"Sarah, stop. It was her idea. She wanted me to take it. All she asked was that I never let my mother know she had it and that she gave it to me."

"Well, maybe it's just as well. She kept worrying about what to do with it, always asking me what she should do, especially lately."

"Could we talk a little?"

"Some other time. I have to pick up my son."

"Please let me know how your mother's doing?" *I don't want to wait years before we talk again. Minnie doesn't have years. Do I?*

Paulus walked into the living room, a frustrated look on his face. "I think I lost some stuff on an upper shelf. Can you give me a hand?" He saw the cigar box. "You smoking?"

"Yeah, I decided my bad blood needed bad lungs to keep it company. The ladder's behind the door, but it's wobbly. I'll hold it for you."

As we walked into the room I couldn't stop remembering the times Max and I had snuggled peacefully on the couch after making love. It hurt to think about how handsome and debonair he was, how well our bodies fit together. He said he loved me. I said I loved him. In the beginning, our marriage was almost like a dream. My fears of not being good enough began to fade. I enjoyed being married. I loved being half of a couple. That people took our being together for granted was a source of pleasure.

But there were other times, in this same room, like the afternoon, about three months after we were married, when Max asked, "Hey, Anna, how did you get to be such a good fuck?"

"Max! I'm your wife." I moved away and covered myself, trying to collect my thoughts. "I don't ask about your love life so why ask about mine?"

"You're great in bed. The best I ever had. It's only natural to wonder how you got to be so good." He pulled me back and sucked my nipple.

"Quit it, Max." I pushed his hands away. He tried to coax me back into his arms. "Stop it." The nuzzling continued. "I said, leave me alone." Max raised himself and grabbed my face.

"Babe, what's wrong? I paid you a compliment." I stormed out of the room. He followed. "Hey! Is something going on? You screwing the mailman? One lousy question and you act as if I'm the prosecuting attorney. Jesus, Anna, act normal for once."

"You wouldn't know normal if it smacked you on your dick." I put on my bathrobe.

"One lousy question. Shit! You don't want to answer? Tell me, 'It's none of your business.' That's what a normal person would say."

I remember feeling trapped. Maybe he was right. One look at the smirk on his face and my doubts disappeared like sun-scattering fog.

"What's normal by you is what you think and you do. That's not exactly—"

"I am fucking tired of your explosions," he said coldly. "You stop it right now or—"

"Or what?" We were on treacherous ground. I was afraid we would start something that couldn't be stopped. Before he could speak, I put my feelings in a box and slammed the lid shut. "You're right, honey. I'm sorry." I burrowed my face in his chest and wrapped my arms around his body. I felt him respond. In a second we were back on the couch, making nice. Inside my head, voices shrieked. *Who cares how I got to be such a good fuck? That's not who I am.*

My heart was pounding and my hands shook as I opened the cigar box and picked up the faded blue leather diary with gold binding. I tried to open the lock but it wouldn't budge. Should I read it? Curiosity won. I got a nail file and pushed and prodded and fiddled. Maybe my mother broke it to make sure no one could read it. I poured peanut oil into the lock, jiggling it with tweezers. When it sprang open, it released as if liberated. I stroked the smooth leather, trying to imagine my mother as a young woman, buying what looked like an expensive diary to write down what she didn't want others to know. I felt weird. Did I have the right to read it without her permission? She thought she threw it out when she put it in the garbage. I took a very deep breath and opened the diary. The entries were undated.

> Dear Diary,
>   I bought you today because you have a lock and a key and I need to talk to someone in private, who won't say I'm bad. I can't tell Minnie. She would never do what I did. When I was walking in the park today I met a man. No, I don't usually talk to strange men but he was looking at a rose and he kept looking at it like there was something really special about it. I got so curious I had to go over and ask him what he was looking at. He didn't even look up at me, just showed me the colors inside the center and asked, "Did you ever see anything so beautiful?" I never looked at a rose so close before. He was right. It was beautiful. And we stood there, looking at the yellow rose, just the two of us, with the sun warming my back. His real name is Avram, which is such a lovely name, but he wants me to call him Avi, a name that's private, just between us. He asked if I wanted to go for a coffee and I said yes. Diary, I never felt like this before. He

smells so good. And he has a smile like—like—I don't know how to describe it. All I know is when he smiles I feel special. Not beautiful, I know I'm not, but it doesn't matter because he's smiling, at me.

Dear Diary,

I went to the movies last night with Avi and he held my hand. Once, he put his arm around me but when I moved a little I guess he thought I didn't like it so he took his arm away. I wanted to say put it back but I was afraid of what he might think. Having his arm around me made me wish I knew him better so I could tell him what I think about. Papa asked where I went but I didn't tell him the truth. I said I was with Minnie. Do I have to tell her to say I was with her in case he asks? I'm not ready to tell anyone about Avi. It's so wonderful being with him it feels like a dream. He knows so much. I have to start reading the papers so I'll know what he's talking about. He keeps saying there's going to be a war. He has to be wrong although something about the way he says it makes me afraid he's right. Even though there's so much I don't know he never makes fun of me, just explains things that I ask. I could tell him anything. All I want is to be with him.

Dear Diary,

I wish I could talk to Minnie about Avi but every time I start, something stops me. She's my best friend and I know she would be happy for me but I'm afraid she won't understand. Avi isn't like anyone I ever met. He's older and he was born in Germany and he's an artist. I don't want anyone to know I went to his room so he could show me his paintings. One of them was a portrait of me. I was terrified. If Papa ever saw it he'd beat me good. I know artists don't make a lot of money and Minnie would say he's not a good catch but I don't care. I can work. I can make money for both of us.

Dear Diary,

Sometimes, when I tell Minnie what Papa does she acts as if I'm making it up or exaggerating, that things aren't as bad as I say they are. She keeps saying he's a good man. He supports his family. That can't be all that matters. What about kindness? I wonder what she'd say if I told her what happened today. Papa burned my poems. Every single poem. He said he did it for my own good because I shouldn't be wasting my time on such foolishness. He says I should be thinking about ways to make money. He says having a lot of money is the only thing that makes you a real American.

My poems weren't bothering him. They weren't taking up any of his space. I usually keep them in my drawer, under my slips, but Lilly was cleaning and she asked me to empty my drawers so she could put new liners in them. I put the poems on my side of the bed, under my pillow. In a neat little pile, tied with a blue ribbon. How did he find them? What right does he have to destroy my writing? I write after I come home from work. That's supposed to be my time. Lilly saw him take them and said she tried to stop him but I don't believe her. She's just as afraid of him as I am. She was crying when she told me but it didn't make me feel better. She says if I wrote them once I can write them again. Is that supposed to make me feel better? Besides, how would she know? Did she ever write even one poem? I'm not a machine, press a button and out comes a poem.

All the more reason not to talk about Avi. I don't want to give Papa any more reason to be mad at me. We already fight so much Mama leaves the room in tears. I'm too tired to write any more, dear friend.

My grandfather burned all my mother's poems? Then how could she destroy what I wrote when I was in high school? I had plans to be a writer, which she wasted no time letting me know was a terrible idea. One night, I was revising a story to submit to a contest and she grabbed the pages out of my hands. After reading a few words, she tore them up. "Do what you're supposed to do and you won't get into trouble," she snarled. Is that what she learned from her life?

I reread the first few entries, feeling her vulnerability and loneliness. She can't even find a way to tell her best friend about the man she loves. The next entry seemed to have been written a few days later. Why didn't she date any of the entries? Although I found myself feeling sorry for the pain of the woman writing, I couldn't fathom how that Sadie became my mother, Sadie? Was she really my mother?

Dear Diary,
I finally told someone what Papa did. And I was right. Avi does understand. He held me until I stopped crying. He said that even though those poems were gone I would most definitely write new poems because I was a writer and writers never stop writing no matter what happens. He only

read one of the poems I wrote because I was afraid to show him the rest. Now they're gone. I know I have a lot to learn as a writer but he says I have a lot to say, and I do.

Dear Diary,
     I'll tell you what I haven't told anyone else, not even Minnie. I love Avi. We're going to be married, I'm sure, even though he hasn't asked me yet. In some ways we're already married, which is scary, but he tells me he loves me so much he would never do anything to hurt me. And I believe him. I love him more than life itself. I know that sounds corny, but it's true. I hate when I have to say goodbye to him. It's like when he's around every thing is in color but when he's gone, it's all black and white.
     I'm so frightened all the time. Bad things are happening in Europe. Avi says he might have to go to Germany to see if he can get his family out. He's very worried about his parents and brother and I don't blame him. He showed me some of the letters they've written. I can't believe the terrible things they say. How is it possible that soldiers would beat up old people while everyone laughs? And how can universities get away with firing all the Jewish professors? I don't believe in God but maybe I can still pray that things will get a little better and he won't have to go. That can't be too much to ask can it? If I don't marry Avi I'll shrivel up and die. The worst thing is I'm a coward. I know I won't be able to kill myself.

I stopped reading, trying to imagine my mother writing, "I love him more than life itself."

Did she love my father more than life itself? Minnie told me even though my mother didn't ever say much about Avi, she couldn't help noticing changes in her after he was no longer around. She said my mother didn't laugh like she used to and got angry for no reason. What would my life have been like if she had married Avi. If he had been my father. Why didn't they marry? Did he find someone else? Is that why she changed? I turned the pages to see how much more she had written. After several blank pages there were additional entries.

Diary, forgive me.
     I stopped writing in you because I've been writing letters to Avi and I tell him everything I would tell you. I keep

writing to him even though I stopped getting letters from him a long time ago. I keep hoping and praying he's in a hospital or even a prison. I keep hoping and praying he'll come back to me but nothing happens. Now I know for sure there is no God.

I put the diary down and tried to picture my mother as a young woman. Loving a man. Not knowing where he was. Unable to talk about him with her best friend. Too afraid her best friend wouldn't understand. Did my mother trust anyone besides Avi? What happened to him?

I went to the kitchen to get a glass of water. Paulus was making coffee. "Want some?"

"Not right now," I said. "Did the mail come?"

"I don't know."

"I'll go see." I came back with a stack of letters and was opening a bill when I heard Paulus mutter something under his breath. I looked up. He was staring at a pale blue piece of paper. His face was grim. "Bad news?" I asked.

He put the letter into its envelope and stuck it in his jacket pocket. "There's a hot little restaurant that just opened up near the paper. It's been attracting standing-room-only crowds and I've been asked to review it. Will you come with me?"

"Me? What do I know about rating restaurants?"

"The truth is, I'm a little nervous. You know how much I want to be food editor, and this could be a test. I have to write about the meal, the service, the ambience, the look and taste and smell of the food. It would help if I could talk with you about it." When I didn't answer immediately, he sighed, "It's okay. Forget I asked."

"Don't tell me what to do. Let's go. A great dinner is exactly what I need right now."

"Are you sure? Not going isn't the end of the world."

I tried to smile. "You never know when the end of the world will come."

Paulus stopped the car at the front door to let me out. I gasped so loud I embarrassed myself. He looked at me as if to say, "What's wrong?"

Max was walking into the restaurant with a slim young woman in a sexy business suit. Her most noticeable feature was long blonde hair that curled in ringlets around her head. They moved in step, hips touching, his hand resting casually on her butt. He was wearing a greenish-blue suit, the color of his eyes. I remember how hard I fought to get him to stop wearing gray, that there was more to life than boring just for the sake of convenience. I couldn't stop staring at his hand on her butt, remembering how often his hand had touched me, in love, and anger, and desperation, and disgust, and desire.

Paulus interrupted my thoughts. "You look like you've seen a ghost." I watched Max hold the door open and felt my heart lurch. The woman turned around, holding her face up to his to be kissed. I saw Max oblige, laughing, as if bestowing a favor. The gesture reminded me of all the times I wanted affection or caring or a sign of connection from him. Yet more often than not, what I got was sex.

*****

We're sitting in the living room, drinking wine. It has been a particularly grueling day and I need to talk about having to confiscate a test from a student I caught cheating. She had rushed to the Dean of Students, complaining that I was picking on her. I lean against Max, nuzzling my cheek against his chest. "Rub my neck for a minute?"

"I'll rub more than that," he says, putting down his glass.

"I'd love a neck rub. It's been a hard day."

He cups his hand around my breasts and tilts my body back, giving me a long lingering kiss that leaves no doubt about what he wants. I move away, determined to get what I need. "What's the matter, Babe?" he asks, annoyed.

"My neck hurts. Right here," I say, putting his hand on my tense muscles.

He touches the sore place and then moves his hands back to my breast. I try to keep my voice light. "Wrong muscles, Max." I put his hands back on my neck. He sighs and gently rubs. It might not be the world's best neck rub, but for me it's heaven. Even so, I worry about putting him in a bad mood.

*****

"Anna? Are you going to stand and stare for the rest of the evening while I die of curiosity and starvation?"

"I just saw my ex-husband go inside."

"How long has it been since you've seen him?"

"Not long enough."

"It's your call. We can go in or leave; whatever you want."

I couldn't stop seeing his hand on her butt. The easy way she'd lifted her face for a kiss. I took a deep breath. *I want to leave. Now.* "Let's go in."

Wedding Daze

The knocking was loud and insistent. Sadie opened her eyes, wondering who it was and what couldn't wait a few minutes. It was her wedding day and she didn't feel like rushing. "Sadie, it's Papa. I need you should come with me. Get dressed."

Sadie groaned. What had she done now? She wished Lilly was here. She knew how to get around Papa, at least some of the time. "Sadie, come now!" She felt a little frightened. Even though she couldn't remember what she had done, it must have been something terrible. Papa sounded awful.

"What about breakfast, Papa? Can't we eat first?" she asked, hoping for a hint of what was wrong.

"After. First I got something to tell you. We'll go to the park. It's quiet there."

It's 7:30 in the morning. It's quiet everywhere, she thought. What's the rush?

When they got to the park, he sat her down on a bench in front of the rose garden. Good thing flowers can't talk, thought Sadie.

"So, Papa," she began nervously. "What can't wait until after breakfast?"

"It's your wedding, day, Sadie." As if I didn't know, she thought. He sat down next to her, stood up, and then sat again. When he stood up once more, Sadie sighed. Whatever she had done must have been horrendous.

"Papa, stay put, you're making me dizzy."

He looked at his daughter. She didn't look so happy. Not like Lilly on her wedding day. Well, that was her business. He could only hope her marrying Heshie was for the best. He took a small box out of his coat pocket and stared at it, hoping he could do what he had to do.

"Sadie." It was harder than he thought.

"Yes, Papa?"

He sat down next to her, holding the box, unable to look into her eyes. "When I was a boy, my papa told us that when the soldiers came, we should hide in the outhouse. He said the smell would keep the soldiers away and we would be safe until he could come and get us. But when the soldiers came the last time, I was the only one in the outhouse. I waited and waited and waited. I don't know how long I waited." Sadie wondered what this had to do with her. "I don't know how long I waited. Papa never came. Mama never came. My brothers never came. I was afraid to leave. When Tante Roshnya found me I was half crazy. I kept telling her I had to wait for Papa. She said Papa wasn't coming, that I had to go with her. But before we left, she looked around. I didn't pay no attention. I heard her say, 'Thanks, God' but I didn't care. As far as I was concerned, God was no friend of mine. If he was, it would have been Papa who opened the door. I was young, but not too young to know that if Papa didn't come, it was because of the soldiers."

Sadie shivered, imagining her father as a child, waiting for a papa who never came.

"Are you cold? Do you want my jacket?"

Sadie shook her head. What was wrong with Papa? He had tears in his eyes. He handed her the box. "Open it," he said in a strangulated voice.

Inside the box, wrapped in worn gray velvet, was a Star of David on a fine gold chain. She stared at her father, wondering why he, who had no use for religion, would give her such a present.

"It was Mama's. Papa hid it in a box in the outhouse when the troubles began. He told his sister, Roshnya, that if something happened to him, she was to dig up the box and give it to me when I became a man. He told her I was to give it to my daughter on her wedding day just as Mama's papa had given it to her."

"But, Papa, Lilly's the oldest—"

"Lilly married a man who'll be rich." He looked away. "Sadie, when I look at you I see Mama. The same eyes and mouth. You even sound like her. It's hard for me to look at you sometimes. The pain is so big. Some days, I don't even want to get out of bed." Sadie looked at the father she thought she knew. Who was this man?

He kissed the Star of David and put the chain around his

220

daughter's neck. "Life for you won't be easy, Sadie. You're too much like me. We're dreamers, and people like us, our dreams don't come true." Sadie refused to think about Avi, how he had kissed her in this very place. "I want you should have this. It's Mama's gift from her to you. After today, you'll have a different name, but I want you should know where you came from, who your people were. The chain was broken when Papa and Mama and my brothers were killed, but you, you're still a link. You and Heshie. You should have known them."

He wiped his eyes. "Sadie, I want you should do me a favor. If it's all right with Heshie, if you have a daughter, will you name her Anna? It was Mama's name. It's all I have left of her.

Walking up the aisle, with Papa's hand in hers, Sadie felt his fingers tighten around hers when they reached the chuppeh. He kissed the top of her forehead and then released her to Heshie, who was waiting, yearning, smiling.

She knew how to be a good daughter. She would learn how to be a good wife.

14

The restaurant was dimly lit. I kept my eyes glued to the back of Paulus' head as he followed the hostess. We were led to a table in the middle of the dining room. I quelled my panic and said, "We'd prefer a more secluded table."

"There are no more tables for two."

I was about to tell Paulus I wanted to leave when I saw an empty table at the back of the restaurant, hidden behind a huge plant. "Look, there's a table. It's perfect. Why can't we sit there?" I pointed. "Those two couples are sitting at tables for four."

The hostess gave me an unpleasant look. People stared. I could feel my face turn red. Determined to sit where I chose, I refused to follow her.

An elegantly dressed man came up and asked, "Is there a problem?" The hostess shook her head coyly, smiled the phoniest smile I ever saw, and led us to the table I requested. I breathed a sigh of relief.

As we sat down, Paulus said, "You look like you could use a drink."

What I need is an emotion transplant. Gratefully, I took the menu he handed me. *I need to stop caring that Max is with a tall beautiful blonde. I need him to disappear into outer space.*

I looked up and there he was, walking to our table, his full attention beamed on me as if Paulus didn't exist. "Hello, Anna. Long time no see." His smile could melt steel. "What are you doing here? I didn't think this was your kind of place." He looked me up and down, grinning, taking pleasure in my obvious discomfort.

I took a sip of wine, amazed I could speak. "How would you know?"

"Same old Anna, always answering a question with a question." He turned and smiled at Paulus the smile he reserved for people who didn't measure up to his standards of valuable. "Aren't you going to introduce me to your date? Or is he your husband?" Furious, I tried to think of a smartass response. I wanted to nail him. My mind went blank.

"Paulus, this is Max. Max, Paulus." Watching the dignity with which Paulus shook hands made me proud of him. *Way to go, Paulus.* "And now, gentlemen, if you'll excuse me, I have to use the ladies' room." I picked up my purse and left the two men to fend for themselves.

All of a sudden I really did need to go to the bathroom. A wave of nausea hit me hard. After washing my face with cold water, I was feeling slightly more human until Max's woman walked in, her perfect hair and face and figure perfectly arranged. She looked like an exotic manikin until I took a closer look. I was delighted to see wrinkles on her face and rumples on her dress. The sight of a small pimple cheered me up enormously.

Paulus was pouring wine when I returned. Handing me a glass, he said, "Here's to you, Anna, a woman who knows how to exit gracefully. Max is quite a guy. Makes a rattlesnake look positively friendly." He had a twinkle in his eye.

"Here's to you, Paulus, a man who knows who he is." He sputtered and choked. I had to pound his back. "What's wrong?"

He shook his head, still coughing. "Nothing."

"Doesn't look like nothing to me."

"When you put something into words, you can't not know it anymore. I'm not ready to admit a part of my life is over—irretrievably broken."

I refilled my glass, not sure how to respond. He emptied his. Poured more wine and drank most of it. *If I drank half that much that fast, I'd be under the table.* He looked like he couldn't decide whether to say something.

"It's okay. You don't have to tell me."

He sighed. "Who am I kidding? Mollie and I lived together for three years. I would have married her if she'd said yes, but every time I asked she told me she needed more time. It wasn't only my frequent changes of jobs—I knew she worried about money—but I'm not irresponsible. I always—shit, what's the use—no sense defending myself all over again. Let's talk about something else. What about you and Max?"

"You sound like my mother, always changing the subject just when we're talking about something important. What good does that do? You're still thinking about her." I gulped down my wine and leaned toward Paulus, pleasantly buzzed. "I definitely and positively think you should keep talking. Get her out of your system. Absolutely."

He laughed. "If I didn't know better I'd say you were drunk."

"My condition is irrelevant. Talk, Paulus. This is your big chance."

"Anna, you're my employer."

"True, but tonight we're compañeros, deciding the fate of this restaurant. Speak now or forever hold your thoughts. Now there's a curse if ever I heard one."

He emptied his glass. "I didn't have the courage to confront her, gave her all my power, and then said, 'Thank you very much' when she used it. I knew she was taking advantage of me, but I told myself she would change."

"How come you lived with her for three years?"

"How many years did you say you were married to Max?"

"Case closed." I emptied my glass.

"Want more?" he asked.

I knew I should say no. "Yes." My head was gently spinning. *I hope I don't pay for the pleasant way I'm feeling with a migraine.* I handed him my wine glass with a not-so-steady hand. "Paulus, if you met Mollie now, do you think you'd be attracted to her?"

"No." He answered so quickly I laughed. Then he nodded ruefully. "I'm sorry to admit it, but I probably would be. I keep asking myself why I stayed as long as I did. I worry that it could happen again. What about you?"

Saved by the sudden presence of the waiter who hovered politely. "Madam, Monsieur, are you ready to order?"

Paulus rose to the occasion. "We'd like to hear the specials one more time." The waiter responded with a graceful description, different enough from the first time for me to know it wasn't memorized. When he left, Paulus and I decided we should have two full dinners, although I couldn't imagine how we could eat that much. Neither one of us felt comfortable leaving food on our plate. But, as he reminded me, we were scoping out the fare, and that called for special tactics. Paulus ordered in what sounded like perfect French. If it were up to me, he would definitely be appointed Food Editor.

Sitting in the expensive and exclusive restaurant, knowing we were seated because Paulus worked for the newspaper, did nothing to diminish my awareness that Paulus wanted me to be here with him, maybe even needed me to be here. When I was with Max, it felt as if I was always the one who needed to be where we were, with him. I looked at Paulus, relaxed, enjoying himself, holding his own with Max, and I realized there was a lot I could learn from him.

Our first course was gorgeous. Tiny shrimps nestled in red and black caviar on a bed of greens for me. He had ordered pâté that sat on finely shredded vegetables of many different hues. I guessed carrots and beets and celery, maybe some green pepper. I was beginning to feel like a kid at the circus, especially when the waiter brought us a basket of steaming hot breads with butter, a dish of olive oil, and hummus. Our secluded table was perfect for sharing, which we did with great glee. We both took notes. Paulus decided two points of view would give him more to consider when writing his account. After we finished the first course, the waiter set a small dish of pale yellow sherbet before each of us—to cleanse the palate. he said. The tart lemony taste was so cool and refreshing I could have stopped right there, perfectly satisfied. Closing my eyes, I savored my contentment until I heard Paulus say, "Anna."

I gasped when the waiter put my entrée in front of me. It was the most perfectly shaped lobster I had ever seen. The meat had been taken out and mixed with something that smelled divine before being artfully put back in the bright red shell. I had never in my life felt so blessed. I couldn't imagine anything better. Paulus beamed. "You said you liked seafood. This is one of the specials the restaurant is noted for." He sighed. "Imagine being paid to do this every week."

"Paulus, how am I going to eat it all? It's enormous and I don't think this is the kind of place one asks for a doggie bag."

"Anna, don't worry about it. Enjoy!" If ever there was a man who had a right to feel he'd been cheated when it came to physical attributes, it could be Paulus. But instead of letting it get to him, he'd found a way to fill his life with joy. How had he learned this? Could I?

I had to laugh at the expression on Paulus' face when his meal arrived. He inhaled the aroma of his baby rack of lamb, beautifully arranged on the plate, surrounded by deep green beans, shredded red something, and roasted potatoes with a heavenly sauce. He ate delicately, savoring every bite. It was the best food I ever ate. "Maybe you should tell your paper they need to hire me as your co-taster," I cooed.

By the time the salad came I was feeling as if the chef couldn't do any better, but I was wrong. The salads we had ordered were small gardens, perfectly matched, and totally different. Mine was mostly reds; his mostly greens. Mine came with a spicy, creamy dressing, his with a pale red liquid that tasted like fresh raspberries. Not knowing ahead of time what was coming only added to my delight. Then I saw Max and his bimbo.

"What's the matter, Anna?"

"He's walking toward us. With his sweetie."

"What do you want me to do?"

"Make him disappear."

"Short of that?"

They stopped a few tables from us to chat but I saw Max looking at me. I smiled seductively at Paulus, took his hand in a decidedly "unemployee"-like manner, and spoke in a low voice. "Can we pretend for the moment that we're in love?"

"Sure. How about a passionate kiss?"

"How about intense conversation?"

He leaned toward me, took my hands in his, and looking into my eyes, spoke in a sexy voice. "Darling, you are the best—the most magnificent—I thank my lucky stars I met you—you are the woman of my dreams."

"Thank you, Paulus. I'd give you a raise if I could. To hell with Max."

And the desserts? Words fail me. Spun sugar concoctions of fruit. Swan-boat pastries filled with white, black, and brown chocolate drizzled with decorations of orange and raspberry glaze. I was in awe of the pastry chef's talent, and of Paulus' culinary knowledge. We sipped dark, hot coffee, in gourmet bliss. I just wasn't sure I could walk.

"Does Max still attract you?" asked Paulus.

I said no so fast we both laughed. *Part of me is not laughing.* "How do you stop being attracted to someone you know is not good for you?"

"I'm the wrong person to ask. There's a woman in the pressroom I'd ask out but she looks enough like Mollie to be her twin sister. So far, all we've done is exchange pleasantries."

I kept my voice neutral. "What's keeping you from making a date?"

"What's the saying? Once bitten, twice shy?"

"Just because she looks like Mollie doesn't mean she'll act like her." *Why isn't he attracted to me?*

"All I know is my body says yes and my brain screams no. For the moment, I'm letting my brain win." He wiped red glaze off his lips. "You think there's something wrong with us? We seem to be looking for love in all the wrong places with all the wrong people."

"I'm not so sure I'm looking anymore." *Even when the person I love is a small girl with huge brown eyes named Marina, there's always pain. Love and pain, pain and love, go together like a hand and glove.* "Maybe we should settle for friendship. Look at us, talking, enjoying each other's company, no complications. Maybe that's good enough." *Who am I kidding?*

*****

I've just graduated from college. Tired of being alone, I muster the courage to go by myself to a dance at a local restaurant. Even though I take an inordinate amount of time dressing and walk slowly to the bus stop, the bus comes on time and I am earlier than I want to be. A few people are dancing, no one I know, even slightly. I wonder if this will be another evening where I hide my discomfort at not being asked to dance by taking too frequent trips to the ladies room. I am giving serious thought to leaving when a guy comes up to me. Barely taller than me, wearing a suit that smells like a Chinese restaurant, at least he's male. For the moment I'm not a wallflower. He turns out to have a great sense of rhythm. Just before the last set he says, "It's nice to be with a woman who knows how to follow."

"You know how to lead, that makes a difference."

"How about I lead you to my place? We can have a drink and talk." I'm not attracted to him, but I do like dancing with him so I say yes. He's very gallant, pays for the subway, and leads me to a seat away from noisy teenagers celebrating a hockey win. As we walk to his place, I worry about what I've gotten myself into and consider telling him I've changed my mind. His fourth floor walkup is small but clean. We move from drinking coffee and listening to John Coltrane to his king-sized bed. He's a surprisingly caring lover. Patient and kind. I'm too nervous to pretend anything, and this seems quite all right with him. He strokes my back and my neck and my face, never once touching my breasts or thighs until we both feel me relaxing. It's a good night.

I think I can learn to love him even though he's a construction worker, a high-school graduate who never reads a book or thnks about the meaning of life. Yet a few months later, instead of making love, he sits me down on his sofa and looks at me with his clear brown eyes. "Anna, I've been thinking about us. I really like you and we've had a lot of good times but I just can't see a future for us. You talk about stuff I never heard of. Books I never read. It makes me feel bad about myself. I don't like to feel that way."

I admire his candor, give him a kiss, and say goodbye, feeling a sadness I can't explain. In the days after we part I think about how I could help him develop new interests, but he is perfectly happy the way he is. At least I'll never have to hear what my mother thinks of him.

*****

Paulus ordered an after-dinner drink. "When you were young, what did you imagine your life would be like?"

"I don't remember thinking about it. I suppose I thought I'd work for a while and then, after I'd been married for a few years, have a couple of kids." I looked away for a moment and saw that Max was now sitting at a table near us, laughing. The warm full laugh that used to fill me with happiness. My stomach cramped.

"Is that what you still want?" asked Paulus.

"I don't know; it just popped out. At least I'm glad I had no kids with Max. I'd never be free of him." Paulus went to the men's room and I allowed myself to float.

"Did you ever think about your forays into inner space as a story wanting to be told through you? Like a kind of gift?" asked Paulus, jolting me out of my reverie.

"Some gift. Makes me feel crazy."

"That's because you're afraid of it."

He pulled a small notebook out of his jacket and pushed it and a pen toward me. "Start writing!" I stared at him and then I did exactly that, as fast as my fingers could move.

Souls—hard, soft, sweet, sour, weak, strong, knowing, unknowing, stiff, flexible. Jealous Shapers curse the soul. Who can undo their curses?

I stared at the paper, barely able to read what I had written. The words looked as if they had been hurled on to the page. Paulus stood up. "We should leave. Artists need to pay attention to their muse when she decides to pay a visit."

"Sit down! Artists make art. My portfolio is empty."

"I'm not so sure. Maybe the urge to say something's been inside you all your life just waiting for you to pay attention."

"So why's it coming out now? Or, more to the point, where has it been?"

"Who knows? I bet if you closed your eyes you'd see something. Try!"

Curiosity got the better of me. For a few seconds I didn't see anything, but then I saw more images than I could describe. "It's like there's a lot of mist and fog. Shapes are forming and reforming. Colors are shifting and changing. Two huge mountains, at least I think they're mountains, with a narrow space between them." I opened my eyes, feeling strangely excited. "You're right. Let's go!"

"Just one moment, my dear Anna," intoned Paulus. "Please do not forget that I am the person who gave you your first notebook. When your work is published I would not refuse a dedication that says, 'To Paulus, who provided me with food for thought.'"

I grinned. Raising my glass, I toasted, "Here's to you Paulus, a man who's willing to listen rather than judge."

He lowered his eyes with mock modesty. "Please, I need no thanks. The dedication will suffice. But I wouldn't refuse ten percent of your royalties."

As we walked to the front of the restaurant, we passed the table where Max was sitting. He winked at me. His girlfriend was talking to another woman, even thinner and blonder. On impulse I stared back, hoping I looked cold rather than interested. Paulus might not be anyone's idea of gorgeous, but he was kind and thoughtful and funny. Three attributes totally missing from Max. "Thanks, Paulus," I whispered in his ear.

"For what?"

"For being here. For being you."

We drove home, my head filled with pictures and ideas, too many to keep track of. Yet when I tried to write, the images refused to form. I went to bed thinking my excitement was much ado about nothing. Toward dawn, I woke up. Something inside wanted to come out. I picked up the notebook and pen. By the time I was snuggled back in bed, leaning against pillows, the words flowed. I sensed Boonah was nearby, smiling.

> It was the time before time, when there was only Great One.
> The way of creation was not clear, but Great One exhaled
> huge breaths of air and suddenly tall mountains appeared
> between a narrow pass.
>   Great One blew many bursts of sound-forming beings,

Shapers, who guarded the entrance to the narrow pass.

Great One exhaled and moved the swirling air until there was light and heat and roundness. Thus was Sun created. When Sun's rays grew hot, Great One exhaled again. Sun grew fainter. Great One quickly inhaled, sucked in a piece of Sun and exhaled. In Sun's place was a pale sliver of faint light—Moon.

Still, there were only gray expanses interrupted by tall mountains. Great One said to the Shapers, "Let us sing a song of yearning to create life." And their singing brought forth earth and water and sky and fire. Great One shook the air with pleasure and brought forth vegetation of all shapes and colors.

"We must rest," decided Great One, "for there is more to create." And so they slept by Moon's pale light until Sun's rays woke them. Great One said, "Let us fill the earth with creepers and crawlers and flyers and swimmers and walkers." Once again Great One and the Shapers shook the air with songs of yearning. Soon creatures filled crevices, corners, and spaces of ocean, earth, and sky. Great One was satisfied. For a time, all was well.

Then Great One felt peculiar. Something was missing. What could it be? Great One and the Shapers sang songs of yearning until Great One understood. "We must have creatures who sing." Great One mixed browns of earth, blacks of night, reds of fire, yellows of Sun, and whites of Moon creating people of all sizes and colors. Great One was satisfied. For a time, all was well.

Then Great One felt peculiar. Something was missing. What could it be? Great One and the Shapers sang songs of yearning until Great One understood. "We must give the power of generation to all living beings so they too can create." Great One told the Shapers, "Create the spirit of every soul so that at birth each will be unique." Great One was satisfied. For a time, all was well.

Then Great One felt peculiar. Something was still missing. What could it be? Great One and the Shapers sang songs of yearning for a long time until Great One understood. People were lonely. Songs were not enough. People needed words. Great One said, "Shapers, when you mix the spirit of each soul, add the gift of speech." So it was. Great One was satisfied.

People told stories. When the stories reached Great One, trouble began.

My mind went blank. What trouble? Nothing came to me. I watched the sun come up, made myself breakfast, dusted the stereo. Nothing. Then, while making a cup of tea, I knew what the trouble was. After a few hours of writing, polishing and shaping, I felt satisfied.

> Each Shaper competed fiercely to create the best storyteller and soon the competition became so intense, the more blessings a soul was given, the more curses it received. Great One ordered the Shapers to stop cursing, but jealousy deafened their ears.
>
> Great One told Sun, "Blind them so they cannot see." The rivalry stopped until Sun's rays waned. Then fierce competition resumed.
>
> Great One asked Moon for advice. "Just as I continue to change," said Moon, "so does creation. Nothing remains the same."
>
> "How will I protect souls burdened by Shapers with too many curses and not enough blessings?"
>
> Moon watched in pain. Great One despaired. Moon spoke. "Weigh each soul as it is created. For every curse there must be a blessing. Blessings will triumph over curses if the soul chooses to prevail."
>
> Great One sang a song of yearning so potent all Shapers paused. The curses and blessings stopped. In that moment a huge scale appeared, barricading the narrow passage in the tall mountains. Now, souls are weighed as they move through the passage, allowing Great One to balance blessings and curses forever.

Boonah touches my cheek. "Yes, Anna, yes! Always remember: Sun gives way to Moon, who waxes and wanes and yet is always Moon."

A Time for Playing

The doctor turned from his patient and said, "Nurse Holder, I want to speak with you, now!"

Jacob kept his face impassive. "Certainly, Dr. Clarkson. I'll just finish the dressing." He deftly taped the bandage around the wound, cleaned up, and walked outside to where the doctor was making notes on a chart. He kept writing. Jacob waited, hoping his fury did not show.

"Nurse Holder, I'm not satisfied with the way the patient's wound is healing. Are you absolutely positive the dressing has been changed regularly?"

"Yes, sir, every four hours, just as you prescribed."

The doctor stared at him. "I'll ask your supervisor to check."

Jacob's jaw muscles clenched but his voice was calm. "Whatever you think best, Dr. Clarkson."

The doctor finished writing. "Here, put this chart back on the patient's door."

Jacob nodded and returned to the patient's room, waiting until he was sure the doctor had gone.

Cursing under his breath, he went to the locker room and changed into his soccer clothes—shorts and a T-shirt. Despite the chilly temperature, he ran up and down the makeshift field until he was sweating profusely. For Jacob, one of the best parts of working in the hospital was the weekly employee soccer game. Suited up in operating room greens, emergency room grays, or shirts and shorts, with numbers on their chests, no one differentiated doctor from janitor. Once, even a patient snuck out and played before he was discovered and sent back to the ward. Jacob always tried to get to the field before the others so he could warm up and practice dribbling by himself the way his coach had taught him. It reminded him of all the games he'd played for his team in Jamaica, before he got tired of his racist supervisor and decided to leave. He still missed the way his team played, hard and fast, with little talk either before or after games, except for suggestions from the coach about how to play better. He shook his head and stretched, concentrating on loosening up his tight muscles.

On the field, he was running, keeping the ball nicely in front of him, when someone intercepted it and started moving it in the opposite direction. Jacob never looked up, just kept his eye on the ball and quickly recaptured it, but his opponent stayed with him and intercepted once again. It became a game between the two of them, each vying for the ball, but when Jacob used the skills he'd once been famous for, and despite the other man's agility and speed, Jacob finally kicked the ball into the cage.

"Well done," cheered his out-of-breath opponent as others poured onto the field. Jacob never looked up to see who it was. He played soccer to get rid of feelings he bottled up inside him each week. It also helped that the hospital soccer game was strictly first come first play. No matter how many showed up, everyone got a chance to play. Jacob, as the scorer, started the choosing. One by one, those watching took the place of those who'd been playing. Jacob was so good no one traded places with him. He got to play the whole time.

The soccer games were always fifteen-minute quarters with a three-minute rest. Two minutes to change players after each goal or quarter. The angrier he was, the better Jacob played. Today, he was unbeatable, charging for the ball, dribbling it as he ran, scoring goal after goal, like a man possessed. What would he do without these games? Open his mouth and get himself fired, probably.

Jacob walked to the dressing room, ignoring a voice calling his name. He was looking forward to his after-game hot shower, the water pounding his tired muscles. Almost as good as playing. Still, the voice kept after him. In the shower the guy cornered him. "Where'd you learn to play like that?"

"Soccer's the national pastime where I come from. Kids start kicking balls almost as soon as they learn to walk. Besides, once you have a ball, you only need a space to play; any empty lot will do. "

"I notice you're always the first one on the field."

"I like to practice."

"Guess you thought about being a professional, huh?"

"Not for long. I may be good but there are lots of guys much better than me where I come from."

"Must be nice to be chosen first."

"I guess." He wished the guy would leave him alone.

"How about some lessons if I can get there early?"

They didn't understand. The way he played wasn't only skill, it was passion. On the field, nothing mattered except the exhilaration of kicking a ball into a net. Maybe he should have tried to play professionally.

15

The writing in the diary changed from neat, carefully scripted words to scribbles.

Dear Diary.

I can't bear to write the words but maybe if I do it will make them real. Ok. I'll write them. Avi is not coming back. Avi is not coming back. Avi is not coming back. I could write them a hundred times and my mind still screams NO! HE PROMISED HE WOULD COME BACK TO ME. I don't know what happened. I just know that if he was coming back he would be here by now. The war has been over for six months.

To make matters worse, Minnie's been pushing this guy on me. She says I look terrible. By her, what I need is a man in my life. She's right. I do need a man. I need my Avi. Every time I hear her talk about this guy it sounds like she's describing a nothing. Minnie keeps telling me he's a good man. He'll take care of me. What does she know? By her, any man who has a steady job is a good man. What about love? Oh Avi—

I stared at the page. Now I understood why my mother had hidden the diary. But why did she keep it? Why didn't she throw it out when she got married? What if my father had found it? And read it? Then again, maybe he had. Was that why he was always taking me on little trips instead of my mother? Without my mother? I began to sweat, seeing myself walking next to my father, him buying me a rose and holding my arm like I was his girlfriend. I pushed away the thought and picked up a letter, also undated, just like her diary entries. It was in an envelope marked: "Returned—address unknown."

My Dearest Darling Avi,

Already I miss you more than I can bear. How will I get through the days and weeks until you come home? I know you told me not to worry, that no matter how long it takes you will come back to me. Life without you is beyond horrible. I'm not really alive. I just go through the motions so no one can see how I feel. Please dearest, take very good care of yourself. I miss you more than you could imagine. You have to come back to me.

The highlight of my day is when the mail comes, just before I go to work. I make sure I'm there before Papa so I don't have to explain to him why I get letters from Europe. It's my business, not his. You say so little in your letters about where you are and what you're doing. Your silence makes me worry. Please my dearest, tell me where you are and I'll send this letter to you by return mail. In the meantime, I keep writing. I put them in a box to keep them safe until I can send them to you when I have your new address.

Your loving Sadie

To keep the letters in the order my mother had written them I numbered each entry. As I wrote the number fourteen my eyes were caught by the first lines.

Avi darling,

I am going crazy. My period is late. Two months! I've never been late before. What if I'm pregnant? I told you we should get married before you left, just in case. You said you couldn't do it, that it wouldn't be right. But if I'm pregnant? Please, can't you at least send me your address? If I knew where you were I'd come to you no matter what I had to do to get there.

Your frightened Sadie

My mother had sex before marriage? After all the lectures she gave me? Was that what she couldn't tell Minnie? Was she pregnant? Did she have an abortion? Wouldn't Minnie have known if she'd given birth to a baby and then given it away? Too many questions and no answers. I read the entry again and again, but I couldn't connect "your frightened Sadie" to my mother. Why did she treat me like a whore after my abortion? Why wouldn't she talk to me or comfort me when she knew firsthand how miserable I was? I thumbed through empty pages until I noticed more writing, even harder to read than the previous entries.

Diary,

I'm in big trouble. Yesterday, Papa took Mama to the hospital. He says that when she's ready to come home I have to quit my job and take care of her because he can't afford a nurse. Going to work is just about the only time I get out of the house without him asking a hundred questions about where I'm going and when I'll be back and and and. I'll kill myself if I have to stop working. Papa says he can't ask Lilly because she has her own family to take care of. I don't want to get married but I can't think of any other solution except running away from home and I'm too scared to do that. Papa's already talking about me as if I'm an old maid. Oh Avi, why couldn't you have taken me with you? No matter what would have happened, anything would be better than this.

Good grief. What a reason to get married. And they stayed married. What kind of marriage did they have? All those endless evening meals, the silence broken only by "Heshie, pass me the salt." "Is the gravy hot enough?" "How was school today?" "Sadie, I won't be home for dinner tomorrow, I have a meeting after work." What would our lives have been like if she had married Avi? Who would I be? The writing in the next entry was so small I had to get a magnifying glass to read it.

Dear Diary,

Yesterday Minnie and I took a walk in the park after work and she reminded me for the millionth time that the guy she's been telling me about keeps asking to meet me. I couldn't stand it. I was so angry I asked her if he's such a great guy why didn't she marry him? She looked hurt and reminded me she already has a man in her life. What can I do? Even if he's the most boring person I ever met I might have to marry him. I don't know what else to do. I'm too scared to kill myself. What if Avi should come back? I don't want to be another Juliet. I told Minnie if he came to the dance on Saturday I would dance with him. That's only four days from today. I wish I believed in God.

What would I do if I were that desperate? Would I marry a man just to get away from home? I pushed away the image of an angry Max crashing into my body. Of me trying to pretend it wasn't happening. Of me thinking if only I were a better wife—

Dear Diary,

Time is running out. Papa and I had a terrible big fight when I told him I wouldn't quit my job. He said I was ungrateful and a bad daughter. Usually when Papa is mad at me I don't say much. I'm afraid of his temper. When he gets really mad he beats me with his belt and Mama never says anything. Even now, when I'm old enough to fight back, something stops me. I think I must be a bad person because I dream about hitting him with his belt so he'll know what it feels like. He's such a bully. If he doesn't get what he wants when he wants it, watch out! I'm such a coward. Maybe he's right. Maybe I am selfish.

There were no more entries. I shuddered. What did she do with her feelings so Minnie wouldn't know how she felt? Could she have learned to pretend so well she didn't know how to stop? Did she want to stop? Did she ever think about it? How did she turn into my mother?

I was spooning muffin batter into pans when Paulus appeared. "Well, well, Sleeping Beauty is not only awake, she's baking goodies?" I flushed and poured him a cup of coffee.

"Be careful, I could get used to this."

There's that flirting tone again.

"Tell me, would it be utterly churlish to ask if this is a special occasion?"

"Nope," I said, putting the muffin pans into the oven. Ignoring his puzzled looks I gave him a small stack of pages. "Have a look."

"What is this?"

"I wrote it early this morning."

"What's the matter?" he asked as my demeanor visibly changed. "Just a second ago you were dancing on air. Now you look like you're drowning in garbage."

"That's probably a more apt metaphor than you know," I sighed, checking the muffins, my back to Paulus. *Shit, old behavior.* "Can I read it to you?"

"Sure." He settled himself into the chair, sipping and listening.

"It was the time before time — You're absolutely sure you're not bored?"

He laughed. "You read half a sentence. What's to be bored? Look, I'm no literary critic. If you want to read, read."

I read, losing awareness of everything except the words in front of me. "Now, souls are weighed as they move through the passage, allowing Great One to balance blessings and curses forever."

I watched him, waiting for his response. When I couldn't stand the silence, I said, "After I wrote it, I felt incredibly peaceful. Am I being weird?"

Paulus munched on a muffin. "Not by my standards."

I felt elated. "Want to dance?"

"Don't know how." He buttered another muffin.

"Of course you do. Dance is our natural birthright. It's the dance teachers who say you don't know how."

"Teachers—maybe," said Paulus, "but a whole lot of girls for sure."

I turned on the radio. "C'mon, dance with me."

"Is that part of our contract?"

"No." I turned off the music.

He went into his room and closed the door. Drawers slammed. Muffled muttering.

I sat down in my chair, taking comfort from my grandmother's needlepoint. Although the stitches weren't perfect, the colors were still glorious and vital, just as she was, even when she was old. I thought about what my mother had written in her diary about her mother. Sounded like she didn't have an easy time of it. Like grandmother, like mother, like daughter? Was misery passed on through our genes? If so, for how many generations? What would it take to stop it?

*****

I'm too scared to give Momma the note I brought home from my teacher saying I talk too much in class. I can't bear for her to know I've been bad, so I ask Grandma to sign it using Momma's name. She says, in her thickly accented voice, "Darling, your teacher will know, believe me. This is not a good idea. You will get into more trouble."

"No, she won't. She just needs a grown-up's signature." I keep at her until she signs the note. She sighs. I snuggle into her ample breasts, waiting for the story that always comes when the two of us are intertwined. This one is a Yiddish story about a poor man who borrows a silver spoon from a rich man and returns it with two, saying, "The spoon gave birth to a daughter," which of course, the rich man is pleased to accept. The next time the poor man borrows a candlestick he returns three, saying, "The candlestick gave birth to twins." The rich man is so happy that the next time the poor man asks to borrow a few dishes he gives him his best set. When the poor man doesn't return the dishes the rich man demands to know where his dishes are. The poor man says, "I'm sorry to tell you but the set had a miscarriage and the mother died." The rich man is so furious he takes the poor man to the magistrate who listens carefully before making his judgment. "If a spoon can give birth to a daughter, and a candlestick can give birth to twins, a set of dishes can certainly have a miscarriage. Case dismissed."

"But Grandma, what does that have to do with faking momma's signature?"

"Do you feel better, Annale?" I nod. "That's what it has to do with."

*****

I stroked the needlepoint and smiled. Even remembering the story made me feel better. It reminded me of another story she told me. About a month after Grandpa died, Grandma told me she went to her rabbi because she felt broken. Nothing made sense any more. He told her that according to the Kabala, in the beginning, creation took the shape of a beautiful bowl filled with light. But as creation continued, the light so filled the bowl it cracked and fell to earth, shattering into a zillion pieces. Consequently, the world is imperfect, chaotic, and in disrepair. Human beings are born into a world in need of healing and we all have the responsibility to mend what is broken, piece by piece, fragment by fragment, as best we can. Then, when we are dying, we will know we have done what we could do to leave the world more whole than it was when we were born. He told her it was called *Tikkun*, the Hebrew word for repair. So we're not born perfect and we're not born into a perfect world. Right from the beginning, the rabbi told my grandmother, we face a rough road. It's up to each one of us to do what we can, in our own way, to make the world a better place than it was for us.

How did I forget that story? And how could I forget what Grandma told me after she finished the story? Smoothing my hair and kissing my forehead, she said, "You see, *mein shaineh maidele*, even you don't have to be perfect."

The telephone rang, shattering the peaceful moment. Shirley's voice got my attention. "Dr. Heisenfelzer said to tell you she scheduled double bone marrow tests for you at the hospital Monday morning at nine. You'll need to go to the oncology outpatient service department on the fourth floor. If you have a fever of over one hundred degrees, you'll have to cancel. Let the hospital know at least twenty-four hours ahead of time. Any questions?"

I put down the phone, noticing a crack in the wall I hadn't seen before.

Paulus came in. "What's happening?"

"I have to have bone marrow biopsies on Monday."

"What's that for?"

"To get a sample of my bone marrow so the doctors can see what the cells look like. This is supposed to help them figure out why my blood counts are so low. The big question is if. Sometimes all they get is dry marrow which doesn't tell them much of anything except my bone marrow is abnormal."

"Sounds awful. Is it?"

"Not if your idea of fun is someone drilling into your bones and scooping up samples of your bone marrow."

"Ugh! How long does it take?"

"Depends. If they get what they want on the first try on each side, maybe forty-five minutes. Sometimes they have to keep trying." *And trying – And trying – And trying –* .

"Do you want some time to yourself? I can disappear if you like."

"To be honest, right now, being alone is the last thing I want." *Imagine! Me admitting I need company –* . I stared at the crack. It was definitely growing wider as I watched. "Oh well, I got through it before. I guess I'll get through it again."

"Could you use earphones to listen to a tape? The music might distract you."

"It's a pain that demands attention. Still, it might work. If I had a tape recorder, that is."

"You have a birthday coming up. Now I have the perfect gift."

"How do you know?"

"It's on the prescriptions. You are planning to celebrate your birthday, aren't you?"

"I don't feel much like celebrating."

"Describe your favorite cake."

I shrugged. "What's yours?"

"Chocolate walnut fudge, with curls of bitter chocolate dispersed over hazelnut liqueur mocha filling and frosting with a sprinkling of finely ground hazelnuts on the top and sides."

I shook my head. "Obviously, you haven't given much thought to the matter."

Paulus walked toward the kitchen and then stopped. "No lectures, please. I do not want to hear how I sublimate my romantic fantasies by indulging in a passion for food, or that abstinence is good for the soul. That crap was devised by skinny prisses who never learned to enjoy themselves. So, while I go into the kitchen and return with my latest 'sublimation,' Anna Baum, think carefully about your favorite cake."

"I'm thinking," I joked.

"Good, and while you're thinking, would you mind clearing the coffee table?"

He brought in a pale-green box tied with dark green ribbon, held in place by a gold seal, the trademark of the most expensive and best bakery in town.

Paulus set the box down on the coffee table and stood for a moment gazing rapturously at it. Then he brought in two plates, two forks, two napkins, and the longest knife I owned, all of which he placed around the box on the coffee table. Ceremoniously, he cut the string. "Ta-dahhh," he sang as he opened the box, and inhaled. "Exquisite, isn't it?"

The cake was covered with dark chocolate icing, which in turn was covered with dribbles of a lighter brown icing and sliced hazelnuts in a spiral design. In the center was an arrangement of different kinds of sliced chocolate that looked like a modern sculpture.

"Wow! It's gorgeous. What's the occasion?"

"I came, I saw, I bought. And soon, I eat."

I stared at Paulus. His whole countenance was transformed.

"I want you to know this is one cake that tastes even better than it looks." He sliced a piece, big enough for three or four people, and gave it to me. "Eat, in good health."

"That's too much, Paulus." He looked hurt, but the next piece wasn't much smaller. *Am I paying for this?* He ate, relishing each bite. "Let me get this straight. You just bought this cake? For no reason?" I couldn't help myself. "It must have cost a fortune."

He scowled, and then gave himself back to the rapture of eating. "It's a present, Anna, for both of us. Enjoy!" He cut himself another piece, equally enormous, and ate it as blissfully as he had the first. When not even a crumb remained on his plate, he sighed. "Tell me," he asked, "what's your idea of a perfect cake?"

I hesitated. *To hell with bad memories of awful birthdays.* "Lemon cake with lemon orange filling, covered with slightly sweetened vanilla whipped cream mixed with bits of lemon peel, and whole strawberries all over the top and sides. If fresh strawberries are out of season, frozen ones just on the top will do perfectly well."

"Awright!" he crowed, visibly pleased.

I felt rather pleased myself as I licked icing off my fingers.

The phone rang. When I picked it up the voice said, "Anna, call me back."

I cut a not-so-small slice of cake and ate it before dialing. "Are you all right?" I asked when my mother said, "Hello?"

"It's a long time I haven't heard from you. I'm not getting any younger."

I gritted my teeth. "How are you feeling?"

"How should I feel? I'm seventy-seven years old."

What does seventy-seven feel like? "How's your arthritis?"

"It hurts. So what's new?"

My good will was fast disappearing. "How's the weather?"

"The weather is the weather — it does what it wants. When are you coming to see me? Like a real daughter."

"I told you, I've been sick."

"You want sick, I'll show you sick."

Touching my grandmother's needlepoint inspired me. "You know, I'm so pleased you gave me Grandma's needlepoint; her work is exquisite and the colors are still vibrant. I love it. Did she make any others?" No answer. "Ma, are you there?"

"Yeah, I'm here. Call me back."

I stuffed another piece of cake in my mouth first. "Why the silence?"

"Stop going on about 'Grandma's needlepoint.' It's enough already."

"What's wrong with admiring her artistry?"

"I don't want to talk about it."

"Why not?" More silence, this time longer than the last one. "Mother, talk to me." Silence. "Mother?" Silence. "Will you please tell me what's wrong?"

"Okay, you asked, I'll tell you. Grandma didn't make the needlepoint."

"She didn't? Then who did?"

Another long silence followed by a deep sigh. "I did."

"What? You made it? When—?"

"I knew if I told you you'd be after me with a million questions."

"But Mother, you're an artist!"

"Artist schmartist!"

"It's beautiful. Your color sense—"

"Okay, now you know. No more talk about it." Silence. "I'm glad you still like it."

"I love it."

"This is costing money. Call me again. Soon."

I've been loving my mother's work? "Good night, Mother. Sleep well." I touched the tapestry as I had done for years. *Why did she lie?*

For the next few days I replayed the conversation. Questions bombarded me. Memories assailed me. Enough missing pieces to make a huge quilt.

I called Miriam. "Any chance you might have time for a lesson today, or is this too short notice?" My fingers ached to make something.

"I'm doing a firing so I have to be here. Two o'clock works best for me."

"You sure it's no bother?"

"Yup, only I better warn you, I'm so steamed I could spit. Not a great time to work on a delicate pot."

"What happened?"

"My mother's lonely. I can't bring back my father. All I can do is listen and be kind and patient. One day it'll be me who's old."

"Try talking to my mother. Conversation with a stone would be easier."

Miriam sighed. "Pounding clay sounds like a good idea for both of us."

She was on the phone when I walked in. "Mamale, it's not a good time. I'm in the midst of a firing and my student is here. I'll call you back tonight, after supper. Yes, I promise. Look, I really have to go. I love you too." Miriam shook her head and handed me a chunk of clay.

"Pound," she advised, "it's a great way to get rid of frustration." I threw it against a wooden plank to soften it and kept throwing. Most satisfying.

"Miriam, do you love your mother?"

She nodded. "What about you?"

I stared at the clay. "I dream of making my own dishes."

She gave me a funny look. "Well, let's start with centering. It's not easy so take your time. Enjoy the feel of the clay and the rhythm of the wheel."

She was right. It was difficult. I used a wire to take off one lopsided mess after another but after a while I noticed that the movement of my feet was connecting with my hands. I felt a sense of power. No matter how many times the clay crumpled or tilted I kept going, fascinated by the shapes my hands and fingers were creating. Miriam and I developed an easy rhythm; she showed me a technique and I practiced. My fingers acted as if they'd been searching for clay forever, yearning to mold and press and pull.

I put a small piece of clay on the wheel and paid attention to the way I was pedaling and forming and shaping. It felt good. I felt good. Although the little bowl that emerged was slightly lopsided, I liked it and continued to shape it. I felt Miriam's presence but kept going. When there was nothing more I knew to do, I used the wire to release the pot, which was sturdy, if not beautiful. I wondered if I should crumple it. Not now. This time it would feel like murder.

"Just in case you have any ideas about crushing this," Miriam said as she took it from me. "It's a fine first effort." *I want to hear it's extraordinary, that I have amazing and hitherto unknown talent –* She looked at her watch. "I'll keep your pot here and fire it with my pots if that's okay with you."

My grin was my answer.

Helping her clean up, I said, "This is more fun than I've had in years. I can't begin to thank you. How much do I owe you?"

"I'd prefer to think about what we can barter. So far, I've gotten bookcases, chairs, my teeth cleaned, a dress – lots of things, all in exchange for pots. Very cost effective."

I started to say, "What do I have to offer?" but changed my mind. "It's up to you."

Miriam snorted.

I took one last look at my pot and blew it a kiss.

Miriam grinned.

I hummed as I walked up the street, thinking I would take a cab home. The sun's warmth brought a smile to my face. I sniffed the smell of streets washed clean by rain, nature's reminder to us city dwellers that spring matters. The return of possibility. I was thinking about my possibilities when I bumped into a pedestrian. Mumbling an embarrassed, "Excuse me, I'm very sorry," I started to walk away. A hand grabbed my arm. I heard his voice and felt the all-too-familiar fear and panic. *Don't hit me — I didn't mean it.* I forced myself to stand tall.

"Anna, this is amazing. Must be fate."

Yeah, bad karma. "Hello, Max." I tried to walk away but he blocked my path.

"What's the matter? So busy with your new boyfriend you can't stop for a moment to talk with your old love and former husband?"

"He's not my—" I caught myself. Old anger and defensiveness flared up as if I'd seen him yesterday. A thousand glib responses should have flashed through my mind.

"I must say, Anna, you can do better than him. You're still a good-looking woman. I didn't think short, fat, and bald was your type." *He thinks I'm good-looking!*

I forced myself to breathe. "That was part of the problem, wasn't it? You never listened long enough to know what I wanted."

"And my former darling, what was the other part?"

I decided not to wait for his inevitable putdown. "I have to go." I pushed by him, almost bumping into someone else, but this time I apologized and kept moving.

In the café, original paintings hanging on the wood-paneled walls caught my attention. I ordered a tall double latte and found a corner table beneath an abstract oil painting with swirling shapes of brown that reminded me of Boonah. I thought about my encounter with Max. At least this time, I had held my own, sort of.

Glancing toward the door, I wasn't prepared to see Paulus walking into the café with a woman. Tall, dark, and handsome were the words that came to mind, along with pangs of jealousy. What was Paulus doing with a woman almost a head taller than him? *What am I doing, being so prejudiced?*

"Anna, what a surprise!" They came over to my table. "Anna, I'd like you to meet Anja. Do you mind if we join you?"

Yes. "Of course not." I moved to make room for them and managed a weak hello. At least the woman, who was even more gorgeous close up, took my mind off Max. I was no competition for her. *Why should you be?*

"Paulus, do I really have time for coffee? I can't be late for this interview," she said. "I'm tired of his snide remarks." *Whose?*

"Anja, you need the coffee. You have the time," he said good-naturedly.

I waited for her to ask me questions but she talked about the new café and the seafood restaurant that the owners, friends of hers, were planning to open upstairs. *You could ask her questions.* "I find the artwork very interesting, sort of unusual to see outside a museum," I ventured awkwardly. She grinned.

"They're Anja's," said Paulus. "Show her a painting from your portfolio." It reminded me of my grandmother's needlepoint—*my mother's needlepoint.* The more intently I looked, the more there was to see, the more I wanted to keep looking. "I really like this. What inspired it?"

"Kaleidoscopes. What I find so fascinating is that you can change the arrangement as you turn the glass but you're always working with the same stuff, whatever's in that particular kaleidoscope. I have quite a large collection; some of the best came as presents when I was a kid. The oldest are the most spectacular."

"Do you also work at the paper?"

She laughed a deep, rich laugh. "No."

I waited, discomforted by the terse answer. Anja smiled ruefully. "I laughed because I'm a horrible writer. I can hardly put together a brief bio for the back of my book, much less a coherent story. Although Paulus is a good teacher, I seem to be a very poor student, much too slow a learner." *Are you in love with your teacher?* She looked at her watch. "Paulus, darling, could you get me a double espresso? If we wait for the waiter, we could be here all day." *Darling?*

"Your wish is my command." He grinned. She smiled. Her eyes were a deep green, so beautiful I had to avoid staring.

Jealousy, go away! "May I ask what you do?"

When she answered, she looked at me as if we were the only two people in the world. *No wonder Paulus is smitten.* "I'm a painter and an illustrator. I'm due to meet my publisher in a few minutes, and it's not a meeting I'm looking forward to. Paulus decided coffee and a piece of chocolate almond cheesecake would help calm my nerves."

"How did you meet Paulus?"

"Across a crowded room." She laughed. "Actually, I was starving, in a restaurant with no empty tables. When I saw a guy sitting by himself at a table for two my growling stomach propelled me to ask if he would mind sharing his table. And he said—"

"The curse of being single is having to eat alone. I'd be delighted if you joined me," continued Paulus as he set an espresso and a piece of cheesecake in front of Anja.

She practically inhaled the steaming liquid and gulped down the cake. Standing up, she said, "I'm off. Wish me luck!" I watched her saunter towards the door, oblivious to the stares of men and Paulus, his face a mask.

"Oh, before I forget," said Paulus still watching Anja, "Pilar phoned. She says to call her as soon as possible."

"What's the matter?" *Has the substitute teacher been hired to take my place full time?*

"She didn't say, but she sounded pretty upset."

I headed for the pay phone, aggravated that I had to wait until two people ahead of me finished chattering. Pilar thanked me for calling back so quickly. "We have a new child, Tamaqua, and she has only one hand. The children are teasing her something terrible. Nothing I've done helps. She's a lovely child; her mother's Thai and her father's West Indian, nice people. I spoke with them but they say it's always like this. I feel so bad for her. It would be terrific if you wrote a story for Tamaqua. You know, something about a girl with one hand who no one likes until she does something so spectacular everyone is forced to see how good and kind and worth knowing she really is?"

The substitute teacher is still a substitute. I laughed. "You mean where the kid single-handedly saves people from the burning building? Oops, pardon the pun."

"We have to do something, Anna. You should see her. She's only four years old and sweet as can be, yet she looks so sad, always hiding her arm."

"I need to think of something we can read to the children without throwing up."

"I'll pick the story up during my lunch break so I can read it to the class after their nap."

"Pilar Escondido!"

"You can do it, Anna." She hung up.

When I told Paulus what Pilar wanted, he laughed. "My dear, the world is conspiring to help you see yourself as others see you?" I punched his arm playfully which he graciously acknowledged by returning the favor. "As an inspiration, I'll treat you to another latte. And while we're at it, how about a slice of hot apple pie, with French vanilla ice cream? A little hot caramel fudge sauce sloshed over the top. And it couldn't hurt to add a few toasted walnuts, ever so lightly sprinkled—"

"Paulus, you are incorrigible." This time I didn't say no. "What about one for each of us? My treat. Oh, and when you order, tell them not to spare the walnuts."

Truth and Consequences

Anja watched the elevator numbers rise. The closer she got to his office, the angrier she felt. He was a good editor, but sometimes his taste in writing turned her off. She wondered how they worked together as well as they did. The door opened and she strode out, stopped, and composed herself. It wouldn't do to get his back up, especially if Diana Clark, his "newest find," was more than just another writer on his list.

Robert Blair was standing in the outer office looking through page proofs when she entered. "Anja, what a surprise. You're here so early," he teased. "Didn't even get to finish the chapter."

She flushed. Everyone knew she worked late and sometimes lost track of time, especially for early meetings. "I asked to talk with you before you left for Boston because we have a big problem."

"What don't I know?" he asked, looking amused.

"Can we talk privately? I'd like to show you some drawings."

"Sure," he said, leading her into his office. The walls were filled with framed illustrations of successful children's books he'd edited and published. Robert Blair was proud of his books and his reputation. Awards of various sizes sat on a large coffee table, evidence of his success. "What's up?"

Anja tried to think of a diplomatic way to describe the problem. "I've been working on Diana's book—"

"Super, isn't it? She's one of the finest children's writers I've seen in a long time. I believe her work will be very well received. She's already got ideas for three more books. The two of you make a great team."

Anja's heart sank. This was going to be even harder than she imagined. "Well, Robert, I'm sorry to have to tell you this, but I'm having difficulties with her story. It's almost impossible to illustrate."

"Why? Her writing is wonderfully descriptive."

Anja spoke carefully. "That's part of the problem. Her work

makes visual images superfluous. She'd do better to write for a magazine."

"Ridiculous. Let me see what you have." He looked annoyed.

Anja started to open her portfolio and stopped. Why pretend? The worst he could do was fire her. "Robert, we've worked together for four years, and in that time we've had our disagreements. So far we've been able to work them out and I hope we'll continue to do so."

"Sounds ominous. What am I missing?" he asked warily.

Anja hesitated then plunged in. "I don't like Diana's writing. Frankly, I think it's a bad book and I'm not going to illustrate it. I don't want my name associated with hers."

Amazement turned to anger. "I don't understand. She's an excellent writer. By all accounts and any standard of judgment, she's a very talented woman."

Yeah, and big tits don't hurt, Anja thought. "Maybe she is, but I can't illustrate a book that doesn't engage my imagination."

"It's the children's imagination we want to engage."

"I'm not going to argue with you. I won't continue working on it."

"Just like that? Aren't you the one who's always saying, 'Let's talk. Let's negotiate.' Why not now? I really like her work."

"I know," said Anja, trying to keep the edge out of her voice.

"So that's it? What am I supposed to tell her? She's under the impression that everything is all set. And so was I."

"If you can't tell her the truth, tell her my current project is taking longer than I thought and you've decided you need to choose another artist."

"Do you have a current project?" he asked sarcastically.

Anja lied. "I think so. I've met a new writer who's shown me some of her writing."

"What's her name? Maybe I know her work."

Shit, thought Anja, lying takes too much energy. "I don't think so, she hasn't been published yet. I'll work with her while I finish McKeever's book. She has a wonderful imagination and an interesting voice."

"I don't understand why you can't trust my judgment. Surely I don't have to point out all the awards my books have won. I'm well known in this business for my discerning eye."

Philandering is more like, thought Anja. "My decision is final. I will not illustrate Diana's book."

"Maybe I need to make a final decision as well," he said, turning his back on her.

Anja felt released. All she could think of was "Tit for Tat." Paulus said he knew a new writer whose work was worth looking at. There were other publishers.

16

Thinking about a story that would make Tamaqua feel better rather than singled out stretched my brain but to no avail. I wrote for hours, tearing up every page. Stumped! *Not a useable pun.* What did she call the end of her arm? Stump was such an unfriendly sounding word, yet I couldn't think of an alternative. I remembered fairy tales where the girl's hand is cut off by a father or brother, but in those stories she always gets her hand back and I couldn't do that in my story. What would make her feel better given that she'd always have only one hand? I didn't relish telling Pilar that not only didn't I have a story, I couldn't even think of a way to begin.

Neither awake nor asleep, I heard sounds, like a cat meowing that grew increasingly persistent. Opening the front door, a scrawny black kitten with yellow eyes stared up at me just before it leapt into my arms, snuggled against my shoulder, and purred. The cat had no collar. I stroked it, enjoying the sound until I realized I was standing in the hallway in my nightgown.

"What am I going to do with you?" When I tried to put it down, it clung to my shoulder, digging its claws into me. "Ouch," I yelled, dropping the kitten, which scooted through the open door and under the sofa.

Wonderful, just what I needed, a strange animal wandering around my apartment. I tried to pull the kitten out, but it avoided my hands. "Okay, cat, if I can't drag you out, I'll fix it so you come out by yourself." I poured a small amount of milk into a dish and waited, but not for long. With quiet dignity, the kitten walked to the dish, sat down, and looked at me.

"If you're hungry, eat." The cat sat, looking at me. "What do you want me to do? Read your mind?" I knelt down and stuck my finger into the milk to stir it, thinking to tempt the kitten into drinking. Instead, it licked my finger. I felt inordinately pleased as the rough tongue cleaned the milk off my finger. After dipping my finger into the milk again the kitten licked it clean, looking up at me when there was no more milk. "What's the matter?" I asked, continuing to feed it via my finger, "you don't like to slurp?" When the dish was empty, the kitten sauntered into my lap, curled into a ball, and fell asleep.

"Now what? Am I supposed to sit here all night and watch you sleep?" The sight of the black ball of fur nestled in my lap was irresistible, making it impossible for me to put it out. "Oh, well, I'll worry about you in the morning." I carried the kitten to my bedroom, put it on one of my pillows, and fell asleep to the sound of its gentle snores.

It was late when I woke up. The kitten was still asleep on my pillow. Shaking my head in disbelief, I went into the kitchen to make coffee. It immediately woke up and followed me. On the counter was a note from Paulus:

> My Dear Employer,
>
> Do we have an unexpected houseguest, or have you taken to drinking milk from a saucer on the floor and meowing in your sleep? I hope you don't mind my telling you this, but the last cat I tried to pet bit me. By the way, be careful where you step. There are several messes in the bathroom, but I didn't have time to clean them up.
>
> Paulus

What if it bit him again? What if it had rabies? How would I know? What if it bit me? I picked up the kitten, holding it at arms' length. It wailed. When I put it outside the door the wails increased exponentially. When I opened the door to see if anyone else had noticed or was ready to claim the cat, it streaked in and darted under the sofa. "Okay, cat, you win. Let's hope that wherever you came from was a healthy place."

I closed the door, cleaned up the messes, and phoned Paulus at work. "You're right, we do have a visitor. It appeared last night and I have no idea where it came from. However there is no doubt in its mind where it wants to stay. How afraid of cats are you?"

"It's more than fear. What about rabies? And fleas?"

"I guess if it had fleas I'd know by now. But you're right; I should get it checked out." I was beginning to wish I'd never seen the kitten. "I'll call a vet and make an appointment."

"Maybe you should keep it locked in the bathroom until we know it's healthy?"

"Right now it's under the sofa. I guess that's as good a place as any. If you come back and find me missing, you'll know the cat is gone too." As we hung up, I saw a bit of black tail swishing, as if it was not pleased with what it was hearing.

Five phone calls later I was scrambling to get dressed, call a cab, find a box, make holes in it, and convince the kitten that out from under the sofa was where it wanted to be. By the time I got it in the box, it had stuck its head through one of the holes. Visions of a cat running loose in the cab were not amusing, so I taped over the holes to make them smaller, and in the process caught a whisker. The kitten yowled and I cursed, but we made it into the cab with only a few indignant meows. The cab driver looked at the box. "What you got in there?"

"A cat that thinks it has the right to choose where it lives."

He grunted. "That's a cat all right."

I'd never been in a veterinarian's office before. As a child, no one I knew had a pet and it never occurred to me to want one. I looked around and noticed the pet owners soothing, stroking, and patting their animals with attention and concern. I couldn't help wishing parents would show their children as much love.

The vet was a young woman who began speaking to the kitten before it was even out of the box. She had a soft alto voice that had a noticeably soothing effect on the cat, who watched the vet's every move as she carefully took it out of the box and put it on the scale. It barely weighed six pounds. "I'm Dr. Keyes. What's the kitten's name?"

I was stumped for a moment. "How about Mystery? I have no idea where it came from or how it got outside my door. I can call it Mys for short."

"What if Mys is a Mister?" laughed the vet.

"I guess you'd know better than I would. And if Mys is a Miz, let's get her fixed, if she isn't already." Ready or not, Mys was mine.

My surprising desire to keep the kitten was stronger than the increasing awareness that I knew next to nothing about how to care for an animal. I continued to surprise myself. Passing a hobby shop, I gave in to my yearning to make more pots, went in, and bought two large packages of clay that could be baked in the oven.

When I got home I saw that Pilar had left a message on my machine. "I'm planning to come get your story today." I gasped. With all the excitement about the cat I'd forgotten about the story. I hung up and started writing. *Thank you, Mys.*

There was once a little girl who had two eyes, two ears, two legs, and two arms, but only one hand. Her right arm ended at her wrist. Everyone stared at it when she went out to play, to a store, to visit family. In school, no one wanted to touch her wrist. When the teacher told children to hold her arm they made faces or whispered nasty words. Wearing an artificial hand, a prosthesis, didn't make things better. Her momma and poppa tried to help, but they could not stop the stares and teasing. Finally, the little girl refused to go outside to play. She hated school and cried every morning as she walked to the bus stop.

One day, while the little girl was playing with her dolls, she heard a loud meow but couldn't find where the sound was coming from. When she opened the front door, in ran a black blur that turned out to be a skinny kitten.

Her momma poured milk into a dish. The kitten just sat next to it, meowing. Her poppa got an eyedropper and filled it with milk, yet when he tried to squirt milk into the kitten's mouth, the kitten ran under the sofa.

The little girl picked up the dish of milk but as she walked toward the sofa, she tripped. Milk spilled all over her arm. She sat on the floor, wondering what to do. The kitten came out from under the sofa and began licking her wrist, the wrist with no hand. The little girl watched. When the kitten licked all the milk off her wrist it meowed. The little girl dipped her wrist into a milk puddle and once again, the kitten licked her wrist clean.

She called to her momma and poppa. "Look, the kitten is slurping milk from me." When the dish was empty, the kitten licked itself clean and curled up in the little girl's lap. Snuggling against her wrist, it purred and fell asleep.

"You saved the kitten's life," said her momma.

"The kitten loves you," said her poppa.

"That's right," said the little girl, stroking her kitten.

Not bad for a first draft. At least I had something to give Pilar. I wondered about using the word prosthesis but decided to keep it in. It was a word the children should know. I plopped down on my bed to rest and fell asleep, only to be woken up by a nightmare in which I was drowning in torrents of blood. I opened my eyes, expecting the moisture to disappear but it didn't. I looked under the covers and saw large red stains. Too stunned to move, I lay there, cold and wet. The phone rang. The world was spinning as I struggled to pick up the receiver. A voice was coming from a far-off place, but my tongue was on strike. Everything went black.

I woke up in the hospital with Paulus staring at me. Once again I was connected to tubes filled with various colored liquids flowing into me.

He spoke calmly. "You had a hemorrhage and fainted while you were talking to Pilar. She called me and I phoned for the ambulance."

"Hemorrhage?"

"Try not to worry. Dr. H. will be in as soon as she can," he said, trying to be reassuring but not succeeding.

Dr. Adams walked into the room and my heart lurched. I could hear myself gasping for breath. "Hello, Ms. Baum," his voice was pleasant. "How are you feeling?"

I tried to mask my fear. "I'd be lying if I said I never felt better."

"I can imagine. Waking up in a pool of blood is not my idea of fun."

"I don't understand. How can somebody just start bleeding?"

"With your platelet counts so low, even a normal period can turn into a hemorrhage. Judging by your counts and color, Dr. Heisenfelzer and I agree you need a transfusion. We've ordered four pints."

"But what about AIDS? Hepatitis?"

"Don't worry. We have an excellent testing program."

"I'll give blood to Anna," offered Paulus.

Dr. Adams looked pleased. "How does it feel to be so popular?" *Am I hallucinating? Is Dr. Adams smiling at me?*

Dazed, I murmured, "It feels fine. I mean I'm very lucky." *Has he had a heart transplant?*

"Mr. Barszinsky, if you want to donate blood, speak to the head nurse and she will make the necessary arrangements." He turned to leave, then stopped. "Ms. Baum, I'm sorry about this setback, but I've studied your records. I still believe you'll make a splendid recovery." *He's been cloned. They gave him an emotional enema.*

As he left, Emma came in, her face a mixture of smile and worry. "Emma!" I croaked. "That can't be the one and only Dr. Adams. Did he get an attitude transplant?"

"He got married. For the first time. At his age. Can you imagine?" She grinned. "Just think what a regular dose of you-know-what can do for the soul."

"Unbelievable!"

Paulus looked relieved. "With Emma here you're in good hands. Try to rest. I'll make sure the children get the story, and I'll see you after work unless you need me sooner."

Emma teased, "I must say, my girl, if you wanted to see me so badly you could have called and invited me over." Her voice grew serious. "What happened? Last I knew you were doing just fine."

"I don't know. One minute I'm taking a nap and the next thing I know I'm lying in blood. What's wrong with me?"

She turned away and tidied up the already neat bed table. "Whatever questions you have, you need to ask Dr. H."

"You don't want to tell me."

"It's a question for your doctor to answer."

"It is leukemia, isn't it? That's why my counts are so low." I took a deep breath. "Tell me what you know about leukemia."

"Well," she said carefully, "there are many kinds but only two forms. One is acute. The person is in a critical stage, in danger of dying. The other is chronic, and there's no immediate danger but it's fatal without treatment. In some forms of leukemia there are too many white cells, in others not enough. Diagnosing leukemia can be tough because the symptoms are often similar to other diseases."

"So what kind do I have?"

"I don't know."

"Acute or chronic? At least tell me that much."

"All right, but this is absolutely the last question I'll answer. They think it's chronic. That's why the docs didn't treat you immediately. They figured you had some time and wanted you to recover from the pneumonia."

"What's the name of what I have?" She checked the blood transfusion. I panicked. The urge to hide my arm and refuse further transfusion was overwhelming. "I want to go home."

"You need the transfusion. Your blood counts are life-threatening."

Suddenly an image of my mother's face loomed large in my mind's eye, a hideous grin on it. "Emma, can I tell you something personal, something I've never told anyone, ever?"

"Of course," she said, moving a chair close to the bed. "Go ahead. I'm listening."

"I know this is going to sound weird."

"Where I come from, white people's weird is our everyday normal."

"Well—It's about my mother. I keep seeing her face. She wants me to die with her so she won't be alone. She hovers over me, telling me I'm no good. I'm selfish, a bad daughter. The only way I can redeem myself is to die with her. Sometimes her face is so real I wave my arms to push it away. But nothing's there."

"In Hawaii, we pay attention to what you're seeing. It's a spirit."

Like Boonah?

"There are good spirits and bad spirits. Bad spirits can't stand love," she said.

I stared at her.

"Look, Dr. Adams was different compared to last time you were here, right?" I nodded. "Well, when we act as if we're unlovable, our life spirit, the good spirit, weakens and the bad spirit, the death spirit, gets stronger. Remember when you first came to the hospital?" I nodded, embarrassed. "You turned your back to us and wouldn't let anyone help you. Then, slowly, you began to change. You talked to me. You talked to Jacob. You had visitors. You felt better. So keep on reaching out. It's medicine for the life spirit."

She checked the blood transfusion and found it needed adjustment. The dripping blood held a morbid fascination for me. I barely heard her say, "Get some rest, love. It's been a hard day." She closed the door, leaving me to the horrors of my imagination.

The excruciating throbbing in my arm woke me up. When the door opened, the relief and pleasure I felt at seeing Jacob momentarily dulled the pain. "It's good you're here; my arm hurts something awful."

"Let me take a look." He adjusted the tubes. "Your hand is swollen. I don't like the color. Let's get you some help." I retreated inside myself. I knew I could trust Jacob to take care of me.

Boonah's tone of voice is serious. "Emma is correct about spirits, my love. Listen to her. She knows whereof she speaks."

"Tell me a story, please, about good spirits." I snuggle into his story, wishing my mother's face would disappear.

"In the earliest days, there were twins who lived with their grandmother. They grew up playing with earth and water, learning the flora and fauna of forests and plains so well they could find their way home even when it was as dark as the middle of a moonless night. Secretly, each boy wished there were other people in the world, though neither spoke about this. Both were ashamed of their yearning.

"One day, the eldest twin played with the energy of his unhappiness. He made clay by mixing earth and water. With it, out of the mud and his

misery, he made figures and dwellings. He and his brother crafted a whole village and then gave each villager a name.

"Unbeknownst to them, in doing this, they invoked the wrath of North Wind who, fearing the twins would now try to create life, determined to stop them. Neither boy saw North Wind blow toward them, a cloud twisted red with fury. It engulfed and separated the brothers. North Wind screamed his anger. The twins shouted out apologies but the raging wind refused to listen, hurling their voices into the howling void.

"Only Grandmother heard their cries for help. Though she was old and weak, love for her grandsons strengthened her voice. 'Out of mud and misery my grandsons have built a village of people. I beg you, Great One, let these clay villagers help my grandsons find their way home.'

"Great One breathed life into the mouth of each clay villager. Most received Great One's warm and welcoming breath, but a few were born by the last bit of air that was cold and inhospitable. The spirits born of warmth tried to help the twins find each other, but the spirits born of cold were mean, delighting in keeping the brothers separated and lost.

"The warm air spirits battled the cold air spirits so ferociously they created a wind even more powerful than the North Wind. The good spirits, who outnumbered the bad spirits, sucked the brothers into their midst and reunited them. Avoiding the bad spirits' wiles and tricks, the good spirits helped the twins find their way home.

"Grandmother and grandsons were so happy to see each other they agreed to help Great One by breathing their warm breaths into each newly-shaped clay figure so the good spirits could multiply and prosper.

"People sometimes think there are more bad spirits than good, for cold weighs more than warm, and bad spirits sit heavily on the soul. But good spirits are always with us, ready to help whenever we summon their power."

"Now, dear Anna, sleep in the care of good spirits who watch over you."

"I love you, Boonah."

Boonah?" asked Jacob as he rebandaged my arm. "What's a Boonah?"

Without thinking, I said, "Boonah tells me stories," and immediately wished I'd kept my mouth shut. "It's hard to explain."

"You know, lots of times when kids made fun of me or I'd hurt myself, Mama would sit me on her lap, put her arms around me, and tell me how I never had to feel bad, 'cause if I sat real still and listened real good, I'd hear all the stories I needed to hear. When you feel better, maybe we can talk about this." His words soothed me to sleep.

I woke up to intense throbbing. Agony. My right arm was more swollen and discolored than before. I could barely move my distended fingers. The nurse took forever to answer the call button. "What time does Dr. Heisenfelzer come in?" I asked, my voice trembling from a pain so excruciating it hurt to breathe.

"I think she's due in at five." Her touch was light as she examined the swelling but the increased pressure was unbearably painful.

"It's really hurting. I need to see a doctor now. I'm supposed to get four pints of blood. How much have I had?" Hope and hysteria collided.

"A little more than two," answered the nurse.

"Isn't it taking a very long time?" I asked, trying not to lose control.

"I would have expected it to be finished by now," she admitted.

"I don't think my body likes this transfusion. I think it needs to be stopped. If a doctor won't do it, I will."

The nurse gasped. "You don't mean that." She fiddled with the lines, trying to improve the flow of blood but didn't appear to be having much luck.

"Yes, I do," I said, hoping this was true. "I would greatly appreciate it if you would find a doctor to stop the transfusion now."

"I'll do the best I can, but promise me you won't do anything until I come back. Okay?" The nurse took my chart, waiting until I agreed before she would leave. Looking at my discolored hand strengthened my resolve, and when the nurse brought a young doctor who looked like an intern, I tried to remain calm.

"What's this nonsense I hear about you wanting to stop the transfusion?"

"I can't stand the pain."

"Don't be silly, you need the blood. Be a good girl and stop bothering the nurses. The doctor ordered four pints and that's what you're getting. I'll tell the nurses to put ice on the swelling." He turned and walked toward the door.

I was so mad I had difficulty keeping my voice steady. "Will you at least call my doctor and tell her about my problem?" He nodded, hurrying out with my chart.

The nurse was about to follow him. I hurt too much to care about dignity. "Please," I pleaded, "contact the senior doctor on call. The pain is getting worse."

To calm my rising hysteria I decided to set a time limit—one hour seemed reasonable. It was now ten minutes past four. I would wait until ten minutes past five, and if by then no doctor came, I would take out the needle. I was afraid to stop the transfusion so I tried to help the blood flow into my arm by imagining my breath going into hurting places, opening up blood vessels, removing whatever was impeding the flow. I even tried speaking to the pain. "What can I do to give you respite?" The pain was too busy to respond.

Feeling his familiar caress eases my fears.
"Courage, dear girl, you're doing fine."
"I think something bad is happening to me."
"Remember the story about good and bad spirits. If you summon good spirits to help you, a doctor will come within the hour."
"How can you be so sure?"
Boonah smiles.

It was almost an hour and a half later and I had just about worked up my courage to take out the needle when Dr. Adams walked in. I found myself becoming tense without knowing I'd reacted. My self split into two parts. The angry self was screaming, wanting to know why it took him so long to respond, but my calm self prevailed. "Thank you for coming, Dr. Adams."

"I hear you have a problem." I showed him my swollen, discolored arm. Once again I was surprised at the tenderness with which he examined me, especially when I thought about how the nurse's touch had hurt and the intern didn't care.

"It's been sixteen hours. Isn't that an unusual amount of time for a transfusion of four pints of blood—and it's still not finished?"

"Yes. I'm surprised it's taking so long."

"The nurse told me I've only had half of what I'm supposed to get, but I don't think my body wants this blood." I held out my good arm as if to caress my angry self and was astonished when Dr. Adams awkwardly patted my arm.

"Ms. Baum, I talked with Dr. Heisenfelzer and we agree you need the full transfusion." I was about to interrupt when he continued. "But we also believe it's important to honor your wishes." My jaw dropped open. I couldn't believe I was hearing Dr. Adams correctly, yet there he was, taking out the needle, calling for a nurse to bring ice as he removed the bandage and board on which my arm had been resting. Amazed, I watched him soothingly place the ice on my discolored hand and carefully move my swollen fingers. "We'll leave the ice on for a few minutes, but if you feel any discomfort, take it off immediately. We don't want to exacerbate the damage. The ice should probably be put on and off a few minutes at a time, for at least half an hour, to reduce the swelling. Would you like something for the pain?"

"No thanks, it's already a little better. I think I can manage."

"No need to suffer unnecessarily. It might help you sleep."

Whatever had happened to Dr. Adams, I appreciated the result, and if it was a woman who worked this great miracle, I was ready to sign up for lessons. I saw my angry self becoming smaller, moving closer to my calm self. Both looked at me with huge questioning eyes. I knew they were asking, "What happened?" He was a different person from the last time I was here but I didn't feel right asking him personal questions. Instead, I said, "Dr. Adams, can they do the bone marrow biopsies now? It doesn't make sense to leave and then come back again."

It suddenly occurred to me I might not be leaving so quickly and I panicked. My hands drenched with perspiration. My head ached worse than my throbbing arm.

"It's late, and you're exhausted. Let me talk with Dr. Heisenfelzer in the morning and then we can decide what's best."

I chose my words. "I'd like to be in on that conversation. As you may have guessed, I have a thing about people making decisions for me."

"No problem. I'll arrange for the three of us to talk."

Tears filled my eyes. "Thanks, Dr. Adams. And congratulations on your marriage."

"How did you hear about it?"

"Oh, we patients have our own news network and we never divulge sources."

He smiled as he checked my arm and took off the ice pack.

"Maybe I'll be lucky the next time." I muttered under my breath. "If there is a next time." I didn't realize he'd heard me.

"I have a feeling there will be. Don't worry about the ice. If you fall asleep, sleep. You need the rest. But if your hand is still throbbing when you wake up, put the ice on it for a few minutes. Good night, Ms. Baum. Sleep well."

"Good night, Dr. Adams."

"Bravo," says Boonah, clapping his hands. You are doing well.
I snuggle into his approval.

As if by magic, or perhaps by wishing, I woke up smelling coffee. I thought I was dreaming so I kept my eyes closed, not wanting to be confronted by a less pleasant reality.

"Wake up, sunshine, time to rise and shine," said Jacob, examining my hand. "Business before talk."

"It's much better," I said, sipping the coffee with my good arm. "Look, the swelling's down and the color's better, not so black."

"Watch your tongue, honeychile. Some of us folks think black is just fine," he teased. "Better get you ready, a whole convention is coming to see you in about fifteen minutes." He helped me move my IV into the shower, where the hot water playing on my body was so soothing it put me into a trance. Then I remembered the kitten.

Paulus came into the room carrying a small suitcase with clean clothes. "It's good to see you alive and kicking. I took your bedding to the cleaners. Is that all right?" I nodded, feeling grateful. "You had two messages on the machine. One's from someone named Sarah. The other was from your mother. She wants you to call her immediately." He paused, choosing his words. "I have some bad news." *He got a job. He's leaving.*

"I don't know how to say this, but the cat's gone. I thought it might be hiding but I searched everywhere..."

"It's okay. She's at the vet's, getting fixed. I was supposed to pick her up today." *Why doesn't he offer to pick her up?*

When Dr. Adams and Dr. H. walked in, I thought they both looked grim. She examined my arm, clucking over it in a satisfying manner. "I'm sorry you've had such a bad time, Ms. Baum, but Dr. Adams and I agree we'd better do the bone marrow biopsies as soon as possible." I felt myself drifting off, worrying about my cat.

"Ms. Baum," said Dr. H., "you look as if you're a million miles away from here. What's the matter?"

"I'm sorry," I said, embarrassed, "what did I miss?"

"We need your permission to do the bone marrow tests."

I began to shake uncontrollably.

Dr. Adams tried to reassure me. "It's not such a bad test. I do it all the time on children."

"So? They're brave. I'm a cowardly adult. What if I say I don't want this test?"

Dr. H. said, "Dr. Adams and I will abide by your decision. We're recommending the biopsies to help us diagnose your underlying condition, perhaps what caused the hemorrhage and why your blood counts are so low."

"What's the point of doing another bone marrow test when the others didn't tell anybody much of anything?"

"Not getting cellular material is in itself part of the diagnosis, but Dr. Adams believes he can get some marrow. He has a very good track record."

"You still think I have a form of leukemia?"

"Yes, but we don't know what kind. We'll know more when we see the test results."

"What difference does it make? It's all cancer."

Dr. Adams spoke quickly. "Every cancer is different, as is each leukemia. You have to figure out what you want to do about your illness. When you make up your mind, we can suggest what we think is the most effective course of action."

"Hah! Life seems to do what it wants without consulting me."

"No need to decide right now," said Dr. Adams.

I was too tired to endure more internal debates. "Do what you need to do." My mouth was dry. Drinking half a glass of water didn't quench my thirst.

Emma came in with a tray. "How's it going?"

"I'm about to become a human excavation site. Can you stay with me while Dr. Adams does the test?"

"Yup. Not only that, I'll hold your hand and you can squeeze as hard as you like."

"I wouldn't do that."

"Others do. The offer stands."

My apprehension grew as the technician came in with a larger tray filled with packages whose contents I didn't want to think about. Emma rubbed alcohol on my back, and the cold swabbing of liquid on my skin made me tremble. As Dr. Adams entered I heard her whisper, "Breathe, Anna, from your abdomen."

Dr. Adams tried to reassure me. "I'll explain everything I'll be doing before I do it. If you need me to stop, say 'Stop.' Okay?" I nodded. "I know it sounds ridiculous but try to relax. Tension produces enzymes that make the test harder for me."

"Any recommendations? For relaxing?"

"Sure." He grinned. "Take a deep breath and squeeze Emma's hand. It'll give you something to focus on." He looked at Emma, who nodded. "The first prick will be to numb your skin. You'll feel a little sting."

As the needle pierced, I gasped. "If that's a little sting, what's the rest going to be like?" I could hardly control my panic.

"Try to take a deep breath," she suggested. But between the pain and the relentless pressure from the drilling, it was all I could do to keep from screaming. Only the thought of the needle breaking inside me kept me still.

When Dr. Adams finally said, "I think we have a sample on this side," I felt relief and despair. Half done. Half to come. I was grateful Emma continued to hold my hand. I tried to visualize Boonah, but the pain was overwhelming.

As he switched to my other side I saw that Dr. Adams' face was bathed in perspiration. "How's it going?" I asked to gain a bit of time.

"I don't need to worry about getting exercise today — I'll have had more than my usual workout by the time we're finished." He gave me a concerned look. "I'm ready to start this side. You'll feel a small prick —."

"God save me from small pricks!" When Emma and Dr. Adams laughed, I realized my double entendre and blushed. "You mean I'll feel as if a gigantic bee has mistaken me for its dinner." Dr. Adams chortled. I felt a little better. When it was over, I lay on my back, sweaty, drained, and depleted. My pelvic bones ached and I was nauseated.

"You've done very well. I'm sorry it took so long, but I did have trouble getting material. You're a real trouper, Ms. Baum"

"How soon will I know the results?"

"A couple of weeks. I'll send the slides off to the National Cancer Institute today." He noticed my look of shock. "You can go home tomorrow if all goes well. Right now, I want you to drink the orange juice Emma's bringing you and get some rest. You deserve it."

Alone in my room, I felt as if I'd done battle with a hundred armies coming at me from all directions. Images of Mys loomed, but I'd run out of worry.

"Boonah, will you sit with me until I fall asleep?"
"Of course. Have a good rest."
"Stay with me."
"Sleep well, Luv."

First Night

Sadie's worries escalated. She wasn't a virgin. What if Heshie decided she was damaged goods and turned away from her? What if he wanted more than she could give? What if he was a virgin and didn't know what to do? What if she knew more than he did? She dreaded thinking about what might happen when they were finally alone, with nothing and no one to distract them.

As the last of the guests said goodnight, her fears swallowed her words. All she could do was nod and smile, letting her parents and Heshie do the talking. Minnie was no help. As she left, she hugged Sadie. "I'm so happy for you. Heshie's a good man. You'll make him happy, I know." How could she know so much?

Sadie shivered at the thought of all the people who had gathered to watch her become Mrs. Hershold Baum. Not one of them knew about Avi. Not one of them knew how she felt. Her flushed cheeks burned red. "You are so beautiful," murmured Heshie as he thanked and nodded and smiled. What mirror was he looking in, she wondered. Who did he think he'd married? Sadie had never in all her life felt beautiful, much less looked it, except those times with Avi, when he insisted she accept his compliments.

She fingered the gold chain around her neck, hidden by the high neckline of her dress. Its warmth felt reassuring and at the same time kindled Sadie's feelings of loss. She knew she had no right to complain—she was alive, she was healthy. So she had married a man she didn't love and didn't want—what was any of this compared to what her grandmother had suffered.

Although Heshie couldn't afford to take time off from work for a honeymoon, he tried to make up for it by booking a room for two nights in an elegant hotel in Manhattan. Momma helped her change into street clothes. "Sadie, I never talked with you about—"

Sadie blushed. "Momma—" She wanted to ask what it was like

to be married, to have promised to love, honor, and obey. Papa's insistent knocking on the door made further conversation impossible.

The ride to the hotel was too short and too long. Heshie's arm around her shoulder slowly drifted to her breast, caressing the fullness, moving more intently. She felt herself responding and for a moment, she was back in Avi's arms, touching his face, tasting his lips, holding him tightly, wanting— She tried not to think about the night ahead.

In the hotel bathroom, more elaborate than any she had ever seen, she heard Heshie talking on the phone. Had he gotten a girl in trouble? Had he waited until he was alone to talk to her? Sadie opened the door just as he hung up the receiver, ready to pounce. "I noticed you didn't eat anything all day, so I called room service and ordered dinner for us."

"Isn't that terribly expensive," she asked. "Can we afford it?"

"It's our wedding night. We're celebrating. Nothing's too good for you."

He touched Sadie's cheek. Caught between her imagination and his reality she stiffened when he said, "I can't believe I'm married to such a beautiful woman."

Was he making fun of her? She wanted to say, "Stop with the beautiful already." Why did he keep lying? She felt like crying.

"Would you mind if I take a bath?" Sadie asked. She needed to do something.

"Do you mind if I pour in the bubble bath?" he asked, grinning.

More nervous than ever, she shook her head.

"There's a bathrobe for each of us hanging in the closet." He touched the top button on her blouse. "Shall I help you get undressed?"

Sadie blushed. "Uh, no, I, uh—" She fled into the bathroom wondering how loud the sound would be if she locked the door.

Heshie followed her, turning on the water in the tub, checking the temperature, pouring half the container of bubble bath he had thought to ask the hotel to provide. Sadie wondered what she should do. Frozen, hardly able to breathe, she stood motionless. He began to unbutton the top of her blouse. Not wanting to be the only one naked, she unbuttoned his shirt. They slowly undressed each other, letting their clothes fall around them. Heshie looked at her as if he couldn't believe what he was seeing.

"What's the matter?" asked Sadie, frightened of what he might say. Sure, she was his wife but she didn't have the greatest figure even though she had gone on a diet for a month before the wedding.

Heshie took her cold hands in his. Their warmth was a shock. He helped her into the bath, watching her body disappear in the bubbles. "May I join you?" he asked.

Later that night, lying in bed, their bodies entwined, Heshie said, "I am so lucky, Sadie. You are so beautiful."

She smiled.

17

"Anna? Anna? It's time to wake up." I was being called back from somewhere out in space. The voice took a long time to reach me and when it arrived, I tried to wave it away. Eventually I bowed to its insistence and opened my eyes. "I need to put new dressings on your back. Can you turn over?" Her touch was calming despite the pain. "You did real well, Anna. You can't imagine how some people carry on. One man howled like a baby."

"Especially for a coward, wouldn't you say?" I grinned.

"You're no coward, Anna Baum."

I shrugged and a moan escaped as Emma helped me to lie on my back.

"I know the pain. I once sold my bone marrow when I was broke. I ached for a week."

"You must have needed money pretty bad."

"Yeah," she snorted. "The next time my bank account registered zero I considered prostitution. Seemed an easier way to go."

"Did you?" I put my hand over my mouth, embarrassed.

Emma laughed. "That's what I like about you. Whatever's on your mind, you just ask. No pussyfooting around. Straight ahead and out-front."

"You'd be surprised how often straight ahead is down and out. I get into more trouble than speaking's worth at times."

"People who don't want to hear the truth aren't worth knowing, though Lord knows you have to deal with them more often than not." She gave me the largest glass of orange juice I'd ever seen. "Drink this, love. It'll give you energy. You'll be having visitors pretty soon. Got to help you look your gorgeous self."

I blushed and shook my head, pushing away the compliment. She looked disapproving. "You telling me I don't know gorgeous when I see it?"

My eyes filled with water.

"What's the matter?" she asked.

"First I can't cry, then I can't stop. I wouldn't mind a bit of moderation. That can't be too much to ask, can it?"

Emma grinned. "My daddy used to say, 'All things in moderation, even moderation.' Let the tears come, love—they're not bothering anyone."

"They're bothering me."

"That's your problem. No appreciation for how much your inner landscape needs a drenching soak." Emma sounded so much like Boonah I wondered if he talked to her. She responded to my puzzled look. "Where I come from we say that tears quench the soul's thirst. Without tears the spirit shrivels. Who wants a shriveled spirit?"

I laughed in spite of myself.

"Well, it's something you either believe or you don't." As she bathed me I allowed myself to luxuriate in the feeling of the warm water on my body.

"There's still blood oozing from where they stuck the needles in, so you'll need to lie on your back for a while longer."

"Isn't it taking a long time for the bleeding to stop?"

Emma didn't answer. She swabbed my back and put adhesive tape on the dressing.

"More proof it's leukemia, I suppose," I said dryly.

"Girl, you're getting so sharp you might as well join the staff."

"You didn't answer my question."

She helped me into a fresh gown and tidied up the room. I kept staring at her. "You're right. It's not a good sign. Now finish your orange juice like a good girl and let me see what's being ordered for you."

If a male said good girl to me, I'd have a hissy fit; but when she says it, I feel cared for. Amazing. "Emma, you're the greatest."

Stroking my hair, she said, "Don't say I told you so, but I'll take feisty patients who speak up any day of the week. At least I know what's on their mind. Don't go anywhere," she grinned. "I'll be back in a bit to check your dressing." Even the thought was comforting.

I suddenly remembered the messages and decided to call Sarah first. Maybe Minnie had asked to see me.

The phone was busy for a long time. When Sarah answered, her voice was flat. "My mother died at four this morning. The service is tomorrow. Paulus told me you were in the hospital, so I guess you won't be able to come to the funeral."

"Oh, Sarah."

"I knew you'd want to know."

"I appreciate your calling. Are people sending flowers?"

"No, we're establishing a scholarship fund." She paused. "Maybe I have no right but I have a favor to ask of you. A big favor."

"Sure, anything." *What kind of help can I give her?*

"When I called your mother I told her we already had the funeral." I gasped. "I know, they were best friends for sixty years, but your mother wasn't my friend. She never liked me. Besides, she's in Florida; she might not even be able to get here in time. Anyway, if she calls, you don't know anything. Not about her death and certainly not about the funeral. Okay?"

"Okay." *What if I can't pull it off?*

"Thank you. You have no idea how much this means to me."

I dialed, hoping I was a good-enough actress.

"Minnie's dead," my mother said as soon as she recognized my hello.

"What?"

"Sarah called me. After they had the funeral. Which she didn't bother to tell me about."

"Oh, Mother, I'm sorry."

"Yeah, well, we all got to die sometime."

"When was the last time you saw her?"

"Before I left for Florida. I kept asking her to come down here by me. Airlines give big discounts to seniors these days. There was even a nice apartment two doors down on my floor. The right size and a good price too. But could she leave the grandchildren? So, that's that."

"I'm really sorry."

"The two of us, it was like we didn't have to speak, we knew without words. What we thought. What we felt. That Sarah—" There was a long silence. "Who's going to love me now?"

I'm running. No matter how fast I run he keeps coming closer, talking sweetly. I try not to listen. His hands grab my body. He forces me down on to a rug. Pain is pushing its way into me, stretching, tearing. The voice is kind and the words are soft. I cry out, "No," but the pain is searing. The man is lying on top of me. I can't see his face.

I see Boonah and yell for help but no sounds come out. I can't get up. I can't make the pain stop. I hear Boonah command me. "Look, Anna. Look at the face of your nightmare."

I'm afraid to open my eyes. Boonah speaks again, more urgently. "Open your eyes, Anna. Open your eyes now!"

And then, because it is Boonah who is asking, I look. I see the face of the voice.

Am I bad, Daddy? Is Momma right? Do I deserve to be hurt?"

Gasping for air, I woke myself up. Tears were pouring down my face. My gown was soaking wet. Ripping off the covers, I turned on the light. My father's face was everywhere. Memories flooded my mind. Too many, too fast.

*****

"I'm taking Anna for a walk," says Daddy, putting on my sweater.

"I'll go with you," says Momma.

"I thought you were going to see Minnie." Daddy buttons my sweater wrong.

Momma starts to re-button it. Daddy pushes her hand away. "Go see Minnie. I'll take Anna for ice cream. You don't like ice cream."

"I like ice cream. I don't like chocolate ice cream. You keep buying me chocolate."

"I don't want ice cream, Daddy."

"Yes, you do." He takes my hand and we leave.

We walk to a house near the ice cream store. We walk up the steps. "I want to go home, Daddy." I try to turn around, but Daddy holds my hand too tight.

"Daddy's going to tell you a story."

"I don't want a story. I want to go home."

"Don't be silly, Anna. All good girls love stories. You're very lucky. Not every little girl has a daddy who knows so many stories."

"Daddy, please. Can't we go home? I don't want to hear a story."

"After I tell you a story, I'll buy you an ice cream cone."

"I don't want ice cream." I stand still, refusing to walk up the steps.

He carries me up the steps. "What flavor do you like best?"

"Put me down, Daddy. I want to go home." I start crying. Daddy looks around.

"Stop crying. Only bad girls cry. Only bad girls disobey Daddy."

*****

I don't want to think about what happened next.

"It's the past, Anna. If you look now it will stop haunting you. I am here. I am with you. Give me your hand. You have the courage to look."

"Boonah, I'm too frightened."

"Daddy cannot hurt you. Look! Your life depends on it."

I look.

*****

I see Daddy unlock the door, still holding me in his arms. He puts me down. I try to run away but he grabs me. "Stop!" he says. He takes the sweater off my frozen body. His voice turns sweet. "Daddy and Anna are going to have a nice time. Daddy's going to tell you a lovely story." He takes off his jacket and his shirt and his tie. He takes off his belt. He unzips his pants and takes them off. He folds them neatly. He puts them on the top of a chair. He takes off his underpants. He leads me to the couch and sits down. He takes off my underpants. He sits me on top of him. He lifts my dress. I'm cold. I shiver. Daddy shivers too. He puts my hand on his swelling. He rubs my hand on it.

I go inside myself. I go to the beach. I play in the waves. Daddy keeps rubbing and moaning. I am turned around. I am lying on the sand. A huge wave washes over me. Salty liquid pours into my mouth. I gag but the wave pushes the liquid back in. It grabs my jaw and holds my mouth closed. "Swallow, Anna. Swallow Daddy's love." The waves hold me down and wash over me. They return to the sea.

Daddy is washing my face. He is dressed. I am dressed. He takes me to the ice cream store. He tells the boy behind the fountain to give me a strawberry ice cream cone. He orders chocolate for himself. Daddy hands me the ice cream cone. I don't take it. He puts the ice cream cone in my hand. He wraps my fingers around it. He pushes the ice cream into my mouth and holds it there until I swallow. He takes his hands away. I drop the cone. I vomit on my clothes I vomit on the floor. Daddy tells the boy to clean up the mess.

We walk home. Daddy says, "Good girls don't vomit. They're happy that Daddy takes them for a walk. They're happy that Daddy buys them ice cream. They want to be with Daddy."

*****

When the retching stopped, I remained where I was, hugging the toilet bowl, my hot face pressed against the cool porcelain.

"One more, Anna. Just one more. You can do it."
"Boonah, am I a bad girl?"
"No, Anna. You are a good girl with a bad daddy."

*****

"Anna wants me to take her for a walk," Daddy tells Momma. Daddy is holding my hand tightly. He is whistling. He is smiling.

"I don't want to go for a walk."

"Of course you do," says Momma. "Daddy always tells me how much you like to walk with him. Don't bring me chocolate ice cream. I like butter pecan."

"Sure," says Daddy. "Anna will even ask the boy to put chocolate sprinkles on it, right, Anna?" Daddy looks happy.

"How many times I got to tell you? I don't like chocolate. Put nuts on top." Momma sounds cross. She looks mad.

Daddy grips my hand too tightly. "Say goodbye to Momma"

"Goodbye, Momma."

"Have a good time, Anna." Momma goes into the kitchen. We leave the house. I know where we are going. My feet refuse to cooperate.

"I'll carry you, Anna. I like to carry you." Daddy throws me over his back and he walks to the room. There is a new rug on the floor. Brown and white. "Look at the rug, Anna. Isn't it pretty? I bought it just for you. Let's lie on it."

"No. I want to go home."

I struggle but he's too strong. When he puts me down. I go inside, to the beach, where the sun is shining and I don't feel my cold naked body on the rug. I lie on the warm sand. I stare at the clouds and the blue sky. I send the pain between my legs to the sun. I send the moaning sounds to the clouds. I don't know what to do with the blood on my body.

*****

Boonah's voice is warm and soothing. He rubs my neck. "Good girl, Anna. You are very brave."

"Boonah, will you stay with me forever."

"I am you."

The End of an Era

Rose was worried. Something must be wrong. Usually, Sadie called or stopped by at least once a day, more if Rose encouraged her, but in the two years she'd known her, Sadie had never gone three days with no contact. It wasn't as if they were such good friends, more geographical than emotional, yet the friendship had served them well enough. Both came from Brooklyn. Each was a widow on a limited income. Neither got along well with her children.

She knocked on the door a few times with no response. Reluctantly, she decided to use her key. Opening the door she saw Sadie sitting on her sofa, fully dressed, in the dark, except for light that escaped from drawn curtains. "Sadie?" Rose closed the door and sat down on the end cushion of the sofa. "What's the matter?" She hoped it wouldn't take too much time. She had a beauty parlor appointment in an hour.

With great effort Sadie answered. "Minnele's dead. Sarah, her daughter, she called after the funeral. Said she knew it would be too much for me to come. You tell me how come she knows so much. Suddenly she's in charge of what I do?" Rose didn't know what to say. Mostly she and Sadie talked about stuff going on in their complex or about movies and TV programs.

Rose looked at her watch and sighed. "Is there something I can do? Make you a cup of tea?"

Sadie stared at her hands.

"So tell me, did you eat lunch?" asked Rose, who believed that food was the answer to almost all of life's problems, and a lot more dependable than people. "I got vegetable soup. I just made it. It's still hot."

"She was my oldest friend. We met in first grade. And when she stole my most important possession, I never said a word. I kept thinking she'd find a way to give it back to me so we could talk. And now she's dead. And I never got a chance to say I'm sorry because her daughter knows what's best for me better than I do. And I never told her she was right about me. And now who knows me? Who knows what happened in my life? Who?"

Rose tried to make sense out of what she was hearing. Out of politeness she spoke timidly, carefully, not wanting to upset Sadie, not wanting to be involved. "I don't understand. Your best friend steals from you and you think you got to say you're sorry?"

"I told her it was garbage because I was ashamed. Maybe you never had such a friend like Minnele. She was so good even if she couldn't boil water." Sadie smiled, thinking of how many times Minnie had asked her for recipes that never tasted like what she made. "I couldn't believe she wanted to be my friend, my best friend. She was so much nicer than me. I mean why would anyone? I got a mouth on me that never quits. Especially since—"

Rose tried to hide her growing bewilderment and discomfort. "Look, Sadie, you're upset. Naturally. Your best friend dies and her daughter doesn't tell you in time for you to go to the funeral. I just made a batch of the cookies you like. I'll get some and then we can have a cup of tea. You'll feel better. Believe me, I know what I'm telling you. I got experience."

Sadie stunned Rose by saying, "Thank you for coming. I appreciate that you came. "

If only she wouldn't get hysterical. Rose couldn't handle it. Already she was talking nonsense. Stealing something that was garbage. And being ashamed? Of what? Should she ask? No. Definitely not.

"I kept thinking I should ask Minnie to give me back the box or that Minnie would tell me she had it so we could talk about it. Now Minnie's dead. The only person I could ask is Sarah. I definitely cannot ask Sarah. She hates me. Always has, from the time she was a little girl. Probably kept Minnie from coming to visit me. Do you think Minnie read the letters? And the diary? But there was no key. I lost it somewhere, in one of the places I hid it, to keep Papa from reading what I wrote."

Rose was baffled. "I'll be back in a second. You need to eat something." She hurried out and returned with a tray of cookies and two cups of steaming tea. "I made your favorite tea, Sadie, with lemon and sugar. Oh, and I forgot to tell you, the movie you said you wanted to see is playing. Leah said she'd join us if we go today; tomorrow's not so good for her. Come to the movie. It will take your mind off what's happened. We can stop by Jimmy's for dinner; they have the early bird special today." Sadie seemed to nod. Rose felt relieved. You can't stop living just because someone you know dies. She walked to the door. "Sadie, I'm leaving, but I'll be back in time for us to go to the movies." As Rose opened the door she heard Sadie moan. She stood at the door, wanting to close it, afraid to leave. She saw Sadie take out an album filled with photographs. They looked old and fragile.

Sadie handled them lovingly. "How am I going to live without my Minnele? What am I going to do without her? Who's going to love me now?"

Rose sighed. Well, she'd done her best. Her hairdresser was waiting.

18

Where was my mother while this was going on? Did she know what was happening? How did it start? Why? How long did it go on for? When the orderly brought my breakfast, the soggy toast, lukewarm coffee, and rubbery eggs stopped the stream of pictures and questions. I looked forward to trying to eat it.

At nine I called the veterinarian. "Dr. Keyes is in surgery. Give us your number and she'll call you back." How long did they keep an unclaimed cat? Poor Mys. She had no friends. I had no friends. There was no one I could ask, "Could you pick up my cat?" There was no one I could tell, "My father raped me." *Why had I chosen to live like this? Did it have to be this way?*

When Dr. Keyes returned my call, I blurted out, "I'm in the hospital but I might be released tomorrow. My doctors think I have leukemia. How's my cat?"

"Mys came through the operation with no problems. We can board her here, but I think it makes more sense to put her up for adoption. Doesn't sound like you need to worry about a kitten right now, even a charmer like Mys."

Every bone in my body screamed *No!* How did I get so attached to her so quickly? "Let's board her for a couple of days. I can't bear the thought of giving her up." We settled on my paying for three days room and board. I forgot to ask how much it cost.

Emma was changing the bandage on my back when Paulus came in.

"How're you doing?"

"Not too bad. Just aches a bit from all the drilling."

"Any news about how long you'll be here?"

"I have more blood tests at five. If my counts are better I think they'll let me go home tomorrow." *What if I wake up drenched in blood again?*

"Pilar called to tell you she read the story to the class. She said Tamaqua smiled and the rest of the kids looked ashamed. When she asked if anyone wanted a copy of the story, she was surprised. She expected Tamaqua to say yes but two other kids also wanted a copy. Seems one of them has a cousin with one leg and the other has an aunt in a wheelchair."

"Maybe the kids can make up stories for the cousin and the aunt."

"Great idea. Why not call her and suggest it?"

"I'm too tired. Could you tell her?"

There was a strained silence. "I'd better go so you can rest."

It's now or never, my girl. Ask! "The cat's been neutered and the vet says she's healthy. Would you pick her up for me?" He looked annoyed.

An insistent knock on the door ended the conversation as a beaming Joe said, "Put your shoes on, folks. The world's newest child is ready to boogie."

"It's here? Already?"

"Correction," said Joe. "She is here. Mother and daughter are doing fine. All cleaned up and ready for visitors. If I stand here one more minute, I'll miss my daughter's first smile. Gotta go." He took off.

"Well, I guess I'll go back to work," said Paulus.

"Didn't you hear the man? He said folks, plural. You and me."

Emma looked as happy as I felt when I told her the news. "While I hook Anna up to a portable IV, why don't you get the wheelchair near the front desk?"

Within minutes, Paulus was wheeling me toward the maternity wing.

"Paulus? The cat?"

He sighed. "I am not a cat lover."

The jealousy I felt when I saw the baby was so powerful it would have knocked me over had I not been sitting in the wheelchair. Only an hour ago she was an it, inside Josie, an unknown. Now, she was a tiny person, her whole life in front of her. Looking at the happiness of the new family made me wish I had a husband and a child. I discovered I wanted to touch the baby with an intensity that shook me. She was the tiniest human being I'd ever seen.

Josie noticed. "Would you like to hold her?"

Yes. "Is it safe? She's barely an hour old."

Josie smiled, cuddling her sleeping daughter. "What's not to be safe?"

With a little help from Emma, I was cradling the baby, inhaling her sweet baby smell. Birth was a miracle. I yearned for Mys, to hold something alive that belonged to me.

*****

Living with Minnie means living with the smells of cabbage and soap that make me sneeze. It isn't like it's going to be forever. Just till Mama comes home from the hospital with the new baby. But I have to sleep with Sarah, who's much bigger and takes up almost the whole bed. When I complain, she says, "Shut up. If you don't like it, sleep on the floor. Anyway, how come you're not staying with your daddy?"

I don't know. "He has to work."

"So? You could have a babysitter." She glares at me, her threatening fingers inches from my eyes. When she moves toward me, I back away.

Playing the only trump card I can think of, I spit. "If you don't stop being mean to me I won't let you hold my new baby."

"There is no baby," she says, wiping her face.

I punch her so hard she reels back. She recovers and pushes me down, kicking me. I pull her down and roll on top of her, ready to smash her. The fight lasts as long as it takes Minnie to run in and yell for us to stop acting like hooligans.

Crying, I tell Minnie, "Sarah says there is no baby. There is. That's why Mama went to the hospital. Tell her to shut up." Minnie glares at Sarah, who is not cowed.

Defiantly, Sarah repeats the hurtful words. "There is no baby!"

"Aunt Minnie, Mama said she's bringing home a baby. When is Mama coming?"

Minnie sits down on the bed and picks me up even though I'm four and much too big for laps. "Anna honey, sometimes, when babies are born—"

Sarah interrupts. "Mama—"

Minnie's voice is sharp. "Go put the kettle on for tea. Now!"

Sarah sneers. "I told you the baby's not coming home. I told you. I told you."

Minnie swats Sarah's behind and she runs out, trying not to cry.

"Aunt Minnie? Did something happen to the baby? Is Mama sick?"

"Your mama's getting better. She'll be home soon." She sighs. "What Sarah said is true. She isn't bringing the baby home. He was born with the cord wrapped around his neck."

"A cord around his neck? Where did it come from? What kind of cord? How did it get there? Was it like my jump rope?" I keep peppering her with questions. The more she answers, the more I ask.

Then it hits me. I'm not going to have a brother. I am still an only child.

I refuse to drink the tea. I refuse to hold Sarah's new doll. I sleep on the floor.

*****

Suddenly, the baby wriggled and whimpered. I felt betrayed by her cries. When Josie took her daughter back, I was besieged by images of my mother cackling, pointing her finger at me. Shaking her head. *I didn't make her cry.*

I needed to go. "Josie, congratulations. She's beautiful. I'm sorry to leave so soon, but I need a nap. Paulus, can you wheel me back to my room?" I gave him directions to the vet, ignoring his stony silence.

In bed, under the covers, I curled into a fetal position, trying to stop the images of my father that kept flooding my mind until I got tired of cowering. "No!" I shouted. "No. No. No." The words had no effect. Images and memories swirled, fought, and crashed.

Throwing off the covers I sat up, furious with him, me, my mother, the world. *All right, Daddy, you want stories, I'll tell you a story.*

"Once upon a time there was a daddy who wasn't getting much from the mommy so he decided to get it from his daughter. He forced her to pretend. He made her eat ice cream. He said it was a story. He told her only bad girls say no to Daddy."

My father's image blurred. "Oh no, Daddy, you are not leaving. Not till I finish this story.

The girl grew up remembering a caressing voice. Hating strawberry ice cream. Thinking she was bad. Afraid she was crazy. Worried because the story hurt her. Because she had nowhere to go. No place to hide. She learned to go inside herself; but even there, there was no escape."

The image was getting smaller. "Daddy, your daughter is not bad. She is not crazy. She remembers the truth." My father's image disintegrated, leaving pieces dangling in the air.

The door opened. A burly middle-aged man with a missing front tooth and a large well-waxed moustache asked, "You Ms. Baum?" I nodded. He twirled the ends of his moustache, looking like a villain from a silent movie. "Time to go." He motioned for me to get into the wheelchair. Before I knew it, he had unlocked the brake and was wheeling me out of the room.

"Hey!" I yelled. "Where are we going?"

"Cat Scan. Liver and spleen." He took one look at my shivering body, whipped the blanket off my bed, deftly wrapped it around me, pushed me toward the elevator, down into the basement of the hospital, and in and out of corridors that all looked alike to me. I was now so cold my teeth were chattering. Mr. Moustache kept going at a clip that would have served us well in a race, moving through swinging doors, taking countless twists and turns without a pause. He pushed open a heavy steel door and a sloppily dressed blonde, looking like the worst night of her life was not yet over, nodded to him, checked my bracelet ID, and told him when to pick me up.

"How ya doin', hon?" She heard my teeth chattering. "Cold, nervous, or both?"

I nodded.

"Well, all you got to do is drink some stuff—we'll take a few pitchas—and you'll be done in no time." I couldn't help noticing her poorly bleached hair, smeared lipstick, and stained uniform. I drank, and it returned, all over her with a smell so awful I retched again.

Don't hit me. I didn't mean to do it. "I'm sorry. I'm sorry." I started crying.

*****

After Grandpa's funeral, we go back to Aunt Lilly's house. There are too many people in the room. I have to get away from the noise and the heat. "Where's Grandma?" I ask Aunt Lilly.

"She's resting. Don't bother her."

I tiptoe down the hallway, making sure that no one sees me. The doorknob squeaks as I turn it. Grandma is lying on the bed, crying. I freeze, not sure whether to go in or run away. Grandma stops crying and sits up. "Come here, *neshomeleh.*" She cradles me on her lap. "You want I should tell you a story?" I shake my head, worrying that I'm being a pest. I start to cry. Grandma brushes the hair out of my eyes.

"It's good you came. You reminded me of a Yiddish proverb Momma used to tell us. "If you need to cry, cry all night, but smile by morning light."

"But Grandma, what if you still feel bad?"

"So a smile's gonna make you feel worse?"

*****

Without a word of rebuke, the technician wiped up the smelly mess. "Hey, hon, that's the way it goes. Some folks just can't keep the stuff down. I'll give you a glass a water and we'll try again. Ya need it for the scan." She washed the front of her uniform that was now definitely the worse for wear and gave me another glass of pink liquid.

When we were finished, she put her arm around me. "Ya done real good, kid. Lotsa folks never keep it down. We have an awful time getting them done." *See, Mother, I am a good girl.*

Mr. Moustache appeared like magic. He whispered into her ear. Blushing, she gave him a kiss on his cheek. When he returned the favor she ducked out of reach. "Take good care of her."

Hear that, Daddy? She knows what good care is.

We headed for my room at the same breakneck pace with which we left, arriving just in time to see a scowling technician pushing his cart down the corridor. Mr. Moustache hurried after him, yelling. "C'mon back. It ain't her fault she was late." After making sure I was nicely tucked in, he left, whistling, guiding the wheelchair with one finger.

The technician was in a bad mood. He stuck the needle into my vein with all the grace of a ten-ton truck. Even before he withdrew the needle I could see the blue mark forming. Daddy's face was all smiles until I rang for the duty nurse who brought me ice. *One way or another, Daddy, you will leave my life. You will not hurt me any more.*

*****

I hate my fourth-grade teacher, so I'm really happy that school is cancelled because of the blizzard. It's been snowing for two days. The big street is quiet—no buses, or trucks, rushing to beat the light. There are a few cars stuck at odd angles with no regard for streets or sidewalks. The quiet of falling snowflakes makes the city feel peaceful. I rush to get into my snowsuit and out of the apartment, ready to make tracks in the perfect white surface. The cold turns drips from my nose into icicles but I'm too happy to care. I lie down and make angels in the snow.

The cold and wet seeping through my jacket makes me think about time. I trudge back to the apartment. At the front door, I put my hand in my pocket. Empty. I can't find my key. I must have lost it in the snow. No one is home. Shivering, I go back outside to look for it. The ice on my eyelids melts into tears. Cold turns me numb.

"Anna," I hear a woman call. I look up and there's Mrs. Sikorsky, a large, red-faced woman who my mother says is the world's biggest gossip, a person she will walk ten blocks out of her way to avoid. "Anna? You locked out? Come up by me."

My mother will not be pleased to learn I've lost my key. How much worse will it be if she knows I've spoken to Mrs. Sikorsky?

"Anna Baum, come up before you freeze to death. I'll make hot chocolate." It is getting dark. "You hear me? Come right now!" I climb the three flights of stairs. Smells of pot roast fill the stairway. While I hesitate, wondering whether to knock on Mrs. Sikorsky's door, she opens it, shaking her head.

"Look at you. Two more minutes down there and you'd have frozen to death. Where's your mother? It's dinner time."

"I lost my key."

"Poor thing. Come in. Take off your clothes. You can wear Rosie's. They'll be a little big but they're clean and dry." I belt the skirt to keep it from falling down. The woolen stockings rub where they've been darned many times, but they warm my cold feet. I thank her for the pair of slippers and try to keep her from seeing how big they are as they dangle precariously. The apartment smells of chicken and my stomach growls loudly. I worry about what I will tell my mother. Maybe I can leave quickly. What about my clothes? There's a laundromat around the corner. I don't have any money.

Mrs. Sikorsky interrupts my worrying as she puts a huge bowl of soup in front of me. "You must be starving. I made a big pot of chicken soup. You like scallions?" I nod. Mrs. Sikorsky deftly slices circles into my bowl. Soon the surface is covered with bits of green bobbing in and around the golden globules. "Enjoy!"

The soup is scrumptious. Beads of fat float on top of the yellow broth, filled with chunks of chicken, carrots, onions, potatoes, and celery. "This is really good," I say, sipping from a large soup spoon as she slices scallions into her bowl.

She slurps unselfconsciously so I do the same. It's delicious soup and slurping makes it even better. When my second bowl is empty she makes hot chocolate, topping it with small marshmallows that melt into the steaming brown liquid. I savor every sip, trying to prolong the inevitable "I guess I should go see if my parents are home."

Mrs. Sikorsky puts her hands on mine. "Come see me any time you feel like it. You hear me? It's nice to have company for dinner."

"Sure," I say, wishing I could. I thank her for the clothes. She gives me a hug. Her breath smells of chicken soup and scallions. Maybe my mother is wrong about her.

"Bring the clothes back tomorrow after school. I'll make you hot chocolate. What kind of cookies do you like?" I don't know what to say. Suddenly the bell rings.

My heart sinks. Mrs. Sikorsky opens the door and my mother rushes in, barely acknowledging Mrs. Sikorsky's "Hello, come in."

"So there you are Anna, we've been looking all over for you. Mrs. Schwartz said she saw you come up here." She grumps a graceless thank you to Mrs. Sikorsky and pushes me downstairs. After making sure I take a bath and scrub myself all over, she returns the clothes, meticulously washed and ironed.

*****

Snuggling deeper into the warm blankets, I wrote an imaginary letter to Mrs. Sikorsky, wishing I'd had the guts to visit her again. How lonely she must have been. How lonely I've been. *I am going where the hot chocolate lives.*

When I heard the knock, for a moment I thought it was Mrs. Sikorsky but the smell was of spice, not chicken soup. I peered out from under the blanket. "Miriam!"

"How're you doing?"

"Waiting. My least favorite activity."

"I can't stay long but I have something for you." Before I could say she shouldn't have, out popped a little pot that looked familiar. "Yup, it's yours. Sweet, isn't it? When you're up and about you can glaze it." I loved holding it in my hands. Even though it was lopsided and thick, it was mine. And, I decided, the first of many.

I thought I had just closed my eyes when a thermometer was stuck into my mouth. "How does anyone expect people to get well if they're always being bothered?" I grumbled.

"Your counts are improving. You can go home tomorrow." My fear showed. The nurse asked, "What's the matter? You keep saying you want to go home."

"True." I mended fences. "Thanks for telling me; it is good news. What time?"

"Between eleven and twelve. That'll give us time to do any other tests the doctor orders."

"With all the blood tests I've been having, it's a wonder you bother with transfusions. First you put it in, then you take it out—what a business," I snorted as she unhooked the IV and I stood up. The nurse was kind enough to smile.

"Free at last," I said before crashing to the floor, waiting for the world to stop spinning before I tried to get up. My body and mind definitely needed to talk. Negotiate. Compromise.

She helped me stand up. I gritted my teeth, walking a few steps with difficulty despite her support. "You're doing fine," she said. I didn't believe her.

"I can finish washing up by myself," I said, hoping it was true.

"Maybe," she said, helping me clean up. When I was sitting in the chair, my father's face loomed large.

"Okay Daddy, you won't go away. Let's talk."

"I love you, Annale."

Daddy, I am learning. This is not love.

Wanting

Sarah put off making the phone call as long as she could. It was true enough that after Mama died she had a lot to do what with selecting which agency to give her mother's clothes and how to deal with the furniture Mama had kept in storage after moving in with Sarah. Then there were the things people wanted. That was the hardest. Although her mother left a will, there was so much she had not mentioned, like the ruby necklace her mother's cousin swore was supposed to be hers. And the set of dishes her cousin Sheila was certain should be her inheritance. It wasn't that Sarah wanted to keep everything. She just wasn't ready to give anything away. Not until she'd had a chance to grieve. Not until she called Sadie.

She still remembered Sadie's voice when she'd called to tell her Minnie was dead and that they'd already had the funeral. It would be a long time before she could stop hearing Sadie say, "You mean to tell me you decided it was too much for me to attend my Minnele's funeral? You?" Sarah had stammered a stupid response like a schoolgirl caught in the act of stealing lipstick from a drug store.

She poured herself a glass of sherry, practicing the meditation she'd read in a book, then picked up the phone and dialed. It rang and rang. Maybe she could just leave a message. That way it would be up to Sadie to decide. "Sadie Baum speaking." Sarah's heart lurched. She gulped a large swig of sherry.

"Hello, it's Sarah, Minnie's daughter."

"I know who you are. You called a few weeks ago."

"Well, uh, I know how close you and my mother were—"

"Now you know? How come you didn't know before the funeral?"

"Sadie, please!" In spite of herself Sarah began to cry, huge wracking sobs that wouldn't quit. She wanted to say she had to hang up and would call back but she couldn't speak.

"Your mother was my best friend. Sixty years we knew each other. You don't find people like her but once in a lifetime. What gave you the right to decide I couldn't go to her funeral?"

"Look, this is really difficult for me to ask, but I need to do it. Everyone's claiming things that belonged to Mama, but before I give anything away, I want you to have what you want. Is there anything of hers you'd like me to send you? Most of her furniture is in storage but whatever you want, I'll make sure you get it."

"Thank you," Sadie said coldly. She wondered whether to ask Sarah about the box with her diary and letters to Avi. But if Minnie had thrown it out, asking would only stir up stuff she didn't want to talk about. Still— What else could she ask for? "I don't really need much down here. My place is pretty small." She took a deep breath and blurted out, "Well, come to think of it, there is one thing, if you don't mind, that is."

"What?" asked Sarah, hoping that the worst part of the conversation was over. "Anything you want. If I can find it, it's yours." She wondered what Sadie would ask for.

She heard Sadie take a deep breath. "She was keeping a box for me. A cigar box. I'd like to have it."

"A cigar box?" Sarah prayed she sounded perplexed.

"Yeah."

"Well," Sarah said, as if she were mentally going over her mother's things. "No, I don't believe I've seen a cigar box. She did have a jewelry box. Is that what you're thinking of?"

Sadie's voice was razor sharp. "I know the difference between a cigar box and a jewelry box. I said a cigar box. I meant a cigar box."

Sarah gritted her teeth. "I don't know anything about a cigar box. Is there anything else you want?"

"Yeah, I want my Minnele. I kept telling her she should come down here, where it's warm, but no, she had to stay and be useful. Said she had to stay in the cold to help with the grandchildren. Said you needed her."

"Are you telling me it's my fault my mother died?"

"Warm is good. It's nice to walk on the sand. That's what I'm saying. She was such a special person. They don't make them like her anymore. You hear me?"

"Sadie, is there anything else of my mother's you would like?"

"What I want I can't have."

"It's not that you can't have it. It isn't there to have."

"Sure," said Sadie. "So what else is new?"

19

I was putting my things in a plastic bag, waiting for the blood test results, when a young technician came in with a cart I recognized only too well.

"I don't need the test," I told him. "I had one yesterday."

"You're on my list. See? Anna Baum."

"So someone made a mistake." The technician kept pointing to my name.

"If you won't check it, I will."

The technician pleaded, "Lady, gimme a break, I'm just trying to do my job."

Ignoring him, I dizzied my way to the nurse's station, holding on to the wall, hoping I could keep upright, ignoring the sweat dripping down my face and the technician behind me muttering about my name being on the list.

Summoning an authoritative voice, I said, "I'd like to speak to the charge nurse."

"She's not here, Ms. Baum. Can I help you?"

"I hope so. The technician came in to do a platelet-bleeding test. He says I'm on his list, but yesterday the doctor told me my platelet count was improving. Tell him I don't need the test."

"If you're on his list, you need the test. Doctor's orders."

"I'm sure it's a mistake."

"A platelet test is no big deal."

"I don't need the test."

"I'll look at the orders, but I'm not allowed to change them."

"I understand," I said, refusing to back down.

The nurse asked the technician. "May I see your list?"

The technician handed it to her. "Sure. See, there's the name, Anna Baum."

"This is yesterday's list." The technician mumbled an apology. The nurse looked embarrassed. "I guess we all make mistakes."

Back in my room, I lay down on the rumpled hospital bed, drifting into the nothingness of space and time, feeling as if I'd done battle with the gods of darkness.

In the distance, floating like a water lily, I see Boonah, smiling. "Well done, Luv." I drift to his outstretched arms.

"Hey, Anna, it's time to go," Paulus said, shattering my reverie as he appeared with a wheelchair. "The car's in a no-parking zone." This time I had no objection to leaving in a wheelchair. Funny what a loss of blood can do to one's confidence.

While riding in the car, I told him about refusing to take the test. "The strange thing is, I didn't do anything wrong yet I feel ashamed of myself. Weird, huh?"

"Early conditioning."

"Fuck! I'm too old to keep blaming my parents."

"Some things we never outgrow," he said, deftly passing a slow driver.

"Well, I intend to do just that."

"How?" he asked.

"I have yet to figure this out." *Is there a connection between what happened with my father and my marriage to Max?* Although I didn't know what questions to ask, it was comforting to remember that if I was opening Pandora's box, along with all the miseries, there was hope.

"Good luck," said Paulus, as if I was embarking on a futile mission. "Maybe you shouldn't think about the past so much. When I was a kid and felt bad, my grandmother would hug me and say, 'No point chasing misery; it finds you all by itself.'"

"Emma's grandmother told her the same thing. I can see it now — millions of gray-haired women getting together over tea and cookies deciding what to tell their grandchildren."

"Not mine," said Paulus. "She'd choose whiskey over tea any time. I don't even remember gray hair. She stood straight as the old walnut tree that grew down the road. And she smoked cigars. Big fat smelly ones." Paulus grinned. "One time, I must have been about five, my parents came home and found my grandmother drinking whiskey, puffing a cigar, with me on her lap, snuggling. They hit the ceiling but Grandma wasn't fazed. She gave me a hug, rumpled my hair, and took a puff before setting me down. I remember her hugs. She'd hold out her arms and wait for me to get as close as I wanted. Not like my other grandmother who squished the breath out of me. Strange what we remember—."

*****

There's a knock at the door, so light I wonder if I'm imagining it. Then the knocking starts again, a bit louder. I hear Momma yell for me to go open the door. She's in the kitchen cooking. I wonder how she hears such a soft sound from so far away. Daddy left an hour earlier. He goes out when Momma's parents come to visit. I open the door. It's Grandma. My grandpa isn't with her. Grandma gives me a big hug and presses a fifty-cent piece into my hand, closing my fingers around it. The last time, Momma saw and made me give it back. She said Grandma can't afford to give any money to anyone. Grandma takes my hand and we go inside. Momma comes out, wiping her hands on her apron. "So where's Papa? What's his excuse this time?"

"Please, Sadie, he works hard. He's tired."

"He's not too tired to see Lilly and her kids. Not too tired to take them to the park and buy them ice cream. I have to sit and listen to Lilly tell me how her kids love their *zaideh*. What about Anna? She's not his *ainikel*?" I sidle out of the living room. I hate it when they fight.

"Anna, come here." Momma's voice is tense. Anything can happen. "Take *bobbeh's* coat and hang it up. Where are your manners?" I look at my feet as I walk to Grandma. I help her off with her coat. She seems fragile. Like if I'm not careful I could crush her bones.

"You shouldn't be so hard on her, Sadie. She's only six. She's a good child. She'll learn."

"You're never too young to learn manners." While I'm hanging up the coat I hear Momma scold. "How many times I have to tell you, don't correct me in front of her."

"Momma? Is something burning?" I don't smell anything but it's enough just to ask. She runs into the kitchen and I'm alone with Grandma, waiting for our special greeting.

"*Mein shaineh maidele*," she murmurs in my ear. It's one of the few Yiddish expressions I know. I love to hear her say it. My pretty little girl.

I give the response that always brings a smile to her face, "*Mein shaineh bobbehle*." My pretty little grandmother. We sit on the couch. She pulls me to her chest and strokes my hair. If I were a cat I would purr.

"Anna, I need you to finish setting the table."

"Yes, Momma. I'm coming." I make no move to get up.

"*Mein shaineh maidele.*"

"*Mein shaineh bobbehle.*"

She gives me a kiss. "Go, your mother needs you." I walk a few steps and then turn around. She whispers, "You're *mein shaineh*, Annale."

*****

I can live on that.

A black wriggling ball of fur greeted me. "Coffee or tea?" asked Paulus, an irritated look on his face when he saw the kitten.

"Coffee! Thanks for picking up Mys."

He made no attempt to hide his unhappiness about having a cat in the house. I hugged Mys so hard she squealed, purred, and then meowed in complaint, refusing to leave my lap when the coffee came. Paulus scowled at her. I inhaled the pungent smell of coffee and sighed. "Except for Jacob's brew, how do hospitals make such bad coffee?"

"Bad beans, dirty pot, no love—it's easy."

I heard love and froze.

"Josie's coming home from the hospital tomorrow," I said, trying to chase away my depression and his bad mood.

"Do they need anything?"

"Maybe we could cook them a couple of dinners."

"Good idea. I'll buy French bread and fresh fruit tarts from the new bakery. And a bottle of wine for Joe and sparkling apple cider for the nursing mother. How does that sound?"

"Expensive."

"I thought they were good friends. Look what Joe did for you." His voice was judgmental.

"I'll make a spinach quiche," I said, knowing we had all the stuff in the house.

Paulus glared at me. "If you have no objection, I'll buy wine for Joe and cider for Josie."

"It's your money. Do what you want."

He slammed a drawer closed.

"Thanks for the coffee. It hit the spot," I said to his receding back.

Mys followed me into my bedroom where the pillow revealed her sleeping preference. I couldn't stop hugging and kissing her. She couldn't stop purring. *Kitty, you are exactly what the doctor did not order.*

I put my crooked little bowl next to Miriam's and cringed at the sight. No comparison. *I will love it anyway.*

Paulus knocked on the door. When I didn't open it, he called out in a voice that was hard and obsequious. "What shall I do about dinner?"

I don't give two shits what you do. "I'm too tired to think. You decide."

"Since your budget is so tight, you better let me know what I can spend."

His injured tone of voice made me furious. I handed him fifty dollars. "This is all I have until I go to the bank." He took it and left. *Fuck you, Paulus. You can sulk all you want, but it's my money and I decide how I spend it, especially since I don't know how long it will last.*

*****

Momma and I are at the beach. I've been making a sand castle, but I have to go to the bathroom. Momma isn't sitting in the chair under the umbrella. I stand up, a little frightened because I can't find her. I keep looking around. Near the boardwalk, I see her talking to a strange man. I try to wait until she's finished talking, but I can hardly hold it in. "Momma, I have to go."

"How many times I have to tell you? Wait until I'm finished talking." She resumes her conversation. I tug frantically at her arm but she pushes me away, all the time talking to the man. Just as I leave to find the toilet, pee flows down my legs making a steaming, smelly puddle in the sand. Momma yanks me toward the restroom as pee dribbles down my legs. I can't stop it. All the time she's screaming, "You're old enough to know better. Can't I take you anywhere? What's wrong with you?" She pushes me into the stall. I take off my stained bathing suit. I hear her washing it, muttering. She throws the cold wet suit at me. I put it on, shivering. She doesn't say a word as I follow her out into a sun so bright it hurts my eyes. I expect her to tell me we're going home, but she walks back to the strange man, ignoring me. He touches her shoulder. She smiles. They continue to talk. I watch them. My suit dries.

*****

"Boonah, will you leave me again?"

A sharp clanging sound interrupts.
The phone was ringing. I tried to separate memory from reality. My body ached as if ten armies had invaded me. The phone kept ringing. I followed the sound until I found it and answered in a shaky voice. Not a voice I wanted to hear.

"Ms. Baum, Dr. Heisenfelzer's nine o'clock appointment for tomorrow morning has cancelled. She'd like to see you. Can you make it?"

"Is something wrong?"

"She wants to check your counts."

"Oh—Okay."

"Good. We'll see you tomorrow at nine."

This is what a hangover must feel like—dry mouth, aching head, double vision. I walked into the living room, my eyes settling on the needlepoint. It was still difficult for me to switch gears, to think about my mother making it. Suddenly my father's face leered, following me, wherever I went, not something I could "unsee" though I opened and closed my eyes. What if Boonah was right? What if the images were a gift from my psyche, a way of helping me uncover at least part of the truth of what happened? One thing I was sure of, the images were filling a void I didn't know existed, triggering memories I had worked hard to forget.

*****

I'm home from school early; the teachers have to go to in-service meetings. I go into the kitchen to get an apple before changing out of my school clothes and hear Daddy call out querulously, "Anna, I'm in bed, sick. Make me a cup of tea."

I pretend I don't hear him, but he keeps shouting. I go to the door. "Stop yelling. I have to wait for the water to boil"

"Come sit by me until it boils." He hasn't shaved and there's a bad smell in the room. He pats a space right next to his body. "Sit over here." He pulls back the cover.

"I think the water's boiling," I say and run into the kitchen. I stick a tea bag in a glass even though I know he prefers tea brewed from leaves, put it on a tray with a piece of sugar, and take it in to him. I set the tray down on the table next to his bed. He leans forward to grab my arm. I run out, slamming the door behind me.

"Anna, come back. Right now. " I pretend I don't hear. "Anna, I'm calling you." I leave, ignoring the increasingly loud and insistent cries of "Anna." Once outside, I realize I haven't changed into my play clothes and I forgot the apple. No way am I going back in.

I walk over to a group of kids playing stickball just as Momma is walking up the sidewalk with two bags of groceries. "Help me with these bags," she says. I take one and follow her, afraid to go back inside. "Why didn't you change your clothes?" I don't answer.

When she opens the door, we hear daddy yell, "Anna, you come in here right this minute or you'll be sorry."

"Heshie, she was outside playing. What's the matter?" asks my mother through the kitchen door as she puts away groceries. I am unusually helpful, which does not go unnoticed. "You sick?" I shake my head and concentrate on straightening the neat rows of canned beans. She looks at me strangely, then goes into the bedroom, and shuts the door. I hear yelling that keeps getting louder. I turn on the radio. I don't want to hear what they're fighting about.

Momma and I eat supper by ourselves and then she fixes a dinner tray for my father and takes it into the bedroom, slamming the door. Once again there is yelling. I put my hands over my ears to drown out the shouting, wishing I was allowed to listen to the radio while I do my homework. Ink dribbles all over my spelling and I have to do it over again. Twice.

*****

I decided to call Emma. She always made me feel better.

"Hey, Anna, how's life?"

Terrible. "All right, I guess." *I shouldn't have called.* "You sound upset, what's up?"

"My husband was supposed to meet me for dinner before my meeting, but at the last minute Sam decides he doesn't have time."

"Come over. I'll make you something to eat."

"You sure? I know it's short notice."

"I invited you, remember?"

"Great. I'll be there in about half an hour. Don't fuss. In fact, I'll be satisfied if I can just have a good cup of coffee."

"What about Jacob's beans?"

"Just before he went for lunch, and beans, he got a call from his aunt. His mother's in intensive care with a possible stroke. I said to leave word on my answering machine as soon as he knew something. She was a classy lady. Did not take no for an answer if she wanted yes."

"Was? She's not dead yet, is she?"

"No. I guess I'm preparing for the worst. Well, I have to finish up. See you in a bit."

Nice I can do something for Emma for a change.

She greeted me with an exhausted look.

"You look like you could use an extra strong cup of coffee," I said.

"Forget coffee—I need a drink." She threw her bag down on the floor.

"That bad a day, huh? How's Chardonnay or do you need something—?"

"That's fine." She slumped onto a chair in the kitchen and closed her eyes. "Some days nothing you do makes a difference."

"Don't be so sure. In the hospital, every time you came into my room, I'd feel better, no matter what. Even when I didn't trust you, I trusted you." I laughed. "One of the only people I might add." *Maybe the only person?*

"What about your mother? Didn't your trust her?"

"I'd sooner trust a witch," I said.

"Why a witch?"

"They make potions, don't they? Make people think they're not who they think they are?"

"A witch. Huh! That reminds me of something I haven't thought about in years."

"What?" She was staring into space. "Tell me."

"When I was a kid, we lived near a black beach—it's black because it's made from volcanic lava. The tide is ferocious so we were never, ever, allowed to swim there unless a grownup was watching. But I couldn't keep away. To me there was something magical about the place. For some unknown reason, it just kept calling to me.

"Anyway, one day I cut school. It was a beautiful day, much too nice to be inside. I walked down to the beach and saw an old woman combing her long white hair. I kept watching, fascinated. All of a sudden she said, 'Come here, my child.' I was insulted. After all, I was almost thirteen. I stood there, trying to decide what to do when she said it again, 'Come here, my child.' She had so much power I had no choice but to walk to where she stood. She finished braiding her hair and held out her hands. My hands reached out for the old lady. She took them like this was what we always did.

"There we were, the old lady and me, holding hands, squatting in the black sand. I waited for her to say something but she just kept looking at me, like she was memorizing my face. Then she let go of my right hand and began to push the sand around. I was ready to tell her I got better things to do with my time than watch an old lady play in the sand, but she was so intense and deliberate, I couldn't stop watching her.

"Suddenly, I was scared. As kids, we'd heard lots of stories about Pele, the goddess of volcanoes, who was known to erupt with no warning. I had just about decided to leave when she finished and took my right hand. I remember her hands were cool and they felt good holding mine, which were hot and sweaty. I thought I was going to faint but when she put my hands in the sand picture, I felt better. Soon I felt a whole lot better, about everything.

"She sang a song I'd heard my grandmother sing once, when my grandfather died. For some reason I wanted to run away, but I couldn't. She kept holding my hands, singing in this amazingly low voice, looking at me, looking through me. I found myself singing with her even though I didn't know I knew the words. We sang, squatting in the sun on the black sand. I forgot about everything except the song and the sand picture. It was like we were in the picture, her hands holding my hands, moving them in the sand."

Emma stopped talking, lost in memory. I filled her glass. "What happened then?"

"That's the weirdest part. What I remember next is sitting in the sand by myself. No old woman. No picture in the sand. Just me, feeling incredibly peaceful, like something magical had soothed my ruffled feelings and healed the hurting places. After that day, I never cut school again. I studied hard, even graduated with honors. I'm the first one in my family to go to university. I can't explain anything about the old woman—how she came, where she went—but I'm sure of one thing—that old lady was real. And she changed my life."

"How did my mentioning a witch make you remember the old woman?"

"I don't know."

"Did you ever tell anyone about meeting her?"

"Not right away. I didn't want people to think I was crazy. But one night, when Mama and I were working in the garden, she said, 'Honeylove, you need to tell me what's on your mind.' I felt relieved. If anyone could make something right it was Mama."

"What did she say when you told her?"

"At first she didn't say anything, just took me in her arms and held me, something she hadn't done since I was little. Already I was feeling better. But then she sat me down next to the vegetables and spoke real quietly. 'Your great-grandmother looked exactly the way you describe the old woman. And she could heal troubled spirits. People were always coming to her, bringing a chicken, some eggs, or fruit—whatever they had to give. They'd put it on her front porch wrapped in flowers or pretty leaves and wait until she appeared. If she thought she could help, she'd take what they brought and motion them to come inside. If she didn't think she could help, she'd take their present and put it back in their hands and cry with them before she turned and went back inside.' I sat real still, afraid to ask what worried me most. Mama kept holding me, sitting quiet, like she had all the time in the world. Finally, I couldn't help myself and blurted out, 'Am I crazy, Mama?'"

"She hugged me. 'No, of course not. Your soul was troubled and your great-grandmother's spirit knew you were at a crossroad, in danger of taking the wrong path. Her love spoke to you. She knew you would hear her. Not everyone can. It's a special gift you have. I've known it for a long time.' I gasped. 'You have? Why didn't you tell me?' She said, 'It's something people have to find out for themselves. Some never do.' Mama gave me a big hug and motioned for me to get busy weeding the garden. After that night, we never talked about it."

"Did you ever see the old woman again?"

Emma grinned wryly. "I certainly have. She is one persistent old lady. Comes when she wants. Says what she thinks. Stays as long as she wants. No stopping her once she gets going. To this day, I've never told anyone except Mama. There was something about her that kept the darkness from getting me, at least when I was young."

"Did that change with your sister's death?"

"Maybe even before. I guess we want our heroes to be perfect and they never are." She sighed, shaking her head, taking a sip of wine.

"Did your sister ever see her?"

"I don't know. She always made fun of what she called, 'that spirit stuff.'"

It was hard for me to see the misery on her face. I poured us more wine. "Emma, you know that story you told me about your sister?" She looked so sad I decided to take the chance and give her a hug. It was just what we needed and it gave me the courage to say, "I think I know something about how your sister might have felt."

"You do?" Her intensity frightened me but I was tired of keeping everything in.

"I think so. But it's hard to talk about. And it's all mixed up, in bits and pieces." I put on water for coffee. "There's something I've never told anyone either." Emma put down her wine and gave me her full attention. I was amazed at how frightened I felt.

"I was—My father—" I felt tears filling my eyes. "You know those things I told you about? The images?" She nodded. "I'm pretty sure they're memories."

Emma took my hand in hers. The stillness was palpable. I was terrified. Like any moment my father would come through the door and call me a liar or worse.

I knew it was now or never. "My father raped me. More than once."

"Did your mother know?"

"I don't know. I remember them fighting about me."

"Oh, Anna," she said, holding my hand.

"Hello hello hello," said Paulus cheerfully. "Nice to see you, Emma." Without either of us hearing him he had come into the kitchen. His entrance burst the bubble of intimacy.

"Hi. Get yourself a glass," I said. My tone of voice was civil. *Leave us alone!* Paulus engaged Emma in friendly chitchat that increased my irritation. I went into the kitchen, boiled eggs, and cut up carrots. There wasn't much to snack on, but I suddenly remembered buying a few cans of peanuts before I got sick. They weren't where I'd put them. I looked everywhere. I also couldn't find the box of crackers or the Melba toast. I guessed that Paulus had eaten them. And not replaced them. I was furious. Rooting around in the refrigerator I found the remains of a huge chunk of cheese and a loaf of French bread that had been stuck so far back in the freezer he must not have seen it. I had to warm up the bread before I could slice it, but when I went to cut it part of it was still frozen. The knife slid off the bread, slicing my hand. More blood.

"Sorry the pantry's a little bare," I said, glaring at Paulus.

Emma took a piece of cheese and a slice of bread. Paulus chomped on carrots. The inanities continued. To stop them, I said, "Emma, check your answering machine. There might be a message from Jacob."

"I'll do it later. I'm in no mood for bad news."

"Aren't you always telling me, 'It ain't over till it's over?' Call!"

Sighing, she listened to her messages, resigned to hearing the worst. Her face lit up.

"What is it?" I asked.

"Jacob says it wasn't a stroke after all. Something to do with her blood sugar. The doctors think she'll be fine." Emma cried. Paulus handed her his handkerchief. She refused. "It's too nice." He insisted. She blew her nose like a small child.

I walked her to the door, but Paulus followed so all I could say was, "Thanks for coming. I hope you'll do it again real soon." I closed the door, afraid of my feelings.

To speak or not to speak ought to have been the question, but I was too mad to think about strategy. "God dammit Paulus, if you're going to eat all the peanuts and all the crackers and all the Melba toast, and most of the cheese, the very least you could do is replace what you've eaten when you go shopping."

The muscles of his cheek twitched. It looked like he was going to say something but instead, he took his glass to the kitchen, washed it, and then went into his room. He was putting on his coat when he came back into the living room. "Is there anything else you think I need to replace?" His lips were hard and tight.

"Think? Think you need to replace? Don't you know what you eat?"

We stood, glaring at each other. *Maybe he didn't eat the stuff. Maybe I misjudged him.*

"Why don't you give me a list of what I can and cannot eat?"

"Why don't you use common sense and replenish what you eat when it's gone?" He nodded and left. I dropped one of the wine glasses on the kitchen floor and when the glass shattered, I dropped the others. The sound was oddly satisfying. I wanted to cry so badly I could taste it, but my eyes remained dry. I swept up shards of glass. It was only when I cut myself and blood gushed onto the floor that a few sobs managed to escape.

Now What?

Seeing the sunlight, Sadie sighed. Another day. She forced herself to get up, put on the kettle, and take a shower. By the time she finished, the water was boiling, so she toasted a bagel, smeared cream cheese on it, sliced a tomato, sprinkled pepper on top, and made herself a cup of instant coffee, her breakfast for as long as she could remember. Anna had bought her a coffee grinder and a small contraption to make fresh coffee, but it was too much trouble so she gave it away. Just too much fuss over something that wasn't worth it. Oh sure, it tasted better, but she was used to instant. She knew how to make do.

Sometimes she wished she'd ordered the newspaper. It would give her something to do while she ate, company of sorts, but she hated reading about murders and robberies and muggings, especially of old people. Not knowing made her worry less. At least she could walk on the street and go into shops without imagining disaster lurking at every turn. Sometimes she wondered if all the crime stuff on television and in newspapers wasn't some huge conspiracy to keep old people so afraid to walk downtown they had to buy stuff from catalogues where they couldn't compare prices or buy on sale.

She ate slowly, postponing the inevitable morning question: "What am I going to do today?" When Minnie was alive she had letters to write. And once a week they called each other, taking turns, although in the past few months Minnie had called more often, making Sadie feel she should do the same. Not that she didn't have the money, she did. Heshie left her a good insurance policy and Sadie knew how to manage money, but for how long? That was the problem. Who knew how long you would live? And if there was one thing Sadie did know, it was that she would never go into a nursing home. It cost too much and took away all your power. Living with Anna wasn't a possibility either, even if Anna would agree, something Sadie wasn't so sure of. She didn't want to share her daughter's life. Didn't want to see Anna make the same mistakes she had. No. Her only option was to stay healthy and die in her sleep. If she could. Even she knew she couldn't control death.

With the coffee cup empty and the bagel gone, she put the dishes into the sink and washed them. Wiped the clean table. Sponged off the spotless stove. Looked for stains on the immaculate refrigerator. Washed the floor only she had walked on. She looked at the clock. It was barely ten. Twelve hours to fill before she could allow herself to go back to bed.

She would have had to shop today if her neighbor hadn't stuck her nose in Sadie's business. Normally Sadie bought everything in small quantities so she had to shop every other day, which took about two hours. Something to do, even a little exercise. But no, Shirley said, "I've got my car. Buy as much as you want. I'll drive you home." Sadie hadn't been able to think of a single reason to refuse her offer. So here she was, stuck with a full refrigerator. No need to shop for another week, at least. Maybe she should go down and buy a newspaper. She made herself a cup of tea and sat down on the sofa, staring at Minnie's letters lying in a big box. Seven years of letters. Sadie picked up the last one and started reading it. She thought of all the things she wanted to tell Minnie. Since Minnie's death she had no one to write to. No letters to look forward to. No one to share her thoughts with. Oh Rose and Shirley and Beaty were nice. They meant well, but it wasn't the same. By the time Sadie got through explaining what something meant, she forgot what she started to say in the first place. It was so much trouble she stopped trying.

Sadie sipped her tea, staring at the stationery she no longer had any use for. She would give it to Goodwill except that Anna had given it to her and had had her name embossed on the top of each sheet and on the envelopes. Who would want stationery with someone else's name on it? She picked up a piece of the fine off-white paper; the quality of the bond had always pleased her. Reluctantly, she put it back in the box and stood up, ready to toss it into the garbage. Such a shame to waste it, but what was she going to do with it now? She looked at the clock . Ten fifteen. Eleven hours and forty-five minutes before she could go to bed. She decided she would definitely wash her teacup and go out and buy a newspaper. Maybe for once there would be some cheerful news. Good things had to happen once in a while, didn't they? She could stop by the bakery and treat herself to a fresh bagel.

She thought about calling Lilly, but talking with her sister was never satisfying. She kept complaining about her husband. He was alive, wasn't he? So he wasn't so great—but he made lots of money. Lilly could buy whatever she wanted. She could even come for a visit if she wanted. What was the big deal about getting on a plane? People did it all the time. And survived. Instead of taking her teacup into the kitchen, she found herself sitting back down, as if her thoughts had their own power. Without thinking, she opened the box of stationery. She took out a sheet of paper and put it on a clear space on the coffee table. She uncapped the fountain pen Minnie had given her and filled it with ink. As if Minnie's voice was guiding her, she began to write.

Dear Anna . . .

20

The sun refused to let me pretend it was early morning. Sooner or later I was going to have to face Paulus. The coward in me hoped he had gone to work, having stocked the cupboard with a pleasant note saying he was so very sorry and would never do such a dastardly deed again. The rest of me grew increasingly nervous. I listened at the door but didn't hear anything. That was good. I didn't smell coffee. That was bad. Then again, maybe he left without making coffee—*It's my apartment. I can set the rules. I'm paying the bills.* I got dressed. *He's my employee. I can fire him.* I was terrified.

*****

Momma finishes rolling the vanilla dough on top of the chocolate dough, making long rolls that she will put into the refrigerator to harden before slicing and baking them. She notices the time and sighs. "I forgot. I have a dentist appointment. I'll be back in a couple of hours. Do your homework and don't let anyone in." I watch her leave before I slice off a chunk. The dough is sweet and cold. I slice off a piece from the second roll. Raw cookie dough is my most favorite thing to eat, and chocolate and vanilla icebox dough is the best. I'm about to slice another chunk when I see that the ends are a bit messy so I slice slivers off until they are as neat as I can make them. In the middle of doing my homework I rush back to the refrigerator and slice off another big chunk. It's only after I finish eating it that I notice how small the rolls are. No way will Momma not notice.

I decide to bake the cookies myself and look up the proper oven temperature. I don't know whether to grease the sheets so I do. At least they won't stick. I try to remember how my mother slices the cookies but even after I decide how thin they should be, it's hard to keep the slices consistent. The dough is soft and difficult to cut; mine don't look at all like the neatly shaped cookies Momma makes. Still,

I put the cookies into the oven and hope I can bake them all before Momma comes home. I open the refrigerator to get some milk and eat a few more of the unbaked slices.

Momma barely opens the door when she sniffs. "What do I smell?"

"I baked the cookies for you. As a surprise." She pushes me aside and hurries into the kitchen. At least I had time to clean up any mess I made. "Where's the rest of them?"

I look at her as innocently as I can. "What do you mean?"

"I made enough dough for twice that many."

My heart is beating so loudly it's a wonder she doesn't hear it. "I baked what was in the refrigerator. I have to finish my homework." I walk out, hoping the dough I ate doesn't show.

*****

If I had waited two more minutes, Paulus probably would have left, but I met him as he was coming out of his room. I didn't know what to say, so I took refuge in pleasantry. "Good morning, Paulus." He nodded. *Now what?* "Shall I start the coffee?" My voice squeaked.

"I'll get some on my way to work." He put on his coat.

I felt myself wanting to pretend nothing had happened. Hoping that if I said nothing we would find our way back to some semblance of routine. But this is what I'd done with Max and nothing had ever been resolved. I was tired of pretending and scared of confrontation. I forced myself to say, "Paulus, I think we have to talk."

"I'm running late. We can talk on our way to the doctor this afternoon."

"We need to talk now."

"You're the boss." He stood, coat in hand, waiting for me to begin.

"We have to figure out how to manage groceries so that if people come, we know there's food to give them." I waited for him to say something. "What do you think?" I stared at him..

He looked as if he was trying to contain his anger. "I don't think anything. You tell me what I can eat. It's your house — you make the rules. Now, if you don't mind, I have to go. We have a staff meeting and I don't want to be late. I'll be back at one to take you to the doctor."

"I'll take a cab."

"Suit yourself."

His hand was on the doorknob. "Stop," I yelled.

He turned. "I told you. I need to leave."

"And I need to resolve the tension between us."

"There's nothing to resolve. You've made yourself perfectly clear. I'm not your friend; I'm your employee. If my work isn't satisfactory you can fire me. It won't be the first time."

So he has pity parties too. "I may be your employer, but we're living in the same space. I can't just issue orders. Let's go sit in the kitchen, I'll make coffee."

"I have to leave." *I don't believe you.*

"Not before we talk." *Keep going, Anna; you can do this.* I stood at the door, waiting until he finally headed toward the kitchen. On the counter were five jars of peanuts and three boxes of Melba toast. When I opened the refrigerator to get the coffee beans there was a huge hunk of cheddar cheese. I made coffee.

"God dammit, Paulus, say something."

"Whatever I say will be wrong."

"Poor Paulus, always at the short end of the stick."

"I don't have to take your sarcasm. It's not in my contract." He stood up.

"And I don't have to take your silence. If something's on your mind, say it. God knows I can feel it." *My stomach doesn't like this either.*

"All right, I will. You embarrassed me in front of Emma. You think she didn't hear the venom in your voice when you talked about the bare cupboard? So I ate the stuff. Is that such a crime? You walk around this apartment like a wounded princess who's been forced to eat porridge while I'm supposed to read your every wish and whim. No thank you. I've had enough of princesses to last ten lifetimes."

"No one asked you to read my every wish and whim. Your duties are quite clear. Do the shopping, laundry, some cleaning and take me to my doctors' appointments. That seems perfectly straightforward to me. And, since you want to talk about bare cupboards, I will. Common courtesy suggests that if you eat a jar of peanuts and a box of Melba toast and most of an enormous hunk of cheese, you replace it. But what do you do? You stomp out of here looking like a bad actor in a Wagnerian opera."

We glared at each other. I refilled our cups. There was more silence, tension growing thicker by the second. I knew Paulus had put himself into a corner and I knew exactly what that felt like. I was in sort of a corner myself.

It's up to me to get us out. "Okay, Paulus, let's make a truce. You're mad at me, I'm mad at you. There's no point in making things worse. Let's agree that we'll put stuff aside for company. If I eat it, I tell you so you can replace it from the money I give you for food. If you eat it, you buy it on your dime. Fair enough?"

He hesitated. I held my breath. "I guess I can live with that."

"Great! What about scrambled eggs and toasted bagel?"

"I told you, I have a meeting."

"Somehow I don't believe you."

"Somehow you're right," he said sheepishly.

"You toast the bagels; I'll scramble the eggs. Want onions?"

"Sounds good." He looked at me with an expression I couldn't read. "Anna, is it okay? I mean, is it finished?"

"If by 'it,' you mean our 'difference of opinion,' it is by me. Is it by you?"

"Yes." The color came back into his face. "You don't have to call a cab. I arranged to have the afternoon off."

Max was wrong. Not talking about bad times does nothing but make them worse. I set the table. It was the best breakfast I ever ate.

So endeth our first catastrophe.

I celebrated by lying down for a few minutes and sleeping for two hours. The urge to talk to someone was growing so strong I found it hard to keep from blurting out my thoughts to Paulus, but he was my employee. I wondered about Emma, but maybe I already said too much. There was Rosa, but she was my colleague. Rabbi Berman would listen, but it had been so long since we last spoke. I felt embarrassed when I thought about how many times she had asked me to come talk. How many times I refused, making excuses she could probably see right through.

Paulus waited for me to get out of the car, but my legs wouldn't move. *Ready or not, here it comes. I am not ready.* A nurse asked if I wanted a wheelchair. That at least got me going. After the blood tests, I waited for Dr. H. Though it was warm in her office I couldn't stop shivering. "I won't keep you in suspense," she said when she came in. "It is leukemia but we have effective medicine for the kind you have. If you'd gotten sick a few years ago, treatment would have been very different and much less successful."

I could barely speak. "What's the prognosis?"

"All leukemia is fatal if not treated, but, as I said, we've had good results dealing with the type you have." Noticing my shivering, she asked, "Would you like a blanket?" I shook my head, disappearing into a safe place inside me. "Ms. Baum, are you listening?" Her voice grew dim. "Ms. Baum, take a deep breath."

"I have no breath to take." Although I kept thinking about leukemia, I never believed I had cancer. I felt punched in the stomach, the wind knocked out of me, a black cloud of fear threatening to smother me. I wanted to run out of the office and keep running until I ran out of run. Even kindness felt bad. "I need to use the bathroom." I hurried out, hoping I'd make it to the bathroom in time. I missed the bowl with disastrous results. Just looking at it made me retch again. I tried to clean it up.

"Ms. Baum, it's Shirley, Dr. H.'s nurse. Can you open the door? I've got a cold compress." The retching continued until there was nothing more to bring up. When I was able, I opened it slowly, afraid that any sudden movement would start me vomiting again. "Wipe your face and neck, you'll feel better." She was right; the cool wet felt good.

"Thank you. I'm sorry about the mess."

"Don't worry about it."

"I didn't do a very good job of cleaning up."

She shrugged. "It happens." She walked me back, assuring me I was going to be fine. Her comforting words slid off me. There was no place for them to come in.

Dr. H. got up from her desk and offered me a mint. "I have another patient coming in a few minutes, but I want to lay out a treatment plan before you leave."

"What do you recommend?" I tried to concentrate as she talked about daily injections of interferon for six months, the frequency of blood tests, lowered counts, side effects—My mind couldn't take it in. Embarrassed, I said, "I guess I tuned out. Do you have information I can read? Maybe I'll make sense of it when I'm home." She handed me four printed sheets of paper with strange-looking diagrams and weird words. "When do I have to decide?"

"At this point I see no reason to delay treatment."

I tried to make a joke. "My mother used to say that if you didn't like what one doctor said, go to another. Maybe I should get a second opinion." I was sliding down a steep black hole.

"That's certainly your right. Tell me the name of the doctor you decide to see and I'll send your records. If you'd like suggestions, I'll be happy to give you a few."

Half of me wanted to say, "Let's start the treatment now." The other half wanted to walk in front of a car. I wiped away the tears on my face. "I don't want another doctor."

Suddenly, something was terribly, horribly, wrong.

*****

I'm bleeding. Daddy is furious. "It's time for ice cream. Stop crying and wash yourself like a good girl. We'll be late if you don't hurry."

I can't move. Daddy yells, "Hurry up and wash your dress. Momma's waiting for us." I wash the red out of my dress and stuff toilet paper into my pants. Daddy is pleased.

"Good girl. Your dress will be dry by the time we get home. What flavor ice cream do you want?" Wet is dribbling down my legs. "I think I'll have strawberry with chocolate sprinkles. Would you like strawberry with chocolate sprinkles, Anna?" I see red stains on my white socks. Daddy takes my hand and puts a cone in it. The toilet paper is sopping wet between my legs. It's slipping out. I can't walk. Daddy is angry again. "Eat your ice cream. It's dripping."

"What happened to your dress, Anna?" asks Momma crossly.

"She fell and cut herself," says Daddy. "We couldn't get the bloodstains out completely. Isn't that right, Anna?"

"Why can't you be more careful?" complains Momma. "You're always hurting yourself. Someday you'll hurt yourself and you won't have us to take care of you. Then you'll really be in trouble. You're such a bad girl."

*****

My underwear was wet. I knew it was blood. Without opening my eyes I said, "I'm bleeding. I can't stop it. It's not my fault." Red was dribbling onto the floor.

"Of course it's not your fault. I'll help you. Don't worry, you're going to be all right," said Dr. H. She called an ambulance. This time I didn't protest when they put me on the stretcher and hooked me up. Wet spread underneath me. My mother's face grimaced hideously. My father's face loomed large and livid.

"We have to stop meeting like this."

"Jacob?"

"The very same. How are you feeling? Can't leave you for five minutes without you getting yourself into trouble."

My eyes filled with tears. "It's not my fault."

"I was teasing. You had another hemorrhage but we've stopped the bleeding."

"I got the diagnosis."

"I know. What about orange juice and a bath? You'll feel better."

I nodded, too tired to speak. "Dr. H. said to tell you she'll be in to talk with you about eleven."

"Eleven? Isn't it past that now?"

"Anna, you've been in the hospital since yesterday."

"Yesterday?" *I missed a whole day of my life?*

He gave me an enormous glass of orange juice. "Here, drink."

"Jacob, I can't tell what's real any more."

"I know the feeling."

"You do?"

"Yes."

"How come? You seem so together to me."

"That's my job. That's what you're supposed to see."

"You do a great job, Jacob." My eyes closed.

The morning sun shines on a small vase that holds gold and orange marigolds. Max is yelling as he storms into the kitchen where I'm washing plums.

"Why does your hearing disappear when I need something?"

"I didn't hear you. The water's running."

"You're always ready with an excuse."

"It's not an excuse. The water's running. I'm washing plums for breakfast. Did you want something?"

"Plums? For breakfast? Who in their right mind eats plums for breakfast?"

"I do. I like plums."

"Normal people eat oranges or grapefruit. You always have to be different, don't you? Tell me, do you actually decide to do the opposite of everyone else, or does it just come naturally?"

I sigh. "What do you want, Max?"

"You're washing plums for a goddamned army. What's going on?"

"I don't know what you mean."

"You fucking well do. You know I don't eat plums. Who are they for?"

"They're for me. I told you I like plums."

His fist smashes me without warning. I fall to the floor. "You're a fucking liar." He hits me again. "I asked you a question. Answer me."

Same scene. Same issue. New imagining.

"Answer me," shouts Max.

"Anna, sweetheart, your husband asked you a simple question. Answer him. Why are you always so stubborn?" asks Daddy.

"He hurt me." I hold my bruised face. "I'm bleeding."

"So he got a little angry. So what? It's your fault. If you would just behave like a loving wife — " lectures Momma.

"No!" shouts Boonah. "No, no, a thousand times no."

I see Max and Daddy and Momma stare at Boonah. Before they can speak, Boonah strides into the kitchen. Behind him is Joe, in full police uniform.

"What's going on here?" growls Joe as he confronts Max and Daddy and Momma. Max and Daddy and Momma cringe, babbling excuses.

"Arrest them," says Boonah.

"For what?" sneers Max.

"Disturbing the peace," responds Boonah.

"There is no peace around Anna. Arrest her," demands Daddy. "She's always causing trouble."

"That's right," agrees Momma.

"Absofuckinglutely," yells Max.

"They're lying," says Joe." I'm a professional. I know when people are prevaricating."

"Who the fuck are you?" growls Max.

"Officer, arrest them for disorderly vocabulary," says Boonah. "They're disturbing the conversation."

Daddy and Momma move closer to Max, knocking over the marigolds. "Arrest them for murdering marigolds, for soul murder," Boonah says to Joe.

"Arrest Anna. She's the one who started this mess," shout Max and Daddy and Momma. Max tries to push Boonah out of the way, but Joe subdues Max, puts handcuffs on his three prisoners, and takes them away.

Boonah picks up the flowers from the floor and puts them in the vase filled with his tears.

I opened my eyes to see Dr. H. enter. "Good morning. How are you feeling, Ms. Baum?" She was wearing a purple suit, so rich in color that not even her white coat dimmed its beauty. Her wedding ring was made of purple stones that matched her clothes.

Still basking in the warmth of my dream, I said, "Fine."

Surprised, she smiled. "Great! Do you mind if I sit down? I'd like to talk about treatment options." I nodded.

Picking up the cup of coffee that had been left while I was dreaming, I drank slowly, waiting to have the courage to begin. "Okay, Dr. H., fire away. What are my treatment options?"

"Are you sure you don't want a second opinion?"

I shook my head. "No. I trust your judgment."

"Cancer is hard to deal with, especially when it's loaded with other issues."

"What do you mean?"

Dr. H. looked intently at me. "I've only known you a short time, but even so, there's been quite a change in you. If I didn't know better, I'd say you've been slaying a few dragons."

I flushed. "You may be right, although I wouldn't have thought to put it that way. Before I got sick, what I mostly did was work. After I got sick, I discovered that part of me was—I'm not sure how to say it—shut down is what comes to mind. When I couldn't take care of myself I panicked. Feeling helpless is worse than being sick." Dr. H. gave me a look that made me want to continue. "One thing I've learned from this whole mess is that change happens, ready or not. I didn't think I was ready but maybe I am."

Dr. H. nodded. "If you realize that, everything else is duck soup."

I grinned. "Honestly Dr. H.—have you ever made duck soup?"

"Nope, haven't even tasted it. Let me see, what about, easy as water falling off a duck's back." We laughed. "I better forget about ducks and stick to what I know." She laid out my treatment options, and this time I listened and followed her reasoning.

Only one thing threw me. "Injections. Every day?"

"At least until your counts have stabilized. We don't know how long this will take."

"I guess if I can learn to give myself an injection I can do anything. This interferon, it's not a cure, if I understood what I read."

"That's right. Initially, we hoped it would be, but we've since learned that when you stop taking it, the cancer cells in the bone marrow proliferate pretty quickly." I retreated inside myself.

"You can do it, Anna. You deserve a chance to live. There's so much for you to discover and enjoy." Boonah holds my hand. "She's on our side." I caress his long beautiful fingers and then twine my fingers in his.

"When do we start?"

"Tomorrow sounds like a good time to me. I'll make arrangements if you're sure. I don't want you to do anything you aren't ready to do."

"No sense postponing the inevitable. I'm as ready as I'll ever be."

"Do you have any more questions?"

"Just one. Do you miss the bowl you gave me?"

"Yes, I do," she said. "But knowing it's in such good hands makes all the difference."

After she left, I conjured up images of my mother and father and Max. My mother's face sagged. My father's was deflated. Max's features blurred. I willed them to disappear. The dream reminded me I wasn't alone anymore. There were people in my life who were willing and able to help. Some weren't exactly friends, and a few were being paid to take care of me. But what mattered at the moment was I knew they cared about me, and that was a good enough start.

On my bedside table was a fat envelope that had arrived while I was sleeping. Just the sight of it made me happy. The children hadn't waited. Jacob came in to take my vital signs. I asked him, "Remember when I said I wanted to be in one place?" He nodded. "And you said you knew the feeling?" He nodded again. "Want to talk about it?"

"Sure do, but not right now. I need to check your breathing capacity."

"Why is it hospital routine always interferes with what's important?"

"Another good reason to go home," he said.

"Would you be interested in continuing the conversation we didn't even start?"

"Sure."

"Could I invite you for coffee? Paulus takes coffee-making as seriously as you do."

"Sounds great." He wrapped my arm with the blood pressure cuff.

Just thinking of asking him for his phone number made me blush—but I did. Just thinking of sitting with him in my kitchen, having coffee, talking, made me grin.

When Jacob left, I kept replaying Dr. H.'s words about me slaying dragons. I knew there was at least one more dragon that had yet to be slain, the keep-it-to-yourself-and-don't-tell-anyone-what's-going-on-beast. Her number was there, in the phone book. Even her voice on the answering machine was comforting.

"Rabbi Berman, it's me, Anna. I'm in the hospital, being treated for leukemia; but when I'm home, I'm going to give you a call. I would like to talk with you."

"Boonah, I feel hopeful. I think I'm going to get well."
"Yes, Anna, most assuredly, we will."

Acknowledgments

Catastrophic illness becomes a watershed, dividing life into before and after. It forced me to ask for, and accept help, something I had done my best to avoid all my life. Because there were months when I had so little energy, crocheting afghans felt like hard work, thoughts, memories, and images I had successfully denied, came flooding in, too powerful to ignore. All of the characters in this novel are imagined, yet as I wrote, I felt guided by a man named Kurt, who, when I was five years old, called me his golden child, and my Uncle Ray, who was always willing to listen to my dreams, even after ALS claimed his body and silenced his tongue. The longer I live, the more I appreciate them and others who continued to care about me under very difficult circumstances.

People in England, Sweden, and the United States, whose steady loving and generous offers of help with food, transportation, visits, calls and letters enabled me to deal with, and learn from, my bouts of leukemia. Friends matter. Their presence and compassion and love made it possible for me to choose life when I was living in a landscape so bleak I thought there was no way out.

I thank my son, Lance, who came to help without being asked.

I appreciate the care Maria Thaddeus gave me when I returned from the hospital in London. She has been a steadying influence, always loving and honest, especially when it came to reading what I wrote, letting me know when I needed to go deeper into the nightmare, yet ready to help when I felt as if I would never emerge from the darkness.

Frances Silverstein, my mother's second youngest sister, listens to my stories without judgment. Her support has been a lifeline to recovering my emotional and physical health.

Gracias a mis tios, Frieda y Roberto Rubin. Les quiero mucho.

I wish to thank Jeanne Walker and Andrew Adleman for their skillful editing and friendship.

Nancy King, PhD, Union Institute and University, has told stories and conducted storymaking workshops throughout the USA, Scandinavia, the UK, Canada, Mexico, and Hungary. Her latest books include *Dancing With Wonder: Self-Discovery Through Stories* and the novels, *A Woman Walking* and *The Stones Speak*. An active member of PEN USA, she writes, weaves, and lives in Santa Fe, NM. Please visit: www.nancykingstories.com for further information.

Nancy King lives, writes and weaves in Santa Fe, New Mexico. Her other books include the novel *Woman Walking,* and *Dancing With Wonder—Self-Discovery Through Stories.* As a member of PEN International she corresponds with political prisoners all over the world.